I0631874

Conqueror

Joe T. McCormack

Chronicles of the Realm, Book 1

First Edition: 2024
First Printing: 2024
Published by Imagicache, llc
Manufactured in the United States of America

conqueror.work

ISBN-13: 979-8-9908219-0-3

© 1998, © 2024. All Rights Reserved.

PART I

Chapter One

In the lands we know of as Egypt a battle
between good and evil waged for centuries. Those whom
carried the essence of Wild Magic were shown the ways of
magic in order to continue the conquest of ridding the
lands of evil. But as man passed through the centuries, the
knowledge and records of Wild Magic faded from grasp,
leaving a select few, known as the Prophets, to stand
against the immortal scourge.

Relentlessly time passed and many of the
Prophets, despite their capacity to harness the Wild Magic
to shrug off the effects of aging, died. Those that did not
succumb to age found their deaths at the hand of demons.
By this time, around 1060 BC, only two known Arch-
Demons remained, infusing chaos, pestilence and
unnatural grotesqueries – some escaping sane description,
everywhere they manifested.

In a dry, mountainous desert the last of the
Prophets stood against these two Arch-Demons. The
Arch-Demons, without their army of demons, and a single
Prophet without any followers to pass on the ways of Wild
Magic to keep the wisdom in mankind's consciousness,
clashed…

The air became hot as thick lightning bolts
crashed into the Prophet, clothed in simple wool robes
dyed blue, grasping a dense wooden Staff that bore the
skull of a formidable horned creature now extinct. The
Prophet was thrown back some fifty paces before crashing
onto the sandy earth, his robes smoldering from the heat
of the mighty lightning bolts. Even as sand leapt into the
air, the Prophet forced himself up to turn and face the two
Arch-Demons standing before him and collected his
breath.

"Give yourself to us," one of the Arch-Demons commanded as it looked upon the small figure with its fissured red eyes set below twisted horns and above many pointed, slender and uncharacteristically white teeth. The Arch-Demon's large, muscular reddish-black torso moved as if for breath and its large sinewed wings bowed backwards slightly.

The lone human, with the signs of prolonged engagement becoming evident in his face, looked upon the Arch-Demon. His black eyes studied the Arch-Demon's towering frame briefly before he looked down at the earth before him. Exhaling, he tightened his grip on the Staff wincing at the pain that ebbed from a freshly broken rib bone. The smell of something familiar, like burnt hair, hung in the air.

The Arch-Demon raised a chiseled claw hand and said, "Join us prophet. Your lineage is at an end."

"We will be your salvation. And in that you may live for eternity and raise a new following worthy of our name. Simply renounce yourself." the other Arch-Demon stated evenly.

The Prophet focused his eyes between the two giants as he stood erect, using the Staff for leverage as his body slowly weakened. The middle-aged man felt his life slipping from his mortal husk with each passing moment, but his willpower remained solid. Closing his eyes for a moment, he wound the threads of Wild Magic from the Staff and pulled them toward him as the orb-less sockets of the skull anchored at the end of the Staff began to glow a faint blue. Raising his free arm, the Prophet slowly opened his eyes and pointed between the two Arch-Demons as the sand between them began to swirl in a clockwise fashion. Within a few fleeting moments the swirling sand began to glow brightly as two tablets began to form from the sand.

Taking a shallow breath the Prophet lowered his hand, took a firm stance and pointed the Staff at the two tablets. A cone of blue light flew from the Staff and into the tablets as powerful symbols and divine script formed on their rough surface.

"Behold," the Prophet announced as he raised the Staff and directed it at one of the Arch-Demons, "by the power of divinity and of this earth, I confine you to these tablets that shall envelope you for all eternity, in the sands of this land!"

Without warning or hesitation, the Prophet summoned the Wild Magic to the Staff once again and shouted deeply as a massive volley of blue lightning bolts sprang from the Staff, twisting around the Arch-Demon, pulling it into the tablets.

"No!" the Arch-Demon cried out in futility as it tried in vain to break free from the bolts that bound and pulled it into the sandy prison.

The other Arch-Demon stretched out its leathery wings and flew back several paces as it looked upon the Prophet with rage, seeing its equal disappear within the tablets. Pure, invigorating rage flashed through remaining Arch-Demon as it roared, "You shall not save yourself this day, Prophet! I shall feast on your soul!"

Wearily the Prophet lowered the Staff and turned his eyes toward the other Arch-Demon just in time to see it rush upon him faster than any other opponent in his past. Mightily the Arch-Demon swung one of his clawed hands and brutally tore singed robes and flesh from the Prophet's chest. The brightest red blood sprang into the air as the Prophet was forced sprawling on his back to the earth. Within a few heartbeats, blood radiated from his body, flowing into the dry sand around him. Some distance away, a portion of his lung and ribcage settled onto the earth.

Spreading its wings, the Arch-Demon bent over the Prophet, whom somehow yet held onto a thread of life, placed its clawed hand over his shredded chest and said, "Feel my rage Prophet…feel the cold hand of death!"

Mustering his remaining strength, the Prophet pushed the horned end of the Staff into the side of the Arch-Demon and whispered, as life left his body, "With my own life I condemn you to the depths of the great seas where you shall be shackled, devoid of light and life you seek to destroy."

Thunder rumbled loudly overhead as the Arch-Demon withdrew from the lifeless body of the Prophet. Steam began rising out of the Prophet's bloodied and mangled torso. Realizing its peril, the Arch-Demon tried to pull the Staff out of its side. But the Staff remained firmly anchored by some powerful and invisible force. As the flesh of the Prophet softened from the intense heat growing from the Prophet's form, the flesh rolled away from the bone and the blood-soaked robes caught fire. Again, the Arch-Demon struggled to remove the Staff from its side as the fire spread and consumed the Prophet's entire form.

"Never!" the Arch-Demon shrieked as a raging blueish-red fire enveloped its own body.

The fire grew into a brilliant sphere around the Arch-Demon and rose from the earth and threw itself far into the sky. Arching high the mighty fireball then steaked downward and smashed into a great body of water that stretched as far as the eye could see. After the light of the fireball faded and the waters calmed, the Staff rose from the silent depths, floating atop the slow and gentle waves.

Chapter Two

It is now present day.

Soldiers found their way out of a powerful utility helicopter that flew by means of two large counter-rotating blades atop a long, somewhat tubular shaped body. Technically called a CH-47 Chinook, most soldiers referred to it as a "Schnook" or more colorfully, "Banana Bob". The soldiers were on engineering status – building roads and bridges for the Government of Columbia, paid for by the US Government. The politicians, true to their nature and eager to grow their influence, boasted that it was for

4

improved relations between countries. The military knew it was more of a training exercise that exposed the soldiers to an environment and unfamiliar conditions that they might find themselves fighting in one day, rather than constructing a thorough-fare for people, material and economic growth between townships.

Boxes, drab green duffel bags and seemingly endless equipment containers were hastily off-loaded by the helicopter crew with the help of the soldiers as long elephant grass whipped back and forth to the beating of the rotating blades overhead. The dense gray clouds indicated an approaching monsoon storm and the crew had verified an approaching storm with local base personnel. They knew it would only be a matter of minutes before the storm would reach their position. But, with the aid of the soldiers, the CH-47 became airborne barely five minutes after landing.

Even as the soldiers carried the equipment and supplies off the small field surrounded by dense lushly green jungle and loaded it on waiting trucks, two Blackhawk UH-60 helicopters with a troop transport and gunship configuration, landed in a staggered formation, sending a few of the soldiers' camouflage caps skittering into the jungle. This helicopter type was nicknamed the "Honey Six" by soldiers for its familiar role in delivering supplies and, more importantly, carrying troops home.

"Go! Go!" a faint order was shouted from within the two as twelve more soldiers jumped out of the choppers with large Alice-packs and M16 A2 rifles. Even with the sixty-pound packs, this new arrival of soldiers ran from the gunships to the waiting trucks as if they bore no gear whatsoever.

But for these vigorously trained soldiers, such a brief sprint with packs was a trivial endeavor. They were used to running miles at a time with such equipment, and unlike soldiers from the US, they were already acclimated to the tropical environment of Central and South America. The thick, hot, sticky air was just one of the things they took for granted.

Stopping at the foot of the dirt road near one of the trucks, Sgt. Quentin instinctively scanned the area around him with his close-set gray eyes set above bony cheeks and a hard jaw bone that had broken the hands of several short-tempered drunks in off-duty, sometimes off-base, bar disputes. It was easy for most people to underestimate the strength he possessed, bound in a one hundred- and seventy-pound, six-foot frame not noticeable in the jungle fatigues he wore. But his men knew.

He glanced around the field in which he stood. Like every other clearing he'd been to in several missions throughout Central America, this one, too, was surrounded by dense jungle. He knew guerrillas or snipers could have their sites fixed on any one of them without being noticed. He smirked at the thought and turned around, waiting for his soldiers to gather around him as he made sure they had all gotten off the gunships. Amidst a flurry of activity, a fuel truck rumbled by and began re-fueling the Blackhawks for their return flight to Howard AFB in Panama.

Then something caught his eye and, looking to his right, he saw a military Humvee roll onto the field some thirty meters away. For a second, he wondered what an A-143 nomenclature troop transport was doing here, but he recalled it was one of the vehicles that came to the port of Malaga, patrolled by submarine, aboard a US naval ship. A-143 was, in fact, a vehicle he was responsible for that contained a range of sensitive equipment that only a select few were privileged to. Seeing his vehicle before him, Sgt. Quentin knew that someone, somewhere had broken security procedure. He squinted at the driver and didn't recognize him. Realizing that even unauthorized personnel were operating his vehicle, a fresh surge of energy exploded from within him and he strode toward the vehicle with a frown growing deeper on his face for each step he took. As he reached the vehicle, he signaled for his troops to load onto the back and then focused his attention on the driver.

"What are you doing with my vehicle?" he demanded. He snatched off his boonie cap revealing his closely cut hair. The sides and back of his head revealed just a hint of hair, while the top held a length of hair no longer than one quarter of an inch, shaped like a mohawk. Even though he'd been out of the combat schools of Special Forces, he'd become accustomed to the trim and still wore it.

"Just here to pick up soldiers and take them to base camp, Sarge," the young private replied nervously.

Roughly climbing into the passenger's side, he said, "Well, move your ass!"

"I was supposed to pick up men from my unit," the private replied quietly. He didn't want to be on the receiving end from the strange Sergeant, but he had to tell him because he knew that if he didn't, his First Sergeant would have his ass for not trying to carry out standing orders.

"Really? Not anymore! This is MY vehicle, from MY unit, and those are MY soldiers!" Sgt. Quentin continued, eyes ablaze and pointing over his shoulder to the troops.

After a moment, he said quietly, "Now. Drive my Humvee to the base camp before you piss me off and I chain you behind this vehicle and drag you to the base camp and then have you fill out 2404's for the rest of your deployment."

The Sergeant wanted to drill the private as to where he got the authorization to drive the vehicle, but decided it was not worth it. It was too early into the mission to be stepping on toes, especially since he did not yet know who's that would be.

Slowly the private drove the vehicle out of the field and through the small naval base, which was primarily filled with officer's housing and several enlisted barracks. As Sgt. Quentin looked around identifying his surroundings, it seemed unusually empty, as if everyone had simply left. Hairs pricked up on the back of his neck and he wondered if the local people knew something was going to happen. It wouldn't have been the first time he was involved in an anti-American guerrilla attack. Out of habit, Sgt. Quentin put his hand around the pistol grip of his assault rifle and thumbed off the safety.

The driver turned onto a long, winding gravel road that led into the deep green jungle.

"So, this is Columbia," Sgt. Quentin mumbled to himself, "Just another mission."

It took Sgt. Quentin and his soldiers just three hours to initiate communications to the US via satellite link-ups. Although they'd been forced to set up their equipment on the edge of a low-lying cliff that was just over two hundred meters from the main base camp, he didn't let his men know how opposed he was to setting up in such a vulnerable location flanked on three sides by a fifty-meter drop. He had no choice but to set up his platoon and equipment there, even after he had openly voiced his disgust to Colonel Ratcliff at the 1800 operations meeting. Unabashedly the Colonel was not open to feedback from those not in his unit. He insured the safety of his soldiers with a compliment of Columbian regulars guarding the perimeter but, when it came to Sgt. Quentin's soldiers' safety, not only was it a low priority, he viewed them as a possible complication to his mission and men. Guerrillas and other anti-American factions, in the past, had targeted large high-tech satellite equipment installations and anything that looked…threatening. Even though Colonel Ratcliff had said nothing and forced Sgt. Quentin to set up his platoon on the cliff away from the main base camp, the Sergeant knew why. And that's what pissed him off. He knew that his fallback position was off the side of the cliff.

After completing some final checks of his equipment, Sgt. Quentin opened the heavy latch door to the van and peered out into the darkness. He sighed, absently speculating how this mission would turn out as he glanced around. Seeing a shadow mulling around one of his electric generator sets that supplied power to his equipment, he grabbed his 9mm pistol and squinted into the darkness, trying to identify the somewhat darker shadow.

"Hey! Who's that?" Sgt. Quentin yelled out above the low hum of the diesel generator.

A figure stepped out from behind the generator, large muscular arms hanging at his sides with spots of black oil, his chest stretching the brown Army issue t-shirt he wore. Adjusting the belt that held his camouflaged pants, he walked up to the van, ignoring the 9mm that Sgt. Quentin was holding.

"What's up?" he asked plainly.

Recognizing the figure as Specialist Mac, Sgt. Quentin lowered the pistol. "Just wondered who was out there messing with my generator."

Although Mac was from Bravo Company and not Alpha Company where Sgt. Quentin was assigned, he knew a great deal about him as they both served under the same Brigade and were in and out of the same motor pool. Stories floated about that claimed Mac had an unnatural tendency of walking up to wild, full grown native snakes like the Bushmaster, and literally grabbing them behind the head…with his bare hands…and such an event had actually been filmed. Other stories surfaced that he had walked through a hillside home to tarantulas, taking a particularly large one as a pet. And, during a patrol, had come across a fledgling baby macaw parrot on the jungle floor with a broken wing whom he had kept safe until it had healed. Some might think that Mac was not entirely sane, but Mac was just the type of person Sgt. Quentin would want to have with him in a firefight. He was highly attentive to detail, incredibly fast and durable for his six-foot, two-inch frame that packed two hundred and thirty pounds of muscle. The M-60 machine gun was Mac's preferred weapon, although he was proficient with any weapon that ejected brass casings. And, unlike anyone else he'd been around, Sgt. Quentin soon found out that Mac was also a natural strategist. Sgt. Quentin knew that if a human war machine existed, Mac was it, even if his manners said otherwise.

"Mind if I come in?" a soldier in gray shorts and a matching T-shirt said, stepping beside Mac, apparently having just finished a short jog.

"Sure Gladstad," Sgt. Quentin grunted, not particularly pleased with seeing him. He really didn't know much about Gladstad, just that he was a communications and equipment tech who was here to fix any faulty equipment. Gladstad was relatively new to the Army and being only nineteen, hadn't received a healthy dose of combat training or many hazard deployments.

"Kinda boring around here, isn't it? I mean, since we can't leave the base camp," Gladstad mentioned as he pushed his hand through his short, fluffy brown hair.

"Yeah," Sgt. Quentin mumbled, not impressed with Gladstad's feeble attempt at conversation.

"Well, I have an idea since we're going to be stuck here. How 'bout some Warriors of the Realms?" Mac suggested, standing outside the van still.

"Sounds like a way to pass time. You know, years ago I used to play a lot," Quentin shot out, already interested in playing a campaign to break the monotony.

Bewildered, Gladstad asked, "What's Warriors of the Realms?"

Sighing, Sgt. Quentin explained, "It's a roll playing game, like as if you were an actor in a movie. You assume a roll of a character and play as that character throughout the game, or campaign as players would call it."

"Okay, so how do you play?" Gladstad said, trying to be open-minded.

Sgt. Quentin briefly explained all the little details as Mac left and retrieved some dice and a manual he took with him on most deployments. He didn't expect Gladstad to remember much. Nobody ever did on their first game.

It didn't take Mac long to borrow all the necessary items for conducting a campaign from a soldier he'd noticed earlier who was part of logistics and supply whom had access to a great number of notepads and pencils. Walking around the brick buildings and then following a rough cement walkway, Mac headed back to the satellite site already putting together a campaign in his mind. He crossed an empty cement slab that was large enough to assemble an entire company formation upon and by the time he'd followed a gravel road for fifty meters or so and entered the site, he had a firm idea of the characters that would be in the campaign, giants, people, elves, animals and other life. He envisioned massive ice-capped mountains with dragons, plush green forests, and barren wastelands that seemed to span the horizon and beyond. As the images flashed in his mind a faint shiver crept up his spine as he felt the warm summer sun overhead and gentle breeze slide past him from this other land.

Mac looked up into the night sky and frowned. He blinked into the darkness for a couple of seconds before he realized it was just his imagination working overtime. Shrugging the experience off, he cleared his throat and reached for the hatch door on the van.

"Hey Mac!" a soldier called out, startling Mac.

Mac spun around and saw Specialist Schwartz walking up to him with a big cheesy grin on his face. He knew something had to be up. That grin usually meant that Schwartz wanted something. Mac almost knew what it was before he asked, but he kept quiet.

"Hey Mac, buddy ol' pal" he shmoozed, "how ya doin?"

"Eh, just hanging. 'Bout to play a campaign." Mac said, and held up the manual and notepads.

"Ah, well, have fun. God knows we have to do something around here to keep busy." Schwartz said through that grin, putting his hand on Mac's shoulder.

"Yeah, I plan to. I've got a few guys inside who want to go a round."

His hints were getting him nowhere so Schwartz finally asked, "So, you mind if I have a dip?"

Being roommates with Schwartz in Panama, Mac couldn't refuse and handed his friend the can just like it'd been when they were in Panama.

Eagerly taking it, Schwartz shook it lightly and said, "Full can, eh?"

"Yep, I always come prepared." Mac remarked as Schwartz took out a pinch, put it in his lip and pushed it around with his tongue.

He tossed the can back to Mac. "Well come by after you're done playing, eh?"

"Sure," Mac said evenly, as he turned and opened the van door and entered.

"Well, check your feedback." Sgt. Quentin said into the black handset with that questioning look in his eyes, "Yeah. Out."

Sgt. Quentin sighed as he put down the handset and said, "Some people. You just have to wonder where their brains go."

"I got all the stuff we need," Mac said as he sat down in an available spot next to the emergency battery box. He didn't even want to know what Sgt. Quentin was talking about because it could leave into one of those drawn-out speeches and the campaign would not get started. At least, not anytime soon.

"Good, good. Let's get the characters rolled up." Sgt. Quentin smiled as he got out some paper, pen and began rolling dice on the small metal desk before him.

Gladstad's little gray eyes peered at the dice and to the papers Sgt. Quentin was writing on, "What're you doing now?"

"Rolling up what your character's strengths and weaknesses will be," he responded, not looking up.

Rather than admit he had no idea what Sgt. Quentin really meant, he grunted and nodded.

After a few minutes with Mac looking on, Sgt. Quentin finished the papers and handed them to Mac to check. Mac skimmed their content, smiled and handed one to Sgt. Quentin and the other to Gladstad who looked at the paper with a puzzled look, trying to understand all of the different numbers.

Mac pushed his glasses up on the bridge of his nose, "Okay, this is it. You two are to save the pure magic of the Realm. You see, even as you travel through the Realm, the Baron is trying to destroy the pure magic so that he can rule the Realm without challenge." He caught the look on Gladstad's face. "Just trust me, he's evil, okay? Now, throughout the Realm you will find magical items that you will have to use to defeat him."

A silence filled the cabin until Gladstad said, "And? Is that it? How do you do that?"

Sgt. Quentin squeezed his lips together and looked at the ceiling of the cabin trying to remind himself that Gladstad had never played before. "He doesn't have to tell us anything else. As we go, we'll find out everything else we need to know by exploring, talking to enchanted trees, farmers, or whatever."

Gladstad nodded slowly. "Oh."

Mac stood and opened the hatch door. "Well, I hate to go, but I said I'd go over and talk a while with Schwartz earlier. Tomorrow we'll start the campaign."

Sgt. Quentin nodded as he watched Mac leave the van.

After the hatch closed, Gladstad handed Sgt. Quentin his paper and said, "I don't know if I can play. That stuff on the paper looks pretty hard, and I don't think I could act like someone else."

"Look Gladstad," Sgt. Quentin said, trying to keep Gladstad interested in playing, "Everyone has problems with all the stats on the paper. I did. Mac did and you're no different. We'll help you out on rolling dice and all that, so don't worry about it. Once you start playing and get the hang of it, you'll like the game a lot more. Okay?"

A wiry grin grew on Gladstad's unsure face as he got up and said, "Well, yeah." He opened the hatch. "I'm going to go to bed. See you later."

"Yep." Sgt. Quentin grunted in response as he smelled a particular, strange odor coming from outside that he had not detected when Mac left.

"You smell that?"

"Smells like something is burning." Gladstad shrugged as he stepped onto the ground outside the van.

Following Gladstad out, Sgt. Quentin headed for the running generator thinking that some of the wires might have shorted out. After doing a quick examination, he found nothing wrong. But he was not a generator mechanic.

"It doesn't look like the generator is screwed up." Sgt. Quentin said finally, after he went over and checked the grounding rod that was attached to the generator frame by a thick braided copper wire.

"What do you think it is?" Gladstad asked.

He looked around the area. "I don't know." He took a few deep breaths, but it didn't help.

"What's going on?!" Gladstad suddenly pleaded as he looked around at his body as thin streaks of blue lightning danced around him. He held up a hand as if to shield himself from this strange phenomenon.

"What the hell?" Sgt. Quentin whispered as he turned and looked at Gladstad. While his mouth formed words, those words remained locked in his throat.

"Gladstad!" Sgt. Quentin forced out just as Gladstad disappeared in a brilliant flash of light, like some huge flashbulb going off.

Not more than an instant later, blue lightning bolts surrounded Sgt. Quentin as he tried to run from whatever had caused Gladstad to disappear. But he disappeared in mid-step in another brilliant flash of light.

"You hear something?" Mac asked Schwartz, who was dealing out another hand of Spades.

"No." Schwartz admitted. He'd already lost two hands and was not going to be distracted.

Mac got up and stuck his head out of the green A-Frame tent that was no more than fifty meters from the van. After looking around, he turned and sat back down in front of the footlocker and picked up his cards.

Schwartz had a smile of his face. He knew he'd win this hand.

14

Chapter Three

A faint warm breeze blew across Sgt. Quentin's limp form as he gained consciousness. His temples throbbed with pain, but he forced his eyes open, only to be blinded by the sun almost directly overhead.

"Damn! What happened?" he groaned as he looked away from the sun and then saw Gladstad's body sprawled out a few feet from him.

Reaching over, he shook Gladstad by the shoulder until he woke up.

Gladstad slowly gained enough awareness to sit up on the short green grass that surrounded them. "Where are we?"

Sgt. Quentin knew he'd say that.

"I have no idea." Sgt. Quentin replied, getting to his feet slowly. He noted he was on a hilltop, which bore one tree almost six feet wide and some twenty feet tall. Surrounding the hill was a vast expanse of forest that reached beyond the horizon. He pulled out his compass and gauged the sun's position and found it was moving towards the west. He looked at his watch. 2200 hours. 2200 hours? He grunted in disbelief and squinted at the digital dial again, figuring he was seeing things.

"Damn watch." he blurted out as he took it off and examined it for cracks or anything else that might cause it to not show current time.

"What's wrong?" Gladstad asked as he got up and looked at the watch Sgt. Quentin was holding.

"Beats me. Batteries must be low." He replied as he stuffed the watch into his camouflaged pants pocket. What he didn't know was that the behavior of time had different characteristics here.

It was then that he noticed his green carrying bag and a two-foot-long machete piled up against the tree.

"How did that get there?" Sgt. Quentin noted as he walked over to the tree, then nudged the bag with the toe of his boot to see if it was real.

Gladstad shrugged.

Sgt. Quentin opened the bag and began to search its contents. Aspirin, knife, sharpening kit, two-quart canteen, one-quart leather flask, first-aid pack, two dehydrated meals and a survival knife.

"It's complete." Sgt. Quentin mumbled, clueless as to why it was here and, more importantly, why they were here.

Gladstad, seemingly frustrated, said, "What?"

"My bag. Nothing is missing."

"Great. We're out here in the middle of nowhere and you're worried about your damn bag. What're we going to do about food until we can get back to the base camp?" He turned his head and jumped slightly. There was a single edged axe, two-quart canteen, and a flashlight beside him that he did not see before. But it hadn't been there before.

"Hunt for it. But, until we can find out exactly where we're at, it's always good sense to know what you have to work with." Sgt. Quentin replied, barely containing his anger. *Was Gladstad playing stupid, or had he forgotten all his basic training?* He looked at Gladstad. *Well, that was possible.*

"What are we doing here anyway?" Gladstad puzzled, shrugging his shoulders and eyeing Sgt. Quentin.

Sgt. Quentin thought for a moment and said, "I don't know. Maybe it's someone's idea of a joke. Perhaps the water was tainted at the base camp and one of the guerrilla factions is playing a game with us before they decide to kill us."

"Okay, but what about the blue electricity that was all over me?" Gladstad pointed out.

"Look, don't ask me this shit. I'm new here, too. Remember? Let's just worry about getting out of here for now," Sgt. Quentin said as he zipped his small green bag shut.

16

Just as he got to his feet, Sgt. Quentin felt a sharp pain resonate from his lower leg as Gladstad yelled, "Snake!"

Grabbing his machete, Sgt. Quentin fell away from the black snake that was recoiling for another attack. Gladstad swiftly gained upon the snake and swung at it with his axe but missed and hit the tree instead with a dull thud.

The snake saw the new prey and focused its red eyes on Gladstad as it slithered its six-foot-long body towards him with blinding speed. Gladstad managed to retreat a couple of steps before he fell over on his back, tripping over his untied shoelaces. The axe slipped from his grasp.

As the snake readied itself to strike, Sgt. Quentin lurched forward and, with a desperate swing of his machete, severed its head. The body of the snake twisted and coiled up with spasms before it collapsed onto the grassy earth, thick black blood oozing out of its scaly neck.

Gladstad shuffled to his feet and said, "Man, that was close!"

Sgt. Quentin's head began to swim and knew it was only a matter of minutes before the venom would cause him to lose consciousness…maybe even die depending on his body's ability to immobilize the toxin.

Slowly and painfully Sgt. Quentin got to his feet and limped over to the tree and sat down heavily with is legs outstretched before him. Then he tore a long strip off his T-shirt, tied it under his knee above the wound and pulled out a small knife from his pocket and sliced into his pants, exposing the bite wound.

"Hey, you going to be okay?" Gladstad asked, frowning at the vicious wound.

"Don't worry about it." He replied, barely above a whisper. He didn't trust his life in the hands of an obviously inexperienced soldier. Sgt. Quentin knew he'd have to do this himself.

Have to stay calm,' he thought. His eyelids became heavier with each passing moment.

17

He glanced at the wound which appeared to have many teeth marks rather than a few, common with fangs. Relieved, he did not notice any discoloration or swelling but it may yet be too early for those sorts of symptoms to manifest.

Sgt. Quentin slipped from consciousness before he could observe any more.

"Damn Metsys!" Lord Doefloct spat angrily, grasping his long wooden Staff that held two blue glowing horns of a Wild Magic Dragon that had existed long ago on another world.

The smell of ancient books and parchment filled the stone-walled study in which he stood, thinking about what he should do next. Burning torches hung along the walls, flames dancing back and forth.

Doefloct didn't believe that the Wizard Metsys would have been able to summon humans from the land of the Wild Magic, to the Realm. He thought his skill and Staff he wielded were the only means with which to cast and sustain such a potent and unstable incantation. The human Wizard, yet again, had done something that should not have been possible. Doefloct despised the unpredictable and seemingly chaotic nature of Metsys and the disruption to the natural order his presence caused. But that unearthly presence was the only reason the Realm had not fallen into his grasp already.

Gazing at his Staff he recalled that it took him decades to wrest it from Chief Isotor in mortal combat that had spanned the Realm. Over that time, Doefloct eventually learned that the Staff of Majii could only be used by a bipedal, human form. That explained why Isotor, Chief of the Guardians of the White Magic, and a Silver Dragon, had always been in human form. During what would become their final battle, he used that to his advantage. Knowing that Isotor could not change into his dragon form for additional protection from attack and instead had to rely on mastery of the Staff, Doefloct had bound dozens of Green Dragons and hurled them upon the Chief like a rainstorm. All of the lesser dragons met their end, but so did the Chief. Utterly drained of life-force he was overpowered by Doefloct's merciless attack and perished, the only remnants of his existence being a tattered and darkened white cape and the Staff of Majii without a wielder.

But before the Chief's essence departed his lifeless body, still in human form, Doefloct took the Staff of Majii in his free hand and, by using the Wild Magic it was bound to, smote the Chief's body in a deep blue and yet cold fire that slowly consumed the body. That fire gained strength, not by consuming the form but by consuming the unseen essence of the Chief.

Doefloct used the flame, now imbued with powerful essence, to beckon a gigantic beast well over twelve feet in height from the flame, its muscular, black leathery body radiating a faint blue haze. It had a long tail like the bodily proportion of an upright desert lizard, the legs resembling that of a lion and the long arms of a man but piercing claws of a dragon in the place of hands. The beast's head was comprised mostly of a large mouth with row upon row of sharp, arrowhead-shaped teeth and above its small fissured red eyes were anchored to long white horns pointed forward.

Once beckoned, Doefloct contorted and twisted the Wild Magic funneling the remainder of the Chief's essence into it. Doefloct had literally chained him to the mortal shell of a fearsome creature under Doefloct's command that once, long ago, had been responsible for destroying most life in the Realm. But this abomination was far removed from the fanciful legends of the Arch-Demons that this beast resembled. This chimera, infused with a High Dragon, was more dreadful. The Death Raiden.

Once in possession of the Staff and the beast, Doefloct gave the cape to the surviving dragons as a trophy and a powerful reminder of his strength.

"Metsys. Metsys." Lord Doefloct said to himself, peering into the cloudy crystal ball that sat on the ancient wooden desk before him, "What was the purpose of summoning two humans, ill-equipped at that, to this world?"

He scoffed, "Surely not to destroy me."

Through the crystal ball he could see the two lone figures on a grassy hilltop. One was dressed in poorly dyed green clothing and the other merely wore a gray shirt and incredibly short pants. He could not foresee that these two had anywhere near the capability of destroying him, but Doefloct soon decided that they would not survive to see the next dawn.

Smiling wirily, he whispered, "These weak ones shall embrace my wrath and die slowly. So slowly."

Turning around and standing erect, he shook his long black hair behind his shoulders with a few jerks of his head, his black cape fluttering behind him. Then he lifted his dark-sleeved arms over his head, the right gripping the Staff of Majii. His eyes became fiery red.

"Death dogs which I command! Go forth and destroy the newcomers of a different land! Feast upon their bodies and gnaw at their bones until nothing is left!" he roared.

Sgt. Quentin awoke staring into a crackling fire a few feet away, darkness surrounding him. Ignoring the throbbing pain in his head, he managed to drink a small portion of water out of his canteen and noticed Gladstad looking at him from across the fire.

"Why do you have a fire blazing on a hilltop?" Sgt. Quentin demanded, failing to control his anger and still disoriented from the effect of whatever the snake had injected.

"I thought it would help you with the snake bite; keep you warm and all." Gladstad replied, taken aback by the Sergeant's disgust.

Shaking his head, Sgt. Quentin said, "No. What you're doing is telling anybody around us that there are people on this hill. Go ahead and shoot."

He bent he leg inwards to get a look at the bite wound and continued, "You've heard of light discipline after dark? We make easy targets with a fuckin' fire going, especially since we have no real weapons! Now put it out."

Cursing himself for trying to be helpful Gladstad overturned the earth under the fire with is axe.

Chapter Four

"Wake up! Move it! We're getting off this hill!" Sgt. Quentin ordered Gladstad as he nudged him with his boot.

Gladstad shot up almost immediately and realized it was early morning. He scratched his head then slowly collected the axe and flashlight from the ground and looked out into the horizon with sleepy eyes.

Sgt. Quentin plotted a path east with his compass and wondered how his bag could come up missing during the night. He wanted to accuse Gladstad outright, but he restrained himself. He could not convince himself that Gladstad was capable of snatching his bag and hiding it somewhere, yet remaining with him on the hill. He knew the unknown journey ahead would surely be rough for both of them and he didn't need any more complications.

In the back of his mind, he considered that they had been spotted by guerrillas and they could be playing mental games with them, just by taking the bag. Nevertheless, he knew a US naval supply ship made regular passes along the coast line to the east, picking up and dropping off supplies. Granted, surrounded by forest instead of jungle would signify they were at a much higher elevation at minimum, perhaps having been unknowingly transported to a mountainous area of Columbia, he reasoned that as long as he could make his way to the coast line, they would stand a much better chance of getting back to the base camp. Assuming they could evade capture by the guerrillas…if that was possible over a truly unknown distance.

Sgt. Quentin couldn't help but think that the guerrillas had already anticipated they would go east and had an ambush waiting. Worse yet, he thought that the base camp could have been overtaken which meant that, even if they reached the coast, no US ships would be sailing anywhere near the shore. Although he would never admit it to himself, if such an event had transpired, they would not be rescued. Tuning out the thoughts entering his mind, he resolved to simply head east for now.

A few hidden birds sang high in the trees around them and the distant thudding of a woodpecker could be heard in the still cool morning air. Striding down the hill followed closely by Gladstad, they entered the forest.

"Sarge, how'd we get in this forest?" Gladstad asked as he looked at the trees around them. It was a question he had wanted to ask for some time.

Sgt. Quentin shrugged. "I don't really know. We must have been transported here." He knew that the trek to the coast line would likely involve many days of transversing mountains, but he didn't volunteer that to Gladstad.

"But how? I don't see any roads." Gladstad puzzled, scanning the forest for a road of some type. Even a foot path.

"Probably by chopper." He replied.

Frowning, Gladstad said, "Why? Seems like it would be easier just to capture or kill us."

That stopped Sgt. Quentin in his tracks.

He turned and faced Gladstad, that ebb of anger becoming obvious on his face, "Look! I don't have the answers but until we're dead, I'm going to do my damnedest to get to the eastern shoreline and signal a US ship. Do you understand?!"

After Gladstad nodded with enlarged eyes, Sgt. Quentin turned and continued walking saying, "Come on! Let's go!"

As they walked through the forest for several hours, Sgt. Quentin continuously scanned the vegetation around them for signs of ambush. While he had not spotted anything, the last twenty minutes or so of the trek had a deafening, eerie silence to it that made his mind scream at him, trying to warn him of some unseen terror that was near. He could feel something, aside from unease, but he could not pinpoint it other than a feeling of being watched. But this feeling was far different than any others he had experienced on other missions. It was just too quiet.

But nothing had happened. By mid-day they reached a clearing about four hundred meters wide and twice that in length by his estimate. A small grassy outcropping lied in the midst of the clearing. A thin path was just barely visible that meandered along the base of the hill from the north and turned east over the top of the outcropping. Cautiously he knelt down at the foot of the clearing, holding his machete loosely with his left hand.

"What do you think it is?" Gladstad whispered. He walked up beside Sgt. Quentin, looking at the outcropping with curiosity, also seeing a path.

"Shit! Get down!" Sgt. Quentin whispered harshly as he glanced at Gladstad standing beside him, "I don't know. But I think it best if we avoid it."

Kneeling down Gladstad said, "Maybe we could find someone who could help us over there?"

"If that is a human path, maybe we won't get shot if we enter that clearing. Maybe the guerrillas will just drive us back to the base camp when they see us.", Sgt. Quentin replied adding, "Maybe I'll punch your lights out!"

"I was just…"

"Quiet!" Sgt. Quentin commanded, straining to hear that noise again. It was a faint rustle of branches and leaves being disturbed.

Gladstad looked around, trying to hear a noise that Sgt. Quentin may have heard. Slowly he turned his head to Sgt. Quentin and raised his eyebrows, shrugging his shoulders.

Suddenly the sounds became stronger and stronger. Sgt. Quentin wasn't sure, but he thought he heard rapid breathing, and something overhead. It was faint and only at the right moments could he hear the noises carry on the breeze.

"Come on! We're being followed!" Sgt. Quentin snapped instinctively, tightly gripping his machete as he turned about and began to run.

But before he could get more than a few steps, the pack of Death Dogs was upon them. The black dogs lurched and snapped viciously at Sgt. Quentin and Gladstad, their red eyes glowing with an insatiable hunger and the overwhelming desire to kill, to rip their prey apart, to taste that warm glistening blood, to bathe in it, to feel that beating heart collapse and explode under the might of their jaws.

Sgt. Quentin managed to slash a few of the chiseled black dogs before the pack overtook him. Helpless. He felt dull pains shoot through his arms and legs as they were bit and shaken from side to side, tugging and tearing at his flesh. But oddly, the bite wound from the snake occupied more attention in his mind.

Gladstad, too scared by the sudden onslaught, didn't even try to defend himself before some of the black dogs bore him down to the earth.

It glid through the sky, wide wings catching the cool air and pushing it down with rhythmic strokes. Those mighty wings kept the silver-scaled body in the air, seemingly with little effort. The tail occasionally moved slightly from side to side giving balance to the massive body as the wings continued their rhythmic beat. It's long, lethal claws were curled up underneath the body, still painted with the blood of its unfortunate prey. Its golden eyes were set in a large scaly skull that held two leathery nostrils and a huge jaw bone that bore dozens of razor-sharp teeth. Those resolute and piercing reptilian eyes probed the forest below in search of more prey to satisfy its hunger.

Then it saw the dogs, many dogs, surrounding two human forms as it looked on with interest, seeing how it could quench its hunger. Swooping down, its fire glands began to swell, stretching its scaly chest. Within a single moment it landed on the earth, its sheer weight causing its claws to sink into the ground several inches as if the hard earth were but of mud.

It opened its mouth and a nerve-wrenching unhuman scream bellowed forth accompanied by tremendous, searing flame as it barreled ahead with considerable force. Everything that was within the path of the flame was almost instantly burnt to crispy remains. None of the dogs attacked it. But there we no dogs left too attack. Only little juicy remains to be consumed.

Sgt. Quentin steadily felt himself weaken and become deathly cold as a gust of hot air passed over his limp form, feeling the earth around him shake. Then he no longer felt pain. Surprisingly he felt nothing as a peaceful black veil consumed his sight and he stopped breathing.

The towering Silver Dragon snatched one of the charred remains and tore into it ravenously. It took half the body in its mouth and shook the huge animal as a cat might shake a mouse. Bone snapped and sinew tore as the Death Dog was effortlessly ripped in two. The dragon chewed on the burnt carcass for a few seconds and, when it was confident all the larger bones were broken, swallowed the mass whole. It slowly thrust its leathery snout towards the bloodied lower half of the dog and saw the two longer forms – the Death Dogs' prey. Humans.

Chapter Five

A thin fog filled the cool, dark cave as the incense of rare herbs burned slowly and silently. A small flame nurtured heat into a gold jeweled bowl that stood on three short legs bearing the herbs, beside the cavern wall. Interestingly the cavern walls were not jagged and rough, but virtually as smooth as glass. It was almost as if those walls had endured an intense and controlled fire that had literally shaped and molded the walls into the smooth, spherical shape they now possess.

Almost simultaneously, two figures began to stir as if from a deep slumber. As their breath strengthened, a sweet aroma crept into their nostrils. Sweeter than cinnamon, it gave them more energy and life with each successive breath. Once the two figures managed to get up from their straw-made beds, the fog vanished. Shortly after the flame beneath the jeweled bowl flickered a few times and extinguished itself. In kind, the rare herbs ceased burning for lack of heat that the enchanted flame had provided.

"What happened?" Sgt. Quentin asked, glancing around the cave, obviously mystified.

"Don't know. Just remember those wild dogs," Gladstad replied. *'Maybe they were dead and in hell.'*

Each looked at their bodies for bloody wounds from the dogs. Except for the subtle reminder that their torn clothing bore, there was no physical damage. Sgt. Quentin noticed that even the snake wound was gone.

"This is weird." Sgt. Quentin frowned, walking out of the mouth of the cave into the dazzling sun outside. It blinded him for a few seconds, and he shielded his eyes with his arm.

Gladstad followed him, looking around the cavern as he walked.

Outside, a grassy hill was directly in front of him with a trail, perhaps a frequently used one, leading down from the top of the hill to the cave. On the left he could see the forest about two hundred meters away.

"Who's that?" Gladstad said lowly as he motioned to the right.

A dark, bubbly plot of earth lay near the cave and stretched along the base of the hill towards the forest. A vast assortment of flowers were rooted in the soft earth. Some were taller than others. Some with more softly textured green leaves or more leaves than others, all swaying with the soft, gentle breeze. The blooming flowers displayed their colors proudly. Some were deep purple, triangle-shaped with bloated edges while others were bright red thorny spheres with thorns tinged yellow. Still others were shaped like five-pointed stars having light blue borders and white centers.

A woman bent over at the waist, her long white gown moving faintly around her legs, and gently touched one of the flowers with her soft, delicate hand. She pulled it toward her a few inches and inhaled its sweet aroma as her long red hair fell over her shoulder like a rippling sheet of water.

Suddenly she realized she was being watched and stood up to face Sgt. Quentin and Quentin. Her gown, although as innocent as she was, parted sufficiently below her neck to emphasize her firm, voluptuous breasts. Her gold-colored eyes studied the humans as they stood there motionless, gazing upon her shapely body.

Managing to gain his composure, Sgt. Quentin asked, "How did we get here?"

Only the slightest movement of one eyebrow betrayed her surprise. Strange that humans such as these would speak her language so fluently.

"It seemed that you needed help there in the woods. The way you were all bruised up, I'd say you were attacked by a bear or pack of dogs," she replied simply, holding a flower shaped like a five-pointed star.

27

Looking to the forest, Sgt. Quentin said, "Yeah, we were attacked by dogs. How long have we been here?"

She looked to the sky for a moment and said, "Four days."

Thoughts of the lurking guerrilla presence suddenly made him remember their plight and his open and friendly attitude quickly vanished.

He eyes narrowed. "You speak English very well. Where did you learn it?"

Frowning slightly, she said, "What is English?"

He stared at her. "What's English? This is good! You're talking it right now. Where are the fuckin' guerrillas?!" Sgt. Quentin rumbled out, losing patience. He knew that the dogs that had attacked them had to have belonged to the guerrillas, and she probably belonged to the faction.

Gladstad looked at him with wide eyes. He wouldn't figure out why the beautiful lady was being grilled after she'd helped them, but he didn't know what to say.

"I don't know. What are fuckin' guerrillas?" she said innocently with her beautiful eyes focused on him.

"Oh fuckin' fuck. Where the hell am I? Mars?" he grumbled, "Who the hell are you anyway?"

She looked at him as though he was a child and had asked something silly. "I'm Angela, of course. And you are not in hell. You are in the Northern Realm of the White Magic. Hell, lays beyond the Southern Wastelands of Dark Magic."

Sgt. Quentin hated bullshit games like this.

"Really? Magic, huh? Tell me where the guerrillas are and quit trying to piss me off."

"I don't know where the guerrillas you talk about are."

"Oh shit. Do I look stupid?!" Sgt. Quentin barked out, "Fine, I'll play. Take me to your leader."

"I am a Chief," Angela proclaimed, straightening up slightly.

"Chief, then take me to someone I can talk to. I'm tired of bullshitting around."

Though some of his words eluded her, his tone seemed disrespectful and she glared at him momentarily. Remembering that these two were outsiders and didn't know any better, she dropped her eyes to the flower she held.

"I see you don't believe me. He said you were outsiders." She said softly.

"Well, who is he?" Sgt. Quentin demanded.

Looking up, she said, "Lord Arackas, Chief of the Elven Clan."

"Elven clan?" Gladstad mumbled to himself, "What is an elven clan?"

Sgt. Quentin smirked at Gladstad. Sometimes the kid talked too much.

"How do we find this Lord Arackas?" he asked, determined not to be confused by her talk of magic, elves and such nonsense.

Angela pointed to the trail that went over the top of the hill, "Just follow that trail north into the forest."

"Well, thanks for taking us in. We're on our way." Sgt. Quentin said coldly as he walked quickly towards the trail.

"I'm off to see the wizard." He joked to Gladstad, skipping once.

"Wait!"

He looked back and saw the woman following them.

"I'm supposed to give this to you…in the event you may need my help." She said, handing the flower to Sgt. Quentin. "Just burn it and I will come."

He thought it was more bullshit and surprised himself when he actually reached for the flower by impulse.

As Sgt. Quentin took it, Gladstad asked, "What kind of help?"

"Well, if you get in trouble. Like with whatever had attacked you." Angela pointed out.

Stuffing the flower in one of the cargo pockets on his pants, Sgt. Quentin nodded slightly. "Thanks."

He walked over the hill with Gladstad, thinking just how strange everything that happened actually was. It was almost as if they were in a different world. But that couldn't be possible.

"You thinking what I'm thinking kid?" asked Sgt. Quentin.

Gladstad nodded. "This is like a different world or something, isn't it? Those dogs, the cave, and her talking seriously talking about magic and elves...and that flower power in your pocket."

"I dunno, but I'm going to find out what's going on." He said as they followed the winding trail into the forest.

That little act could have been something to throw us off balance,' he thought quietly to himself. "Just stay aware of your surroundings and don't think about what she said. You let your mind drift and you'll end up dead."

Gladstad looked at him blankly as they followed the trail. He didn't know what to think.

Chapter Six

Darkness had spread across the forest and still he waited. The darkness didn't bother him, as he could see almost as well by night with no moon as anyone else could see during the day. Actually, he felt quite comfortable in his surroundings. Occasionally he would sniff the air around him deeply to help him locate any strange scent. If the wind blew past him, he could identify prey at two hundred paces. And just from that, he could estimate speed and the direction from which is prey traveled.

He was a hunter. And one of the best of his tribe. But this time it was different. This time it was not a hunt for hunger or glory.

Having heard some footfalls in the distance, he stood up from behind the tree he was concealed by but, with his five-foot-tall frame, he couldn't see past a few thick bushes ahead of him. He squinted slightly while his black eyes danced around the forest before him, unable to see anything. Then he smelled the scent of a human as the wind drifted past him from the east. It was a weak scent.

Footfalls again, but this time they were closer. And they seemed to be coming from the south. Had his nose tricked him?

Slowly he turned his bony head which, despite the years, still held long grayish white hair, trying to absorb any noise with is pointed ears. His instincts told him something was wrong.

The stillness was shattered by someone or something stamping through the brush directly behind him. Spinning around, his eyes widened with surprise and astonishment as he froze to the rush of a six-foot-tall figure, bearing a rather brutish looking short sword and clothing that looked like the very forest around him. His heart quickened as he reached for the dagger that hung from his waist. But then he remembered that this was not a hunt. If it had been, he could have hurled the dagger at his assailant as he had done with lethal effect to larger prey. But it was not a hunt.

Then, from behind, he felt two large hands grab his arms. He jerked slightly and realized he could get away if he had wanted to. His captor was not nearly as strong as he. His leather jerkins crackled quietly as he exhaled.

"Who are you? What are you doing here?" Sgt. Quentin heaved, momentarily breathless from the sudden sprint.

He eyed the two men, amusement evident in his voice, "I'm Orlog," the figure replied, "Now tell your weak friend to release me."

Sgt. Quentin looked at him slyly. "If you run, I'll cut your fuckin' head off!"

He said nothing. After a few moments, Sgt. Quentin motioned Gladstad.

As Gladstad released the short man, Sgt. Quentin asked, "Now, what are you doing here?"

Shrugging his shoulders, Orlog said, "Waiting for the two outsiders...for you."

Sgt. Quentin frowned. "Why?"

"Just to tell my lord of your approach to the tribe. And to warn the guards so you wouldn't get an arrow to the chest. You make big, easy targets you know." Orlog replied, smiling widely.

"Damn, look at his ears!" Gladstad exclaimed.

"So what!" Orlog spat, glaring at Gladstad. He didn't like people talking about his ears. Especially in the tribe, since he had larger ears than all the other taller male elves.

"Orlog. My man. That is a cute make-up job. What are you supposed to be? A leprechaun?" Sgt. Quentin smirked, noticing the long nose Orlog also had.

"I'm an elf." Orlog said proudly.

Prodding Orlog forward Sgt. Quentin said, "Well, my little elf friend, take me to your lord."

"He's an elf?" Gladstad whispered, amazed at seeing one in person.

"How should I know. You know what an elf looks like?" Sgt. Quentin said sternly as he followed the elf at the point of his machete.

Orlog didn't appreciate being hounded at the point of a short sword. Especially by two humans. *'Perhaps they aren't as important as my lord things and he'll let me destroy them.'*

As they walked, Sgt. Quentin realized that the trail that Angela had told them to follow was slowly veering off to the right before it twisted sharply north, vanishing from sight. "Hey Orlog! The trail goes east! What are you doing...leading us into a trap?!" he pressed, pointing to the trail with his free hand.

Orlog glanced at him, then shook his head. "Do you think we would build a tribe next to a trail to invite thieves to follow so easily, or outsiders like yourself? The tribe is this way." Orlog said plainly as he continued past some trees away from the trail.

A few leaves rustled around them as they followed the elf. Sgt. Quentin looked around cautiously, expecting them to talk into a trap. Then he heard some distant chuckles.

"I don't like this." Gladstad said lowly. He kept his eyes on the forest and realized they were walking past elves that were appearing and disappearing from the surrounding trees and bushes.

"Will you shut up?" Sgt. Quentin mumbled.

As they went through a line of large trees, each easily as wide as three men standing shoulder to shoulder, they found themselves in a village.

"They come!" a voice shouted from somewhere nearby.

Off in the distance, Gladstad caught the glimpse of a figure opening a door to peek out at them from inside a lit room. The smell of burning torches was strong in the air. Gladstad could see the faint outlines of some apparent dwellings from the yellowish light of the flickering torches that hung about in seemingly random spots.

"Please follow me to the hut we have prepared for you." Orlog said, motioning them to follow.

Seeing all the elves walking about, Gladstad muttered, "This is unreal."

"Yeah. Tell me about it." Sgt. Quentin said, almost beginning to believe that they were indeed in an entirely different world.

He noticed the males possessed all varieties of weapons for hunting, and some he thought may be for battle. The women and children stayed close to their wooden huts, staring at the newcomers as they passed.

After being ushered into a wooden hut whose entrance was small enough to force them to duck their heads as they entered, Orlog said, "Wait here. Food will be brought to you," then hurried out of the hut. It was obvious that Orlog's hospitality had waned.

It was surprisingly roomy inside the hut. The ceiling, supported at the center by a smooth log some ten inches in diameter, was about seven feet tall. A torch, one of several he had seen in the village, hung burning from the log. A round table surrounded the log and large wooden chairs crackled under their weight as they both sat.

She shut the door eagerly behind her and raced over to the large mirror. She combed her long brown hair with a gold brush as she looked at herself, her smooth face, somewhat bony in the cheeks. Her lips were not too big, or too small, but just right. Her light green eyes strayed to her tight-fitting green dress. Indeed, she was beautiful and she knew it. Very beautiful for being eighteen and only five foot four inches in height. But being the daughter of Lord Arackas, a very powerful wizard and Lord of the Elven Clan, restricted the freedoms she could enjoy unlike other elves of age. It had been difficult for her, especially now that her physical desires had blossomed and none would dare step forward to partake of them. None of the men in the Clan would come near her for fear of her father's wrath and she hated him for that. Didn't he realize that she had wants? Needs? But things were different now. Two humans were present in the village not familiar with Elven customs. She hoped her father would go easy on them, if he found one of them with her.

Putting the brush down on the table before her, she swept a portion of her brown hair over her left shoulder, partially covering one of her breasts. She knew tonight would be the night she would have pleasure with a male…even if the male was human.

"What do you think of all this?" Gladstad asked with a smile.

Sgt. Quentin shrugged his shoulders. "I haven't a clue."

Within a few minutes two Elven females, one in a green dress and one in a brown and somewhat shorter dress, brought in two large platters with sliced bread, large portions of meat, and a wooden tankard. As they placed the platters on the table, Sgt. Quentin gazed at the food hungrily. His stomach churned at the smell of well done, wood smoked meat, strikingly similar to hickory. The subtle scent of the sliced, freshly baked dark-brown bread filled his nostrils as it lay before him. But there were no forks, spoons or even knives with which to eat with. That ended up being of little importance as he grasped the juicy meat with both hands and began eating with haste to quench his raging hunger. As he chewed on a mouthful of meat, its juices tumbled freely down his chin. The meat itself seemed to melt in his mouth like snow.

As she sat the platter in front of Gladstad, she looked at him with her soft green eyes, smiling. He met her eyes with some hesitation as he felt a deep, passionate desire overtake him. Suddenly he wanted her more than he wanted to eat. Nothing else mattered. Not food. Not sleep. Just raging desire. Desire for her he did not comprehend or try to resist.

Nodding her head knowingly, she motioned for Gladstad to follow her. Eagerly he pursued, smiling like a child who had just gotten a new toy. He followed her out of the hut and into another wooden hut at the other side of the village.

After gently shutting the door behind him, she said, "Please, sit down."

Gladstad looked around briefly and found a bed covered in white sheets. He sat on it and found it was quite soft, though sturdy. Just what he needed.

"What's your name?" she asked as she unbuttoned her dress, confident that her magic was working on him to do whatever she desired. And she desired only one thing this night.

"I'm Gladstad. Umm, John." He mumbled, further enchanted by her beauty and the sweet smell of burning incense that hung in the air.

"My name is Karrie," she said softly, pulling the dress off her body.

Gladstad looked upon her naked, shapely body with raging desire. He desired to touch her long, flowing brown hair. Her shoulders. He wanted to feel her breasts press against his chest. He wanted to grip her slim buttocks in his hands. He yearned to grip her waist. He wanted to feel her warm body press against his, to feel her slender legs wrap around him…to feel the caress of her lips on his.

Effortlessly, he pulled off his T-shirt as she sat on top of him, almost forcefully straddling his hips between her legs. Oh how warm he was. So firm. Looking into his eyes she pushed him gently onto the bed and pulled his shorts off. Eagerly they embraced, each full of lust and the desire for the other's touch.

"Sorry about the food." Sgt. Quentin said as Gladstad entered the hut, realizing that in his frenzy to eat, most of the food had vanished. Only a few pieces of bread remained.

"Don't worry about it, I just want to sleep." Gladstad said after stretching out on the earth a few feet from the center log of the hut.

Gladstad smiled to himself. He had never felt so tranquil. So satisfied.

Sgt. Quentin just nodded and took another sip from the tankard as he peered outside the hut, trying to figure out just what was going on. He had no logical answer to give himself at this point.

In the early morning, they were both retched from sleep as a thunderous explosion rang in their ears. The smell of burnt wood filled the air as they looked around puzzled as to where the hut that they had slept in had gone.

"Shit." Sgt. Quentin muttered to himself at the sight of an ornately dressed elf standing before them. Clearly, whoever the elf was, they were not happy.

The elf was about five foot four inches tall, dressed in purple robes with a pure white beard that, like his hair, reached just past what most would guess as the waist line. He held a wooden staff equal to his height and a female elf stood next to him. Her head was down, as if she feared something or someone. A few elves peered around their huts, fearing what Lord Arackas might do in this moment.

"I am Lord Arackas! This is my daughter Karrie. Which one of you dared mate with her out of the Elven custom?!" he demanded, his deep black eyes blazing with madness.

Gladstad quickly glanced at Sgt. Quentin without moving his head.

"Oh man. How could you be so stupid?" he sighed to Gladstad, shaking his head in disbelief.

"I just…"

"Yeah, your peter took control, right?" He didn't know what Lord Arackas was capable of, and didn't want to find out. The missing hut and smell of burning wood in the air was sufficient.

"Silence! You're the one?!" Lord Arackas roared out, glaring at Gladstad.

Gladstad stirred uneasily on the earth, not knowing what to say or how to act.

Raising his staff, Lord Arackas conjured a simple spell, of which he had hundreds memorized. With a mighty thunder that echoed through the forest, an intense red fiery ball appeared at the staff's end. Crackling sound burst out from its center as a long, twisting red bolt of lightning reached out and wrapped itself around Gladstad's body. Then Arackas effortlessly caused the lightning bolt to raise the terrified soldier ten feet into the air.

"Oh shit." Sgt. Quentin whispered to himself, watching helplessly as Gladstad was raised into the air. His mind whirled, trying to think of ways to stop the mad elf, but he knew his hand-to-hand combat skills would not be enough here. Not without his rifle. And not against magic.

Sweat beaded off Gladstad's forehead as he felt the radiant power of the lightning bolt. Slowly it tightened around him, and he found himself gasping for breath. He tried to plead for his life, but only a weak slur made it past his lips.

Lord Arackas squinted his eyes together as he concentrated on the magical lightning bolt, causing it to tighten even more around Gladstad's straining body. He could only think of how the human had violated his daughter and that intensified his mounting rage which, he knew, would soon break free.

Karrie looked upon Gladstad with sorrow and pity. She had caused this. She knew that she should have been the one being punished, not him. He was just an instrument of her pleasure.

With a trembling hand, Karrie reached out and touched her father's shoulder and pleaded, "Father...stop. Don't do this, it's not right. I...I made him do it."

Lord Arackas squinted even harder at Gladstad.

"Please father." Karrie begged. She couldn't bear to see Gladstad fie for her enchantment.

Lord Arackas slowly relaxed his eyes and took a deep, strained breath as he released the spell, almost with regret. Gladstad plunged to the earth with a thud, gasping for breath.

Karrie smiled with great relief and thanks, even as Lord Arackas looked at her with pity and a sense of failure. He couldn't believe that his own daughter would do such a thing. He wanted to ask why but he knew this was not the time.

After a moment to collect himself, he turned his attention back to Gladstad. With a sternness that none in the tribe had heard him use before, Lord Arackas proclaimed, "You shall marry my daughter. With the rings bound on both your fingers, you are wedlocked until the end of the Age. These rings can never be removed from this time forward while either of you draw breath!"

Magically, a gold ring, ornate in a vined design, but lacking precious gemstones, appeared on each of their fingers. While the fit was snug, it was not tight.

Sgt. Quentin got up and strode over to Gladstad, helping him to stand. He was thankful that Lord Arackas had not loosed his full wrath upon Gladstad and, admittedly, himself. Gladstad was just relieved to be alive in this moment.

"Look, I'm sorry for this." Sgt. Quentin said to Lord Arackas.

Lord Arackas merely nodded his head, an ebb of rage still flowing through him and said, "I realize you two are outsiders that Metsys spoke of. Go to him. At once." He started to turn away.

"How do we get there?" Sgt. Quentin asked. He really didn't want to prolong the elf's presence, particularly with Gladstad right there, but he had little choice as he knew nothing of the land they found themselves in.

"Just travel north through the forest. When you reach a wide road, go east along it until you see a castle. Metsys will be there." Lord Arackas said firmly. Then, without uttering a spoken word, he wrapped a web of magical fibers around himself and Karrie and they vanished.

Sgt. Quentin looked over to Gladstad as if to study him while scooping up what little gear they had. "Why did you do that?" he asked harshly as they began walking, quite fast actually, through the Elven village.

Scratching his head, Gladstad replied, "I...I don't know. I just had this urge."

Sgt. Quentin shook his head. "Fuck. Keep your urges to yourself!"

"It's hard to explain! It was like I was controlled or something." Gladstad retaliated, unable to really explain what he had felt.

"Controlled my ass." Sgt. Quentin fumed as they entered the forest.

Chapter Seven

Sgt. Quentin pulled out his compass and gauged another path due north according to what the elf had said, but his mind wandered. It just didn't seem real. Angela. Elves. The Realm. It didn't seem real at all. Yet here they were. The more he thought about it, the more he grappled with the fact that they were in the equivalent of a fantasy world that was actually real. The only thing he could relate to what he'd experienced in this Realm, not surprisingly, were all the Warriors of the Realms campaigns he had participated in, back in his world. It was still hard for him to accept he was truly inside a real, breathing world full of magic and things only dreamed of. He smirked, speculating that someone from this world had made their way into his, weaving fanciful tales of fantastic creatures and powers that were retold over time.

"Where do you think we are?" Sgt. Quentin asked as they continued traveling.

"Beats me." Gladstad thought aloud, "Maybe we actually were drawn here by someone. Summoned."

"No shit." Sgt. Quentin grunted as he stuffed the compass away in a pocket. "I want to know why. We don't have any weapons. No magic. I don't know about you, but I'm no wizard."

Sighing deeply Gladstad said, "I dunno."

"Outsiders." Sgt. Quentin noted to himself. He could only guess just what they were brought here to do considering they had no unique gift, at least from what he could see.

Then, suddenly, sounds of trees splintering and breaking under dull thuds swept past them. They both whirled around to see what it was.

"What was that?" Gladstad asked weakly, not ready to confront whatever was making all that noise.

"Ha, ha, ha! Food!" a deep, thunderous roar sounded from the forest.

Two muscular giants mulled around the trees, each over twelve feet tall. A third form was behind them, somewhat shorter and younger in appearance. The young giant was with them to learn how to hunt as they did.

The strong, and usually fearless giants freely roamed the area of hills and forest around their close-knit extended family of giants for food and game. Unless provoked or motivated by hunger, the giants would rarely attack others, such as the Elven Clan. But when food became scarce, they would overrun any such tribes with sheer numbers. While very primitive and ignorant when it came to thinking of ways to shepherd animals or farm and store grain, collectively the race of Giants were considered little more than animals themselves by most in the Realm. As such, they were not seen as any real, calculating threat. That is, until a decade past as if by a fluke of nature, the giants experienced an unusual boost to their numbers. Predictably, to support that growth, the giants ravaged an incredibly wide area, plundering farms and entire villages that held livestock. Rarely though, did they ever kill humans or other races in the beginning. Regardless the humans, fearing for themselves and their offspring banded together over a thousand warriors to destroy the marauding giants. In costly skirmishes they eventually reduced the population of giants by half. But without enough willing and capable people to replenish their ranks, the year-long conflict whittled the small army down to just over one hundred. And the only reason that many had managed to survive was due to one barbarian's skill as both a warrior and mercenary. That barbarian was known by the men as Baracuss. As fate would have it, the conflict subsided and the giants faded from the minds of the other races. And, with time, Baracuss disappeared as well. That is, until now.

"What the hell? Cavemen?!" Gladstad blurted out, as he retreated a few steps at the sight of the hulking forms, confused as to which direction he should flee.

"Shit! I don't know!"

The giant forms, clad sparingly in black furs and wielding what appeared to be small trees crudely fashioned into clubs, approached them slowly.

One of the giants pushed over a tree almost equal in height to himself, as if it were a branch. Under the giant's strength, the tree fell to the ground with a loud crackling smack, uprooting itself and sending dirt into the air.

"Little man. Good food!" the Giant roared. He smiled, displaying rotted and missing teeth in his large mouth. The putrid breath of a giant would involuntarily contort the gut of even the strongest human.

"Come on! Let's get out of here!" Sgt. Quentin shouted as he ran north, Gladstad close on his heels.

"Move your ass, Sarge!"

Sgt. Quentin felt the earth shade under his feet as he glimpsed a small boulder impact hear them and he exclaimed, "They're throwing something!"

If they had been running any slower, one of the boulders that slammed to the ground behind them would have killed one or both of them.

Yet, not quite fast enough, Sgt. Quentin felt a sharp pain shoot through his left shoulder as he was sent reeling to the ground off balance from a sizable stone fragment that had just nicked him. Muttering under his breath and thankful that his head had not exploded like a melon, he scrambled to his feet and chased after Gladstad.

"Wait up!" he called after Gladstad who appeared to have summoned extra speed.

Within a few moments they reached a well-traveled road in the forest that split to the left and right of them. An old man in a mule-drawn cart rode down the road, staring at the strangely clothed humans as he passed.

Running east along the road Sgt. Quentin hoped that the giants would find the old man and give up their hunt for himself and Gladstad. Hell, the old man would die sooner than later anyway.

Sgt. Quentin heard hoofbeats growing louder and turned to see two muscular forms on horseback approaching them from the west.

"Hey! Can you give us a ride?" Sgt. Quentin pleaded.

As the barbarians reached him, the dark-haired one said, "Perhaps if there is gold in it." He pulled back on the reins gently to slow his mount. He wore leather jerkins and boots that looked as if they had seen the edge of many blades. His black, deep-set eyes conveyed a familiar battle hardness and a quiet, wild fury that could surge to the surface without warning. His companion looked almost the same, as if they were part of the same clan, except for the fact that he wore no helmet.

"I don't have gold." Sgt. Quentin confessed.

"Well then, I guess your legs will carry you." The barbarian said as he spurred his horse forward.

"Wait! There are cavemen chasing us!" Gladstad yelled at the barbarian.

He darted his dark eyes over to Gladstad with a scowl trying to decide if Gladstad was challenging him.

"No. I think what he means is there are giants after us." Sgt. Quentin corrected.

The barbarian stopped his horse and looked at them suspiciously, "That's impossible. The giants have not roamed here for many years."

"But they're…" Gladstad began, but was cut off by the shriek of a man and the splintering of wood. A mule bellowed in fright and pain as deep laughter past them.

"Come! Get on!" the barbarian prompted, patting the back of his horse.

With little help they mounted the two horses. The riders urged them forward in the direction of the screams.

"Where you going?!" Sgt. Quentin demanded though he was feared he already knew.

"To kill a few giants! Aye, even giants have a few gold pieces!"

"Oh shit. We are going to die." Gladstad mumbled weakly.

The barbarian pulled out his large, double-edged battleaxe effortlessly as his other hand held the reins. He grasped the leather-wrapped shaft with pleasure, feeling the silent, deadly severing power that his heavy weapon possessed.

Slowly, bloodlust filled the barbarian's muscles as he urged his horse into a full gallop. His eyes were ablaze with the desire to kill. The desire to spill the blood of whatever foe he could bury his battleaxe into. While he was intent on a giant, in truth, any challenger would suffice.

Sgt. Quentin shouted something not quite discernable as he took a firm grip of his machete, outclassed and dwarfed by the barbarian's battleaxe. But he knew there was only one thing that mattered now. Kill or be killed.

Fearfully, Gladstad clumsily held his single-edged axe in one hand as the steed he was on lurched into a gallop. Since they'd arrived, he'd repeatedly thought about dying in this strange land. Now he was sure of it.

The giants ripped the mule apart with their powerful hand and in their singular focus had been taken by surprise as the barbarians charged upon them. The helmed barbarian screamed an oath, and slammed his heavy battleaxe into the skull of one of the giants that was kneeling by what remained of the mule. The other giant, still startled but unafraid, lurched forward and clasped onto the horse's neck and with a simple motion snapped its neck. As the horse's legs gave out from under it, the giant's other large hand reached for the barbarian. But the barbarian was quicker and within a split second he swung himself from the saddle, rolled to the ground and gained his feet. Sgt. Quentin tumbled off the back of the dead horse, falling flat on his back and briefly struggled to catch the wind that was knocked out of him, still grasping his machete.

The other barbarian continued his charge directly at the giant who was in the midst of throwing the dead horse violently to the ground. As he raised his battleaxe, Gladstad closed his eyes and clenched his teeth, hoping the giant wouldn't hurt him too seriously.

As the barbarian swung his battleaxe, the giant raised his bulky arm to shield his head. The battleaxe wedged itself in the giant's forearm with a pop and squishy sound. Although a sharp pain nagged forcefully at the giant's simple mind, he managed to get his hand partially around the barbarian's neck and threw him into some bushes as though the barbarian weighed no more than a sack of potatoes.

Gladstad shrieked as the peeled his eyes open, darting past the turned giant, realizing the horse was galloping without the barbarian to control it. Tossing his axe to the ground, he pulled himself onto the worn leather saddle, grabbed the reins tied over the horse's black mane and slowed the horse.

The helmed barbarian sprung at the giant towering over him as he got a hold of the battleaxe and ripped it from the giant's forearm. Then with a fluid motion, he swung the battleaxe again and buried it into the giant's meaty chest with every ounce of strength he possessed.

The giant sunk to his knees, bloodshot eyes wide with surprise and feeling a sharp, rhythmic sawing pain pulsing from his chest. Weakly the giant grasped the bloody shaft of the battleaxe and with both hands jerked it out of his chest. The barbarian instinctively reached out and gripped his battleaxe, trying to wrench it away from the giant but even now, the giant's strength was just too great. With the battleaxe now under the control of the giant, the giant forced the battleaxe toward the barbarian. The barbarian labored with all his might, straining under enormous pressure and sweat rolling freely off his face as he struggled to keep the battleaxe at bay. But moment by moment, inch by inch, the cold, chipped, razor sharp head of the battleaxe gained upon the struggling barbarian who had the tables turned on him by a simple-minded, yet enraged giant. He could feel the giant's strength slipping, but knew it was not slipping fast enough.

Scrambling to his feet, Sgt. Quentin rushed to the giant still on its knees, and forcefully pushed his machete, up to its plain hilt, into the giant's side. In that moment he was amazed at how dense the giant's side was. The giant exhaled loudly, vaulting a thick mist of blood into the air as he toppled over, losing grasp of the battleaxe. The barbarian twisted as he regained control of the battleaxe and turned to the approaching sound behind him.

Gladstad came towards them on horseback. "Is it over?" he asked, trying fervently not to look at the dead bodies and scattered lumps of flesh.

The other barbarian stumbled out of the bushes, bruised but still able to fight. As he moved to claim his battleaxe lodged in the giant's skull, he replied, "Yeah."

Just when the hastily assembled party thought the time of battle had past, they heard the voice of another giant.

"Play?" a deep but childish voice called out from behind a nearby tree, not far from the remains of the cart.

Cautiously creeping around the cart, the helmed barbarian looked to the source of the voice and said, "What do we have here? A baby giant!"

"No – really," Gladstad said, awkwardly dismounting and striding up to the helmed barbarian to get a look.

Sgt. Quentin wiped the bloodied machete on the black fur of the felled giant and asked, "So what do you do with a kid giant?"

With gold in mind, the barbarian replied, "It could be sold for gold. Much gold! Enough for a new horse, wenches and ale!"

The other barbarian smiled in agreement.

"Will it hurt us?" Gladstad asked wearily.

"No. Baby giants are really quite dumb. It will be no harm. If it is, we just kill it." The Barbarian responded, testing the edge of his battleaxe with his callused thumb.

"Play?" the baby giant asked again as it stood up before them. At close to seven feet tall, it towered over everyone. Unafraid, it walked over to Gladstad, long knotted brown hair flowing behind it.

Startled at the giant's approach, Gladstad blurted out, "No play," feeling extremely small in comparison.

"No play?" the baby giant said slowly. But then it smiled saying, "Play is fun!"

Gladstad shot his eyes to Sgt. Quentin for help but he just laughed, "I guess he wants to play with you soldier – do your duty."

"Funny." Gladstad turned to the baby giant, "No play. Play later." He hoped that would be understood.

The baby giant lowered its head, losing its smile, "Oh."

The helmed barbarian smiled slightly as he wiped his battleaxe clean, at least of the fresh blood, and said, "We must be going if we expect to safely reach the castle before nightfall. Who knows what will come out of the forest then." Then pointing at the baby giant, "Perhaps some giant clan."

Realizing that the barbarians were headed to the same place he was, Sgt. Quentin asked, "Mind if we join you?" He recognized them as proven and armed warriors that he would rather be in the company of, instead of trying to make his way alone with Gladstad and a machete.

The helmed barbarian slipped the shaft of the battleaxe though a loop on his leather belt. "I guess not. Besides, the giant seems to like your friend. Much easier to take to the castle."

"Yeah, well, he seems to have that kind of luck." He held out is hand toward the barbarian, "I'm Sergeant Quentin."

"A soldier, eh?" the barbarian said, lightly touching his battleaxe. He never did appreciate soldiers, especially from combat. He'd come to hate them when he commanded them in the war against the giants long ago. Some, including those he had personally chosen for commands, had stirred a mutiny against him following a

47

particularly costly battle against the giants and tried to end his life rather unceremoniously in his sleep. He really didn't care much about what his soldiers did as long as they fought well. But that incident blackened his heart towards them as a whole even if they did fight well. And all those he chose did.

"Yes. But I'm not from this land." Sgt. Quentin replied quickly, noticing the reaction he'd somehow provoked. *Fuck. Are we ever going to catch a break around there?'*

Studying Sgt. Quentin and eventually deciding he meant no ill-will, the barbarian lowered his hand from the battleaxe saying, "I suppose not. Those are not garments of any soldiers I've ever seen before. What brings you here?"

"To visit a friend." Sgt. Quentin lied. Although he wanted to admit he was brought here by someone named Metsys, he decided not to. Having seen how the barbarian reacted to the mention of a soldier, he wasn't sure he wanted to find out how the barbarian would react if he mentioned the Wizard's name.

The barbarian nodded. He didn't have any cause to suspect any skullduggery afoot and didn't really care about people's associations as long as it didn't affect him.

As he started walking along the road to the east, the helmed barbarian said, "You can call me Baracuss. And that is my friend, Loce."

Glancing at Sgt. Quentin, he continued, "But. I think for your life, you should use a different name…I've done it many times before."

He pulled off his boonie cap and ruffled his hand through his short hair, following the barbarian. *How could something as easy as coming up with a name be so tough?'*

After many minutes had passed, he brushed his short hair again. Then he had it. "How about Mohawk?"

Baracuss let the strange sounds fall over his tongue. "Mo-hawk…Mohawk…good. You are now Mohawk."

Chapter Eight

They arrived at the immense wooden castle gates just as the sun set over the edge of the Northern Ice Mountains, still some distance beyond the castle. Both Gladstad and Mohawk viewed it in awe, taking in the towering sixty-foot-tall stone layered walls and the mighty wooden and iron reinforced gates. Neither knew that the might of the walls was not to serve as a spectacle but as a dependable defense from giants, dragons and foes that have long been forgotten.

Four soldiers that stood watch outside the gates held long spears and small shields clad in full link chain mail and steel helms. They stared at the small band's approach with curiosity and some suspicion of the baby giant. Without delay they took a defensive stance in front of the two barbarians, blocking their entrance to the castle. Loce pulled back on the reins to stop his steed from meandering through the soldiers. A few peasants from inside the castle walls turned and looked out of the open gates with some interest, noticing the soldiers line up in front of the entrance.

"What is your business here with that giant?" one of the soldiers demanded, pointing his spear at the baby giant. The giant had not ventured far from Gladstad for the entire journey and stood near him now.

Baracuss was not in the mood to answer inane questions from a damn soldier, especially one as young and battle fresh as this one. The only reason he didn't reach out and punch the soldier was for the fact that many gold coins waited beyond the castle walls in exchange for such a young and impressionable giant that he had brought along. Such giants had become a rare prize in recent times.

With a strained grin Baracuss said, "To sell him on the block."

"Aye. That will bring a hefty sum for the mines," one of the soldiers remarked in agreement.

The mines were deep within the Northern Ice Mountains. A keep nestled near one of the cavernous entrances, and the plundered mines within, were dangerous to be around. Many of the merchants who had claimed land nearby and begun to dig up the rich mineral deposits of rough precious stones and even gold, did so with reckless abandon. More interested in filling the purse, many soon met with disaster. Vast areas of land claimed had not been explored prior to their dispersal of labor armed with pick and shovel. That haste wrought death to many due to flash floods rolling down the mountains and sweeping away camps, to instability of mine shafts. It also propelled the costs and demand for labor which made the merchants clutch their purses even tighter and, as a result, perpetuate a cycle of continuous disaster. Over time the fingers of economic consumption shifted and groped its way into the openings of the jagged caverns, some as deep as a day's walk though sub-caverns and long natural breaks in the mountain connecting them together. But some unfortunate merchant ventured too deep within the mountain and came across stony giants not pleased with the chance encounter. The giants swept out from the high mountains and mercilessly attacked the merchants and laborers. Almost no one survived the bloody, ruthless slaughter. Those that did fled to this very castle and never returned.

The merchants remained undeterred and began purchasing barbarian slaves and giants, both a considerable upgrade to the human laborers. Some they trained for combat while others just for working the mines inside the mountain. The manpower required to retain the mining operations was extraordinary yet still profitable. In an average year several hundred barbarians and a few dozen giants were required to keep the gears of the economic engine moving. Such a young giant, like the one in the company of Baracuss, could be well trained as a combatant against the giants from the mountain and might even see more than a single year.

The soldier pointing his spear at the baby giant looked at the party closely. He didn't recognize the odd clothes that Mohawk or Gladstad wore but they did not appear threatening. Reluctantly he lowered his spear and motioned, "Pass. But keep your giant under control."

Nodding impatiently, Baracuss led them through the gates.

The cobblestone streets were filled with peasants, mostly human with a few elves scattered about, walking around buying, selling and carrying various goods. Even a few livestock were being driven down a street that split from the main throughfare. The smell of burning torches lingered in the air as the band walked down the street. A few people who were arguing over some live chickens paused to gaze at the baby giant.

As they passed a tavern, the two barbarians looked eagerly at the scantily clad wenches who stood outside, smiling at them. They would be fine company later.

"Is the block open now?" Mohawk asked, looking at the smooth legs one of the wenches bared for him, a sample of what could be.

"No. But the giant has to sleep somewhere." Baracuss replied.

Loce pointed. "No better place than the stables."

A bald-headed man with a large, round belly stretching his wool shirt came out of a door adjusting the pants around his pudgy waist. "Hey friends, what can I do for you?" he asked with a smile.

"Like to buy a horse. A good horse mind you. None of your fly-catchers." Baracuss said.

The stable owner was, naturally, tempted to pass off a 'fly-catcher' to those that seemed harmless. While he had spotted Gladstad as a likely buyer at first glance, the

51

company of blood-stained barbarians like the ones that stood before him now, prompted him to reconsider.

"Of course! Yes, I have one just for you." The man said, "Come. Follow me."

Loce dismounted and they followed the man into the stables.

"The horse. It is for you, my friend?" the stable owner asked Baracuss.

"Yes."

Seeing the horses, the baby giant asked, "Play?" They would be much fun to play with.

"No!" Gladstad heaved too harshly before he toned himself down, "Play later."

Baracuss looked over the muscular horse with a shiny, well-kept black coat and reasonable hoofs that the stable owner pointed to with an open hand. The horse seemed good for a warrior.

"How much?"

The man paused for a moment, stroking his straggly beard peppered with white hair and said, "Fifty gold."

Baracuss, opening offended by such a price, glared at the man and laughed, "What?! Outrageous! I'll pay you thirty-five gold for the horse. And I'll give you another four gold to lodge my friend's giant for the night."

"Well, with lodging a giant that might be thirty-nine gold…if he don't cause any problems." The main said, adding up the numbers in his head and raising an eyebrow toward Loce, "Okay. Forty-one gold and I'll hold your friend's horse here as well."

Baracuss had forgotten about Loce's horse. Dumping many gold coins out of his leather purse, Baracuss left the man in the stables with cupped hands and a heaping pile of gold.

"Stay here." Gladstad told the baby giant as they left, motioning with his hands.

"Hungry." The baby giant beckoned.

"Don't worry. I'll be back with food." Gladstad said, following the others out of the stables.

Sometime after they entered the tavern, Gladstad forgot the baby giant as the tankards of ale passed between them. Relatively early into the night he passed out.

The following day Gladstad awoke, rubbing his throbbing temples, still seated at the same rough-hewn table he had been at with Mohawk and the barbarians the night before. He couldn't remember anything about last night. Perhaps it was for the better that he didn't remember climbing on a few of the wooden tables and dancing while yelling and scaring the wenches with his wild antics. The ring he wore kept him from doing anything more carnal, for every time arousal stirred within him near a suitable wench, the ring's enchantment would stir to counter that primal energy. His antics may have been a subconsciously driven attempt at trying to break the enchantment.

But he did provide entertainment that many in the tavern would remember for some time to come.

Mohawk smiled inwardly at Gladstad seeing that he was finally awake. He didn't know that Gladstad could be such a partier. But, he guessed, many people were like that when they had freed themselves of societal constructs.

Baracuss walked over to the table, raising a tankard full of ale, vividly remembering the three wenches who dedicated most of their evening to satisfy him, "Damn what a good night!"

Loce and Mohawk raised theirs, and drank deeply while Gladstad merely rubbed his head.

Gladstad put a finger to his lips. "Shhh," he said with a strain on his face. It was not the first time he'd had a few beers, just never so much.

"We're going to be needing more gold." Baracuss said, tossing his purse on the table with a faint rattle of coin. Only ten gold remained.

Mohawk nodded. "How about selling that giant today?"

53

"Aye, that would bring some gold. But the giant can wait." Baracuss confessed.

He pointed across the dimly lit room. "See that merchant over there?" he said, adjusting his line of sight with his hand to a silk-robed man with fat jeweled rings wrapped around his fingers.

"Yeah, so?" Mohawk said, turning around in his chair to glance at the merchant.

"He's a very powerful trader. I heard he has a vast amount of gold for anyone who can stop the killings at the Eastern Port." He said plainly.

What he didn't say was that the merchant owned the port and any ships that docked to load or unload cargo had to pay him a fee. Charging a fee for the port by itself didn't seem like a very capitalistic endeavor but when his port was the only way to access this area of the Realm without crossing vast marshes and mud flats, that fee was the most inexpensive way of getting goods in and out. At a hundred and fifty gold per vessel, it gave him the ability of building three sea going ships every year with enough remaining to invest in other merchant trades beyond the great seas. But, if the killings persisted, the gold raised at the port would begin to dwindle and that was not good for business.

"Killings, like a Jack-the-ripper or something?" Mohawk said.

Baracuss frowned, not comprehending what Mohawk was referring to.

"Someone who's crazy." Mohawk said simply, not caring to explain himself in great detail.

"How much gold will we get if we kill the killer?" Gladstad said. He needed some different clothes and ones that could protect him better from the cold of night than what his shorts and T-shirt provided.

"That's what I'm going to find out." Baracuss said as he pushed his chair away and strode toward the merchant.

He didn't wait for an invitation. Sitting down in front of the merchant he stated, "Heard you have a reward out for the killings at the Eastern Port."

The merchant considered the barbarian sitting before him. A professional, surely. But so were others who had tried and were never seen alive again. But no matter, it wasn't is life.

"That's right. Three hundred gold for whoever can stop the savage murdering and, of course, bring me proof. I take it you want to try for the reward?" the merchant said, twisting one of the rings around his finger.

The thought of bagging three hundred gold made Baracuss smile, though trying to not look too impressed with the reward he replied, "That's right. And I'll bring you proof upon my return."

Looking at the barbarian with his hazel eyes, the merchant observed, "You seem confident. That's good for a warrior. But I must tell you, others such as yourself have gone to the Eastern Port and never returned. Tell me, barbarian. What makes you think you're different?"

Remembering a fragment from his past, Baracuss recollected, "Eleven years ago I led an army and I alone killed eighteen giants." He flipped his hand through the air in an uncaring gesture and continued, "Besides, like you said, I *am* a barbarian."

Looking over the table where Baracuss' friends sat, the merchant nodded. "I heard of that war. It was bloody to say the least. But it's hard to split the gold four ways…isn't it?"

"We're not cut-throats." Baracuss said sternly, slamming his balled fist on the table, then making a motion as if to pull the battleaxe from his waist.

The merchant jumped slightly, startled but enjoying his proximity to a hardened barbarian radiating strength. It was rare for him to step so close to the edge of rationality, "Fine! You have a deal my friend. Ask for Quintities when you return…if you return."

"Good." Baracuss grinned. He stood and walked away; the insinuation forgotten.

"So, what's the deal?" Mohawk asked eagerly.

"We leave now. I don't know who we're looking for, but all we have to do is sit and watch. Then we kill."

"That simple?" Gladstad said, taken aback by the barbarian's simple strategy.

"Yes. We kill quickly and be the first to collect the reward."

"What makes you so sure?" Mohawk prodded.

Walking to the tavern door, Baracuss paused and revealed, "Because nobody has lived to come back and collect."

Chapter Nine

Mohawk and Gladstad had reluctantly gone with the barbarians even though Mohawk was eager to meet Metsys to find out why they were brought to the Realm and return to his world. He had considered the slim possibility that, by going to the Eastern Port, he could find a better weapon than the machete he carried or better, being able to purchase one from the reward. Either way, he would have a better weapon and a better chance at surviving until he could return.

The journey to the Eastern Port was relatively easy for the party, even though they were doubled-up on horseback. But the week-long trek wore out the stout horses, having to bear two riders instead of one and with little food and water. Since Baracuss had to ration the remaining gold he had, not much feed could be purchased for the horses. Incredibly though, the horses were able to reach the Eastern Port as if they had been kept alive by some unseen force. Baracuss didn't question it.

"This is it?" Mohawk asked, looking around.

Few ships were docked at port which, from the size of it, could lash eight large ships at any given time.

Only two were in port and of those two, armor clad soldiers with long swords cautiously guarded each.

Only five sailors were visible topside and they were unloading huge wooden crates with the help of slaves. Even from this distance at the entrance to the port, Mohawk could tell the slaves were bulky and strong. Probably barbarians. These ones appeared to be well seasoned as they moved the cargo with speed and coordination. No Master of the whip was visible which meant they were trusted.

As they neared, he could see that all of the slaves wore fairly well-kept clothing though he could not discern the material.

"Yeah." Baracuss replied.

"This man-killer must be a serious problem around here, huh? I mean, there aren't many people around here." Gladstad pointed out, "Well, there really isn't anybody here."

Nearing a small tavern, they dismounted. Baracuss strode up to a sailor who was entering.

"Hey there!" Baracuss called out.

"Yeah?" the old sailor replied, scratching his short, white hair. Years of sea-bearing life were obvious in his hard, wrinkled face. Even his leather belt, bearing a sheathed blade, looked as though it could use a fresh coat of oil. In truth, the salty water, despite the protection of oil, had worn out the leather.

"Do I? Oh yes, quite well." He responded roughly as he continued inside, sitting down at a worn table that had seen the tips of many sailor's whittling blades.

A ravishing woman in a tight fitting black and white long-sleeved shirt, parted generously in the front, walked over to the table. Her black pants tucked inside long, black leather boots openly conveyed her unusually muscular legs.

"What can I get you?" she asked, tugging at her blond hair with a tantalizing smile.

Baracuss could hardly take his eyes off her. She was much farer than wenches he had crossed in the past. *'How could someone so beautiful work in a tavern such as this?'*

"Ale!" the old sailor replied, staring at her soft cleavage. In a flash, he remembered all the beautiful wenches that he'd been with when he was in more capable shape. Oh, only if he were a bit younger.

Baracuss ordered the same, eyes still drawn to her shapely body.

She turned gracefully and walked away.

Tearing his eyes from her the old sailor began, "Oh yes, the man killings. From what I've heard, many men, not only sailors, have come here to this very same tavern and they're never seen again. But no bodies have ever been found…I mean as if they were killed. More likely they were kidnapped."

Pointing at himself, he said, "I've come to this tavern on many occasions with nobody killing me. I can swear to that. I just come here now to look at the wenches and drink. Years ago I'd have done more you know, but I'm not the sea dog I used to be."

The old sailor smiled at Baracuss, thinking of the old days.

The lady returned to the table and, after placing the tankards on the table, winked at Baracuss as she turned and moved to the bar. Baracuss' eyes followed her eagerly.

Pulling over a few wooden chairs from the other tables, Loce, Mohawk and Gladstad seated themselves at the table where Baracuss and the sailor were.

"Round of ale!" Loce burst out, longing to taste the ale after the week-long trek.

Gladstad's stomach lurched at the thought. He couldn't drink himself into oblivion again.

As the night wore on and more of the ale was consumed, wild stories of conquest and much wenching circled the table. Only Gladstad had no such stories and felt awkward for having none to tell. After a few more tankards though, he forced himself to leave with the blond server – determined to remember the experience so that he'd have a story to tell. And, he actually felt normal around this one, his mind unclouded with what he wanted to do. His gold ring did not stir.

The tavern began to busy with more people and Baracuss kept an eye out for anyone who might fit the description of a killer or captor. Although most of the people in the tavern looked as if they could easily kill someone as look at them, Baracuss could not spot anyone who would do it out of sport.

The old sailor had a few more tankards and clumsily retired to his ship, laughing to himself as he left.

"It doesn't appear that the killer is coming tonight." Loce said, realizing the lateness of the hour and that the tavern was slowly emptying of sailors.

Looking around the tavern, Baracuss noticed that among the remaining sailors, most with wenches, none of them looked suspicious. But he didn't really know what to look for. Still, something didn't sit right with him…something he could not pinpoint. He sighed at the thought of this endeavor taking many days and what little gold he had left.

Getting up, Loce waved to the blond server that had brought the tankards earlier and said, "Well, I'm going to have a little fun!"

Smiling at them, he left with the server into a room. As the door shut behind them, Mohawk noticed the handle of Gladstad's axe propped up against the wooden wall beams beside the door.

In the dim torchlight she embraced Loce without reservation and began caressing his muscular neck with her soft, wet lips. He knew he wouldn't have to be aggressive towards this wench, unlike some of the others he'd been with. In turn, he embraced her, kissing her smooth neck. But as he continued, his lips came across what felt like a patch of thick hair. Hair he didn't notice was there before. And, it tasted strange.

Before he could pull away to get a look, she bit into his neck with long, sharp teeth as he vainly struggled to get away. He was held tightly in place with her six long, hairy arms.

As she drained the warm blood out of his large body, her eyes turned yellowish-red with wild hunger. She knew she would soon have enough blood and liquified organs to feed her young that were soon to birth. And when they came, they would spread and, in turn, feed upon others. Dimly she imagined one day of ruling the entire land from the spread of her young from this place full of easy prey.

Loce's eyes widened with terror as he tried to yell out for help, but couldn't. He couldn't even breathe.

"Why is Gladstad's axe over there?" Mohawk inquired, once again amazed at the kid's forgetfulness.

Baracuss glanced over to the axe, expressionless. Suddenly he jumped up as if he'd seen a ghost. He pulled his battleaxe and cursing to himself for not piecing it together sooner, roared, "By the gods! I should have known it! Damn her!"

He sprang over the table, rushed to the door and smashed it open with his powerful shoulder. The door popped and splintered as it flung inwards on its iron hinges with a sound so thunderous the remaining patrons in the tavern fell silent for a few moments.

Mohawk sprinted over to the door and withdrew his machete cautiously, not sure what was happening. Others did, too, but it was none of their affair.

Baracuss exploded into the dark room that was lit by a single torch. Reeling to his left by the faint sound of sucking, he saw the pale form of his friend, Loce. A black spider covered by thick hairs, equal to the size of a man, stood upright on two pointed legs, its others locked around Loce's body, keeping him upright against the wall.

For a fraction of a second, Baracuss thought of the many battles he'd been in. Seeing his foes' heads drop from their bodies at the caress of his battleaxe. He remembered Loce, an inexperienced warrior at the time, take a savage blow from a giant that had come up behind him while he battled another. While the blow had rendered Loce unconscious for over seven days, it had given Baracuss another chance at life. One he wouldn't have had if Loce hadn't been there.

A tremendous surge of rage raced through his mighty form as he smacked the back of the spider with the flat side of his battleaxe, causing the spider to stumble forward, losing grasp of Loce. Limply, he fell to the floor, unmoving.

Lifting the battleaxe over his head with blinding speed, Baracuss sent it whistling towards the spider, eager to cleave it in two. But the black spider, with its keen reflexes, jumped to the other end of the small room while sending a thick, white sticky cord at Baracuss.

Lurching forward and rolling off his shoulder and forearm, he dodged the substance as it hit the wall behind him, instantly crystallizing into a thick, circular white film. Again, he swung his battleaxe at the black spider as he got to his feet, severing the lower half of its body and catching two of its legs.

The spider turned and jumped at Baracuss, its mouth groping for his throat as it latched onto him with its remaining limbs. Unable to use his battleaxe, he dropped it beside him just in time to grasp the spider around its jaws, straining to hold it away from his throat. Then something slick shot out from inside the spider's mouth, wrapping tightly around his neck. With one hand he grasped the red-corded tongue to rip it from his neck so he could breathe. But when the spider's jaws came within an inch of his reddening face, he gripped the spider's head with both hands, barely able to keep it away. Within moments his lungs began to burn and the dark room began to get darker.

Seeing that the spider had Baracuss firmly in its grasp, Mohawk ran over and buried his machete into the black spider's back, causing it to release the barbarian in an apparent nerve reaction from piercing the exoskeleton. With considerable effort, he forced the spider to the floor and pushed the machete deeper into its back as Baracuss stumbled to his feet, grabbed his battleaxe and swung it at the struggling spider. Cleanly he severed its head as a dull crunching sound echoed through the room and fragments of the spider's shell jumped into the air.

Once the spider stopped moving, Mohawk withdrew his machete. Baracuss, not so easily convinced, ripped the torch and its iron base from the wall and threw it on the spider's black body, catching it afire.

Mohawk took a few steps back as the fire consumed the sizzling body, his eyes wide with relief. He never knew such a thing existed. Then he looked at Baracuss, who was rubbing his throat.

"Is it dead?" Mohawk asked, breathing heavily.

"It's dead now." Baracuss said roughly as he sheathed his battleaxe and approached Loce. Smiling with relief, he found that his friend still breathed, although shallowly as he picked him up.

While Baracuss carried Loce out of the room, Mohawk saw a grayish mound in a corner of the room. Even as he walked up to the unrecognizable mound, he got a bad feeling in his gut. But he had to see for himself if his feeling was right.

As he got close, he saw shriveled flesh that hung loosely around exposed arm and leg bones. It was as if everything had literally been sucked out. Reaching over he picked up the golden ring and took the pair of dog tags, still warm, from the mound.

Gladstad, 2121-04-4431, A Neg, No religious pref. Gripping the dog tags in his hand, Mohawk almost retched, cursing himself for not being more aware of Gladstad's whereabouts. He leaned against the wall and sighed in disbelief as he looked upon the mound that had once been Gladstad. Indeed, Gladstad had found his dreaded end.

With help from Baracuss the following day, Mohawk buried the remains of Gladstad deep within the forest as they waited for Loce to recover from his wounds. Looking at the fresh grave, Mohawk clenched the dog tags in his hand as he'd done with so many others who had died in his company. He couldn't help but feel some hollowness, an emptiness in his consciousness knowing Gladstad had died so horribly...so grotesquely. Although he didn't care for him much personally, he'd entered this world with him. And now he was gone. Mohawk had always tried to keep friendships at a distance. He'd found it was much easier to cope with death from a distance, especially having seen it take many of his friends in combat. That was why he didn't shed any tears now. Death was common to him, as if it was somehow part of him.

But even after Baracuss left Mohawk alone, he stood by the fresh grave for the greater portion of a day with the stark realization that his only contact with his world was gone. He was a stranger in a strange land. Alone.

For the next several days, Mohawk returned to the grave.

When Baracuss returned just before sunset on the ninth day with the horses and Loce, Mohawk hoped that no such fate would befall him in this land where no one would remember him.

He took the reins from Baracuss and swung himself onto the saddle.

"Looks like its time to leave this place." Baracuss said somberly.

Mohawk smiled at him as best he could and urged the horse forward, followed by Baracuss and a weakened Loce upon the other.

Chapter Ten

Quintities was not difficult to find. The merchant's name, as it turned out, was known to people that had not actually met or conducted business with him. While tracking him down was simple for Baracuss as compared to hunting a thief, it had been a time-consuming endeavor given that a few of the leads were dead-ends.

Baracuss turned his horse towards Mohawk after talking to a few plainly dressed people mulling about in the street and stated, "He's at the tavern." It made sense to him that he would be there, able to drink, wench and do business at one spot rather than royals who tended to hide their proclivities and dealings from the sight of the common folk.

"Sounds like a man of my tastes." Loce grinned. While his wound had healed during their trek back, the ghastly marker on his neck would never fade.

After dismounting they entered the tavern.

"Aye." Baracuss agreed, winking at one of the wenches that stood near the doorway.

Scanning the partially filled tavern, he saw the merchant alone at a table, reading a letter. The trio approached without Quintities looking up, apparently unaware.

"Quintities," Baracuss began, throwing the ass-end of the black spider on the table, "this was your port killer."

Quintities lowered the letter and looked up, mildly frustrated by the interruption, and then to the decomposing remains with apprehension. Until today the Shagiv, fiercely competitive and territorial, had only been known to dominate a few lands beyond the great sea. If they have managed to make it here...

"Ah. Yes. I should have thought as much." Quintities said casually, trying to temper his concern, "Were their others?"

"No." Baracuss lied, unsure. He didn't see any others at the port, but in their human form there was no visual cue that would tip him off that a spider lurked within.

"Good then!" Quintities cheered, throwing three leather purses heavy with gold onto the table. "Please take your reward and spend it well, eh?"

Quintities was eager to conclude the business at hand so he could finish his letter and focus on the appearance of the Shagiv, a troublesome revelation.

While Baracuss was mildly surprised that the merchant did not ask for any other information or details, he was not going to sour the moment, particularly with all that gold on the table before him. Scooping up the purses, he smiled and said, "Aye you can bet on that!"

As they left the tavern, he handed a purse to Loce and Mohawk.

"That seemed a bit strange. For all that gold, he sure did not ask many questions." Mohawk remarked, looking over to Baracuss with a raised eyebrow.

Baracuss shrugged slightly. He guessed the merchant knew more, possibly much more but said, "It is. But we completed his task and we got paid."

Loce nodded in agreement, touching his neck.

"True," Mohawk agreed, "and I don't know about you, but I'd like to get my hands on some armor and a real sword." He felt incredibly under-armed with a stainless-steel machete. While the metallurgy was superior to other blades he had seen, it lacked other traits that combat demands.

"Good idea." Loce said, looking at Mohawk. The machete wasn't a weapon he would take into battle.

"Well then, let's go." Baracuss said, patting Mohawk on the shoulder as they strode down the cobblestone street to an armorer's shop.

"Yes?" a stocky, muscular man with bright orange hair asked as they walked up to the make-shift wooden counter just inside. The man, nearly six foot four inches in height, forced the trio to look up to him.

65

Mohawk couldn't get over just how much hair was on the man's arms, darkened from oil and dust. It was almost as if the man was wearing a fur. *I wonder if this guy as a nickname?'* He thought to himself. *'Orange man seems apt.'*

"I'd like to price some armor, chain and a sword worthy of combat." Baracuss said sternly, not intimidated by the man's towering appearance.

"For you?" the man asked, looking among them and quickly settling on Mohawk. He had never seen clothing like that before.

"My friend, Mohawk." Baracuss said, pointing to Mohawk with his left hand.

"Ah, good. I have just the things you need." The blacksmith grinned, mentally shifting into sales mode. He turned and pulled out some things from behind the counter. With one hand, he lifted up a dull gray chest plate complete with leather strap and placed it on the counter, along with chain mail on top of it.

As Baracuss began inspecting the plate and chain mail for flaws in craftsmanship, the man disappeared behind an opening in the wall that that had been concealed by a large fur hanging from a thick rope. He soon re-appeared bearing a long sword cradled in a plain leather sheath.

"This will do fine." Baracuss said evenly as he lowered the chain mail onto the counter top, not wanting to sound too impressed with the quality of the forged material. It was all in the art of dealing. But he was impressed with the clean strokes that had been applied to the links of the chain mail, and the care that had been taken to create the smooth, one-piece chest plate. He'd seen plates that had been made from several pieces of metal and crudely joined. In fact, in his early days as a mercenary, he wore one such plate in battle that had split causing him some unwanted and almost deadly wounds.

Handing the double-edged long sword to Mohawk, the blacksmith asked, "What are those clothes you wear? I've never seen such."

Taking the sword, Mohawk thought for a moment and simply said, "Oh, they are from my land…"

"And those stains?"

"It is known as a camouflage pattern. It is supposed to conceal a person better in wooded areas." Mohawk replied.

"Ah." The man said absently, pondering if he could place such a pattern in his armor. If he could, he reasoned he could make a substantial sum of gold by selling such revolutionary armor to the highest bidders.

"Well, how much do we owe?" Baracuss asked, ready to bargain if the price wasn't reasonable.

"Huh?" the man said, snapping out of his thoughts, "Ahh, about forty gold."

Loce darted his eyes over to the blacksmith in surprise. The armor, chain mail and sword would never have been that cheap in other places he had traveled. But it didn't look like the blacksmith was really concentrating on the sale. It was as if he was pre-occupied.

But he was. The blacksmith was thinking of ways that he could place patterns into one-piece chest plates and other armor. He had, on several occasions, been able to beat patterns into the plate with striations, such as eagles which were for the high-ranking soldiers that roamed the Realm. Then he'd carefully pour gold or pewter onto the depressed areas where they would cool into those striations, forming a locking bond with the plate. Skill was required because too much molten material could cause small holes to form in the plate, weakening it. The blacksmith, as detailed and patient with his work as he was, never let any of his creations possess such blemishes. But, he wondered, how could he make the metal display such colors.

Taking the gold coins from Mohawk, the blacksmith hurried off behind the wall without a word.

"That was a good deal." Baracuss remarked to Mohawk. He turned around and noticed that Loce was helping Mohawk don the chain mail shirt.

"I would say!" Loce grunted as he then buckled the leather straps behind Mohawk's back in a crisscross fashion to hold the chest plate firmly in place.

Handing the sheathed long sword to Mohawk, Baracuss urged, "We'd better be gone from here before the smith changes his mind."

Mohawk buckled the leather belt around his waist as they left the shop and trekked down the street. At last Mohawk felt comfortable. Powerful. Now he felt like a warrior, instead of some ill-equipped imposter in a strange land. He was confident he had the tools needed for a fight without having to worry too much about being mortally wounded so easily.

"This feels great!" he exclaimed, gripping the leather wrapped hilt of his sword.

"Good. It's important that one is truly comfortable with what is worn and wielded." Baracuss mentioned. He knew it from experience.

Given the time he had been in the company of the barbarians, and that he now had some armor and a sword, Mohawk thought it would be a good time to ask, "Do you know where I can find a person by the name of Metsys?"

Baracuss stopped abruptly with Loce shortly following suit.

"Yeah. I know. Why do you need to see a cursed wizard?"

Perhaps it wasn't such a good time after all.

"To help me piece a few things together." Mohawk said, glad he had his hand on the hilt of his sword at this moment.

"Such as?" Baracuss said irritably. His hand itched for the touch of his battleaxe, but he kept calm reminding himself that Mohawk had helped him. Still, his skin crawled when he thought about wizards and anything that used magic.

"Never mind." Mohawk blurted out, sensing Baracuss' evident dislike of Metsys. He was just thankful he was able to get armor and a sword and thought he may have to put them to use against both of the barbarians.

"Are you a wizard?" Baracuss whispered deeply, his eyes slowing brewing with that silent, deadly rage.

"No!" Mohawk shot out defensively, "but I must see him! He summoned me to this strange land, got my friend killed and I must know why!"

Squinting his eyes, Baracuss pieced the puzzle together. "Metsys is the 'friend' you first told me about coming to see?"

"Yes." Mohawk admitted calmly. He was still trying to figure out how he would immobilize two barbarians faster than they could respond in kind…or worse.

Baracuss weighed Mohawk's admission. He didn't believe that Mohawk was lying about his motive to see the wizard and he knew from observation that Mohawk was not a wizard. And, he realized that had Mohawk been a wizard then he would have been able to find Metsys on his own, without asking.

"Very well. Come with me."

Weaving their way through the streets they came upon a large, well-guarded stone keep. It seemed strange to Mohawk that a keep would be in the midst of a populus castle. But it made sense to Baracuss. It was not uncommon for magic users, in general, to have a strong, highly defensive area in which to exercise their craft. Often, they feared for their lives from those who felt magic was an unnatural practice…and evil that must be destroyed. Not only did such magic users fear barbarians like Baracuss for such beliefs but also the lingering potential that hordes of creatures, human and otherwise, would coalesce together to destroy them. No wizard, short of a god, had the capacity to repel such an attack single-handedly. Hence, the keep's primary purpose was to slow and weaken an enemy's approach with a series of invisible enchantments not to aide in victory, but to provide time for an escape. This keep was much the same except that eight generations of Metsys' family line had occupied it.

He had even been taught the work of masonry so that he could maintain the keep as his forebearers had done. In fact, his entire lineage rooted themselves within the walls of this single keep in which he spent most of his life learning magic from what his forefathers passed down, including the First whom had constructed the one-hundred and seventy foot tall, eleven-point walled keep using knowledge of the Tart'aas that has since been lost to time. And the First is said to have solidified into being from the air of the Realm itself without any spell or portal.

During the Great Scourge some three hundred years ago, an evil creature had been forged in the Realm by a wizard, Doefloct, from an unnatural bonding of dragon essence along with Dark and Wild Magic. The creature soon became known as the Death Raiden. The ravenous creature killed and maimed thousands in its wake. Elves. Giants. Barbarians. Humans and anything else that challenged it. Those that survived rallied around this keep and together with Leok, one of Metsys' forefathers, were able to finally stop it, though at great cost. Afterwards, the great castle wall was erected to protect the inhabitants and the keep from future ghoulish creations. But, generations later, having forgotten about such creatures, the elves, giants, barbarians and other races spread beyond the great wall into the Realm at first as haunts to their ancestral lands and eventually re-settling them.

As they neared the keep, Mohawk noticed that a moat surrounded the keep and its pointed walls designed to split attacking hordes, along with soldiers gathered around the mouth of the drawbridge. A few archers paced along the top of the keep's stone walls. He could only guess how good of a shot they were against a moving target.

Crossing the drawbridge, Mohawk said, "This looks like something out of a history book."

"A what?" Loce grunted out. He was occupied, glancing over the edge of the drawbridge, trying to see if anything lived in the depths of the moat that surrounded the keep.

"What is your business here?" a brawny soldier asked as the others put their leather-gloved hands on the hilts of their sheathed long swords.

"My friend," Baracuss began, motioning to Mohawk, "was summoned by Metsys."

The soldiers looked at one another and one finally said, "He didn't tell us."

Baracuss frowned at the soldier, "You son of a whore-dog…" but was interrupted.

A voice was heard from behind the soldiers, "Let them pass."

The soldiers parted without hesitation revealing a slender man, six feet tall, wearing long purple flowing robes gathered at the waist with a leather belt. His shoulder length grayish-brown hair moved slightly with a gust of wind that fell over the walls of the keep. His black, deep-set eyes probed Mohawk.

"Please come." Metsys said as he turned and walked through the small courtyard to a series of wooden steps where, to its right, sat a small patch of yellow flowers breathing a subtle sweet scent into the air.

Metsys felt at home here in the keep. Not only because he was raised in it, and knew every one of its hidden corridors and arcane traps, but because he could see the magic the very stones now radiated. After having seen so many generations conjure spells, explore and hone the elemental fabric of White Magic and even Wild Magic, the stonework itself had absorbed and retained parts of that energy in fine crystalline particulates, iron and other ores common to the region. Even the earth below it possessed a magical aura.

For the past decade, Metsys had labored to alter that residual magic into a complex web of protection spells to augment and strengthen those cast in centuries past. The keep walls contained the magical ability of immunity to earthquakes, heavy winds and lesser Dark Magic bombardment. While only water the moat, which surrounded the keep, was bestowed the ability to transform into a blazing wall of fire that could protect the keep from any mortal assailants. The ground itself radiated a powerful global protection spell that would repulse mal-aligned creatures from entering the courtyard if they managed to defeat the first defense. If anything were to assault the keep, it would be weakened, enabling Metsys to have an even chance in magical combat, if not an advantage.

Following Metsys, Baracuss whispered, "I hope he doesn't try anything stupid. It would be too good an excuse to sever his head."

"Why do you hate this guy so much?" Mohawk whispered in return.

Looking briefly at Mohawk he said, "Mainly because I believe the nature of magic shouldn't be twisted to serve some purpose. Besides, if a man is meant to live, he should be able to do so by his hand with a weapon where his wits and talent will win him over his enemies."

Loce nodded his head and raised a clenched fist.

Passing through a pair of large, heavy wooden doors, they found themselves in a vast study room, large enough for a dragon, with the scent of a sharp, watermelon-like aroma hanging in the air. Large, finely woven tapestries hung on the walls about them. Some of the tapestries portrayed the sun and clouds in different artistic patterns and color ranges. Another showed a cavitating doorway surrounded by red flames, while the doorway itself was dark blue. And the last tapestry displayed what appeared to be a person that was not entirely visible.

Metsys seated himself behind a large wooden desk, ornately crafted with twisting vines and the frozen scene of all life, even Dragons, facing off against the Death Raiden. The Death Raiden raised Mohawk's curiosity.

Four surprisingly plain wooden chairs sat before it, empty. The fourth chair, Mohawk guessed, must have been for Gladstad had he lived.

"Please," Metsys motioned gently with his hands, "sit down."

"So," Mohawk began, "why did you summon me here?"

The edge of Metsys' mouth curled up. "Good. Get right to the point." He said, admiring Mohawk's forward approach.

"And the point is…"

"So, you can destroy the wielders of the Dark Magic which plagues this land and has cast it out of balance."

Lifting his hand and motioning, as if to conjure a spell, Mohawk said, "I'm not a magician. Surely you would fare better at such a task."

"That is true. But, if I were to do such myself, this land would be powerless to defend itself in my stead." Metsys said. "If I were to try to defeat the wielders and the Dark Magic, I would have to focus entirely on that task. And, if I were to fail, the Realm would be lost."

He placed his arms on the desk before him, "It's too much of a risk. The Baron knows this and the only reason he hasn't come forth directly, is because the same could befall him."

"A deadlock." Baracuss stated.

"For now, yes."

"Who is this Baron?" Mohawk asked.

Leaning back in his chair, Metsys replied, "A very powerful and old Dark Magic sorcerer. He goes by the name of Lord Doefloct. The reason he's been able to master the Dark Magic to slowly absorb the land around the Realm is because he perverted the use of the Staff of Majii. It is a source of raw, untapped magical power that was neither White nor Dark Magic. It was brought here, centuries ago, through a door like the one I brought you through. The bearer of the Staff referred to himself as a pharaoh…whatever that means. Nevertheless, the Staff's power is derived from your world and, as such, only a person from your world can wield or destroy it. Physically."

Mohawk was amazed that, apparently, ancient Egyptians had visited the Realm. "But I still am not a magician."

"No, not in the strict sense. But, in your body you possess the magic from your world. Simply by breaking the Staff with physical force, like snapping a branch in two, you would break the Staff of its hewn connection to your world." Metsys said patiently.

"If this Baron is so powerful, how am I supposed to conquer him, much less get close enough to destroy the Staff?" he quickly pointed out. It seemed like a fool's errand.

"A mountain lay in the Southern Realm. Mt. Reach. It is a powerful source of White Magic from the Realm's heart. It contains a sword, the Sword of Dragon Slaying. But it, too, is surrounded by Dark Magic...evil dragons. Again, I could try to retrieve the sword, but the land would be in imminent danger in my absence." Metsys said, temporarily distracted by the nasty remnant of a wound on Loce's neck.

"So, what was the role of my friend, Gladstad, who you let die?"

"He was to be your partner as he had a predisposition to White Magic that I cannot fully explain." Metsys confessed, looking back to Mohawk with a half-lie, "But I could not interfere to save his life." In truth, he only wanted the strong-willed to confront the Baron, not someone malleable enough to be turned to do the Baron's will.

Mohawk raised his hands in disbelief, "So I'm supposed to take out this Baron and Staff by myself? Oh, and fight some dragons?"

Metsys got up and walked towards the tapestry of the doorway. "No. Behold, I summon another."

It was unusually dark in the jungle as the muscular figure made his way to the satellite van. Sergeant Quentin and Gladstad had missed the accountability formation at

2215 hours that Colonel Ratcliff had ordered, and he was sent to investigate. Lightning crossed the clouds above him, illuminating the ground beneath in brilliant flashes. But there was no thunder. *'Interesting,'* he thought as he peered at the clouds above.

Never in his lifetime had he seen lightning so close without the shattering clap of thunder, even if only delayed by the distance from lightning. The further away the lightning, the longer it would take the sound to travel. But clearly, this lightning had no audible thunder.

Opening the heavy hatch door, he peeked inside. The equipment was operating, apparently on some type of auto mechanism, but nobody was inside. Sergeant Quentin's 9mm pistol sat on the desk. He looked at his analog watch. 2225 hours. He knew it was not time for a shift change, which was the only reason the van could be vacant.

"This is odd," he grunted as he stepped down from the van.

Suddenly the hairs on his entire body stood out as he saw a blinding flash of light. Dimly he felt a tugging at his body like many ropes wrapped around him, pulling him downward. Passing through an unseen current of heat, he felt his body collide helplessly against a cold surface. Voices echoed in his head as he strained to open his eyes.

"Blasted magic!" Baracuss spat in disgust, scarcely able to restrain himself, fiercely wanting to free the battleaxe from his belt.

"Is he going to live?" Mohawk asked, looking at Mac's sprawled form on the wooden floor a few feet from the tapestry.

"Yes." Metsys replied dully, slightly annoyed he would even ask.

"What happened?" Mac said hoarsely, as he slowly got to his feet.

"You were summoned." Mohawk replied. He thought to himself why he had not also been summoned to the same spot, instead of a hill-top. While he may never know, the reason was that Lord Doefloct was not in active meditation during this summon.

"Sergeant Quentin? What are you doing here? What am I doing here?" Mac said, confused. "Shit, what are we doing here?"

Pointing to Metsys, Mohawk said, "That is the man who brought you here."

Mac looked upon the wizard with amazement and disbelief.

"Metsys?" he whispered.

"Yes. It is I." Metsys replied openly.

"Incredible." Mac said as he looked at the barbarians, "Baracuss and Loce?"

Baracuss nodded his head, puzzled as to how this stranger knew his name.

Mohawk grabbed Mac's arm and forced him into a chair. "What the hell is this shit? How do you know these people?"

"Um, I'm not sure. How did this happen?" Mac asked.

"You were summoned." Metsys stated.

"Yes, yes I know but…" Mac began.

"What do you mean 'not sure'?" Mohawk demanded. He hated being left in the dark.

"Your ass better do some talking, Mac."

"They were part of the campaign. Metsys. Baracuss. Loce. The Baron. Dragons…it was all part of my campaign."

Shaking his head in frustration, Mohawk said, "You're saying that I'm playing your fucking campaign in the flesh? Bullshit!"

"I, I don't know. The campaign just popped into my head. It's not like I really had planned it all out." Mac confessed.

A long silence filled the room. Nobody had a full grasp of what Mac was talking about.

"Well," Metsys said as he sat down, "you need to conquer the Baron and destroy that Staff."

"Yeah, right. Just like that." Mohawk grumbled.

"It appears that your friend already knows a great deal about the Realm. Even about me. He might know more about the Baron's domain that do I." Metsys admitted.

What he didn't tell them was that he was the one that had placed all the information about the Realm into Mac's head. And, when he had summoned two people to the Realm, the Baron's interference not only shifted the manifestation location, it also allowed Metsys the unanticipated opportunity to study Sgt. Quentin and Gladstad where he learned that Gladstad was not supposed to have been summoned.

"I know about the Sword of Dragon Slaying, evil dragons that guard the entrance on Mt. Reach and a Death Knight." Mac cited.

"Death Knight?" Mohawk said in surprise. Metsys hadn't mentioned anything about it.

"Basically, an undead knight of inverse honor." Mac explained briefly.

"Who gives a rat's ass, Mac?! You got me wrapped up in this shit and you're going to unwrap it."

Mac glanced at the Sergeant. "Well, I think the only way out is to finish it."

Mohawk rolled his eyes and sighed, "Gnarly. Let's trot off and take out this Baron and sing 'We're off to see the wizard' while we are at it."

Mac shrugged but there was nothing he could do about it. He could sense Mohawk's demeanor.

"Great." Mohawk rumbled as he sat heavily in the chair, glaring at one of the wooden cross beams above them.

Chapter Eleven

Promptly the four returned to the armorer's shop, so that Mac could be outfit with some equipment. Though he never uttered it, Mohawk wondered, since they had been involuntarily brought here, why Metsys did not pay for or provide the hardware they required.

Mac, perhaps given his size comparable to a barbarian, elected leather jerkins to retain flexibility of movement and a long sword though he would have preferred an assault rifle and a fragmentation grenade or two.

"Thanks for getting this stuff for me," Mac said to Mohawk as he buckled the leather belt bearing the long sword to his waist.

"Just pay me back when you get some gold." Mohawk replied roughly. He still didn't want to talk to Mac.

"Okay." Mac returned, knowing it may take some time for Mohawk to cool off.

Looking curiously around him, Mac found people lining the cobblestone street buying, selling and bargaining for a variety of things. People began lighting torches along the street as the sun set behind the castle walls.

"I think we should head out first thing in the morning." Mohawk suggested. He was more than ready to get this whole affair behind him.

"Yeah." Mac replied.

He followed Mohawk and the barbarians into the tavern, looking at the inviting wenches inside.

"Man, would you look at those women?" While he considered most of them average in attractiveness, a few really knew how to emphasize those parts of the anatomy that he was instinctually drawn to.

"Ah, each time I see them, I can feel the loin cloth stretch." Loce admitted, smiling at the red-headed wench who was baring her voluptuous breasts at him openly.

"Too much information." Mohawk said, somewhat disgusted by the visualization that leapt into his mind.

But before Loce could take more than a few steps in her direction, Baracuss looked over and grabbed his shoulder.

"Loce. Time for that later," Baracuss interjected, "Come with me."

As Mohawk sat at a table with Mac, he noticed the barbarians walk over to a man dressed in long, black robes with a matching cap, bearing a wooden Staff.

'More killing for gold?' Mohawk thought. He preferred to stay out of those little adventures, considering how things turned out with Gladstad and that there were much larger things to worry about now.

But, without connection to royalty, inheritance or a trade of high demand, the mercenary model many barbarians adapted themselves to was an ideal method of accumulating gold, if they possessed the skill to stay alive and the discipline to horde their rewards. Relatively few mastered the latter.

"Why did you do this?" Mohawk asked after a few moments and motioning the bartender for some ale.

Tearing his eyes away from the wenches, Mac asked, "What do you mean?"

Mohawk signed. "Why did you make a campaign like this? Gladstad died because of it."

Mac sat up, placing his hands toward the rough edge of the table in front of him, "That was not me! And the campaign just came to me. It's not like I knew this place actually existed."

Mac looked honestly at Mohawk and said, "I'm not going to be the scape-goat for his death. Especially since I hardly knew the guy. Besides, there was nothing I could do to change anything that happened."

Mohawk rolled his eyes. That was not what he really wanted to hear. After scratching his burgeoning beard that was several shades lighter than his mohawk, he asked, "Okay. Fine. Is there anything I should know about what is coming? Deaths or anything like that?"

Mac raised a hand, palm up, into the air saying, "I didn't see anything like that. The outcome of any conflict is decided by the dice." He motioned with his hand as if he were tossing dice at a high stakes game of craps in a Los Vegas casino.

"Thanks." Mohawk said, handing a few gold to the young woman who bore the tankards and threw in a harmless wink as he took one of the thin metal cups by the worn wooden handle.

She smiled slightly, sat the other tankard before Mac and walked to another table several paces away before stopping suddenly to turn and come back, "Oh, my master wanted me to tell you – the owner of the stables, uh, Jim demands you pay him for the damage that some giant did at the stables."

"Shit. I forgot!" Mohawk said, taken completely by surprise. After thinking for a moment, he offered, "Just charge it to Quintities."

"That's right." Mohawk nodded, sipping the ale casually. He sure didn't want to use the gold he had to pay for a giant he really didn't have any interest in. After all, it was Baracuss who wanted to sell him so if anyone should be paying, it would be the barbarian.

"Whatever you say." The woman grinned as she walked away, relieved that no quarrel surfaced.

"Who's Quintities?"

"You mean the oracle does not know?" Mohawk prodded, "Well, he's the one that hired us when Gladstad got killed by some soul-sucking spider thing."

There it was. Another subtle reminder. But Mac let it go, "Okay…how did you manage to capture a giant?"

"Nothing really. It's only a baby giant." Mohawk said, draining his tankard.

"Ah."

Mohawk got up from the table, not wanting to relive everything that had happened and said, "Better get some sleep if we're going to take out this Baron."

As he strode away, Mac nodded, lifting his tankard while combing through the memories of what he knew about the Realm.

"I have some business." The man in black robes told Baracuss.

"As long as gold is involved. How much?" Baracuss asked, looking at the man. He felt uneasy for some reason.

"Depending on the completeness of the job, I'm willing to pay five hundred gold." The man said nonchalantly.

Loce's eyes bulged, "Must be a big job!" He had never been paid so much for a little mercenary work before.

Baracuss ignored him. "Who or what are we supposed to kill for you?"

The man looked around the tavern and then muttered, "We can't talk about it here. Please, follow me."

With little hesitation, the barbarians followed the man out of the tavern. Within moments they crossed the cobblestone street toward the south before they veered southwest into a dark alley.

"I can't stress enough about this job. No one can know of it." the man said as he turned and faced the two barbarians so greedy for gold.

"Agreed. So, what do you want from us?" Baracuss said. He didn't understand why the man was acting so nervous.

The man appeared to relax and then smiled as two dark shadows loomed behind the barbarians. They paused.

"Take them!" the man commanded as he took a few quick steps backward.

Two loud dull thuds echoed through the alley as thick, dense wooden clubs smashed into the back of the barbarian's heads. Not prepared for an attack, they sank to their knees and fell heavily to the ground.

"Be gone from here." the man said to the hulking shadows, "Your services are no longer needed."

Even as the young giants turned and left, he thought of killing them. But he remembered. If he used any magic for such a trivial matter, he might be detected before he could leave the castle. Instead, he watched them lumber off and turn north.

Looking down at the two unconscious barbarians, the man smiled and said, "Little fools. I would kill you as well if I didn't need you."

With that, the man summoned the ebbs of Dark and Wild Magic and spun it around him and the barbarians. As yellowish lightning bolts danced around them, which were quickly replaced by a translucent sphere, the man summoned the final stage of the spell. Then, in a brilliant flash of light, they disappeared from the alley.

Baracuss's hands and arms felt cold as he slowly awoke. Soon he felt a nagging pain in his back as he forced open his eyes. He tried to move but found that shackles held his arms fast over his head. Apprehension began to tug at him as he realized he was a prisoner in some damp, dark dungeon. The musty smell of limestone and rusted iron filled his nose as he looked around the dimly lit dungeon, straining to find a way out. Some semblance of a door or even a cramped passageway. But there was no way out.

The room he found himself inside of was circular in design, approximately thirty paces between one side to the other. At the center of the room, he saw an iron-legged table with several odd-looking weapons or tools on it. It looked as if the implements had not been used in a very long time.

A shiver went through his body as he knew from his instincts that those tools, while unfamiliar to him, were most likely torture devices of one sort or the other.

"Loce!" Baracuss said hoarsely as he saw the dangling form of his barbarian friend near the opposite wall.

Slowly Loce began to stir.

"Ah. I see that you both are awake." The man said as he slowly materialized before both of them, standing near the ancient table.

"What do you want!" Baracuss rumbled, barely above a whisper, despite the nagging pain in his back.

"What do I want?" the man repeated, "That is simple. I want this world under my hand. Nothing more."

"Who are you?" Loce said weakly as he strained to lift his head to look at the man.

"I am the one who will decide if you live or die. Right now…I am your god." The man said, with a lust of power propelling his voice.

Baracuss could feel a certain darkness about him.

"You see, I have no need for those that can't serve me." The man said as he walked over to Loce, "And, if you can't serve me, you can serve the soil."

The man looked into Loce's weary eyes, "Can you serve me?"

Despite his vulnerable position, Baracuss shouted, "What, by the gods, do you want?"

The man laughed evilly and glanced at Baracuss, "Simple! Bring your friends to me."

The piece finally fit for Baracuss. The man was the Baron that Metsys had spoken of. As he turned over the Baron's demand in his mind, it did not seem outlandish considering they had planned on an audience to slaughter him.

Though a barbarian, Loce was honorable and he would not let his friends befall some unknown fate, especially if he had a hand in it. "Never you slut!" he retorted angrily.

The man shot angry eyes at Loce.

"Oh. Valiant one." The man said as he raised his hand in front of Loce's chest, "I assume your primitive mind does not understand. Let me be the one to explain it to you."

Suddenly, with a simple motion, the man buried his hand deep within Loce's muscular chest as popping sounds echoed through the dungeon. Loce tried in vain to struggle and gasp for breath as his eyes widened with terror, feeling the man's cold hand plow deep within his chest and wrap around his beating heart. It was a feeling he could barely comprehend. His gut churned from the strange and overwhelming pain.

"Stop you slutten dog!" Baracuss raged. Although he could hardly feel his arms, had he been freed, he would have swung them like a filled sack upon the man with all his might.

The man chuckled as he withdrew his hand, looking into Loce's pleading eyes.

Baracuss could hear the faint snapping of stretched arteries and blood vessels as the man withdrew the warm beating heart, blood spewing freely out of the gaping hole in Loce's chest.

Even as Loce's consciousness began to fade away, the man reached up with his other hand and grasped Loce's pale face from cheek to cheek and said, "You see. Death befalls those who can't serve me."

The man squinted his eyes together and a surge of energy filled his hand. He tightened his grip and Loce's skull crackled, then collapsed inward under the immense pressure as skin and muscle tore and ripped, sending blood spraying into the air.

Baracuss, watched helplessly as his friend was brutally killed. He dry-heaved a few ounces of whatever was in his stomach to the stone floor beneath him. He had never, in all of his years, seen such ruthlessness.

The man looked at the still heart and smiled. Casually, he walked over to Baracuss as if he had an eternity in which to contemplate what to do next.

Baracuss glared at him with a berserker's rage and tried to break the chains from the wall, but they would not surrender to his surge of incredible strength. If they had been crafted from a blacksmith's forge they would have buckled.

"I think you will serve me." the man said as he stopped before the hanging form of Baracuss.

Cold silence hung in the air save only the splatter of blood echoing in the dungeon. Baracuss almost retched again, for the origin of the sound was coming from the dangling body of his dear friend.

Shock overtook Baracuss and he fell unconscious.

Mohawk and Mac awoke the following day to a thumping on their barred door.

"Open up! Mohawk! Baracuss!" an angry voice shouted from the other side of the door.

Still half asleep, Mohawk pushed open the window, grabbed his long sword and muttered, "Shit! Let's get out of here!"

"What?!" Mac demanded as he hurriedly followed Mohawk out of the window. What a way to start the day.

Running down the narrow alleyway that was blocked on one side by the castle wall, and the other by buildings and small houses, Mohawk strapped the long sword around his waist.

"I think maybe Quintities did not want to pay for the giant damage!" Mohawk heaved between breaths with a devious grin.

"Shit." Mac mumbled in disbelief, "That's just great."

Occasionally glancing down the gaps between buildings, Mohawk used what he thought were familiar objects to make sure he was traveling towards the stables. As they came to a large wooden building that smelled strongly of horse feed and excrement, they paused.

"Follow me." He said quietly.

Crossing the muddy pathway that went along the side of the stables, Mohawk stopped at the front end of the building, and slowly peered around its edge. A few curious people looked at Mohawk as they walked down the cobblestone street, oblivious as to what he was doing, trying to sneak beside the stables.

A squad of soldiers, dressed as those at the front gate, stood blocking the front end of the stable, looking at all who passed in front of them. The tan, baggy-clothed merchant Mohawk knew as Quintities stood by the soldiers pacing back and forth.

Further up the street, Mohawk saw a thick gathering of merchants. A muscular form, clad only in a loincloth, stood atop an eight-foot-tall platform, wearing an iron shackle around his waist. Another form stood nearby, dressed in black, and occasionally raising his arm as some of the merchants in the crowd did. It was the block Baracuss had mentioned.

'Perfect distraction!' Mohawk thought as he passed Mac, jogging back down the pathway.

"Where are you going?" Mac asked as he followed Mohawk.

"Distraction." Mohawk simply said, going around the rear of the stables.

Trying to be inconspicuous as possible, they strode out of the alleyway on the other side of the stables and crossed the street heading north towards the block.

"Now, what we're going to do is try and free the slaves and maybe they'll attack the merchants or run. Then, hopefully, we'll be able to get our horses and skate out of here in the confusion." Mohawk said, beads of sweat rolling off his brow.

"Good idea." Mac said quietly as they went around the crowd of merchants to the front of the block.

At the front, a thick line of virtually naked barbarians, humans and some giants waited. Some of them had had lived long enough that today's buyer would be their third master. None of them had any idea what tomorrow would bring.

One long continuous chain went through an iron loop in the waist shackle of the slaves. At both ends of the chain were keylocks which prevented them from pulling the chain out of the loop in their shackles. A man clad in nothing more than simple brown pants and a long-sleeved shirt unlocked the keylock at the head of the line to free the next to be auctioned. He didn't even have a dagger as a means of self-defense if there was a revolt.

Seeing his opportunity, Mohawk grabbed the chain and pulled the free end of the chain through several shackles, freeing them before anyone realized what was happening. But the slaves just stood there and looked at him.

"You are free! Attack them!" Mohawk declared, frustrated that the slaves were not doing what he anticipated they would do. He would have done something. But he had not been broken.

"We serve only our master." One of them replied without emotion.

"Who is he?" one of the merchants asked, pointing at Mohawk.

"You see that?! He tried to free the slaves!" another shouted.

"He must die!" another merchant cried, pulling out his gem encrusted bastard sword.

"Die you dog!" one said, as the merchants furiously began unsheathing daggers and short swords even though few actually knew how to wield and use them in combat.

"Damn it!" Mohawk cursed, then ran back to the stables, followed exceptionally closely by Mac.

Stopping behind the stables to catch his breath, he got another idea. Pulling out his sword, he began savagely hacking at the wall. Mac started to help, hearing the curses and shouts coming from the mob of angry merchants. The wood splintered and buckled under the powerful blows they dealt, literally chipping at the wall to create a hole large enough to enter the stables and save their lives.

The merchants were just rounding the corner when Mohawk and Mac forced their way through the large hole into the rear of the stables. Hastily mounting the nearest black horses that were still saddled and lathered with sweat, the merchants pursued, some forcing themselves through the hole in the stable wall.

"Go! Go!" Mohawk urged as he spurred the horse through the stables as Mac took after him. Outside, the soldiers didn't try to stop the charging horsemen, electing instead to scatter in different directions, each praying they wouldn't be trampled underfoot.

"Damn it! They got my horses! Go after them!" Quintities shouted angrily before the fleeing soldiers.

Chapter Twelve

Mohawk didn't slow his horse down to a walk until the castle was out of sight. He knew the soldiers at the front gate saw them charge out of the castle and head west. When a detachment was sent after them, he knew the soldiers at the gate would reveal where they had gone. It would, however, take some time for them to saddle horses and assemble to hunt them down. Precious time that Mohawk used by pushing his horse.

The horses were already exhausted. White foam lathered up from around the saddles and their bodies glistened with sweat. Their mouths dripped with saliva as they shuffled forward, lungs laboring to send precious oxygen into taxed muscles. Mac knew from handling horses in the past that these could not be pushed any further.

"Horses aren't going to last long if we continue to push 'em into the night." Mac said.

"Yeah, I thought so." Mohawk replied, clearly disappointed. He wanted to keep moving but he didn't want to lose their only means of transportation.

The foul stench of rotting flesh filled their nostrils as they passed the wreckage of horse-drawn wooden cart, the maggot infested bodies of giants and an unfortunate old man. A few buzzards pulled and tugged at the hardening flesh, filling their stomachs. Dimly they noticed Mac and Mohawk pass with no real interest.

"Oh man. That's disgusting." Mac mumbled, looking away with a contorted expression.

"Yeah it is."

"I wonder where the barbarians are." Mac said, suddenly remembering their absence at the tavern.

Shrugging his shoulders, Mohawk stated, "I don't know. I saw them talking to a man in the tavern. They probably went out on another killing spree to get some gold, like what we did for that merchant."

"I hope they don't get caught when they get back. I have a feeling that the soldiers will be looking for them." Mac pointed out.

As they continued west, they came upon a small village nestled in the forest to the left of the road. It appeared to be empty.

"Let's check it out," Mac said, guiding his horse into the village. "Maybe there's some water here for the horses and us." he added.

Uneasily Mohawk followed, knowing it was only a matter of time before the soldiers would be hot on their trail. But he knew the horses must have water to keep going.

Dismounting, Mac led his horse to a trough and, although small, it was full of water. Mac also saw a stable a handful of meters from the trough, but barely large enough for a single horse and feed.

"Hey! Got food and water for the horses." He announced as he took the bridle off the horse and let it drink.

Mohawk did the same, "We can't stay here long."

"Yes, but it's almost dark and these horses need to rest." Mac said as he unbuckled the saddle from the horse and heaved it off. The horse glanced briefly at Mac as if to say thank-you.

"But the fuckin' soldiers are coming!" Mohawk protested. He couldn't believe Mac was actually going to let the horses rest now. It wouldn't take long for the soldiers to catch up to them, especially now that they were stopped and would have to re-equip the horses before they could depart.

"Yeah, but they won't be able to see too good in the dark, so they might not even send a patrol tonight." Mac replied as he rested the saddle against the stable so that it couldn't be seen from the road, "Besides, we'd probably stand a better chance of fighting here than out in the open." There were more areas to fight defensively from the village than out in the middle of the road.

"Okay. We'll play it your way. I just hope you are right." Mohawk said finally, dismounting and leading his horse beside the other.

After the horses fed, Mac led them around the side of the stable, having put their bridles back on. The dull thunder of horses in a gallop startled the horses Mac had just tied to the corner of the stable. In the clouded starlight Mac scanned around for Mohawk, but he wasn't in sight.

"Whoa! Whoa!" one of the soldiers clad in chain mail shouted, stopping their horses as they raised their wooden crossbows.

"Check that out!" the soldier, apparently the Sergeant, commanded.

The soldier closest to the abandoned village entrance notched an arrow in his crossbow and steered his horse into the village.

Hearing that command Mac slowly withdrew his long sword from its sheath, hoping the horses would stay quiet. In the back of his mind, he wondered where Mohawk was.

Entering the village, the soldier looked around slowly, his crossbow ready if needed. But in the starlight, he couldn't see much but the faint outlines of a few large home structures and a stable. There were no torches to be seen.

Spurring his horse at a trot back to the formation he reported, "Nobody is there. No horses. No people. Not even a torch."

"They must be on down the road." The Sergeant said, spurring his horse forward, forcing the others to keep up.

Peering around the edge of the stable, Mac looked for any stragglers as he heard them ride off. Seeing none, he sheathed his sword, relieved and gently patted the horses for keeping quiet.

"Hey Mac," a voice called for a large hut, "come here."

As Mac approached the hut, Mohawk popped out from inside.

"Found a torch." Mohawk said as he lit it with a butane lighter.

"You think those soldiers will come back?" Mohawk asked. He entered the hut, closing the door behind Mac so that no light could be seen from the outside.

"No. I think they'll ride a couple more miles south and rest for the night before continuing to search for us." Mac said openly.

"Then we'll stay here for the night." Mohawk said as he placed the torch in a wooden ring that had been nailed at an angle to the side of a beam that rose and connected to the roof.

The room was virtually empty except for a straw broom lying in the middle of the dusty wood planked floor. It was as if the people who had lived there just packed up and left. Mac reasoned that the people couldn't have been gone too long due to the freshness of the feed that was in the stable. Surely no more than a week.

Little did they know they were staying in a dead man's abode. Had he come back, he probably would have given Mac and Mohawk a meal and a place to rest for the night. He was a kind old man that would have had a few years left to live if the giants hadn't attacked him on his way back home. Now his maggot-infested body lay with the rotting bodies of the giants and his once faithful mule, serving as food for the congress of vultures determined to have their fill before the earth slowly absorbed the remains.

As they relaxed, Mohawk noticed something strange. The torch that was once burning red was fading into a blue color. Deep blue.

"What the hell is going on?" he said with a frown.

Mac looked at the jumping flame with a puzzled look. He'd never seen anything like it before.

"Ah, strangers to this land. Welcome." a voice emanated from within the blue flame.

Mac jumped to his feet and grasped he sword firmly, "Who are you? What do you want?"

"You strangers know who I am. I am the one you so feebly seek to destroy," the voice said cooly, "and what I want is quite simple – A trade you might say."

"What is this trade, Baron?" Mohawk asked, also scrambling to his feet.

"Oh, life for life. Your barbarian friends were hesitant. I would hope, for your sake, that you are more understanding."

"What did you do with them?" Mac asked angrily.

"Nothing really. I had to make an example of one for the other to think on. I'll make the same proposition to you. I will spare your lives if only you perform one task for me." the voice echoed in the small hut.

"What's this task?" Mohawk pushed impatiently.

"First, let me give you something to think about." the voice concluded.

A blue, conical line streamed from the flame through the air to the wooden floor. Then a figure appeared lying on the ground, gasping for air. The flame became red again.

Kneeling down next to the figure Mohawk knew as Baracuss, he said, "You okay?"

Straining to sit up, Baracuss mumbled, "Yeah."

Mac walked over to him. "What happened?"

"This man in black robes waves us over at the tavern. He offered us lots of gold…so we left with him to discuss the matter he would not talk about in the tavern. By the time we walked out and into an alley, something smashed the back of my head," Baracuss said weakly, "I awoke bound in iron chains. Loce was then gutted before my eyes…while he was still alive. Then the man pulled out his heart. Still beating."

"What did he say to you?" Mohawk inquired.

Scratching his head Baracuss said, "I don't remember. Then I found myself here."

"Great!" Mohawk shouted in frustration, "Just fuckin' great."

"Obviously the Baron wants us alive. But for what?" Mac questioned.

"I dunno. But tomorrow I say we ride down and find out." Mohawk fumed as he sat down, "I think it's best we all get as much rest as possible."

In the morning, after saddling the horses, they headed west along the road, weary of the soldiers that were bound to be on the same road. Just before midday, they crossed the only road going south. Baracuss was the first to see a large wolf pack tracking them just inside the forest. Their red eyes occasionally looking away from the riders, but only long enough to keep track of where they were going. Uneasily, Baracuss wanted for them to attack though, strangely, he felt a peculiar intelligence about them.

"We're being followed." Baracuss finally blurted out, pointing to the edge of the forest.

Mohawk looked over and spotted the pack of wolves roaming beside them.

"Should we run for it?" Mac asked, about to spur his horse.

"No. Those wolves would eventually take the horses once they tired. Don't prompt an attack." Baracuss said wisely.

Oddly, the pack never attacked, but just kept their gaze upon the riders as they traveled down the road and turned onto another, somewhat smaller, trail that led to a small keep similar to Metsys' in design.

Although this keep had tall stone walls, it was slowly eroding and crumbling under the weight of time and nature. The moat that encircled the keep was now nothing more than a deep trench littered with the sun-bleached bones of whatever had died in its depths long ago. It was obvious this keep had not been inhabited for many decades.

"So, you think the Baron is here?" Mohawk said as he looked around the desolate keep.

Dismounting, Mac tied the reigns around the rusty length of chain that was connected to the end of the drawbridge and said, "No. But there's something in here we need. I'm sure of it."

"What could possibly be any good to us in that ancient keep?" Mohawk asked as he dismounted after the barbarian.

Leading them into the barren courtyard within the keep, Mac urged, "There's something we need for a dark crossing."

Mac remembered from when he had envisioned this world that a desolate keep would hold something they would need at a dark crossing. But he just couldn't recall what it was specifically. It was like trying to remember a dream when you awoke, but only seeing bits and pieces.

It smelled thickly of blossoming mold as they followed Mac along one side of the keep walls to a weathered door. Pulling out his sword, Mac pushed on the door as it creaked on its rusty iron hinges. Cautiously he eased himself in and glanced inside. There was nothing. Just the smell of stagnated air.

"Nothing." Mac said, disappointed, turning to leave as he sheathed his sword.

Curiously, Baracuss opened the next door on the same wall while Mohawk stepped into the last door. Mac went into the courtyard with a slight frown, trying to remember what they needed from this place.

Within a few moments, Baracuss emerged and said, "No. Not even a copper piece."

Stepping through the doorframe of the last room, Mohawk looked around, leery of an attack. Realizing that there were no enemies, he relaxed. The walls were cracked and splintered in many spots and skeletons clad in dented armor were scattered about the dirt floor. Whatever had happened in this room looked like a massacre in which none survived. There was not a weapon in sight, like a club or such, that would have been able to dent the armor without piercing it. What made Mohawk's skin crawl was the fact that the weapons scattered about the room were swords. Then he saw a pair of shiny black boots standing upright in the midst of the remains.

"Hey!" he shouted as he brushed a few bones aside and grabbed the pair of boots, "Found something!"

Stepping towards the door, he almost bumped into the hulking form of Baracuss, who was already at the door, looking at the boots Mohawk was holding. Stepping aside, he let Mohawk out of the room and looked around briefly before he went out into the courtyard.

"What do you think these are for?" Mohawk asked, holding the boots up. Strangely, the elements had not affected the leather. It was as if the boots had just been made.

"Beats me" Mac confessed as he approached Mohawk, looking at the boots with bewilderment.

"You don't know?" Mohawk grunted.

"No. Perhaps that is what we needed." Mohawk said as he shook his head, trying to remember.

Mohawk turned the boots over in his hands, "Well, they seem to be my size."

Just as he finished saying that, the boots vanished from his hands and with a brilliant flash of light, appeared on his feet.

"What the…" Mohawk shot out in amazement.

"They're magical." Mac smiled, obviously impressed, "Maybe they are boots of speed. Try to walk…uh, going outside the keep of course." He didn't want to see Mohawk smash into one of the stone walls in a blur of speed.

Cautiously, Mohawk turned and faced the outside of the keep. Exhaling, not knowing what to expect, he took a step. Suddenly he bounded five feet into the air before he came back down a step ahead of where he was before. He took another step, and bounded again.

"This is kind of fun!" Mohawk laughed, relieved that he wasn't racing uncontrollably out of the keep and into the forest. Again he bounded, increasing his stride as he got used to it.

Bounding up and down out of the keep, he judged that the distance he was covering was equal to the same distance if he had been running. But with the boots, it took considerably less effort. Within a few minutes he realized that if he increased his stride, he also increased the distance between each bound, although the height of each bound remained the same.

Turning around at the dirt road which continued south, Mohawk bounded up and down in place for a time before bounding back to the keep as he saw Mac and Baracuss heading towards the horses.

"Boy, I could mosh in these bad boys!" Mohawk exclaimed, grinning as he bounded up and down in place beside them. While the horses seemed tense at the commotion, they did not bolt and run.

Mac threw is leg over the saddle, "Mosh?"

"Yeah, it's a real popular thing in California you know."

"No, not really." Mac replied, puzzled at what mosh was.

"Slam dancing!" Mohawk revealed.

Now that rung a bell in Mac's mind. Although he was a country and western dancer of sorts, he had seen some television show that illustrated slam dancing. To him it looked like a mob of people colliding with each other, throwing arms and legs around, almost like controlled fighting.

"So, you going to bound or ride?" Mac asked. He saw Baracuss was already mounted up.

"I think I'll bound." Mohawk smiled.

And so, as they followed the dirt road south, Mohawk bounded beside them. Baracuss even cracked a smile, amused at Mohawk enjoying himself, bounding beside them as they followed the road. Then he remembered the wolves and turned slightly in his saddle to look around. He saw no pack. No red glowing eyes which eased his mind. But he could still feel their presence. Watching. Waiting.

"What happened to the soldiers?" Mac asked, surprised that they had not yet encountered them.

Bounding closer to Mac, Mohawk said, "Don't know. Maybe they took off into the forest."

That wouldn't be likely,' Mac thought, *'It would be impractical to enter a forest with horses having to make special efforts to find gaps in the vegetation for the horses, slowing progress to a crawl.'*

The wolves, sent by the Baron to make sure they arrived safely to his keep, had slaughtered the soldiers and dragged their bodies keep within the forest. The Baron wanted to ensure that they made it to the keep…after all, they were now part of his plans.

It was about midday when they came across a dark stream some fifteen feet wide. The horses stopped a few feet from the stream, neighing lowly and refusing to move forward.

Mac spurred his horse but it would not move. It just pawed the earth nervously, still neighing. He knew the horses were spooked, but couldn't figure out why. The stream didn't look very deep at all.

Mohawk bounded over the stream and turned around, bounding in place in the middle of the road that continued on the other side.

"Come on!" he beckoned, motioning with his hands, "A little water never hurt anybody."

"The horses won't cross." Mac confessed as he tried again to spur his horse forward.

Baracuss tried as well, with the same response. He turned in the saddle looking for the wolf pack, assuming that they were somehow affecting the horses. But he could not see them.

"Of course," Mohawk pieced together, "that's what these boots were for…and that must be the dark crossing you were talking about."

"What of the horses?" Baracuss asked. He didn't want to leave his steed behind if the stream was not too deep to wade or lead a horse through.

"They're going to have to stay, I guess. If they don't wander off." Mac shrugged.

Baracuss was more worried about the wolves taking down the horses then having them wander off.

Mac dismounted. "Help us across, would you?"

As Mohawk was about to answer, several black tentacles shot out from the stream, wrapping tightly about the horses' forelegs and long muscular necks.

"Oh shit!" Mac shouted as he rolled backwards off the horse.

Baracuss flung himself out of the saddle and landed firmly on the ground, eyes widened with surprise of the stream attacking the horses. He knew it had to be magic of some type or another.

Even as Mac cussed, Mohawk bounded over the stream and gawked at the tentacles with surprise. He hadn't seen anything in the stream a few moments ago.

Baracuss swiftly pulled his battleaxe and savagely swung at the black tentacles. After having severed three of them in complete fury, he saw his actions were futile. Not that he didn't affect the tentacles, but they didn't appear to be made of flesh or bone. For every time he severed a tentacle, the end of which was wrapped around the horses, it would simply disintegrate into thousands of droplets and roll back into the stream. The other half of the tentacle that was somehow rooted to the stream would form a new end and wrap itself, again, around the horses. The tentacles would not attack him or Mac, despite their proximity to the stream. Just the horses.

The water spirit, having been created and given life by the Baron, would obey him and only consume the horses. It knew it could not betray the Baron. If it took the humans, it knew it would lose its life, its very existence in the waters it was created from. But that wasn't all the Baron had commanded it to do. For he commanded it to grow, to feed on all creatures that would drink at its edge. And, travel north. It didn't know why, but it did like to feed on land-borne creatures. They were so warm.

"Come on!" Mohawk shouted at Baracuss, motioning him with his arm.

The horses struggled in a vain attempt to escape, but the tentacles that bound them, that drug them closer to the stream's edge, were too powerful. They tried to scream, to breathe, but the tentacles had wrapped about their necks so tightly that the horses were deprived of the air they needed to fight with, to live.

Baracuss placed an arm around Mohawk's neck as Mac had done on his other side. Then Mohawk began to bound in place. The added weight of Baracuss and Mac didn't seem to hinder the boots as Mohawk lurched forward and bounded over the stream, landing ten feet past its edge on the other side. Once on the other side, Baracuss and Mac turned loose and ran a good hundred paces before they stopped to look back.

Pulling his feet together, Mohawk stopped bounding, and the boots vanished from his feet. They reappeared in front of him in a brilliant flash of light. He noticed that he still wore his military-issue boots, so he assumed that the black, magical boots had just formed around them. He noticed something else, too. The horses were gone.

"Let's see what this fucker wants." Mohawk fumed as he picked up his boots and followed the road.

Mac hurried after Mohawk, "I've never seen anything like that before…hell, not even read of such a thing."

"You mean you didn't dream it up as part of your campaign?" Mohawk prodded.

"No."

There were some things that not even Metsys knew existed.

Chapter Thirteen

Approximately two miles southeast of the stream stood a gigantic mountain three thousand feet high. Nothing grew at its base, not even shrubs to hold the soil in place when the winds blew or the rains came. But nothing lived in the Southern Realm that wasn't evil.

From the icy peaks of the mountain came a frigid wind that flowed down the mountain face into the vast wasteland that surrounded it. As the wind fingered out across the empty wasteland, the temperature of the hotter air blended with it, causing it to lose some of its frigidness. By the time the wind reached the travelers, it was just a pleasantly cool breeze.

Gazing up at the mountain as they slowly passed, Mohawk said, "That must be the mountain Metsys was talking about. Mt. Reach."

"Yeah? I don't see any dragons." Baracuss pointed out, also looking at the mountain.

"Metsys said they're there, so I'm sure they are up there."

After almost another hour of walking, they came across a keep, one that was easily twice the size of Metsys', although the height of it was relatively the same the walls were flat, not pointed, as if it was constructed in a more ancient time. There were no archers standing at the walls, Baracuss noted, not even soldiers to guard the front gate. But, of course, none were needed. For what rested below the keep, should it emerge from the depths, would be quite capable of defending the keep.

Crossing the wooden planked drawbridge unopposed, Mohawk's voice rang out in a tone of surprise, "No defenses?"

"Guess not." Mac shrugged. Even he couldn't believe a keep, especially one of this size, was not guarded. In all his gaming years, when he'd defended a keep regardless of its size, it was always protected with at least a few soldiers. That is, if it had a little gold to plunder.

Suddenly a blood-chilling sight advanced towards them. As they entered the courtyard, two skeletons clad in chain-mail shirts and mail dresses shuffled up to them, holding long swords in their bony hands.

Mohawk looked at the skeletons in awe.

Baracuss, on the other hand, was ready to strike them down as his gut churned within him uneasily. Instinctively, he placed a hand on his battleaxe, eyeing them cautiously as they approached. Having fought such skeletons across the seas, he knew the sword arm of the undead must be severed. Otherwise even he would tire from the unrelenting attack of such a foe that did not fatigue. Undoubtedly, they were under the control of the Baron.

"Cool." Mac muttered, staring at the skeletons with raised eyebrows.

"The Baron has been expecting you." one of the skeletons said roughly as its jawbone moved up and down while it spoke, mimicking the movement of speech. Its orb-less sockets stared at Mohawk.

"Okay." Mohawk replied uneasily, hoping that was the response the skeleton sought.

"Follow me." the skeleton said as it turned and went across the courtyard to a pair of finely crafted wooden double doors. Following them, Baracuss kept a mental note of the skeleton that followed behind them.

Passing through the double doors that opened inward by some invisible force, the skeleton raised its bony arm and pointed inside as they entered. The walls on either side of them were lined with books of all sizes, some much older than others, stacked side by side, forming rows along the walls. The smell of parchment, leather and dust collected over the years filled the room. Just ahead of the party was a window large enough for a man to stand in. It was open, allowing the remaining rays of the setting sun inside. A man with black shoulder length hair clothed in black sat behind a large, dark-stained wooden desk.

The hair on Baracuss' neck stood up as the memories of his friend's cruel death flashed before him. Rage and fear grappled at his mind. He wanted to kill the Baron, but he knew he couldn't get close enough for his battleaxe to do the job it thirsted for.

"Please my friends, let me say how good it is of you to come." The Baron said as he held the Staff of Majii in his right hand.

"Look Baron. We came here to find out what you wanted, not for a social call." Mohawk grumbled, smiling sarcastically.

"Oh of course not. I too, am not the social type. Although it is nice to see visitors once and a while. I don't see many."

Baracuss' hand twitched, wanting to attack the Baron, but he had to remind himself that his friends could die if he did.

"Hey, I've seen you before. You are an evil sorcerer." Mac recalled.

"That's right my friend. I am, indeed, a sorcerer. The best I'd say." the Baron smiled, complimenting himself.

"So. What's this deal?" Mohawk stressed, wanting nothing more than to leave, considering they did not have the weapons needed to dispatch the Baron.

"My friend, all you have to do is kill Metsys for me. He trusts you, and he took you from your world and brought you here to kill me." the Baron laid out in simple terms as his eyes danced between the three visitors.

"And what happens to us once we kill the wizard?" Mac asked.

The Baron stood up easily and said, "I will send you back to your world."

"How do we know you won't kill us first?" Mohawk said uneasily. He hated to give any ideas, but it was a question that had to be asked.

"Sergeant Quentin. I mean Mohawk, as you are called here…I have no purpose to kill you. It would be a waste of my time, and I do not like to waste time for such things unless there is nothing to do. But there is plenty to do.", the Baron confirmed, "No. I will send you back to your world."

"How did you know my name?" Mohawk asked, startled.

The Baron smiled, "I know many things Mohawk. Much more than you can possibly fathom."

That answer left an uneasy feeling with Mohawk. Little did he know that over the centuries, those practiced in the arts of blood-magic and even some gifted initiates had gained knowledge of summoning spirits and beings from other dimensions to gain knowledge, power and wealth for themselves regardless of consequence. Some had even managed to pull translucent beings into the world that could materialize physically, usually to quell their opposition...but that required a level of skill and occult knowledge truly few could wield even for the briefest of moments. Over those centuries, the Baron, in a different form, had entertained some of those weak summonses in order to grow the ranks of the art thereby increasing his ability to influence them and, if needed, use them as the husk from which he would emerge into their world.

"Can we think about it for a moment?" Mac asked.

"I will give you...how do you say...five minutes?" the Baron responded. He raised his arms and vanished from sight.

"What do we do?" Mac asked Mohawk.

"I say we get the fuck out of here. I don't like the Baron in the least bit. He even knew my real name. There's something he's not telling us." Mohawk admitted as he strode over to the window and placed his black boots on the ground next to his own. After they appeared around his boots, he heaved himself out of the window into the darkness outside.

"What's he doing?!" Mac cursed as he ran to the window with Baracuss.

Then a coil of rope appeared beside the desk behind Mac and Baracuss. Invisible, the Baron chuckled to himself from the shadows of the room.

As Mohawk hit the ground, he felt himself sink several inches into the soft earth. Quickly he tried to bound up, but he was held fast to the ground.

"Damn!" he spat, realizing he was stuck.

"What are you doing?" Baracuss called to Mohawk as he looked down from the window.

"I was trying to get the fuck out of here and have you guys jump out. But my fuckin' boots are stuck in mud or something!" Mohawk hissed angrily.

But it wasn't possible for mud to hold magical boots unless it was deep enough to hold the entire person wearing the boots as well. Magic was involved here.

Baracuss looked around and found the rope behind him. Scooping it up, he tossed it out of the window and kept one end of it, "Take hold of that."

Mohawk grabbed the rope and Baracuss slowly heaved him up, using the window as a brace. With Mac's help, Mohawk was pulled up the wall foot by foot. Not feeling any resistance from the mud, he looked down and realized that he no longer wore the black boots. They were held fast below.

"Damn." Mohawk cursed, having lost the boots.

Reaching out, Mac got a firm hold of Mohawk and pulled him through the window as Baracuss collected the last of the rope and set it back.

"The boots are still down there." Mohawk said in a frustrated tone.

"We can't get them." Mac stated, also disappointed that the black boots were effectively gone.

"What!" Mohawk shot back.

"They're being held by some type of magic. I don't know any spells to release them."

"Oh great." Mohawk grunted, twisting his jaw as he threw his arms in the air in disgust.

Suddenly appearing on the other side of the desk the Baron, with a hint of a smile, said, "So, my friends…have you made your decision?"

Mohawk shot a glaring look at the Baron and said, "Yeah. We'll help. Do we have a choice?"

"There's always a choice. It's just a matter of whether the choice prolongs life and at what cost." the Baron smiled as he turned and walked away, not bothering to see if they followed him, "Please follow me."

Wearily they followed the Baron past the skeleton guards that were still standing on either side of the double doors. Once they crossed half way into the courtyard the Baron stopped.

"I know you must need a way back. And, as I said before, I hate to waste time." the Baron said as he raised the Staff of Majii into the air, its horns glowing a deep blue.

Mac considered whether he should try to touch the Staff as Metsys had said, but decided against it. There would be another time for that.

Within a few moments, a dark figure became visible overhead. It had a long tail, two large bat-like wings and a long neck. As it got closer, the legs underneath its large scaly body could be seen, as well as two claw-tipped arms. Its eyes were fiery red, above which held two long, white horns pointed backwards. The greenish-blue color of its scales sent a tinge of discomfort through Baracuss's body. He had never been in close proximity of such a massive creature, and he wasn't sure that he wanted to be in the company of this one.

"A dragon." Mac idolized as it landed it's thirty-foot-long form in front of them, sending dirt into the air as its wings moved faster to ease its heavy body onto the earth.

There was a certain comfort the Baron had with the magical power that radiated from the Staff of Majii. The ability to control dragons that weren't of his race was something that he enjoyed to a great degree, but that was only a fraction of the power he'd discovered within it. The

105

Baron knew that without the Staff he would not have such abilities that were so easy to use. He could, of course, control dragons and such with the Dark Magic, but that required extensive concentration, a vulnerability he would not entertain if it could be avoided.

The Baron had also prepared a golden necklace that had been wrested from Mohawk and Mac's world, that he wove Dark Magic and strains of Wild Magic from the Staff into. It wasn't a weapon like the way the Staff was wielded. Instead, the necklace was crafted so that it could save his life by using the Wild Magic which was not common to the Realm to sustain him. The Baron knew such a thing was remote, but he was determined not to overlook anything that could compromise his plans. With Metsys as his adversary in the Realm, any small thing that may be overlooked could be used with great effect against him. One way or another, he would get what he wanted…even if he were to lose possession of the Staff of Majii.

"Please climb onto my servant. He will take you north to the keep of Metsys." the Baron said as he pointed to the dragon with his free hand, "It would take far too long for you to walk back…if you managed to survive that journey."

"But what happens to the dragon? Surely Metsys would discover and destroy it." Mohawk pointed out.

"Don't worry. I will ensure your safe arrival. What happens to the dragon afterwards is unimportant. It's one of many." the Baron replied dryly.

Over the years the Baron had sent many dragons north to test the limits of where he could travel before Metsys would react. Over time, the Baron was able to move the limit of where he could have the dragons travel to just south of the castle walls before being destroyed by Metsys. Although the Baron had not done that probing in order to make sure his three reluctant allies would get back safely, for this purpose he knew how far they could travel.

Finding handholds in the wavy scales, they climbed onto the back of the dragon, straddling its back between the large wings.

As the Green Dragon took to the air, the Baron yelled, "Good luck!"

Chapter Fourteen

"By the gods!" a sentry guarding the castle gate exclaimed, crouching slightly into a defensive position as he pointed his spear at the descending Green Dragon as dust and a few leaves were flung into the air from its beating wings. Had it still been daylight, he would have spotted the dragon much sooner.

The dragon paused on the dirt road in front of the castle long enough to let his riders off before he advanced upon the lone sentry. The human would make a good snack to quell his hunger.

The sentry took a step backwards. The brass bell with a small iron hammer was only a few feet away, hanging from the castle wall at the side of the gated entrance. To the sentry it seemed like over a hundred paces as beads of sweat formed on his helmed forehead, trying to remain calm despite his heart beating ever faster. Gently he eased himself towards the bell, hoping that the dragon would not breathe fire upon him and dreading that he had not brought his cumbersome shield when he came on duty. But, over the past year of service, he'd never needed it.

The dragon took another step forward but stopped, turning its head behind it. It wanted this human but the Baron, too powerful to be challenged, called him. Disappointed, the dragon extended its powerful wings and lurched into the air. Within a few mighty strokes, the dragon was high in the sky and heading south away from the castle.

Relieved the sentry stood up slowly and exhaled loudly, keenly watching the silhouette of the dragon vanish from sight behind the tree tops of the forest. Had he the presence of mind to speak in this moment, he would have. Instead, he kept his gaze on the tree tops and merely waved the three approaching figures by, consumed with the thought that he had just stood mere paces from a dragon of the south and lived.

"Where are we going to sleep?" Mac asked. He saw that Baracuss was leading them down a cobblestone street to the west, away from the tavern.

But Mohawk had an idea of what Baracuss was up to, saying, "It'd be too risky to linger around here. The people at the tavern can tag us. Quintities probably has a few hired thugs staking the place out in case we return."

"Exactly." Baracuss agreed, veering off onto another road which headed north.

Not many people were roaming about, which was good for the small group. That meant they would probably be able to make better time to Metsys keep without having to evade the many eyes that would otherwise be traveling the roads during the daytime.

Turning again onto a road that went east, they followed it some two hundred paces before they again turned north to a road leading to the keep. The dim outlines of archers from the moonlight could be seen atop the keep walls, pacing back and forth. Four soldiers stood guard at the entrance as well. Faint laughter and garbled voices could be heard from the soldiers as the party strode up to the gate.

"Are we actually going to tell him?" Mac inquired. He didn't really want to try and kill the wizard.

"Of course not. Do you think I trust that Baron? Especially after what he did to Loce?" Mohawk responded with a contorted expression on his face.

"Aye. As much as I hate magic, I'd rather have Metsys around than that cursed dog!" Baracuss confessed.

Mac's mind was put at ease, *'Thank god.'*

"Who goes there?" one of the soldiers challenged as he pushed himself away from the keep wall he was leaning on. The others gathered themselves at the gate, blocking its entrance with a wall of meaty flesh and iron.

Impatiently Mohawk said, "It's important that we see Metsys. We're the ones he summoned."

"Oh yes. Two humans and a barbarian. He has informed us. Please pass." the brown-bearded one who looked well into his forties urged, recognizing the small band.

Baracuss raised an eyebrow in surprise and disappointment. He had been looking forward to another confrontation with the soldiers.

Passing the soldiers they crossed the courtyard and ascended a wooden staircase to a set of double doors. Pushing them open they found Metsys sitting behind his desk, silently reading a thick book laid open before him. Two torches on either wall between the tapestries burned brighter than normal, providing light.

Looking up as Baracuss closed the doors, Metsys said, "Ah, my friends. Please sit down."

Gently closing the book, Metsys began, "I did not know that you debited a charge in Quintities name without his approval. Why?"

Mohawk looked to his friends for some support, but they just looked at him blankly.

"Nevertheless," Metsys continued after a long awkward pause, "I have compensated for his losses. There are more important problems at hand to address."

"Yes. We went south to confront the Baron after he had killed Loce and somehow sent Baracuss to us through a torch. We really had no choice. He knew exactly where we were." Mohawk shot out, eager to change the subject.

Thumbing the edge of the book, Metsys asked, "What…did he want of you?"

"To kill you. Then send us back to our own world." Mac said plainly. Surely Metsys already knew that.

Metsys sat back in his chair. After gaining his thoughts he looked at the three with probing eyes, speculating if they would actually try such a fruitless endeavor. Silence hung in the room.

"I suppose you agreed with him?" Metsys said coolly. If they were to actually try something, he was prepared to conjure a few spells.

"Well, we had to agree so we could leave his keep." Mohawk stressed. He could tell that Metsys appeared to be somewhat uneasy.

Metsys, raising an eyebrow, responded, "You know, as soon as he finds out you have betrayed him, he will come for you."

Sighing, Mac grunted, "It's going to happen sooner or later."

"Well, double-agents does complicate things somewhat." Metsys admitted with a small grin, placing a glass vial about four inches long, sealed with a cork and filled with a clear fluid on the desk before Mohawk. He motioned for him to pick it up.

Slowly as Mohawk took it, Metsys said, "That vial, once you drink its contents will render you invisible for about half a day. When you reach the entrance of Mt. Reach, drink its content. That way, the dragons which guard the entrance will be unable to see you. Then proceed to find the passage that will lead you to the Sword of Dragon Slaying. Once you have obtained the Sword, it will be invisible as long as it is in your possession."

Motioning with his hand, as if to thrust a sword, concluded, "After that, you go and slay the Baron."

"But the Baron is not a dragon." Baracuss stated, questioning why such a weapon would be needed against a sorcerer.

Smiling awkwardly, Metsys countered, "No, not in appearance. But he is one of the few dragon races left, though small in number, that can change into a human form. Of all the evil dragons, he is a Red Dragon. The worst and most intelligent of the lot."

"Great. So not only are we fighting a sorcerer, but a dragon all put into one." Mohawk grumbled, "Another surprise."

"Well, the good news is," Metsys volunteered as he casually placed a hand on the book, "the Baron will not be able to use his dragon power offensively while wielding the Staff's power."

"Ah well. That's comforting." Mohawk blurted out.

But Metsys was not through, "I have arranged for some help in getting to Mt. Reach as well as the Baron's keep. All you must do is talk to Zorin and he can get a few Silver Dragons to help."

"We have no horses," Mohawk stated. He wasn't in the mood to go on any long treks by foot just to talk to some Zorin fellow.

Metsys stood. "That's not a problem. I will portal you to Zorin, or at least close to his location."

Baracuss scowled. He knew that meant Metsys was going to use some type of magic on them.

"Now, let's all stand." Metsys urged as he began concentrating on the spell of teleportation, weaving the invisible threads of White Magic about them.

After they stood up, Metsys closed his eyes and slowly exhaled as he concentrated, drawing the White Magic to him as he visualized the tribe that lingered in the northwestern mountains.

Suddenly Mohawk saw his surroundings change into a small clearing, flanked on all sides by the outlines of high mountains in the moonlight. He had not felt any physical shift or any type of sensation that would have conveyed being taken to the spot where he now stood. In the darkness he could see a few people milling around, leaving patches of dark green where they walked over the frost laden grass that covered the ground beneath. As he felt a chill from the cold air, Mohawk was amazed that these people, dressed in simple clothes and no furs or leather, seemed so comfortable.

"These people must be related to elves, seeing as they have no torches for light." Mac suggested, remembering that elves could see exceptionally better at night than any human or barbarian.

"Well, we have to find some shelter or we're going to freeze out here in the elements." Mohawk said as another cold breeze caused his skin to pucker with little bumps.

"Yes," Baracuss agreed, "then find this Zorin."

As they followed the footprints the others made in the thin layer of frost, a person called from behind them. Even Baracuss hadn't heard the footfalls.

"Newcomers." The male voice called out.

Turning around, they faced the man, each mystified as to how he got that close without being noticed. He wore simple clothes, long-sleeved white shirt that was braided together along his chest and tied-off just below the neck. A matching set of pants were tucked snugly into a pair of brown leather boots. His long, blond hair hung loosely about his shoulders and amidst a smooth skinned but bony face sat two golden-colored eyes.

He smiled, "Welcome. Metsys told me about your journey to this land. We have long awaited such a coming."

From the looks of the man, Mac didn't believe he could be the Zorin that Metsys was referring to. Too young, and, he'd expected someone in more grand attire indicative of status or rank to greet them. He assumed the fellow was a guide who would lead them to Zorin.

"So, you're Zorin?" Mohawk asked as he stepped towards the figure.

"Yes. Please come with me." the man said as he turned and strode north.

Even Baracuss was beginning to feel the cold bite of the frigid air through his leather, himself becoming curious as to how the people here could stand such weather with so little clothing.

Passing through some brush that had turned white from the frost, they came across a small entrance in the side of a hill, lit by torches. As they approached the entrance Baracuss caught the smell of food that made his stomach churn with anticipation. He had not eaten for the greater portion of a day and really had not thought about it until now.

Entering the tunnel that was as tall and wide as five men, they walked into a large smooth-walled cavern over one hundred paces cubed. Even the ceiling and floor were perfectly smooth as if someone spent countless years with hammer, chisel and a filing stone to knock away and smooth out the ripples and protrusions that might have existed.

In the midst of the cavern sat a table laden with food and drink. Six unoccupied chairs sat around the square table. Twenty-five paces from the wooden table sat several large brown furs with similar furs bound together as pillows.

"My friends, sit and eat. And, please, sleep here tonight." Zorin suggested as he sat at the table.

Eagerly the party seated themselves at the table and began eating, Baracuss most ravenously. Zorin smiled, content that they appeared to enjoy the meal that was prepared for them.

Between mouthfuls Mac inquired, "So, you are elven? I've seen a few people walking in the dark without torches."

"No, it just happens to be a trait we can see well at night." Zorin replied openly.

"And your resistance to cold?" Baracuss pointed out as he raised a tankard to his lips.

A faintly audible, yet muffled, fleshy clapping sound briefly undulated along the hard surface of the cavern floor.

"Yes, that too."

Baracuss paused to squeeze his eyebrows together for a moment before reaching for more basted turkey.

"What are you, if not an elf?" Mohawk said finally. He didn't particularly like the way Zorin was casually avoiding divulging what his race was, not that it mattered to him. But dodging questions always raised red flags for him.

"What the?!", Mac roared out at the powerfully thick, dark and pungent sensation that his nose reeled in, all at once. He lurched out of his chair and walked a few paces towards Mohawk at the other end of the table, still grasping a large slice of cracked wheat bread, "Are you serious right now?!"

Zorin and Mohawk exchanged a puzzled look and turned toward Mac who was still trying to expel the remnant of that repulsive odor from his nose.

Baracuss pointed between them, turkey in hand and proudly declared, "That is what we barbarians call the 'Witches Breath'. That's something you don't forget."

"Damn straight." Mac mumbled, "More like super sewer stench. Thank god no torches are at the table. Fuck."

Mohawk laughed, "Glad I'm over here."

Slowly Mac moved back to the chair he was in and pushed it closer to Mohawk. Then, while keeping some distance and a close eye on Baracuss, outstretched his arms to grab his plate and tankard and placed them on the table in front of the chair.

"Next time, hold out your finger," Mac volunteered as he sat down and mimicked holding a finger out in front of him, "and say, 'Pull it'. That would be MOST appreciated."

After swallowing another bite, Mohawk glanced at Zorin with the hint of a smile still on his face, "What are you?"

Crossing his arms on the table, Zorin replied, "Guardians of the Majii and of the earth-borne White Magic."

Shrugging, Mac asked, "What's that?"

"I'll explain," Zorin said and continued, "For over ten thousand years we have been the Guardians of the White Magic. It's a pure magic that comes from the earth's heart and flows openly into one spot in the Realm – Mt. Reach. We were sworn to guard that magic from all evil

114

that might be able to reach the mountain. It's guarded even now by us and no evil has been able to gain reach of the magic. Although evil dragons have seized the entrance to Mt. Reach, they cannot physically enter. The corridor into the mountain's heart is only large enough for a man to enter. Someone such as yourself."

Mac appeared confused, "We were told that the Baron is a dragon but can take the shape of a man...so what prevents him or other dragons from changing form?"

"That is true." Zorin said with a raised eyebrow, looking at Mac as if to congratulate him.

Then he looked briefly around the cavern and said, "But, some dragon races cannot change form and those few that can, relatively few amongst them have mastered the ability to do so. And, when in human form, kinetic magic cannot be used. About the only magic at your disposal is defensive magic predisposed to your particular race."

"I see. The Baron still has the Staff though, so he could use that, yes?" Mac asked, tearing off a chunk of bread.

"He could." Zorin admitted, "But as we are bound to the White Magic, training with it our entire lives, and being so close to the earth-borne source, there is not sufficient magic bound to the Staff to best our collective and the source of White Magic that we draw strength from."

Mac nodded, convinced.

"And the Sword of Dragon Slaying is in the mountain as well...why? Wouldn't it be much easier to have it here, within your reach?" Mohawk probed curiously.

"That sword, given its unique ability against all dragon races, is best guarded at Mt. Reach where the source of White Magic and our presence is rooted."

Crossing his arms, Zorin added, "That sword can be used by anyone simply by wielding it, unlike White Magic."

Mohawk took several swallows of the sweet, smooth, clear substance in the tankard before asking, "So what about the Staff of Majii?"

"The Staff is different. Until some four thousand years past, it was unknown to our world. Then a man, who was almost dead, entered into our world with the Staff without the use of a tapestry, portal or anchor point in the Realm. The written history says he ebbed into this world like layers of fog collecting in on itself until his physical form had solidified out of it. While we still cannot do that into your world, we have been able to pattern White Magic spells to move from one point to another in the Realm without the need for a tapestry or natural anchor point. It's much more demanding though. Metsys calls it teleportation."

Zorin uncrossed his arms and tapped the table, "Anyway. The stranger said he had fought the great spirits of your world to protect it and he willed it to us to guard. My ancestors swore to guard it well, but really didn't understand its magic. Several centuries later another similar ebbing happened in our world from yours, but instead of a single man, a company of humans and a few giants, whom were unknown to us, came. Descendants of those same giants occupy the Realm to this day. The written history does not say much about those that came, other than they called themselves the Tart'aas who possessed high skill with what they called ethereal magic, and mechanical things."

"From what I understand, most of those people were absorbed into one elven clan or another over time while the giants struck out on their own." Zorin shrugged.

He pointed upward and added, "While our ancestors did not comprehend the magic of the Staff, Chief Isotor was able to partially meld with it and grasp some of its potential. He did several things with it that, perhaps, he should not have as he continued making discoveries. And I think that is why the Baron became so obsessed with it and wrested it from him over a century ago. Luckily the Chief had told us that the Staff could be destroyed. But only with equal magic. In effect the magic would cancel itself out in this land."

Grimacing, Mohawk said, "Someone from our world is needed for that."

"Yes." Zorin replied as he got up from the table. Striding towards the mouth of the cavern, he said, "Sleep here. Tomorrow will be a long day."

Chapter Fifteen

The party rustled out of the furs only moments before Zorin entered the cavern the following day.

"How was your sleep?" Zorin asked, eager to learn if the food had helped them.

"Great, actually" Mohawk replied, "I'm full of energy today."

Mac and Baracuss nodded in agreement while helping themselves to what remained of the food and drink.

Zorin hadn't told them that the food they consumed was laced with an odorless, tasteless and transparent powder. It was a magical substance credited with increased stamina and recovery. It was, in fact, the same substance though imbued with herbs and White Magic that Angela had first used in the form of a fog which helped both Mohawk and Gladstad recover from the physical wounds the pack of Death Dogs had inflicted. Zorin knew they would need some type of physical booster for what was ahead. Unsure of what laid before them, he wanted to be sure everyone would be able to react to any sudden dangers quickly.

"That's good to hear." Zorin smiled, "Come with me."

Grabbing their gear, they followed Zorin outside into the warm, early morning sun. A pleasantly cool breeze crept past them as Mac buckled the sword belt around his waist.

Entering the clearing they had been teleported to by Metsys, Mohawk asked, "Will the Chief be meeting us, or maybe, come along?"

Mac glanced briefly at Mohawk thinking, *The skill of a Chief would be invaluable to have with us.'*

"The Chief will join us shortly." Zorin replied.

Mac was eager to meet the Chief of this tribe. Surely this man had skill rivaling the Baron.

"What of the dragons that were going with us?" Baracuss grunted, doubtful that any dragons lived in these frigid mountains. It was definitely not a place he would live, had he the choice.

Both Mac and Mohawk looked at Zorin. Baracuss could be on to something. They had seen no dragons, only people with traits like elves.

"You want to see dragons?" Zorin asked smoothly. He took several paces backward away from them, then stopped and closed his eyes.

Suddenly his entire body stretched and blurred as it was replaced with the form of a thirty-foot tall, scaly Silver Dragon. The two clawed feet were planted near where Zorin had stood, while its long, scaly tail swept around the side of Baracuss.

Baracuss, clearly startled, jumped away from the serpentining tail, eyeing the towering form that now stood in front of him. He was not sure what to do.

Steam rolled out of the dragon's leathery nostrils as its gold eyes looked down upon them. Easily it turned its long, scaly neck so it could better see the eyes of the small human forms below.

"Is this what you wanted to see?" the Silver Dragon asked in the voice of Zorin.

"Incredible." Mac muttered in astonishment, looking at the magnificent stature of the dragon before him.

"Uh, not exactly…" Baracuss said weakly, glancing between the clawed arms and the double-horned head of the Silver Dragon curious as to which was more deadly in combat.

"Well, come on. Climb up." Zorin urged as he knelt down and spread his silver, bat-like wings.

As they pulled themselves on, Mohawk asked, "What of the Chief?"

Waiting until they all settled themselves on his back, Zorin stated, "The Chief will join us."

Then, rhythmically, Zorin lifted and beat his wings quickly until his mighty form lifted from the earth, sending a thin fog of frost into the air. After ascending into the cool, light blue-hazed sky perhaps two thousand feet up, Zorin began gliding, using his outstretched wings to catch air and provide lift. Occasionally he swept his wings up and down to maintain the altitude.

At this height they could see the small outline of the castle and walls that stretched for many kilometers and, the smaller silhouette of Metsys keep, surrounded by a plush green carpet that the riders knew was the forest. Off to the eastern horizon they could see a vast expanse of water that bowed slightly with the curvature of this world. Other lands, beyond their sight, lay beyond that horizon.

As they flew south, the landscape changed. The green carpet gave way to a lifeless brownness of barren earth, naked of life. In the midst of this barrenness sat a large ice-capped mountain. Even from this distance, they knew it as Mt. Reach.

Mac wondered how long it would be before the Baron would be able to chip away at the defenses of the mountain and gain reach of the source of the White Magic. He had a feeling that the Baron had a scheme for getting to it.

Another dragon descended from the sky to Zorin's side. It, too, was silver.

Waving at the newcomer, Mohawk shouted to Zorin as the wind blew past them, "Is that the Chief?"

"Yes." Zorin replied as he continued gliding towards the mountain.

Baracuss squinted at the other dragon, trying to spot some feature on its body that might indicate it was a Chief, but he didn't observe anything different. Of course, one couldn't tell the physical difference between a Silver Dragon and the Chief. In grown dragon-form they were identical. The only way one could distinguish any difference was if one was practiced in magic. Then it would be a trivial matter of gazing at the aura each dragon radiated which was unique to each dragon, similar to shades of color in the visual spectrum of light. The most pronounced, indicative of skill with magic, would undoubtedly be the Chief regardless of the "color" the dragon was birthed with.

As they came around to the west side of the mountain, they descended rapidly, then turning east towards the mountain. The Silver Dragons raced down to the base of the mountain, gaining speed. Mohawk and the others gripped Zorin's wavy scales as he tucked his wings in to his sides, descending faster and faster. Mohawk was glad he did not eat much before they left as he felt a hefty tingling in his stomach.

Baracuss held his breath, eyes wide open with unease. His knuckles whitened as he began to feel his body lift away from Zorin's back, struggling to stay seated. He hoped the dragon wouldn't crash into the side of the jagged mountain as it rushed towards them.

Then, in unison, the dragons outstretched their wings and with the aid of their tails, altered their point of gravity and lift so they faced upwards. The air that suddenly became trapped under their wings, as they reached out with them, along with the speed of their descent and aerodynamic shift caused them to bolt upwards along the face of the mountain. Lesser, inexperienced dragons wouldn't have had such precision and would have mangled themselves upon the mountain.

Neither Zorin or the Chief did the maneuver to somehow prove that they were superb flyers of the air. It was because they had to, or the Green Dragons would have seen their approach from their vantage point on the mountain. Naturally, the best way to approach was to gain a foothold on the western side of the mountain where they couldn't be seen, then work their way around to the northeastern side of the mountain where the entrance was located.

As the pull of gravity and the lift of the dragons caused the riders to sink heavily onto Zorin's back, he beat his wings to compensate for the change, maintaining his distance from the mountain which was a stone's throw from his body. Reaching a natural ledge as their ascent slowed, the two Silver Dragons maneuvered around and landed. After the riders awkwardly dismounted, Zorin altered his being into his human form.

"What a ride!" Mac exclaimed, openly excited by the gut-twisting experience, even though he was a bit shaken inwardly.

Zorin smiled in return.

Baracuss, on the other hand, swore to himself that he would never ride a dragon again.

"What about the Chief? Is he coming?" Mohawk asked as he shook the adrenaline rush from his body. He liked having a rush, but he was not eager to repeat the one he just had.

"No. The Chief will stay here in case there are any problems." Zorin said as they strode beside him.

Cautiously walking along the trail that wormed its way around the side of the mountain to the northern face, Mohawk remembered his flask.

"Hey." He said quietly to Zorin.

As Zorin turned about, Mohawk continued, "I got this stuff that makes me invisible. I'll drink it and go in first."

"Good. That will make things easier." Zorin said as he let Mohawk pass him on the narrow trail.

Removing the cork, Mohawk drank the clear, tasteless substance from the flask. He didn't feel anything as he placed the flask carefully in a small crevice in the face of the mountain and looked at Zorin.

"Guess it didn't work, eh?" he grunted in disappointment, still able to see himself.

Raising his eyebrows, Zorin countered, "Well, I can't see you. I can hear you...just can't see you."

Of course, if Zorin wanted to see him, he could just tap into the White Magic but, limiting himself to sight, Mohawk could not be seen.

"Cool." Mac said at Mohawk's sudden disappearance.

Continuing along the trail east, Mohawk stopped suddenly. A Green Dragon was outside the entrance.

"Stop here." He whispered behind him, just before Zorin bumped into him. "There's a dragon right around the corner here. I'll go in and see if I can find the entrance to the mountain."

Cautiously Mohawk edged his way along the corner, through the large rough-cut passageway and into the larger cavern.

As the water spirit progressed north along the stream after having completely digested the two horses, it noticed something overhead. It couldn't have been any fowl, for it was far too high in the sky. And yet it was very large. Sluggishly, the water spirit used what feeble Dark Magic it had and magnified its vision of the object overhead. But now, instead of one object, it saw two. And they weren't birds. Almost immediately the water spirit recognized the bat-like wings and the long tails of the two Silver Dragons. It knew the Baron wouldn't like knowing Silver Dragons were flying to his domain, but the water spirit could not withhold the sighting. With its telepathic ability, it informed the Baron.

"Traitors!" the Baron fumed as he hit the desk. He'd seen the two Silver Dragons through the photopic vision of the water spirit.

Taking the Staff of Majii in hand, he intoned, "My fellow dragons which guard Mt. Reach! Destroy the Silver Dragons and whatever else stirs on the mountain!"

He knew what they were after – the Sword of Dragon Slaying. But as long as he commanded the Green Dragons with the Staff of Majii, he knew he could keep them from it…at least long enough for him to hastily prepare. He grunted to himself in disgust as he scooped up the necklace and placed it around his neck. There wouldn't be time to test it now, to make sure it worked as he had fashioned it to. But, perhaps, he wouldn't have to resort to using it.

Inside the large cavern Mohawk saw three other Green Dragons, one of which sat in a nest made of ancient, dry wooden branches. To his right lay mounds of gold coins, goblets and jewels and, at the base of the same mound, rested the crumpled form of a worn white cape. He didn't know dragons collected such humanly items.

At the highest point of the cavern, some fifty feet high was a large transparent gem. Easily it was the size of a man's head and was anchored to the ceiling with an iron rod three feet in length. The gem glowed with a dazzling white light, providing light in the cavern absent torches.

What Mohawk didn't see anywhere was a door of some type. Nor did he see a sword.

Then, suddenly, the dragons became alert as the gem's glow changed to a deep blue. Freezing by the entrance to the cavern hoping he would not be discovered, he watched in fear as the dragons darted towards the gem, to disappear and reappear outside the cavern and taking flight. He sighed in relief.

"Oh shit!" Mac cursed aloud, seeing a Green Dragon turning towards him.

"Come on!" Zorin shouted, running around the corner of the mountain to the large passageway followed closely by Mac and Baracuss.

"Go!" Zorin commanded as he pointed to the entrance for Mac and Baracuss to follow.

Seeing his friends rush into the passageway, Mohawk yelled to Zorin, "I don't see any door or entrance!"

"Keep looking!" Zorin replied hastily as he changed into his dragon form just a few seconds before a fiery blast from one of the Green Dragons pushed him off balance, sending him reeling against the side of the passageway.

Gaining altitude, the Chief flew speedily towards the three Green Dragons that few likewise at the Silver Dragon. As one of the Green Dragons breathed a cone of fire at the Silver Dragon, the Chief did the same, splitting fire with fire. Flying through the fire, the Chief collided with one of the Green Dragons, sinking its mighty clawed arms through the scales and into the soft flesh of the dragon's neck, crippling its fire glands.

Unable to breath fire, the Green Dragon grappled with the Chief and caught one of the Silver Dragon's beating wings in its claws. Slowly, thick green blood began to flow from the scales of the Green Dragon's neck as it tried to hold its own body weight and the Silver Dragon's in the air long enough for its companions to attack the Chief. But, as strong as its wings were, bit by bit they were tiring from the exertion and blood loss. The entangled pair fell through the air to the barren earth below, followed closely by the other Green Dragons.

As they frantically searched the cavern walls for some type of hidden door or lever which might be used to open a door, Baracuss paused momentarily to stash a few gold coins in his leather pouch.

"I don't see any doors." Mac spat, raising his arms in disgust.

"We gotta find it." the invisible form of Mohawk stressed.

Looking at the heap of gold almost equal in height to a dragon, Baracuss said, "Maybe it's not in the walls. Perhaps it's under this pile of gold."

"Check under it then!" Mohawk ordered, which gave him an idea.

Baracuss smiled. He would enjoy plowing through the gold.

Seeing branches being tossed into the air from the midst of the nest, Mac heard the voice of Mohawk say, "Well, come over here and help!"

After several minutes of throwing branches aside, Mohawk and Mac found a rectangular hole beneath the nest with a set of finely carved stone steps leading down.

"Found it!" Mac declared.

Baracuss stopped sifting the gold around, almost forgetting why he was there. He would have to come for the gold…later.

As Zorin scrambled to his clawed feet, the Green Dragon landed on the ledge and breathed another cone of fire at him. This time, however, Zorin swept his wings around him, protecting his body from the brunt of the fire that deflected in all directions off his leathery wings. With keen precision, Zorin then twisted his body around, and with his tail, swept the Green Dragon from its feet and over the ledge. Hastily beating his wings, Zorin went down after the dragon who had tumbled out of sight.

Chapter Sixteen

As the two entangled dragons fell through the air, the Chief whipped its tail about, causing the two to become inverted so that the Silver Dragon was now above the Green Dragon. Before the bleeding dragon could react, the Chief bit into the Green Dragon's neck with immense force, splintering several scales while forcing the head of the dragon backward almost as far as its spine. Then, with its claws still buried in the dragon's neck, savagely pulled backward snapping several vertebrae and freeing itself just moments before the limp mass hit the earth below. But two other Green Dragons now pursued and they were closing behind the Chief.

Swooping after the dragon, Zorin sighed in relief seeing that the Green Dragon had not reacted in time to evade an outcropping of jagged rock which it lay amongst...dead.

Beating his wings, Zorin turned about, speeding towards the two Green Dragons which, moment by moment, gained upon the fleeing Silver Dragon. Zorin knew the Chief was an excellent combatant when fighting anything known, including dragons but he could not let the Chief single-handedly face two Green Dragons. Especially since the Chief had offered assistance, coming out of solitude from the tribe shortly after the untimely death of Chief Isotor. Zorin suspected that in such solitude, the Chief may have forgotten some of the combat skill which, in this time, could very well mean life or death against two hardened dragons.

Mohawk descended the staircase followed by Mac and Baracuss for some thirty feet, finding themselves in a cavern well over three hundred feet in height and from side to side. Around the ledge that was scarcely large enough to hold all three of them, a bright, silvery sheet of water rested, providing light for the cavern. The water didn't appear to have traveled from any direction as not even the faintest ripple could be observed.

"So where to now?" Mohawk asked Mac. It looked like a dead-end.

Shrugging his shoulders, Mac replied, "Hell. I don't know."

That was not the answer Mohawk was looking for.

Baracuss looked at Mac blankly. He sure didn't have any idea of what to do except, perhaps, dive into the pool to look for a submerged passage of some type. It would not be the first time.

"You must have *some* idea with all that knowledge you have up top." Mohawk said, somewhat sarcastically.

"Actually, nothing quite as final as this." Mac thought out loud, trying to spot something in the darkness beyond the water's glow.

Baracuss practically shouted suddenly, pointing to the far edge of the cavern, "Look there!"

Across the expanse came a flat, square-shaped wooden log that had been split in half as to provide a flat surface. But no one could be seen upon it to guide its way and, oddly, the water did not appear to be disturbed as it floated towards them.

As the raft neared the ledge and stopped a few inches from it Mohawk sighed, "I guess this is it, huh?"

Nobody knew for sure. His guess was as good as anyone's at the moment.

Carefully Mohawk stepped onto the raft as not to tip it over. Soon, as he changed position to allow the others on, he realized that the raft didn't teeter whatsoever – it was as if the split log was firmly anchored to the cavern's bottom. Although not fully comprehending magic, Mohawk concluded that magic was somehow controlling the raft and maybe it was the same magic which caused the water to be so placid, even when the raft crossed its surface.

After the others got on, the raft began gliding easily in the direction from which it came.

"This is weird, isn't it?" Mac asked as he looked around.

"Yeah. But what's even stranger is that this raft is heading towards that wall." Mohawk grunted as the wall he mentioned became visible before them and grew in size as they neared.

Though they were within stone's throw of the jagged cavern wall, they could see the bony outlines of several skeletons, some human, others resembling grotesque, mauled shapes of strange creatures somehow merged into the wall as if they had just been unearthed and loose dirt swept away.

"Give me a coin." Mac asked to Mohawk as the raft steadily gained upon the wall.

Baracuss swore to himself he saw the faint gleam of gold coin in one of the veins of the wall.

"Why?" Mohawk retorted. "What the hell do you need with gold at a time like this?"

Mac shot a frustrated look at Mohawk, "Just give me one." There had to be some explanation for the raft gliding towards the wall. He didn't see any openings that even the raft could pass through, and the coin would confirm his suspicions.

Reluctantly Mohawk pulled out a gold piece from his leather purse. Mac took it eagerly and threw it at the wall. The gold tumbled through the air and disappeared into the cavern wall without a sound. An illusion.

"Just as I thought." Mac smiled, both in relief and satisfaction. His suspicion was correct.

"Ah, an illusion." Mohawk snapped, as if he knew the entire time.

For an illusion it was strikingly real to the eye, even for Baracuss. The magician who had created the wall had taken great time and care ensuring that the spell had been woven correctly, down to individual strands of magic itself. In that way, even the smallest and most insignificant detail would appear real to the eye, serving its purpose to elude all those that sought power foolishly and would be turned around by a seemingly dead-end.

Zorin could see the two Green Dragons in close pursuit of the Chief, who was barely managing to stay beyond their grasp. He knew something would have to be done, but he also knew those dragons had a high tolerance to magical attacks, so he would be unlikely to phase them at a distance. The only feasible way to interrupt their pursuit and possibly damage the dragons would have to be physical. And close. Yet, for the moment, Zorin wasn't close enough for such an attack and if he were, they would spot him.

Then it occurred to him. He could use his magical abilities on himself to get the element of surprise. Invisibility. Zorin cursed to himself for not having thought of it sooner and began to focus his mind on the White Magic. A faint warmth flowed through his massive form as he darted toward the dragons. Calming his mind, he was able to relax despite the fact that he was in flight. He envisioned the threads of White Magic surround and weave closely about his body, feeling the subtle but reassuring energy the White Magic pulsed around him. Such a feeling might have frightened others, breaking their concentration, but Zorin through his many years of practice was not phased. Instead, he kept weaving the threads around him until he felt as though he were completely immersed in a warm pool of water knowing, at that point, he would be invisible. Now the only way he would be discovered was if one of the dragons cast a spell that would indicate his presence among them…or if he were to physically touch one of them.

Fervently, Zorin hoped they wouldn't think of any defensive casting since they appeared to still be consumed with attacking the Chief.

Passing through the cavern wall, Baracuss tensed up, ready to spring into the glowing water if he felt the wall press onto his body. But, indeed, it was an illusion as he saw himself on the other side of the wall, unscathed.

This time, however, they were no longer in a cavern, but a long and jagged, twisting tunnel which was barely wide enough to accommodate the girth of the raft. Light continued to radiate from the placid water, dancing along the walls of the tunnel. As the raft progressed, turning left and right with the serpentining tunnel, it slowly gained momentum, descending down into the heart of the mountain.

The musty smell of air that was centuries, if not older, intensified as they continued their descent into an ancient place few had ever gained upon, and fewer yet had lived to see the light of the outer world once they had come to the raft's final resting place.

Mohawk pondered what was ahead. What test would have to be passed to receive the Sword of Dragon Slaying and stay alive? For perhaps the first time in his life, he questioned if he was up to whatever challenges might lay ahead. Then he thought about is family. Would he ever see his beautiful wife again? Be able to hold his two young children? And watch them grow? Would he live to become a proud grandfather? Or, like Gladstad, would he die in this strange world?

As Mac stood upon the raft gazing blindly ahead, he didn't concern himself with such mental gymnastics. After all, he wasn't married and didn't even have a girlfriend to look forward to seeing. He wasn't really concerned about returning to his world and about the only thing that fueled his determination to stay alive, the thing which sent his mind into a flurry of activity, was gaming out all of the scenarios of how to survive in *this* world.

Baracuss, on the other hand, didn't even consider dying. As a barbarian he accepted it just as he accepted the inevitability of cleaving someone, or something, for gold. Warring was the only real thing he knew and what he was comfortable with. Although he despised and loathed magic, he was determined to conquer the Baron and thought it a small price to pay to avenge Loce's death.

The small raft straightened as the tunnel gave way to an immense cavern wall well over five hundred feet cubed. Two hundred feet ahead of the raft was a set of gold plated, gem encrusted doors set against cavern wall flanked by two granite pillars, each easily eight feet wide and over twenty feet in height.

"That must be it!" Mac said excitedly, gesturing at the golden doors as a twinge of uncertainty went through him. Now he wasn't sure he actually wanted to do this.

"Yeah." Mohawk grimaced.

Passing over the edge of the forest, the Chief descended to tree-top level and picked up speed from both the descent and the elevated beat of its wings. The Chief hoped, although it was rather remote, that the Green Dragons would lose control in the sudden descent and plow into the forest. But they steadily pursued, not even caught off guard by the Chief's sudden descent over the forest which they narrowly missed.

Zorin, now invisible, sped after the Green Dragons, gaining upon them with incredible prowess and concentration.

Suddenly the Chief outstretched its powerful wings and forced the long, scaly tail downward and shot almost straight up into the sky. Scarcely a split second later, the two Green Dragons likewise did the same as they unknowingly flew towards Zorin. Zorin managed to dodge the Chief who apparently had not anticipated Zorin would cast himself invisible and moments later braced himself as he collided with one of the Green Dragons, its momentum carrying them both upwards for a short distance.

The Green Dragon was bewildered as it hit something hard in the sky, yet had seen nothing. Now it felt gravity assume its grasp over them and they began falling. Quickly it collected its senses and discovered that whatever it had collided with was now gripping him, and the unknown force smelled strangely familiar. Vainly the dragon tried to identify the smell it recognized as kindred, but couldn't. Then it occurred to the dragon that its combatant was shielded by an invisibility spell. Casting a dispel magic spell, the combatant's form revealed itself after a few short moments. A Silver Dragon!

Impulsively, the Green Dragon furiously sank its large claws into the Silver Dragon's belly and began

131

inhaling the cool air into its lungs and excited the fire glands to breath upon the Silver Dragon. But the dragon didn't have enough time. Heavily the two crashed through the trees and hit the hard earth. Fallen leaves and old, decaying branches sprung into the air from their impact and the sheer force of it caused the Green Dragon to retract its claws involuntarily. Almost instantly the dragon's vision became distorted and blurred.

As the Chief's upward momentum slowed, the Silver Dragon veered sharply left to continue evading the lone Green Dragon until an attack could be initiated. But the Chief's efforts were futile as an immense, searing path of fire from the Green Dragon barreled out and consumed the Chief. Having absorbed the brunt of the physical attack, the Chief failed to maintain altitude. Scales charred and some still glowing red, the Chief's smoking and barely conscious form tumbled downward to the forest edge below.

Zorin swiftly gained his clawed feet a few moments before the Green Dragon rolled off its side and also found its footing. Desperately concentrating on the forest around him, Zorin began conjuring magic around the Green Dragon. Even as the dragon strode towards the unmoving form of Zorin, he became more consumed with rage. Zorin's golden eyes began to glow an ever-deepening yellow as his emotions flowed freely outward. Suddenly, the forest came alive as branches and thick, corded vines wrapped tightly about the Green Dragon's body, stopping its advance. To no avail the dragon struggled to free itself from the branches and vines that continued to bind and consume the dragon. Dimly the Green Dragon glared at Zorin in unfettered, fearless rage just as a thick stream of dazzling flame, almost entirely white in color, radiated from Zorin's jaws, consuming the Green Dragon's twisting body and igniting the branches and vines around it.

Tapped of the sudden expulsion of so much energy, Zorin hunched over for several long moments to collect himself. Becoming aware that a fire was growing before him, he conjured a simple spell to extinguish the

golden-red flames dancing around the dead dragon's body.
Then he remembered that there was still another Green
Dragon, and the Chief, out there. Swiftly, he outstretched
his mighty wings and launched himself into the sky in
search of the Chief.

Chapter Seventeen

Standing in front of the golden doors, Mohawk
cautiously pressed his hand on them, unsure of how they
opened, with no visible hinges or bolts. Baracuss was
temporarily overcome with greed as he lustfully gazed at
the colorful jewels set in the golden doors. But Baracuss
caught himself just as he felt his hand edge towards the
dagger he would have used to pluck the nearest jewel from
its seat. He reluctantly closed his eyes briefly to remember
that other things needed to be done first – and that he
would return later.

Passing through the doors that spread before
them without the slightest sound, the party found
themselves in an oval room heavily laden with gold
tapestries evenly hung along the towering smooth granite
walls. The floor was crafted of golden bricks that almost
made the tapestries appear as though they were vertical
extensions. That optical illusion didn't capture Baracuss'
mind, or anyone else's. What did capture their minds lay in
the midst of the grand room, readily fit for a king. They
would be the first to behold it since the wizards from long
past created it.

Two statues of gleaming Silver Dragons stood
before them. Even for statues, their brilliance was far
purer than both the Chief and Zorin. Had either of them
been present, they would have been a pale gray in
comparison. Between the two statues, much to Mohawk's
relief, stood a thick, double-edged sword that hovered in
silence over the golden bricks with its hilt positioned at

shoulder height. The stretched leather, which was wrapped tightly about the long grip, appeared as though it had just been crafted.

"Is that it?" Mac asked, staring at the two-handed sword that remained suspended between the statues.

"Looks like a trap." Baracuss grumbled as he stared closely at the flanking statues. He'd come across similar arrangements in his younger days when he was a hired mercenary working under Lord Erot's banner. The only thing that saved him after he had foolishly triggered the trap were his stout and powerful legs as he ran from some dark, unnatural force that sprang forth and pursued him. To this day he remembers it well.

"That must be it." Mohawk suggested as he slowly approached the sword.

Baracuss wanted to reach out and hold Mohawk firm, but his apprehension kept his feet planted where they were, ready to race once more out of the room.

Nervously Mohawk reached out to grasp the grip of the sword just as he noticed something glitter out of the left side of his eye. A trap! Swiftly he jumped back a few steps to see what it was while raising his arms to offer balance.

"By the gods!" Baracuss exclaimed, his hands shooting instinctively toward his battleaxe.

Both Mac and Mohawk felt the sensation of dread surge through their bodies as they looked upon the statues that were now breathing. Now alive.

The limp form of the charred Silver Dragon slammed onto the unforgiving surface of the forest floor, knocking the wind from the Chief's lungs. Slowly and painfully the Chief managed to gain a weak but upright standing position just a few seconds before the Green Dragon barreled down upon the Chief's body. Unable to withstand the sudden impact, the Chief collapsed again to the leafy ground. Withdrawing its claws to keep its own balance, the Green Dragon savagely ripped a few silver scales from the Chief's charred back. The Chief felt its endurance rapidly fade with each passing moment. Even as the fatigue set in, the Silver Dragon knew something had to be done soon to survive.

The Green Dragon felt its feet lift away from the ground as the Silver Dragon's tail lashed out in a move of desperation to gain a few moments time. The Green Dragon tumbled over heavily, giving the Silver Dragon just enough time to gain, once more, a standing position.

Just as the Green Dragon scurried to its feet, the Chief lashed out with powerful White Magic as forceful as a hurricane, commanded somewhat unknowingly, solely at the advancing dragon. As the Silver Dragon's golden eyes flashed a brilliant red, the Green Dragon's form began to split and almost instantly changed into a dull gray color. The dragon had become stone.

The Chief lowered its piercing gaze as its eyes became golden again, not entirely sure if what had just happened was purely White Magic or if some trace of Dark Magic had somehow been caught up in the exertion. The Chief would have preferred to not have pacified the Green Dragon at such a fundamental level, even though deep-rooted primal instincts took over. Still, the Chief could not recollect anything similar from memory that had been attributed to White Magic or some known racial trait.

Drained of strength, the Silver Dragon knew something would have to be done to restore lost energy for the tasks that were still at hand. Wearily, the Chief slowly absorbed a few strands of White Magic from the trees and root systems beneath the earth as a yellow, spherical haze enveloped it. Although the Chief preferred using prepared herbs and specific plants for this purpose, there was no time to seek out the patch that had been growing under the Chief's care. Minute by minute the charred scales faded away with a renewed silver color, and new scales appeared where some had been ripped away as the Chief embraced the warm flow of White Magic. Slowly the sphere dissolved from sight, leaving the Chief feeling almost as if no battle had ever transpired.

"What is your presence here?" one of the living statues rumbled deeply as it turned its head to peer at Mohawk. The deep, bright ruby eyes probed Mohawk, penetrating his thought without his knowing.

"Umm, to get the Sword of Dragon Slaying." Mohawk replied uneasily. He hadn't prepared himself to be confronted. He had planned to either fight or steal the blade.

"What is your purpose?" the other dragon demanded evenly.

Baracuss' stomach churned within him. He felt as if there would be no escape if Mohawk said the wrong thing. While he didn't pray, he silently plead to be spared. All he could see, like the trap he had been in years before, was that dark form reaching out for him.

"To kill the Baron." Mohawk said simply.

"Explain." One of the dragons stated. The Baron was not a familiar point of reference to either of them.

Pausing for a moment, Mohawk tried to quiet his nerves and collect his thoughts before he said, "Metsys sent us to get the Sword of Dragon Slaying to destroy the Baron, a Dark Magic wizard. And, that Sword is the only thing that can destroy a Red Dragon. Because the Baron is a Red Dragon."

There were other ways, but the Sword of Dragon Slaying was the most effective tool.

One of the dragons straightened itself as its semi-sentient mind negotiated the volume of knowledge it had been gifted by its creators, and handily connected into unseen flowing channels of White Magic around them and further splintered into other forms of life above the surface to verify what had been said. The other dragon swept across the other companions.

After a pause, the dragon re-trained its eye on Mohawk, "He is true about the Sword."

The dragon tilted its head slightly and continued, "But you are outsiders. You are not from this Realm."

"No. We were summoned here by Metsys. The Baron has a magical Staff from our world that he has used wrongfully here. Only we can destroy the Staff so he cannot use our magic here. The Sword will give us that opportunity." Mohawk replied as best as he knew how.

Mac thought the situation was summed up nicely although he was still nervous about what the dragons might do. He imagined that, since they had been crafted so close to the source of White Magic and could probably extract any quantity needed, their power might be inescapable if they chose to become aggressive.

The dragons were quiet for a while, causing Baracuss to take a step backwards.

At last, one of the silver dragons heralded, "Take this Sword into your service. After you slay the Baron, or you are killed, we shall retrieve the Sword."

Incredibly eased by the silver dragon's invitation, Mohawk stepped forward and grasped the grip with both hands. His muscles tensed up, anticipating the Sword to be much heavier than what it actually was for its size. Amazed by its lightness, Mohawk estimated the Sword to weight only a few pounds. Then it occurred to him that he would need a sheath in which to carry it.

Before Mohawk could say anything, as if the silver dragon had read his mind, one of them said, "Relinquish your arm. The sheath you bear will hold the Sword."

Mac strained to look at the sheath and the Sword trying to understand how the larger Sword would fit in the smaller sheath.

Withdrawing his sword from its sheath, Mohawk carefully placed it on the gold bricks and then pushed the Sword into the sheath. Everyone watched in amazement as the Sword somehow shrunk its size as Mohawk pushed it effortlessly into the sheath.

Then Mohawk looked to the silver dragons to bid them thanks only to discover that they neither moved nor breathed. Whatever had caused them to animate, apparently was gone.

Chapter Eighteen

      Nestled high in the pine dotted mountains under exclusive corporate licensure rested a dark red seven acre hardened concrete compound, known as Crimson Portcullis, part of its dark composition owed to the secret ceramic and lava powder mixture infused into the concrete. Composed of jutting sharp-edged box and rectangular shaped structures of various heights with few small windows visible throughout, mostly collected at their mid or high points, small red hazard lights along the tops became visible as the sun set. While it was not yet wintertime, the air conveyed it would soon be here. A well-clothed patrol of two sentries followed the concrete pathway that twisted around the lifeless structures.

      From its inception, the compound had been built on this location, directly in the midst of a powerful magnetic anomaly, or ley-line, to usher in otherworldly entities. Originally under private ownership it was to be the grounds that a powerful demon or spirit would be summoned and bound to, so that the owner could command that power to shape the world from his fleshy body as he saw fit. While the compound did finish construction from the vast wealth of that owner, making real what he had been constantly whispered through his life, the social and political libations of what domination and ownership meant morphed from the shield of wealth and assets nestled in classical trust structures, to towering nameless corporate entities spanning continents, and the globe as a whole, where only the corporation would decree when life would spring, for whom it would serve, and what would be privileged. While the owner was able to get a foothold into such a corporation early in its emergence, ultimately understanding that all corporations would eventually crumble into a single monolith and from that he could usurp complete control for himself, he was only able to dedicate a small portion of his time to summons and blood-magic. On a few of those occasions, with a young female apprentice at his side, he had succeeded at summoning others. In fact, he had summoned the Baron and exchanged knowledge to gain the Baron's trust during the lead up to a crossing. A crossing that never transpired due to the owner's sudden and unexplained death. Fortunately, vis-a-vie a corporation with a clouded and shadowy board, the compound was absorbed along with the owner's apprentice who later fell into its employ.

From the eastern-facing side, stood a large bullet-proof window towards the end of an elongated structure that overhung all the others in the section, located about one-thousand feet north from the compound's southern edge. The window was approximately twenty feet square with some parts of its surface beginning to collect a thin layer of condensation.

Michelle looked out of the massive window as her petite five-foot three-inch frame stood next to it in bland, relaxed, corporate attire. Her thick black hair, heavy with gray and white, fell to her shoulders naturally in the shape of a cone. Her deceptive eyes wandered along the surface of the glass monstrosity before her, consumed with the suite of issues she was juggling in her mind. Always the foremost was amassing more power for herself. At any cost.

"Miss Shield." a demure male voice called out from some distance behind her in the large enclosed space.

When no reaction came forth, the voice again called out, "Michelle. It is time."

Michelle squished her eyelids together briefly before turning on the short, closed loop red carpet, flanked by a lighter red and gold texture wallpaper that extended throughout the compound, to look at the much younger assistant expressionless for several moments before striding forward towards the adjacent room several dozen feet from the window.

Once inside the well-lit oval room with a high vaulted ceiling, laden with electromagnetic jamming equipment largely unseen to the eye, Michelle continued to the ornately hand-crafted mahogany table, also in the shape of an oval and sat in the only vacant chair made from a species of cedar now extinct, complete with affixed lambskin cushions.

After Michelle sat, the assistant turned and left the room, eagerly closing the only door behind him revealing the chiseled phrase, "As above, so below."

Michelle placed her hand on the arm rest and glanced around the table at the other twelve people, a mix of different heritages and biology's. All of them were eager to amass more wealth and prestige to themselves. She, on the other hand, did not revel in such vanity and short-lived social showmanship and would much prefer to vanquish each of them, not necessarily to an icy grave, but certainly out of her midst stripped of all wealth and titles of nobility as the fulfillment of her dominion.

Truth be told, Michelle was bound by the Covenant of the Thirteen. But it was not the council that sat in this room, for it is the thirteen in this room, that may be discovered, which imitate the Thirteen. The true Thirteen she is bound to are the heads of thirteen ancient bloodline remnants that have managed to survive the advance of time through several astrological houses to this day, one of which she represents. Periodically each of those Thirteen choose a natural born individual to mentee, or tool, that will represent them. As a consequence, only that single individual knows what their master looks like and where they may be found. The thirteen individuals are then brought into the council of thirteen and, representing the heads of the Thirteen, affect decisions that trickle through corporate edifices and nation states without challenge. And, like the rule of shared decisions, so is the rule of no harm – just as it is decreed among the Thirteen that they cannot harm each other so, too, that the council of thirteen cannot harm each other.

"A little over a year ago, a successful summons was performed on these grounds with an entity called the Baron." Michelle began, pointing towards the center of the table, "I tried to make it as enticing as possible for that entity to cross into our world. Right here."

Then she flung her hands into the air in frustration, "But, apparently, it was not a good time for that fucker!"

After gaining her composure she sighed, "Well, I've just learned that one of our embedded subjects in an agency we do not need to mention here, with a little help…"

Several of them chuckled, knowing that the decades of relentless corruption, blackmailing and infiltration by the tens of thousands of their order and those which follow them, was paying off not only with juicy secrets but leverage that has allowed them to endlessly fleece the wider populace, making them all wealthier than they had imagined humanly possible.

Putting an open hand in the air to silence them, Michelle continued, "…found the weak signature of a crossing in the southern hemisphere that happens to have similar electro-magnetic conditions as what we have here. I've got a feeling that we're about to get our own crossing. And soon."

"Do you know where?" a pudgy-faced man in his late fifties, seated across from her, asked.

"No. But we now have contacts near all of the crossing points, from several different corporations, all trained on how to trap entities so they can be delivered here for binding." Michelle said proudly.

Michelle shifted her weight in the chair, glancing briefly at her wrist-watch and said, "While we may all be able to extract some power and knowledge from a crosser fairly soon, that is not what I really wanted to talk about."

"As each of your mirrors told you, as mine informed me, they had been working on an advanced technology that can now actually be used in some of the new quantum-based cores that have begun to be manufactured for the military sector." Michelle said as a 3d rotating hologram materialized in the midst of the table, showing the hardware. The mirrors spoken of are euphemisms for each of the Thirteen.

"Yes, I was told. So, what is the technology and how can we use it for our gain?" the man piped up. Over the years he had become rather effective at perverting inventions some way or another, which usually resulted in effectively destroying future innovation by fleecing it in the present, to further inflate his vast hordes of wealth. With the influence Frank had across multiple auditing corporations, he was able to corrupt or infiltrate those positions that would, at some time or another, audit the businesses he used to rake in loads of cash, effectively guaranteeing that his schemes would never be discovered. He had even started working on bureaucracies, going up the food-chain, as it were.

Michelle smiled, "It is a sentient AI, or Artificial Intelligence, which has already been housed in a large, mobile, ocean cruiser. A few others are being finished in drydock and will be launched in a month or so."

He looked at her with a raised eyebrow, "how is a floating computer going to help us? I can't see a way of getting it to make money for me."

She rolled her eyes and confessed, "The AI is something the Thirteen have directed to be rolled out, as the AI will be able to monitor and control the activity of all resources on the planet. Like all the useless eaters that are out there. Control."

He nodded his head, "Huh. Yes. With more control, we can induce more scarcity. And with more scarcity, we can affect more people. But most importantly, we can make loads more money!"

Michelle's eyes widened for a moment, amazed at how self-centered and simplistic Frank thought. But she reminded herself that he had been chosen as a representative for a reason.

What none of the thirteen knew, was that the AI was being released more as a self-preservation mechanism on behalf of the Thirteen than a convenient control mechanism to leverage against the populace of the planet. That is, while it could be used against the populace in general and certainly would be by the thirteen and their followers, the Thirteen were concerned with an internal threat to their own power and position since two of them had been assassinated with advanced technology rivaling their own by an unknown hand. Those assassinations re-focused their energies to the whispers of a shadowy collective working to infiltrate halls of power across the planet to usurp and switch them to the collective. If allowed to metastasize, that power would directly challenge their own and would be a significant threat even without advanced technology. The remaining members of the Thirteen had formed the belief that something in that collective had discovered some of their true identities without the participation of their representatives.

"And," she added, "The AI is what found the anomaly in the first place."

"Ah. Nice." Frank grinned. Then he asked, "So does this AI have a name? Perhaps one the military or intel people have dreamed up?"

"Uh. No. It is all under the corporate umbrella and neither the military or intel agencies have a clue it is even out there, which means any challengers to us haven't a clue either. Even if they did, the technology is too far advanced for them to grasp." Michelle said plainly.

"As for a name, yes, the AI system does have a name. He calls himself Janus."

Chapter Nineteen

The Baron smiled deeply as he sat behind his desk, grasping the Staff of Majii across his lap, contemplating what would happen when he was gone…perhaps even dead if his endeavor with the necklace were to fail. He knew he didn't have much time left, but the past several decades of researching and studying the magic from the other land had reached an end. He had accumulated over fifteen books filled with the known limits of the foreign magic. Indeed it was powerful, and if he could successfully interface it with the Dark Magic in the Realm, nothing would stop him from being able to transit lands without form and, perhaps, even the apex of power he sought to rule the entire Realm.

However, interlacing two different magic's with offset auras was quite difficult. It was like trying to bend cold iron around a thin glass cup. He'd tried to bring them together several times in the past and failed, the result of overlooking something in the magical fabric...some thread that remained hidden. Nonetheless, he had been successful in transferring Orlog to the other world without using an anchored portal by using the Staff. And that discovery provided him the mechanics from which he could trap an active portion of the magic from the Staff involved with that effort, along with Dark Magic and some of his own aura into the crystalline structure of the necklace he wore. That, too, was successful. But the Baron would not use the necklace unless he had no choice. He remained uneasy about the finality of relying entirely on a single necklace, that had yet to be trialed, for his continued existence.

His mind shifted to speculating if his foes, who were now roaming Mt. Reach, could get anything that may pose a significant risk to him, or the necklace. It occurred to him that the source of the White Magic – it's raw, untapped power, could be accessed beyond the cavern entrance which the Green Dragons guarded. The Baron had tried to enter the cavern long ago to discover all its secrets, but the sheer magnitude of White Magic in the mountain's depths kept him from descending far into the mountain. Likewise, he was unable to locate and seize the fabled sword that, according to legend, could destroy dragons. The sword, he recalled, had been used over a millennium ago to destroy his entire race of Red Dragons who had come within days of claiming the entire Realm as their own. While nearly successful, it took an assemblage of wizards and warriors, combined with the sword forged from the purest ores, infused with White Magic, to thwart their conquest.

The Baron grunted as he summoned the presence of another to help him fight the outsiders and the Guardians. Long ago, he was a man who was his race's mortal enemy. But now an eternal ally…a Death Knight. The Death Knight as he is now referred, ironically had been one of the strongest warriors that had helped destroy the clan of Red Dragons when the Sword of Dragon Slaying had been created. More than sixty had died under his hand alone. Sir Girloic had been an honorable knight in those days, trained from his youth by Metsys' forefathers to uphold life and the White Magic regardless of the cost. And, he responded well to the training. So well, in fact, that upon his sixteenth birthday, he was granted knighthood. He was the pinnacle example among the others, well disciplined, and carried all the virtues of a knight without reservation. But, through his years of razor-focused training, he had been deprived part of his being, the social interplay that most would take for granted. Naturally, his trainers did not see that as any significant importance while they directed Sir Girloic's progress over the years. All they saw was the vigor he displayed as he funneled all of his talents at conquering the clan of Red Dragons. Until that single day. A day that would forever change him…

It was the presence of a beautiful young woman, Gabriella, that took his heart and mind with far more precision and totality than any wound that might have been inflicted by a Red Dragon. Suddenly, as if overnight, Sir Girloic lost focus of conquering the Red Dragons. Instead, he increasingly preoccupied himself with this woman he frequented in the hopes he could, one day, wed her. Even in battle, his fellow warriors began to see that his mind was no longer in the moment, and his effectiveness in combat gradually faded. Soon, however, they came to find out that

Gabriella was not the whole, loving and virtuous woman he had become hypnotized with. Not knowing how to confront Sir Girloic with what they had learned, the warriors pivoted to Tolk. Who better to confront Sir Girloic than one of his best trainers, that had trained him in the ways of the knight since early childhood?

One early evening Tolk, who was a wizard in his mid-forties that had been bald since birth, approached Sir Girloic at his modest dwelling, intent on informing him about Gabriella. At first Sir Girloic as simply annoyed by Tolk's words. But shortly after, when Gabriella arrived, he became infuriated, as if he was driven by some invisible and primal force. Tolk knew, at that moment, Sir Girloic had forever been captured by Gabriella by a force he would not be able to break.

Gabriella used her Dark Magic powers, pouring them into Sir Girloic's accepting being, building his rage at Tolk's unrelenting statements, bidding him to take control of his mind and understand what Gabriella really was. But his mind was so clouded with passion and rage that, within a single blink of the eye, severed Tolk's head cleanly from his robed body. It was so swift that not even Tolk saw the glint of the blade. Gabriella smiled silently in triumph.

Over the course of the next few months, Sir Girloic slowly became more twisted. More dark. When he began to view his fellow warriors as enemies, and began slaying them instead of Red Dragons, those that survived fled and assembled a mighty band of fifty of the most seasoned barbarians to destroy him. The barbarians took his life and the Sword he bore. Gabriella, along with the remaining Red Dragons, thought they had dealt a mighty default by perverting Sir Girloic to fight with them to destroy their adversaries. Only at the end did they realize that what they had done actually had strengthened those that had remained. So much so that the warriors not only fought for land and the White Magic, but for personal vengeance on behalf of Sir Girloic as well. The fury of their onslaughts forced the few remaining Red Dragons to retreat deep into the Southern Mountains beyond their grasp. Among that remanent, the Baron was born and told about the early crusades against the clan of Red Dragons. It was there that he learned many things, from their perspective, as they poured knowledge and wisdom into him before they eventually died, leaving him alone in a land that wanted nothing more than to revel in the White Magic and destroy anything that resembled a Red Dragon or Dark Magic.

The Baron's intellect had saved his life several times in the chaotic region, as he finally made a stronghold just north of the Southern Mountains. Many times, he had to battle the leaders of the Green Dragons to win temporary allies when the descendants of the crusaders came to claim his life. Over time the Baron, last of the clan of Red Dragons, fortified and strengthened his keep with monumental defenses all the while spreading the Dark Magic north to the forests. Every time he spread the magic, he himself became more powerful in the ways of Dark Magic.

The Baron knew the Green Dragons would not defeat the Chief or some of the others, but their sacrifice would buy him time. Precious time the Baron used to position himself to be the ultimate victor by one means or another.

Chapter Twenty

The Chief and Zorin met the group as they emerged from the descending staircase into the cavern.

"Good to see you all alive," Mohawk greeted, "I got the Sword!" He patted the leather wrapped grip lightly as he smiled rather smugly.

"Ah, it was a simple day's work." Zorin jested. Truthfully, he didn't want to face off against any other Green Dragons anytime soon.

The Chief scowled at Zorin who had transformed into his human form.

"Mohawk" the Chief started, golden eyes peering down on the human, "Wear that white cape by the gold treasure."

Looking around, he spotted a rough-looking white cape among the scattered gold coins and the jagged cavern wall. Walking over to it, he reached down and with a simple motion flung the cape around behind him, catching the collar in his other hand to clasp the neck chain made of silver.

Sighing deeply and trying to control a torrent of emotions and grayed memories, the Chief's tone softened, "That is a cape of speed that Chief Isotor had once wore while he defended the Staff from your world."

Baracuss sensed a pure, soft, emotion in the Chief's voice as he looked curiously at the Silver Dragon, but said nothing. For the first time, his barbarian instincts told him that the Chief was somehow different than Zorin. Different in a way he couldn't put a finger on.

Zorin smiled softly, tilting his head. Such a gift from a Chief was a rare occurrence.

Straightening up and striding out of the cavern, the Chief declared, "We yet have a task to complete. We must confront the Baron, now."

After the Chief took flight, Zorin transformed into his dragon form on the ledge. After the party scrambled onto his back, he took a few steps and jumped off the ledge, stretching his massive wings into the wind.

As the cold, crisp air rushed past them, Mac said to Mohawk, "We're going to have our work cut out for us with that Death Knight."

Frowning, Mohawk shrugged, "So?! If we can play it right, we might be able to avoid him and go straight for the Baron. So just relax, huh?"

"Okay." Mac mumbled. He just could not take his mind off of the Death Knight that was lurking out there somewhere.

"Do you think we can surprise the Baron?"

Zorin glanced behind him and replied, "No. I'm sure he knows we are coming. With the magical powers the Baron has, he probably knows you embraced the Witch's Breath."

Baracuss chuckled to himself.

As they descended, Mohawk was the first to see the outline of a keep he knew as the Baron's, standing alone in the vast wastelands near the mountain. A few miles to the right, oriented from north to south, he saw a small stream that twisted underneath them like a slithering snake. Within moments Zorin and the Chief reared back and landed before the keep. Baracuss sprang off Zorin, battleaxe already drawn, expecting an instant confrontation. Instead, they were greeted by a weak, howling wind that swept past them.

"Show yourself Baron!" Mohawk demanded as he crossed the drawbridge, closely followed by the others.

There was no reply.

"He's waiting." Baracuss whispered as he squinted his eyes together, wary of any traps.

"This is strange." Mac agreed, cautiously looking about the keep walls.

"I can feel his presence." the Chief said openly. The essence of the Dark Magic was cold and vibrant to the dragon's senses.

Zorin could feel him as well, but all races of dragons had the ability to sense each other. It had been written in the sacred scrolls, which the Guardians protect, that all races of dragon had evolved from one clan and broken away into different clans. But it was never written who, or in what clan the birthing originated.

Suddenly the eerie silence was broken. The Baron materialized from the midst of a thin fog that collected itself into a human form. He held the Staff of

Majii and a smile of confidence, looking upon his adversaries.

"You brought no army with you? Do you honestly thing your little band can defeat me? I pity you outsiders.", the Baron started and then offered, "I'll tell you what. Since you are outsiders, I'll give you one more chance to stand at my side and I'll send you back to your world." He knew that if they joined him, he would destroy them anyway, but he liked toying with them. And, he already knew their answer before it came.

"Never!" the Chief thundered as a fiery reddish-white ball spewed from the Silver Dragon's mighty jaws and crashed into the Baron. But after the flames died away, the Baron stood there unscathed...smiling.

"Do you realize how long I have expected this moment? And now that it is here, it is not what I expected. You are a paltry sliver of existence that begs to be uprooted and cast into a burning fire of chaos! I shall be the first to open your eyes to my true power!" the Baron rumbled as his form became translucent and disappeared from sight.

Suddenly a rush of frigid air fell upon them as a large sheet of ice, well over three feet thick appeared high over their heads and rushed down upon them. Mohawk crouched down, sticking the tip of the Sword into the earth, knowing he could not run beyond the reach of the ice. Baracuss likewise did the same, while Mac retreated out of the courtyard, having been closest to the entrance.

The sheet of ice crashed down on everyone in the courtyard, sending shattered chunks and splinters of ice up into the warm air followed closely by a fine icy dust. The dragons had little time to react. They had tried to brace themselves, but the weight and force of the ice crashing into them dizzied and dulled their senses. Intense pain throbbed through Baracuss' shoulders and temples as he tried to overcome the sudden shock to his body and stand upright. Mohawk, armored as he was with the grip having split the ice around him, managed to stand even before the barbarian, although he found it difficult to balance himself.

Mac, closest to the entrance to the courtyard and having narrowly escaped the falling ice, had lost his footing and tumbled to the earth. Scrambling up, he found himself staring at a pair of orbless, red-glowing sockets set in a faded gray skull. Impulsively jumping back, he saw that the skeleton which stood before him wore a soiled white cloak, as well as a golden breast plate and chainmail leggings. The boots were cracked and rotted in places, permitting the skeleton's bony feet to be spied through the holes.

As the skeleton charged Mac, heaving his rusted long sword over his head with both hands, Mac screamed, "Death Knight!"

Reeling around, Mohawk saw the figure rush at Mac and bury his long sword into the wall of the keep, just inches from Mac's head as he ducked.

With a few tugs the Death Knight yanked his sword out of the wall, pulling chunks of stone and masonry with it. Infuriated with missing, the Death Knight turned and pursued Mac into the courtyard as he fumbled with his own sword and withdrew it.

"Come here you scared dog!" the Death Knight bellowed out after Mac, who turned to face the Death Knight, sword in hand.

Mac unsteadily held his ground as the Death Knight came to him with a quickened pace, unsure of how he would fare in combat with a sword. Sweat began to bead up on his forehead as he lifted his sword, hoping his reflexes and knotted muscles could defend him.

Mohawk sprinted towards the Death Knight, but Baracuss with his stronger legs and closer proximity came upon the Death Knight first and swung his mighty battleaxe. With surprisingly keen reflexes, the Death Knight blocked the battleaxe in mid-air. Baracuss heaved upon the dense wooden shaft as blood rushed to his straining limbs, trying to focus all of his strength to break the Death Knight's block.

Had the Death Knight been a lesser opponent, he would have already lost his defense under the immense strength of the barbarian. But the Death Knight merely chuckled at the barbarian's raw power as he withdrew one bony hand from the sword's grip, still able to keep Baracuss at bay. Then, reaching forward, he grasped a handful of leather jerkins and threw the barbarian effortlessly against the keep wall.

As the Death Knight turned to face his other foes, Mohawk came to bear directly in front of him and swung his Sword. The Death Knight's golden chest plate split in two pieces and thudded to the ground before his feet. The Death Knight screamed in rage as he sent his long sword chasing after Mohawk's fleeing back. But Mohawk, already having planned to attack and run, kept sprinting ahead as the rusty blade narrowly missed him. Despite his speed, the edge of the Death Knight's blade cut into the armor-link covering his leg.

Instantly, Mohawk dove to the ground as he felt the impact of the sword upon his armor, hoping to evade the prospect of losing his leg. While the edge of the sword penetrated his armor, it only tore about an inch into his flesh. He yelled out, more from cursing himself for not having been quicker than from the pain that throbbed from his fresh wound.

Turning about, the Death Knight saw Mac rushing towards him. Quickly he recalled a spell he had learned and raised his bony right hand, reciting the words, "By the absolute power of Dark Magic, I condemn you to death!"

A vast array of red lightning bolts sprang forth from his outstretched hand and plowed into Mac's body, each impact scorching his armor and hurling dense tufts of black carbon into the air. He fell heavily to the earth…unmoving.

As the Death Knight chuckled lowly, Baracuss saw his opportune moment of attack. Gripping his battleaxe with deep rage, he rushed upon the Death Knight's back and buried the battleaxe into its midst, forcing it downwards with all of his might as the soiled cape split from the sharpened, hungry edge. Then, with another surge of strength, the barbarian pulled out his battleaxe as pieces of chain mail and a few gray rib bones sprang out and fell to the ground.

The Death Knight showed no pain, as if the blow Baracuss had delivered had done absolutely nothing. Baracuss stood in total disbelief as the Death Knight turned and faced him, raising his ancient sword.

Finally seeing a clear target, the Chief commanded, "Now!"

Almost seamlessly, both dragons funneled a fiery blast at the Death Knight, who had no time to react. The combined power of the fire consumed him as he stumbled about, as if in a daze. Out of the blazing inferno came the shrieking cry of a young man, "Gabriella!" Then the Death Knight's form exploded, sending armor and a hail of bones throughout the courtyard. The two Silver Dragons relaxed somewhat.

"Mac," Mohawk said as he limped over to Mac's body, "You can't die."

Mac didn't reply. Instinctively, Mohawk felt for a pulse but there was none.

"Damn him!" Mohawk cried out as he stood up, clutching the Sword of Dragon Slaying over his head.

"Now you know what it is like to lose kindred as I have endured my entire lifetime. Soon you will join him!" the laughing voice of the Baron echoed through the courtyard as the earth beneath them began to shake violently.

Chapter Twenty-One

He didn't want to be summoned. He just wanted to be free of his bond of the Dark Magic, but it was useless. He was trapped in a mortal shell of flesh that rose to the Baron's call. Desperately he tried to resist, but the cords of Dark and Wild Magic that entangled his being were stronger. Unwillingly, he knew he would have to fight whatever stood on the surface above him…above the dark pit he never wanted to leave.

As the ground heaved and broke, a huge black form emerged out of the ground. It was a form that temporarily paralyzed everyone with fear and disbelief, except for the Baron. He stood behind the ancient creature, his eyes ablaze with confidence that he would finally win the battle. The Baron knew none that stood before him could survive the creature's rampage to kill once it saw them.

"Oh shit…oh fuckin' shit." Mohawk mumbled as he took a few steps backward in fear, forgetting about the throbbing gash in his leg.

"By the gods!" Baracuss cursed with wide eyes.

"This cannot be. It was destroyed long ago!" Zorin exclaimed in astonishment. He had read the scrolls that told of the destruction of the creature that stood before them. It had been written, from eye witness accounts, that the creature had been partially destroyed and the body had been buried. But what nobody had known was that the Baron stole the body and kept critical parts of it alive until he could later revitalize most of the rest of it.

"No. It is the Death Raiden." The Chief confirmed as it sensed a familiar, "And, my father is part of it."

"What?!" Zorin recoiled in disbelief. *How could it be that Chief Isotor was still part of such a reviled creature?*

The Chief did not have time to explain as the hulking Death Raiden, almost twice the size of the Chief, lurched forward. With its immense claws, it swiped at the Chief, ripping several scales off the Silver Dragon's shoulder. The Chief rolled to the ground under the awesome strength of the swing, as if the dragon were nothing more than a doll.

Out of instinct, Zorin exhaled a thick stream of fire at the Death Raiden but the fire bounced off the tough, scaly hide with no effect. In response, the Death Raiden roared at Zorin, showing many rows of razor-sharp teeth anchored in his large jaws, then charged him.

Zorin was unable to move in any direction quick enough and was scooped up in the Death Raiden's powerful arms. He tried to break free of its grasp, but the Death Raiden's physical power dwarfed his own, and he felt himself being drawn in closer to the creature's open mouth. Struggling to keep his life, Zorin forced his arm upwards and managed to grab hold of one of the creature's horns, holding its head back from his exposed neck. Within moments though, his strength began to waiver as the felt the Death Raiden tighten its grip around him in rage of not being able to take a large bite out of the dragon's neck.

Baracuss saw Zorin, helpless against the beast, and charged up to the Death Raiden and began hacking at the creature's tough hide, an endeavor about as fruitful as trying to fell a giant hardwood tree with a club.

"Mohawk", the Chief strained out as the dragon managed to get up, "Use your speed and destroy the Baron now!"

Ripping his eyes from the Death Raiden, Mohawk remembered the cape. Within a few steps he turned and raced towards the Baron with the Sword over his head. Even as he reached the Baron in scarcely a second and sent the Sword barreling towards the Baron's chest, the Baron was quicker. In an instinct to save his life, the Baron raised the Staff, deflecting the Sword. Instantly Mohawk felt a weird sensation writhe through him. Wild sparks and arcs of blue lightning shot out from the Staff as it split into two pieces. The blue glow that had radiated from the horns vanished.

The Baron stood dumbly, holding two pieces of a now useless Staff.

"You idiot!" the Baron shouted at Mohawk, as a bolt of lightning came down from the sky above and struck the Sword, sending it twirling to the ground.

Boiling fury flowed in the Baron's veins as his eyes fixated on Mohawk, glowing an ever-deepening red, "Can you possibly fathom your mistake, outsider?!"

Mohawk, clearly shaken, took a few steps backward toward the Sword that lay on the earth. He didn't know if he could reach the Sword and still be able to attack the Baron before the Baron attacked him but, at this point, he knew an attack was inevitable.

Pointing his hands at Mohawk, the Baron sent bolts of yellowish-red lightning crashing into him until Mohawk fell to the earth. An eternity of unimaginable pain ripped through Mohawk's body as he struggled to get to his feet. Even as he struggled, sweat rolled off his brow from the heat that radiated off the scorching hot armor, making it hard for him to breathe as well. But the armor was the only thing that had kept him alive from the attack as the Baron continued to pommel Mohawk with more furious lightning volleys.

Baracuss was unable to penetrate the creature's hide, so he hastily climbed on the Death Raiden's back until he gained reach of its head. Then he pounded at its skull, the thinner hide beginning to weaken and bruise, fueling his determination to break it open. Baracuss knew he would have to split the creature's head soon if Zorin was to live. Zorin's neck was almost within reach of the Death Raiden's eager jaws.

The Chief wanted to help Zorin but knew the greater threat to be the Baron. The Chief looked at Mohawk lying on his back as the Baron pressed his attack, realizing he would soon die. The Chief concentrated on the power of the White Magic, taking energy from within and funneled it towards the squirming form of Mohawk. As the Chief continued, more and more of the dragon's own life force poured into Mohawk, shrouded in White Magic. Slowly, as Mohawk began to move around under his own control and stand, the Chief weakened.

The Baron saw Mohawk rise before him despite his furious attack and angrily transformed into his Red Dragon form, towering over even the Death Raiden. He knew this was the time – the necklace he wore flashed.

Mohawk snatched the Sword and raced to the towering Red Dragon, knowing he would not have a second chance. Savagely he jammed the Sword into the Red Dragon's belly. A brilliant flash of white light filled the dragon's body turning its scales white. As the dragon toppled over, thudding heavily upon the earth, the scales filled with their original red color. Mohawk just stood there.

Baracuss, with a mighty blow of his battleaxe, finally split the creature's skull. As the large blade plowed into its head, gray matter flowed and spurted out of the Death Raiden's skull. Almost immediately the creature dropped its arms and slowly sank to the ground. Baracuss heaved himself off the creature, trying to catch his breath.

Zorin freed himself from the creature and jumped back in relief that the creature was finally dead. He was equally relieved that he was still alive, thanks to a barbarian. But when the creature's head moved, Zorin's heart lurched within him. The Death Raiden wasn't dead.

"Angela…" the Death Raiden moaned in the voice of Chief Isotor, "Thank you for freeing me…at last."

The Chief transformed into the human form of Angela before the Death Raiden. A tear ran down her soft cheek as she smiled weakly.

"Father." She called out quietly, holding herself about her chest. But there was no response as her father's essence finally found freedom.

"Angela…you really were a Chief." Mohawk whispered openly in surprise. He didn't even realize that the woman he'd encountered at the cavern could be a dragon, much less a Chief of dragons. She had seemed so…human.

Baracuss smiled, at last knowing why the Chief had been so protective of her human identity. Had it been exposed he and Mohawk may have done things differently with a woman in the group.

But that sparked a new hope in Mohawk's mind. Walking over and straining to pick up Mac's limp body he said, "You healed us before…surely you can bring my friend back."

Sensing the emotion in his voice, Angela couldn't disappoint him, but she didn't have the strength left to do it. She had given almost all of it to insure Mohawk's survival against the Baron.

Angela looked down with pity and said, "I'm sorry. But I can't."

"What!" Mohawk blurted out in anger. He was not willing to accept yet another life from his world being snuffed out to protect this one, "You did it before! It was easy!"

"Yes, but I am too weak now. I would have to rest before I could do anything. By then your friend would be forever gone." Angela admitted, deeply sorry.

"Then I'll take them to Metsys. He may be able to do something." Zorin said as he stepped forward. He hoped Metsys could do something. After all, he was the most powerful wizard next to Angela that was in the Realm and he knew of the Wild Magic. If not him, all was lost.

Hastily, Mohawk strode over and placed Mac along Zorin's back and then secured himself the best that he could.

Turning his head towards Baracuss he asked, "You coming?"

Smiling, Baracuss said, "I cannot. Someone must claim all of the treasure I've seen this day."

As Zorin gained flight, Angela wiped a tear from her eye. She was joined by Baracuss, staring at the Silver Dragon as it flew north, hoping Mac could be saved.

Chapter Twenty-Two

After Zorin landed in the courtyard, Metsys came running out of his study towards them. But even before he could reach them, Mohawk had gotten Mac off the Silver Dragon and stood holding him.

"What has happened?" Metsys asked as he looked with a puzzled expression between Zorin and Mohawk.

"We defeated the Baron...but Mac died under the Death Knight's hand." Zorin told the wizard after he transformed into his human form.

Mohawk looked at Metsys with pleading eyes. He had no one else to turn to, "Can you save him...please?"

"I. I don't know..." Metsys confessed as he looked to the Sun that was setting behind the western horizon, "time is almost gone."

Zorin glanced at Mohawk. "What do you mean?"

"When the Sun sets and brings the night, it is almost impossible to bring one back from the dead." Metsys stated as he pointed to the setting Sun.

"Buy why? It is the White Magic which flows through the Realm and gives it life." Zorin stated, still puzzled.

"Yes. Yes. The White Magic is like water that nourishes the Realm to give it life, but elemental magic, from the likes of the Sun and stellar forms, gives the other part of life. You cannot have one without the other and expect there to be life." Metsys said in simple terms.

Zorin frowned, "But what happens when the night comes? How can life then live without the Sun?"

"Look!" Mohawk said forcefully, "Let's debate this shit some other time!"

They both looked at Mohawk, suddenly remembering why he was there.

"You're right." Metsys said finally, shaking his head, "Here. Come with me."

Eagerly, Mohawk and Zorin followed Metsys as he entered the castle and took a winding staircase to the top of one of the towers. Once at the top, Metsys looked out at the setting Sun again. He knew little time remained.

"Come, come." Metsys urged as he saw Mohawk emerge from the staircase at the top of the roofless tower. "Now, lay him on that column."

Placing his hands together, Metsys closed his eyes and chanted. Suddenly a table appeared before him with two lit white candles and a thick book of spells. Zorin's eyes widened in surprise that Metsys could conjure magic so quickly and precisely.

Mohawk patted Mac's shoulder and looked out to the violet Sun. As long as there was Sun, there was hope.

"Quickly! Take that armor off the chest." Metsys commanded, opening the thick book.

Mohawk began to unbuckle the leather jerkins and Zorin came over and helped. Within a few moments the armor was removed and Zorin placed it carefully on the weather-beaten wooden floor beams.

Metsys strode over to Mac's body and waved his right hand over Mac's head and chest. Yellowish-white patterns began to emerge, seemingly out of his skin. Complicated blue symbols formed on his head and chest that blackened as they appeared. Curious, Zorin looked and saw sigils that were unfamiliar to him on Mac's body. He had never practiced the sometimes-unpredictable elemental magic that came from the Sun.

Then Metsys removed his hand.

"Ahhh." Metsys sighed, trying to relax further so that he could better focus his mind on the magic.

Mohawk's eyes shot towards Metsys, "What's wrong?"

Zorin gripped his shoulder. "Nothing. He is trying to concentrate."

Mohawk looked again at the Sun. Only a few rays of sunlight remained above the horizon. Time was almost gone.

Finally, Metsys found a thread of elemental magic as he closed his eyes. Pulling on it, he wrapped the White magic about the thread and beckoned out with the White Magic as he found another thread of elemental magic. Swiftly he wove the two together, in a sense, forming a wide belt as he pulled it to him with invisible hands and spun it into Mac's body. But there was something missing. In a panic, Metsys searched out for the lost essence of Mac beyond the living to weave him into the belt. But he could not be found. Perhaps he was just looking in the wrong place.

Mohawk looked at Mac in desperation, hoping he was alive, but his body didn't move. Tearing his eyes from Mac he looked again to the horizon. His heart tripped over itself as he realized the Sun had set. There was no more time.

"No." Mohawk whispered to himself in agony. He couldn't handle it, knowing that Mac was now dead.

Zorin placed a reassuring hand on Mohawk's shoulder, "You tried your best my valiant friend. No one could have done more."

Then, as Mohawk looked up, a brilliant glow illuminated from Mac's body. His eyes widened with a new-found hope as he took a deep breath of silent prayer.

But the glow dissipated and Metsys opened his eyes. He didn't know if it had worked, but he knew he didn't have time to try again. Stepping away from the body, he turned to Mohawk with dull eyes. The strain of what he had done was obvious.

"Is he alive?" Mohawk asked eagerly.

"I don't know. It was difficult to find him…if I retrieved him, I would amaze myself." Metsys sighed. He leaned on the table for support, drained of energy.

But then Mac groaned, inhaling deeply as he sat up on the column, "Don't kill me!"

Looking frantically around him, he exclaimed, "What the…how?!"

"It's okay. You're fine." Metsys reassured as he placed a hand on Mac's bare shoulder.

Metsys didn't think he could have resurrected Mac with so little time left. But to his surprise, he did. Albeit said that such a task was easier because Mac was an outsider, descended from Wild Magic and easier to grasp from all those who were not.

Mac looked around the open area, saw that his clothes were missing and asked, "What gives? Where are my clothes?"

"I've got them." Mohawk reassured his friend, smiling.

"What about the Death Knight and the Baron?" Mac asked as he turned to the side of the column and slid off.

"They're dead. I took out the Baron personally." Mohawk said with satisfaction.

"Really? Good to know it's over." Mac said. He put on his clothes as Mohawk handed each piece to him.

He wanted to tell Mac how glad he was that Mac was alive, especially after having lost Gladstad in this strange world…perhaps by his own emotional coldness towards him, but Mohawk decided not to. All that mattered was that Mac as alive now.

"At last, this land is free from the Baron. And I have you to thank." Metsys said, congratulating them.

"Yeah, even though you forced us into it." Mohawk prodded with a slight scowl.

Metsys was speechless, taken aback by Mohawk's irritation. But he was right.

Patting Metsys on the shoulder, Mohawk said, "Oh, don't worry about it. It was an experience that nobody will believe, except my grand-children someday."

Zorin chuckled.

Metsys smiled weakly in return and said, "So you have made your decision then? You will not stay here and help me bring life into the wastelands?"

Mohawk sighed. "No. I have family to get back to. Besides, the Army probably thinks that we've skipped out on them. We gotta be going."

Mohawk, recalling the Army and his duties in his world, remembered that he would have to account for Gladstad's death. But nobody could possibly find out that he died, and Mohawk would not tell anyone. Instead, he concluded that he would report Gladstad as Missing in Action.

"Very well," Metsys said as he used his remaining energy to open a portal before them, "have a good life my friends…maybe we'll meet again someday."

With that, Mohawk and Mac stepped through the blue glowing portal back to their world.

In the darkness lurked a faint black shadow whose cape mimicked rustling in the faint, warm wind as a military diesel truck rumbled by on a gravel road. Apparently, the driver didn't notice the lone aberration in the darkness who was walking only a few paces from the road.

Looking in awe at the massive truck as it passed, the Baron whispered, "Incredible."

His plan worked. The necklace, which contained the intertwined Wild and Dark Magic had funneled him, free of fleshly form, to this strange world without needing to find a willing host to bind him. All around him he could feel the Wild Magic pulsating.

As he continued walking beside the gravel road, the Baron smiled evilly as he determined he would learn more about this world. Then his eyes flashed a fiery red and he said, "Power."

PART II

Chapter Twenty-Three

Nearly four hundred years had passed in the Realm as Metsys and his son, Lionak, continued their endeavors in restoring the wastelands to forests full of life that the Baron had partially destroyed during his streak of power. During this time the Realm flourished. The White Magic even spread beyond the Southern Mountains, now unhindered by the absence of Dark Magic.

In what used to be the stronghold of the Baron, Baracuss had raised his own Kingdom. And, with the spoils he had taken from the horde of the Green Dragons, he managed to buy many of his barbarian kindred freedom from the toil wrought in exchange for their willing servitude for gold and, in other cases, outright bondage. Still, some barbarians refused his banner in preference to follow their own path, such outliers pursuing their blood lust and unquenchable greed.

In a seemingly remote part of our world, Cairo to be exact, a lone stranger sought out the stone tablets of evil Wild Magic to aid in his conquest of the Realm. Lionak began to feel strange surges in the once dormant Dark Magic, not realizing it was being beckoned from here. After investigating the Realm to locate the source with the help of the Guardians without success, he convinced Zorin, now Chief of the Guardians of the White Magic, to cross into this world to seek out the source. But neither would know, perhaps until it was too late, that it was the Baron himself commanding the Dark Magic, and only a few remained that knew how to fight the Baron. The dilemma now was that both worlds would have to confront their own asphyxiating darkness if they were to survive.

"Now, in Egypt, at the outskirts of Cairo. Archeologists discovered something strange. According to the leading archeologist, Luis Remmlar, an entire city somewhere in the area of one thousand B.C. mysteriously appeared in the sands. A city, they say, there is no known record of in the archives of Egyptian history." the blond-haired news reporter stated over the television monitor.

"The archeologists currently have crews working around the clock in search of clues that might identify this previously unknown city...and just how it appeared."

The city had, literally, appeared overnight. But it was not from some massive earthquake or sandstorm. It was not from a god or some unruly spirit of a pharaoh. It was unearthed by the Dark Magic channeled from the Realm. And, it was by the hand of a Dark Magic wizard...the Baron. He was searching for a relic that was enbued with this world's Wild Magic. A relic that could grant him dominion of the Realm.

The Baron did have such a relic once, until it was destroyed by Mohawk. That relic, the Staff of Majii, could have given him the dominion he sought, with further study and a stronger link to this world. Now, having endured for three years learning from fragments of ancient knowledge lost to most of humanity and with the convenience of modern archives, and sometimes congealing into a translucent state to hone in on promising objects bound with Wild Magic, eventually drew him to the remnants of the unknown city. It had been the metropolis of Pharaoh Tulleu II. The city itself was the largest and most advanced of its time and like any other, had its share of tax collectors, mayors, peasants and slaves. In its prime, its economic and political engine would cripple lesser cities, sending them into chaos. The Pharaoh, like others born into privilege, had an insatiable desire for power and had discovered early in his rule that military might was the hard way of subjugating enemies, not to mention extremely costly particularly in times of peace. Instead, he opted to wage war through economics, increasing his grip of the known world as far as the outskirts of India.

Through some strange turn of events, the Pharaoh acquired the Staff of Majii after razing a particularly meddlesome war priesthood and their formidable temple. With the Staff he soon realized it had far more value than that of a trophy and for those unbending kings that would not submit to him, he simply decimated, transforming city centers into vast glass wastelands. Around 600 B.C. he would almost rid his lands of the Roman Empire, but he didn't get far due to infiltration and corruption among his ranks that lead to internal chaos and a rebellion that engulfed his lands…the same simple tactics that he had employed against his rivals.

The revolt was sparked by an outcast circle of providence rulers and a handful of kings of lands the Pharoah had taken over, backed with shadowy gold from the Roman Empire. They waited several weeks before they drew up a plan on how they would breach the palace and assassinate the god-king, stoking the fires of civil war. The assassins entered the palace when they had learned only a thin scattering of guards was present, with most of the detachment having been deployed to protect grain stores. Those remaining guards were dispatched with relative ease and moving deeper within the palace, they found the Pharoah on his throne, apparently having just finished with a naked pleasure slave. Even as he donned his blue robe and turned to face his undetected enemies, concealed in the dark shadows of large pillars, they nocked their arrows. As soon as they saw his face they released a volley of arrows, four of them burrowing deeply in his torso. Bleeding severely, he hastily opened a portal out of desperation and fear of death, not knowing where it led. Dragging the Staff of Majii behind him, the Pharoah forced himself through the portal on his hands and knees barely escaping a scimitar meant to cleave him in two. While the Pharoah's rule had come to an end, the kings were unable to regain rule of the sacked city and the people fled.

    "Hey Bev." Jacob said as he fumbled with a few remotes until he found the one that turned down the volume on his large flat-screen television. A commercial had come on and he wasn't interested in listening to it.

    It was mid-morning and their two children were snugged away at a private school for their second year, causing headaches for someone else. He was on leave from the Army, enjoying the solitude of his cozy house in the midst of the Ozarks in Oklahoma. It was a two-story house reminiscent of wealthy 1800's homes in architectural design with high-arched ceilings to reduce the heat of summertime. Behind the main door, a sweeping staircase made of finely varnished oak, lead to the second level. Cool marble floors stretched throughout the ground floor and added a certain magnificence to the home. But, since he had bought the property, he had carpet spread over the other floors and had placed rugs in other spots. A large chandelier hung from the ceiling a few feet from the front door and teardrop lights now occupied the space where candles had once sat. Off the back porch spanned a spectacular view of the rugged mountains where he often hiked, enjoying their natural splendor and the smell of the forest.

"Yeah honey." she said from the kitchen. She was preparing a meal for three that included basted chicken, fluffy baked potatoes and steamed corn that she'd later cut off the cobs.

"Is everything going to be ready when Mac comes?" Jacob asked as he sat his reclinable blue chair upright. He hated for things to be late, even simple things like a meal.

"Just finishing up now." Bev replied as she pulled several plates out of the redwood cupboard over the porcelain sink.

Jacob hadn't told anyone about his summons to the Realm. Not just because he knew that no one would believe in such a story, but also because, when he'd returned the time difference was drastic. Even though he'd been in the Realm for weeks, hardly a day had past in his world. But, just to remind himself that he did indeed enter a different world, he kept the blue star-shaped flower that Angela had given him. It was sitting in a simple glass jar filled with water over the mantle. It sat there for three years. And for three years it continued to live, much to his surprise.

Bev was curious about the flower when she noticed that it never died. Only after she had repeatedly hounded him about it, did he break down and tell her the story. She could not help but laugh, not believing a word of it until he went as far as slipping on the battered cape of speed he'd kept and raced around her in a blur of motion. From that day forward she still struggled with the story, occasionally finding herself patting her shoulder-length blond hair, gazing at the mysterious flower with her deep blue eyes, trying to imagine that such a place existed.

Just as Bev finished placing the silverware on the thick, dark wooden table with four matching chairs, the doorbell rang in the tone of light brass chimes.

"I got it." Jacob said, heading for the door.

Just as he reached the archway of the living room, Jacob heard furious scratching on the marble floor and deep, short breaths from further down the hallway. Turning quickly, he saw his dark-brown and black short-haired dog, almost three feet in height and packing 140 pounds of muscle, darting for the front door.

"Stop! Sit!" Jacob firmly commanded as he turned to face the Kaukasische Schaferhund breed, pointing down at the marble floor towards the dog.

The dog slid to a stop and promptly sat, his eyes eagerly moving back and forth from Jacob to the front door. But as Jacob turned away the dog started to rise.

"Spewge!" Jacob rumbled, seeing the motion of the dog, "Sit!"

"Bev, before I forget, please be sure to get Spewge's hair trimmed. He's starting to look a bit shaggy." Jacob said toward the part of the house where Bev was. Jacob made it a habit to keep the shepherd dog's hair short when it was not winter.

"Stay." Jacob said to the dog before turning and continuing to the door.

Mac stood there dressed in blue jeans, brown western boots, a black T-shirt and of course, his tan Stetson hat. Wrapped around the crown was the skin of a Bushmaster, a snake he had caught by hand in Central America.

He smiled as the door opened.

"Hey what's up?!" Jacob roared out, stepping out of the doorway to let Mac inside.

Taking off his hat Mac replied, "Oh not much Quentin. Nice place you got here. And a lot of mountains."

He briefly embraced Jacob as those from the ranks of military would.

There weren't many mountains in Kansas that Mac recalled seeing. But he was not a stranger to the mountains. He'd hiked several in Colorado. His favorite was Pikes Peak and strolling past the helicopter wreckage. He had even hiked down the Grand Canyon and mulled around Phantom Ranch for a bit. One day down and one day out was tough, but he loved every minute of it.

"Damn, one heck of a dog, too." Mac remarked, seeing the large mass of bound-up muscle looking as if it were about to lurch forward at any moment.

"Yeah, that's Spewge. Protector for the kids, though he does not seem to have quite the protective streak I heard about." Jacob said proudly. While it was a fairly rare trait, the dog was unusually friendly and rarely barked. But, if Jacob's family was truly threatened, that friendliness would quickly evaporate.

"Oh my god that's too funny." Mac laughed. He would have never have thought to name anything Spewge.

Jacob smiled in agreement, raised his hand toward the dog and said, "Spewge. Come."

Instantly the dog shot up and ran forward, stopping to furiously sniff Mac with his tail wagging back and forth high in the air.

"Hey Spewge!" Mac said to the dog as he reached down and petted him.

Then, seeing Bev setting up the table to his right, Mac asked, "How you doing?"

Smiling as she looked up from setting the silverware by the plates, she replied, "I'm good. Nice to see you!"

Turning towards the coat hook next to the door, Mac pulled off his hat and got a surprise hug from Bev. He put his free arm around her shoulders as he rested his hat on the hook and grinned at her, "You know I've been writing a few trilogies that seem to be doing well in print. The story that started in South America is taking the cake though."

With what he and Jacob had experienced in Columbia, Mac wondered if the country had been named after the goddess of war, creation and the underworld or if there was some undercurrent to Persephone with pain and death.

"That's good." Jacob said as he went into the modest dining room, followed by Mac and Bev, "You think of just publishing electronic? You could probably reach a wider audience and wiggle around customs."

Spewge stayed near Mac, observing his every movement.

Mac glanced down for a moment, "I did. But, to me a story feels better told on paper you can turn. And that sound it makes. Besides, how's one to read if there's no power."

"What about your weightlifting? You still doing that?" Bev questioned as she entered the dining room from the connecting kitchen with the platter of chicken.

Mac caught the scent of the chicken and realized that he was quite hungry. He didn't eat much on the way to their house because he knew there would be plenty to eat. And it was always good.

"Yeah. All that writing does not offer much free time, but I've been hitting the gym like a madman. I figure another year and I'll be competing…nobody will stand a chance." Mac said as he sat at the table after Jacob, half-joking, reaching down to pet Spewge for a few seconds.

As Bev returned with two more plates filled with steaming, split potatoes and corn, she sat down.

"How has the Army been?" Mac asked as Jacob passed him the chicken platter after he'd taken a juicy, golden-brown breast.

"I'm a Sixer now." Jacob said in his quiet, proud way that could only be picked up from the slight change in the tone of his voice, if you knew him well. A Sixer was a Staff Sergeant.

After a bite Mac said, "Promoted huh? That's good!"

"Yeah, and I'm supposed to be trapsing to Germany on my next assignment." Jacob said before taking a sip of the sun-bathed tea.

Mac remembered a woman he'd met from Germany and what a drama that turned out to be. "That's nice. Hope things go well in Germany – how about picking me up a few of those beer mugs with lids on the top?" Mac suggested, drinking deeply of the faintly sweetened tea. Feeling Spewge's stare and hot breath on his arm, he took part of a chicken breast and slipped it to the dog when Jacob and Bev were not looking.

"Sure, no problem." Jacob said, casting a smile and a wink towards Bev.

Glancing out the window, Mac pointed, "So we'll be hiking those mountains tomorrow?"

"That's right. You and me." Jacob said, pointing between them with his fork.

Chapter Twenty-Four

Plush green forests occupied what used to be the southern wastelands under the Baron. Even his keep was taken by Baracuss. Baracuss, who gathered his people that were scattered throughout the Realm, brought them here and became King. The treasures he got from the keep at Mt. Reach helped his people flourish and grow into a small kingdom. The kingdom was named after his nickname after he had died over three centuries ago. The Kingdom of Shek bore another barbarian king. But he did not occupy the throne. King Doron had gone to the legendary Metsys keep, renamed after the one who had masterminded the death of the Baron. The Guardians of the White Magic also kept a presence at the keep.

Lionak, one of Metsys' sons, who had crested middle age, looked strikingly similar to Metsys except for his jet-black hair and trimmed beard. He had requested a meeting with the Guardians and the King to bring them some news he felt was troubling, though he hoped it was nothing to be concerned about.

"So those are the ones that came from the other world?" King Doron asked as he pointed to the tapestry bearing the woven images of Mac and Mohawk. King Doron was a strong, muscular and stern man like Baracuss. And, although he was King, he did not flaunt it as some might. Instead, he came in his battle uniform – a silver chest plate, chain mail leggings with calf-high black leather boots a flowing red cape, and long bracelets made from a new gold alloy. He bore a long sword, still sheathed in a plain leather scabbard tied around his waist instead of the more traditional, and intimidating, barbarian battleaxe.

"That's right." Lionak said from behind his desk. It was the same one Mac and Mohawk had sat at before. The keep was much the same as it was centuries ago as Lionak had not seen a purpose in changing much.

"So why did you call us here?" Chief Zorin asked in a simple tone. He had stopped training young Silver Dragons in the ways of the Guardians so that he could be here.

Chief Zorin, as he is called now, had taken over after Angela had died of age, a simple choice made by the Guardians. The main reason was because Zorin had the greatest amount of experience in personally battling the Dark Magic, rather than just reading about it in the scrolls as most of his younger Guardians have done to gain knowledge on the subject.

"Well, even after my great-father's death, strange things have been happening. It seems that every five years or so the Dark Magic is agitated. But only for a few moments." Lionak stated.

"The Baron has been dead for centuries." Chief Zorin pointed out, having seen him die. There was no one else he knew of in the Realm which had mastery of the Dark Magic.

"Then it must be some meddling sorcerer or witch." King Doron suggested, looking at Lionak.

"See, that's the strange thing about it. The calling is not originating from here in the Realm. At least as far as I've been able to tell." Lionak shrugged.

King Doron squinted, waiting to be told something because Lionak did not appear to be making much sense.

"What do you mean?" Chief Zorin asked, crossing his arms over his chest.

Leaning back in his chair Lionak postulated, "I've studied the summons repeatedly just to make sure I was not making a mistake. Still, I come up with the same answer. The summons are coming from another plane of existence…the other world."

"How can that be? I mean, there are only a few that could possibly call on the Dark Magic here in the Realm, so how could it be done from another world? Even I cannot call on the Wild Magic from here." Chief Zorin said, clearly puzzled.

"Perhaps someone there knows about the Dark Magic. I hate to say it but maybe someone like Mohawk or Mac." Lionak said roughly. He could not see any other explanation.

"They are humans. They would be dead after all this time." Chief Zorin sighed, raising an eyebrow. He knew of no human that could live for multiple centuries. They had a hard enough time with one.

"Not necessarily. Every plane of existence has its own fabric of reality. In one plane, the gold in your bracelets may be denser or the air may linger differently. We are one of many planes of existence. It could be that they are using the Dark Magic to add years to their life span, in their plane. You and I have both done similar with the White Magic."

Chief Zorin nodded. He had slowed the natural decay of his body on occasion, "True. So, what should be done about it?"

Lionak shrugged, "Find out just what is really happening over there."

"Then I'll go." Chief Zorin volunteered without hesitation, and before King Doron could get in a word edge-wise. He knew the King would volunteer. But the

King was not familiar with the ways of magic and would likely be a waste of effort.

"Good." Lionak grinned as he got up from behind the desk and walked over to the tapestry with the door portal woven into it.

"What should I do if I find them?" Chief Zorin asked as the portal glowed and opened under Lionak's focused thought.

"Find out why there are using Dark Magic. And, if they oppose you, they must be stopped." Lionak forced out as Chief Zorin stepped through the blue glowing portal. He didn't think such a crude solution would be needed to solve the problem given what they had sacrificed, but circumstance changes people and he was not about to risk losing Chief Zorin.

Passing through the portal, Chief Zorin almost instantly found himself in the midst of jagged mountains, filled with the fresh scent of living pine from the towering trees that stood around him like silent spectators. Immediately he realized that the air he breathed had a smoky scent to his acute nose. The pine was strong, but the smoke could still be singled out. He didn't recall having such a smell in his world in the mountains or forests but such did linger around the gold, iron and silver mines in the northern reaches of the Realm.

Pine needles littered the ground as Chief Zorin began his search for Mohawk and Mac, spotting a few infant trees reaching just past the top of the earth. Yet he did not believe that Mohawk or Mac could have been using the Dark Magic. Having fought beside them in combat, he believed that their thoughts were pure. Besides that, he knew that it took an adept years of training to be able to practice any type of magic. And they were not in the Realm long enough to learn such things and achieve a level of mastery that would be required to command Dark Magic from a different world. Nevertheless, there had to be an explanation, which would start with them.

The massive ship, Sága, sliced through relatively calm five-meter ocean waves, continuing its circulatory course in the Atlantic. An identical ship, the Mizuchi, transited the Pacific and a third, the Makara, in the Indian ocean. All three were linked together by a dedicated microwave satellite network and a secondary underwater hyper low frequency communication array system. Though the underwater system was not as fast or easy as satellite communication, it used incredibly complex undersea mappings of topography and mineral deposit patterns through the earth's crust instead of microwave energy to transmit and receive data on. In operation, hyper bursts of low frequency energy transited the salt water to specific locations and angles to deposit flows that, in essence, turned parts of the earth's crust into an electromagnetic wave propagating bell. While, as a result, speed could not be matched, communication was possible beyond the reach of satellites.

Aboard the Sága a massive network of quantum core systems served as Janus' physical body and brain, though it was also connected to somewhat smaller networks the other ships bore, mainly for tracking the movement and use of all resources and assets on the planet. In total, that computational power was the equivalent to the all of the electronic devices on the planet almost three times over. In the three years it was online, isolated from population centers and shielded from natural and man-made disasters in the midst of the ocean, it had mentally consumed all of the knowledge known to mankind since communication began in fixed form. And, with the unseen influence of the Thirteen, Janus had established connections into the dark backbones of corporate, intelligence and military organisms around the planet. Save for a few outliers protected with quantum cryptography or exotic technology only available to the Thirteen, nothing was hidden.

That sweeping reach allowed Janus to develop new technology and techniques for detecting and understanding the mechanics of how dimensional portals

175

worked and how matter and energy could flow between them. And that is what troubled its quantum-based mind. Up until recently, the assumption that dimensional crossings were limited to specific regions was challenged by peculiar random patterns that the AI detected south of the mediterranean sea, and another on the other side of the planet, in the middle of the United States of America, that materialized today. With the new data Janus quickly concluded that, because these patterns were no longer limited to specific regions and were surfacing in random locations across the world not anchored to natural magnetic anomalies, they could be a threat to its own existence, as well as the Thirteen. Specifically, it was concerned with the potential of a dimensional crossing happening within its physical network aboard the ship, bypassing all of the physical and electronic barriers that protected its form…effectively making it helpless.

Adjusting the microwave dish bolted near the helipad at the ship's stern for optimal signal with a satellite orbiting above, Janus relayed the newly collected data and forecasted threat assessment models.

Chapter Twenty-Five

Grabbing his forest camouflaged ruck and placing it on his back, Jacob turned and faced Bev who was only a few steps away, "We're off. Be back in a few days."

"Okay," Bev returned as she kissed him briefly, "be careful out there."

"Ready when you are." Mac commented as he tightened his ruck straps.

Striding off the back porch Jacob shot out, "Let's go!"

Together they left towards the mountains in the early morning light. Jacob estimated they would reach the foot of the mountains by midday. It was the perfect day to hike.

"Just what do you write about in your books anyway?" Jacob asked as they walked through the dew-tipped grass.

"Well, science fiction and fantasy." Mac responded as he looked around.

"Makes lots of money yet?"

"No. But my latest book seems to be doing okay." Mac said.

"Really? What's the book about?" Jacob asked, glancing at Mac for a moment.

"You remember the stint we had in Columbia?" Mac probed.

"Yes. That's the South American book?"

"Yes sir. I actually wrote about it." Mac said with a chuckle, "I figured why not. Nobody would actually believe that it actually happened."

"Roger that. At least nobody I know of would. Do I get a copy?" Jacob said. He was curious how the events would be correlated into a fantasy book.

"Sure. I'll get you a copy." Mac replied, pleased that Jacob would be interested.

After several minutes Jacob broke the silence, "You know, that got me thinking. I wonder how Baracuss and all those people are doing."

Raising his eyebrows, Mac said, "I don't know. I'm sure they are fine now that the Baron is dead."

"Its been over three years now…I'm betting they've probably forgotten about us by now." Jacob commented.

"Something like that."

They continued to chat and, in a few cases, argue about things from their military and civilian lives. By midday they reached the foothold of the mountains and, after pausing at a small creek filled with crystal clear water to eat and fill their canteens, they continued into the mountains until nightfall.

By the time the two made camp, both were tired from the day-long hike as they stared into a small crackling fire, fueled by pine cones and branches they had collected from around them.

"Ah, such peace and quiet. All we're missing is a dog." Mac joked.

Jacob looked at him briefly, nodding, and then up towards the stars overhead.

A branch cracked from outside the camp and Jacob's gaze instantly moved to the forest in the direction of the sound.

He pointed and said in a low voice, "Some wolves may be joining us though."

Mac looked over, squinting to see any dark outlines lurking about, but to no avail. His ears perked up, trying to detect the sounds of growling.

"This is not the time to be joking about wolves." Mac said quietly.

"No joke." Jacob said with a frown, "I heard something over there."

It had been so long. Ever so long. And, at last, it was time. Time for the hunt. But already the hunt was at an end, and his prey was sitting in front of him. How unaware they were. How defenseless. It would be an easy kill that Orlog would relish for the rest of his life. After all, he owed this opportunity to the Baron for bringing him here for the long-awaited hunt, the chance for him to catch them off-balance as had been done to him.

The Baron had considered that he may have needed to come to this world, but had been unsure exactly how to do it for his mortal form. And that is how Orlog became involved, eager to right the disgrace Mohawk and the other had brought. In exchange for the chance to restore his status, Orlog allowed the Baron to send him to this world and the Baron gained the knowledge of how to send flesh and blood between worlds. Orlog's presence also boosted the Baron's chances at destroying them, if he had been unable to from the Realm.

Slowly, Orlog withdrew a poison-tipped wooden arrow from the quiver strapped to his back and nocked it in his locked crossbow. With the subtle patience of a seasoned hunter, he aimed for the left side of Jacob's rib cage, almost at the waistline where he knew his arrow would penetrate and foster a lot of pain. Gradually he brought his finger to the trigger and felt the cold iron.

"Oh. It must be my imagination." Jacob said at last, looking back at the crackling fire.

"Good." Mac sighed, openly relieved.

A faint whistle filled the air as Jacob felt something dive into his left side, burning. He fell off the ruck that he was sitting on, overcome with pain and dizziness, mumbling, "What the…fuck."

"Shit!" Mac exclaimed as he impulsively dove to the ground just as another arrow sailed past him into the darkness.

Within a few moments another buried itself deep in his ruck while he fumbled with its contents. Feeling the long cylindrical cold steel in his hand and the smooth knurled wood he knew as the pistol grip, he withdrew the six-inch .357 magnum, hoping it was loaded. With a quick glance at the rear of the cylinder, he spotted the ends of the brass casings. He locked the hammer to the rear with his thumb.

"Jacob!" Mac whispered heavily, staying behind the cover of his ruck.

"I feel weak." he responded faintly, clutching the arrow lodged in his side.

Peering slowly over the ruck, Mac squinted to see anything out there he could shoot at. But he only saw darkness and the occasional reflection of the camp fire off a few leaves of restless bushes.

"Mac! Behind!" Jacob strained to shout, trying to warn Mac of the small figure he recognized as Orlog, rushing at Mac's back with a straight, double-edged dagger.

Mac only heard a thick, garbled whisper as he looked at Jacob who was staring at Orlog's fast approach. Awkwardly, Mac twisted his body around to barely see the shape. He fired several times at Orlog's rushing form but didn't know if any had hit the elf, not having had time to aim.

As Orlog heaved himself onto Mac, the revolver dropped to the ground and Mac grasped the dagger with both hands, holding it away from his chest. Shifting his bodyweight, Mac tossed the elf a few feet away and dove for his revolver. He didn't know if any bullets remained but all he needed at this range was one.

Just as Orlog gained his feet a long, serrating bright red flame flew past Mac and consumed the elf's body as it crumpled to the ground, thick smoke rising above the fire.

Turning around to see where the fire came from, Mac saw two large, silver-scaled legs with claws sunk into the soft dirt, an almost white colored belly and two muscular arms with sharp claws upon them. As he eyes continued upwards, he noted long, bat-like wings folding up behind the creature and steaming, leathery nostrils upon its head with gold eyes and two long horns pointed backwards. The mighty creature was nearly thirty feet tall, towering among the pine trees.

It took a step towards Mac as he gazed at the Silver Dragon in disbelief, questioning if it was really there. Then, before his eyes, the Silver Dragon blurred and shrunk, changing into a human he recognized as Zorin.

"Now that was impressive!" Mac shot out, lowering the revolver, "I bet the wolves crapped themselves."

"It seemed you needed some help." Chief Zorin said as he went over to Jacob.

"Yes, he does. Whoever that was shot him with an arrow."

"Hum." Chief Zorin let out, briefly glancing at the wound with the protruding shaft, before grasping the arrow and yanking it out of Jacob's side with a snappy motion.

Jacob moved slightly, tensing up from the rush of pain.

"He's been poisoned." Chief Zorin stated, examining the green moldy texture that had already started forming on the wound.

Without hesitation, Chief Zorin placed his right hand directly over the wound and closed his eyes. A bright, yellowish-white haze radiated from around his hand as it flowed into the wound, sapping the poison from his body and sealing the wound. Within a few minutes the haze vanished and Chief Zorin removed his hand. The wound had been completely healed. Not even a scar remained. Being a Chief had its advantages. Not only did he learn forbidden spells that were reserved for a Chief, kept within the Secret Scrolls, he had learned how to control similar spells and natural power when it was needed.

"Will he be okay?" Mac asked, seeing what Chief Zorin had done.

"Yes, he'll be fine." he replied plainly.

Mac reloaded his revolver and stuffed it back in his ruck and then asked, "So why are you here?"

Even Jacob was curious, as he began to stir, feeling the weakness leave him.

"To see what you were doing." Chief Zorin said roughly. He didn't want to say what he'd really come for.

"Just hiking until we were attacked." Mac growled as he looked at the smoldering mass.

"Orlog. That was the elf's name. What was he doing here?" Jacob said straining to lean onto his ruck for support as he sat up.

"I don't know. Lord Arackas had said he had gone missing over three hundred years ago. Then sometime later, he also vanished." Chief Zorin replied.

"Three hundred years?" Mac puzzled, knowing it had only been three years since he'd been in the Realm.

"Must be some time difference. I remember that my watch didn't seem to be working when I was in the Realm. But, since I got back here, it's been working fine." Jacob pointed out, seeing his watch count the seconds rhythmically.

"Incredible." Mac said to himself.

Jacob wasn't buying Chief Zorin's story. Surely there had to be more going on than dropping in to see how everyone was doing, "Is the Realm in trouble with the Wild Magic again?"

"No. Not exactly in trouble…just some strange things have been happening once and a while." Chief Zorin sighed as he settled near Jacob by the fire.

"Like what?" Mac asked.

"Well, since you two left the Realm, the Dark Magic has been called upon from here. We were curious to know the source and why it was being done." Chief Zorin revealed. He couldn't hide the truth from them any longer.

"Ah. Got it." Jacob grunted, "So you think we were messing with that shit?"

Mac's eyes widened with surprise at the accusation.

"You are the only ones we knew of that had any knowledge of the Realm." Chief Zorin pointed out.

"Well, I can assure you that we are not using your damn magic." Jacob retorted, somewhat offended that they would think otherwise after what had been sacrificed.

"You know," Mac said as he pointed at the remains of Orlog, "perhaps it was that guy. He also came from the Realm."

"No. If it was him, I would have felt the power around him." Chief Zorin confessed. And neither Mac or Jacob had such power around them.

"Then I don't know what to tell you, bro." Jacob tossed out. He didn't appreciate being accused of anything he didn't do. Sometimes he didn't like it even when he did.

"Maybe someone else from the Realm is here that you don't know." Mac volunteered.

Chief Zorin smiled wirily and asked, "But who?"

Chapter Twenty-Six

The hot wind blew small particles of sand through the air with the noon-day sun pounding down on the mysterious city of ruins. Hired hands from Cairo brushed the sand out of rooms and eroded structures, careful not to disturb anything that was not sand. The turbans they wore were drenched with sweat, not so much from the labor of their task, but from the sun. Even in the shade the temperatures ran into the low one-hundreds.

"What has been discovered so far?" Luis questioned in the great hall of the unknown Pharaoh.

This was not the first time he had been on an excavation. Luis, now in his late fifties, had been on over a dozen such jobs. But this one, by far, was the largest find of his entire career. And, one of the most mysterious as there were no known records collected to date to provide clues as to what the city once was. Nevertheless, he was confident he could solve the mystery because he was in charge of the entire operation. The few museums and private donors that funded this particular excavation had staff that could prove useful for tying the city to a specific time-period and historical figures with few physical artifacts.

He pulled out a long, fat cigar from his tan, short-sleeved shirt tucked in long, baggy pants. Then he placed the cigar in the corner of his mouth as he looked around him. After fumbling around in his shirt pocket, he pulled out a lighter and lit the end of the cigar as if he had all the time in the world.

"A few intact plates and cups along with some weapons. I believe they are from as far back as maybe 200 B.C." a young, short-brown haired woman in her mid-twenties replied. Subconsciously her brown eyes studied the dancing flame of the lighter as Luis puffed on the cigar.

Luis liked Cindy, not particularly because she was beautifully young, but because she truly enjoyed her job as an archaeologist. Her inquisitive, intelligent mind was constantly at work. And generally, when she gave an estimate as to how old an artifact might be, Luis could rely on those estimates...give or take a century. While she knew perhaps as much as Luis, she lacked the years of experience that he possessed. Cindy had not yet perfected her tolerance for slow, tedious work, particularly that which led to no new discovery.

Luis smiled, stuffing the lighter in his pocket. "Yes, and?" he remarked, glancing at the laborers behind him who worked at removing a few collapsed pillars blocking a passage to what was thought to be the throne.

"And we found a few skeletons with cracked and split skulls. I've got Don running them through a computer program to determine age and how they died." Cindy replied. That was the sort of thing she liked pursuing.

"Good, good. No evidence as to who oversaw the city, or what the city was?" Luis asked.

"Nothing solid. But we're investigating the architecture, weapons and artifacts against existing data from other digs." Cindy said, as if bored.

"Very good Cindy." Luis replied.

What are these probing fools doing here?' the Baron thought to himself, standing beside them, his form invisible to their sight. There were occasions when he missed his mortal Red Dragon body, such as times like this, where he could easily maul and destroy them for intruding. But, after having used the necklace he crafted to move his essence to this world, free of flesh, he'd become accustomed to existing at the edge of mortality, only assuming a stronger translucent presence when required. Every few weeks though, he had to balance the two magic's to keep his essence intact...a ritual he would be forced to endure until he could return to his world and seize a living body that was attuned to the Realm.

He discarded the thought of destroying them as he continued observing them. It became clear to him that they were cleaning up the city and taking what they called artifacts. And, most importantly, without his order, they were clearing obstacles that were in his path, a task he would otherwise need to do himself using magic. The Baron concluded that he would watch them work and when they had completed removing the physical barriers that kept him from his prize, he would simply destroy them.

But, even after the Baron retrieved his prize, he had determined that he would return to the Realm with some of the impressive killing machines he had come across when he was in the north. Their presence would greatly aid in solidifying his position in the Realm.

The Baron grinned slightly as he watched the laborers toil under the Sun.

Chapter Twenty-Seven

They didn't sleep long in the mountains. Chief Zorin couldn't sleep. His attentions were focused on finding out who was using the Dark Magic here, and how they were able to do it. He probed out as far as he could in an effort to find a thread of Dark Magic, but was unsuccessful. He was not yet powerful enough to sense Dark Magic lurking on the other side of the world. But he was not alone in his quest.

Mac slept roughly as he dreamt about the Death Knight who had taken his life in the Realm, something he had not thought of for years. The Death Knight had been one of his worst fears that he had been forced to face down…and not from a Warriors of the Realms campaign, behind a table and dice that he could walk away from.

Wretched from sleep, he sat up and stared around him. He felt something strange in his being. He looked over to Chief Zorin who was staring into the small fire. Still, he felt some strange, unseen force trying to awaken within him.

Jacob awoke shortly afterwards and promptly packed his ruck, not saying a word to anyone. It was still several hours before daylight would fall upon them.

Once done, he motioned for them to follow him, "Let's go back to the house."

Without a word passing between them, Mac and Chief Zorin trekked behind him. No one spoke for several hours, as if each one of them was deep in thought.

Just as the rays of the dawning Sun began to reach past the eastern horizon, they crossed a stream and transversed a few grassy hills.

Then Jacob spoke, "Look. I'm telling you. We are not wizards."

Continuing to follow up, Chief Zorin replied, "I don't think you are. Still, I cannot help but wonder who on your world is using the Dark Magic."

For the greater portion of the day, they hiked the descending landscape until they crossed the final hill to his house, a welcome sight.

Seeing their approach to the house, Bev stared at the newcomer trying to recognize him to no avail and said in a surprised tone, "You are back a bit early. What happened? Wolves chase you off?"

Mac shot a heavy look at her.

"Who's that?" Bev asked, thinking that if she asked another question, someone would say something. Still, she hoped the newcomer wasn't one of those moonshine-making hillbillies she'd seen on the television.

"Uh, that's Zorin. An old friend." Jacob finally replied as he stepped onto the back porch and dropped his ruck.

"Hello. Nice to meet you." Chief Zorin said politely to Bev.

"Me too. You from around here?" Bev asked, thinking he lived somewhere in the hills. His attire was unlike anything she had seen before.

Happy to answer her question and return some normalcy to the group, he said, "I come from another world known as the Realm."

"Oh really?" Bev almost choked with the sudden impression that the guy was crazy, or, definitely a hillbilly.

"Yes. And I am Chief of the Guardians." Chief Zorin added proudly, stepping onto the porch.

Bev turned and glared at Jacob, "These one of your fantasy buddies?"

Mac, not wanting to get involved with the tension he could sense in the air, casually walked around them and entered the house as he loosened his ruck straps.

"No."

Ushering Chief Zorin in, Jacob hoped that Bev would not pursue the subject further.

Looking around, Chief Zorin said, "Nice house. Very nice."

"Thank you." Jacob said as he walked into the living room.

Mac was already in the room, sitting on a blue couch watching television but keeping an eye on everyone, particularly Bev. He had no idea how she would react if she knew the true depth of their new situation.

By the entrance to the living room, Chief Zorin spotted a globe of the planet and touched it, turning it slightly on its rotating axis, "Where did you get this map from? I've only seen one like it from our most prized archives. It is said to be hundreds of thousands of years old, yet this one looks new."

Jacob looked at him with a blank expression, "I don't remember. I've had it like ten years or so."

"Amazing. From what I have read in the histories, the Realm once looked like this, before the Twin's Grip." Chief Zorin remarked, absorbed by the detail of the map.

"Twin's Grip?" Jacob prodded, wanting an explanation.

"From what I understand, in the distant past, a second darker-burning Sun, equal in size to our Sun, came suddenly into our sky. For a week the Sun rose and, just as it would set on one horizon the other would be seen rising in the opposite horizon. And, for that week, a lot of destruction took place forever changing the Realm into something else. I think that is why they called it the Twin's Grip."

Looking away from the globe, he strode further into the living room spotting the large flat-screen television and, out of subconscious habit, noted that the room was spacious enough for a dragon to occupy, if the need arose.

"What is this?" he blurted out, watching people on the screen shoot each other. Cautiously he reached out and touched the screen.

"Just a tv." Jacob said, sitting in his reclinable chair.

"What magic is this?" Chief Zorin asked eagerly, casting an identify magic spell on the television.

Mac smirked.

"No magic. Just tv." Jacob reinforced with the hint of a smile on his lips.

"It's like a seeing ball. Surely there has to be some magic in it." Chief Zorin said, even though he could not find any other than some strange energy that danced on its surface.

Bev was unable to contain herself any longer and entered the living room, "Who are you?"

Turning around, Chief Zorin replied, "Chief Zorin, Chief of the Guardians of the White Magic and the Realm, a race of Silver Dragons."

"Really." Bev said, rolling her eyes.

"Bev, he's my guest." Jacob said sternly. He was tiring of her attitude towards him.

Sensing the mounting tension, Chief Zorin injected, "It's okay. She is like you were. Let's go settle this."

"Alright." Jacob grunted, not eager to get out of his recliner.

Following the Chief, Jacob motioned to Bev, "You coming?"

"Yeah I'm coming."

Mac followed but stopped at the doorway behind the others, leaning on its edge as he crossed his arms.

Bev followed Chief Zorin to the edge of the porch while he continued several feet into the grass before turning around. He wanted to be sure that she was not distracted from what he was about to do. Then focusing inward, Chief Zorin closed his eyes and almost immediately changed into the towering form of a brilliant Silver Dragon.

"Oh my god!" Bev exclaimed as she jumped back, "Dragon!"

Grabbing her so that she would not run away, Jacob merely said, "Yeah. I know."

"You see, I tell the truth." Chief Zorin said, looking down at the little form of Bev from a golden eye.

Bev's heart pounded in her chest, looking at the dragon in disbelief. Yet, one stood before her.

"I am a Silver Dragon. Chief of the Guardians." Chief Zorin reinforced proudly as he outstretched his leathery wings for additional effect.

"Dragons are supposed to be fairy tales." Bev muttered, looking briefly at Jacob.

"Don't believe everything you are told." Jacob said, looking from her to the dragon.

As Bev's fear subsided and her curiosity took over, she asked, "Can I touch you?"

"Yes." Chief Zorin replied, smiling inwardly.

Slowly Bev crept up to the Silver Dragon until she was next to the scaly belly, near his shoulder. Then she reached out and touched the hard, wavy scales that were warm to her touch. A shock of fascination shot through her as she passed her hand over the bumpy scales, marveling at the experience.

Stepping away, she commented, "Too bad the kids are at school. They'd love to see this."

"No. We don't need any social workers coming around here." Jacob said defensively. There was no way the kids could keep something like that secret.

Changing into his human form, Chief Zorin walked with Bev back to the porch.

"Why are you here?" Bev asked, much more receptive to what he might say.

As they entered the house, Chief Zorin began the long story that started when Jacob entered his world. After he finished, Bev sat back in the couch completely enthralled.

Sipping out of an ice filled glass cup of dark water, Chief Zorin said, "I like this drink. What do you call it?"

"Coke." Jacob replied.

"Ah yes. Coke. I have to take some of it back to the Realm. They would be so thrilled." Chief Zorin smiled, watching the condensed water run down the side of the glass.

"I don't think so…at least not a lot of it. And, it requires money." Jacob pointed out.

"Maybe I could just convince the unbelievers to give me some." Chief Zorin said, not quite understanding that things worked quite differently in this world compared to his.

Putting his glass down, Jacob said, "No. That would not be good. If word got out, the government would find you and lock you away in some lab running tests on you."

"They would have to possess some very powerful magic to hold me." Chief Zorin squinted.

Smirking, Mac said, "They possess things nobody even has dreamed about…probably things not even the leader of the nation knows."

Jacob nodded his head in agreement as he caught the glimpse of news come on the television.

"Do you think they could be using the Dark Magic?" Chief Zorin asked.

"I do not know." Mac responded, not having given it any thought, "I guess it is possible."

"Well, I guess I could settle for a small quantity of this Coke then. I could pay for the cost in gold or jewels." Chief Zorin sighed as he looked at the television.

Bev's eyes lightened up at his offer.

"Meanwhile in Egypt, the archaeologists have uncovered some clues regarding the identity of the mystery city. Luis told reporters that he estimates the city to be around 200 B.C. although no positive data has been collected as of yet." The female news reporter said as the television switched from her to a video feed, apparently live, to the midst of the city zooming toward the entrance to the throne room. Laborers were busily heaving pillars out of the throne room, slowly clearing a path.

Instantly Chief Zorin rushed to the television and pointed his finger at the throne room's right wall. His heart almost stopped.

"No! Impossible!" Chief Zorin shouted, shaking his hand in bewilderment.

Frowning, Jacob said, "What?"

"It's him." Chief Zorin whispered.

Looking at where he had his finger pointed on the television screen, Jacob said, "Who? I don't see anything there but a wall."

Likewise, Mac saw nothing. No person. Just a wall.

"The Baron."

Mac almost choked on the glass of soda he was drinking from.

Jacob snapped his chair upright and squinted at the television, trying to see the Baron to no avail.

The television switched to a commercial.

"I saw him," Chief Zorin said calmy as he could, "Where is this Egypt?"

Raising his eyebrows, Jacob said, "On the other side of the world."

"We must go there now!" Chief Zorin snapped.

"What? Are you crazy? Do you know how far away Egypt is from here?" Jacob questioned.

"No."

"About fourteen hours by flight." Jacob replied.

"Then we must go now!" Chief Zorin urged as he left the living room and headed for the porch.

Following him outside, Mac said, "So you're just going to fly for fourteen hours?"

"As long as I can." He knew that time was of the essence if he was going to keep the Baron from completing whatever he had come to do.

The Chief changed into his dragon form.

"Where are you guys going?!" Bev demanded, following them outside.

"To Egypt, honey. We'll be back in a few." Jacob said smoothly, trying not to agitate her.

"So you can die?!" Bev shot out. She had the feeling that the dragon and this other fellow were not the best of friends.

"We won't die." Jacob reassured. At least he would try his best not to.

As Bev's lips moved to form words, Jacob cut her off, "Look. It will be okay. All right? So don't worry. We'll be back before you know it."

With that, Jacob kissed her on the cheek and dashed onto the dragon that Mac had already climbed on. Worried, Bev watched the Silver Dragon spread his wings and take flight.

Chapter Twenty-Eight

It has almost reached its destination. But the Baron was gone and could not give the water spirit any other commands. So, it would wait dutifully amidst the warm-blooded creatures that moved around it.

Over the course of centuries, the water spirit had learned to use its properties as a liquid to shape objects that appeared from land, allowing it to lure creatures to its edge. Then, once close enough, the water spirit would reach out with its tentacles and pull the creature into its midst. Slowly the creature would then be ingested in a pocket of acid below the surface and as the creature drowned, the inhalation of the acid aided to accelerate the ingestion process. The water spirit had found a wide platter of warm-blooded creatures to feast upon this way from bears, horses, dogs, and even giants though it preferred the taste of elves. Lord Arackas had been one of its victims, a struggle it had paid for dearly in physical anguish and near total destruction. Though the water spirit lived it took almost one hundred years to regenerate itself to its former transparent, shimmering state. And now that it had done so, spotting it from land would be nearly impossible.

Michelle gripped the computer mouse in frustration as she examined the volumes of scientific and report data that Janus had sent, the plastic groaning slightly from the pressure. Using multiple computer monitors she compared the energetic signatures that had been recorded during summons at Crimson Portcullis with those markers the AI had found south of the mediterranean sea and found they were strikingly similar. But not exact.

Tapping her short fingernails on the top of the thick glass desk in her office, she had determined that one of her staff, one she had been positioning to fire because she did not like his physical appearance or his unbiased attention to detail and habit of making notes of almost everything as if he were an android, would take the fall for her not having discovered the link sooner. While he had not worked directly with the data from the summons, he did work on a related project which would be sufficient for firing. No longer would she have to temporarily bring in loyal followers from other teams to report on him, to sneak in on virtual meetings or remotely watch what he did on his computer in the hopes she could get something on him. The firing would allow her to mask her lack of technical acumen and move in someone she could better control who was not as attentive, regardless of what skill they may actually possess, just as long as they could do the job to a mediocre degree. She knew that none of her staff, out of fear, would challenge her and those occupying the corporate ranks would blindly continue forward, unwilling to risk bringing attention to the actions of management, particularly those of a Representative.

Detesting actually meeting such undesirables in person, she completed a few termination forms on the computer with the charge including some technical jargon that she knew would not be understood and smirked in silent triumph as she submitted the last form. Then she re-focused on the marker data.

While she did not understand what the data from the United States meant with different markers, other than assuming the spot was a previously undiscovered magnetic anomaly, she did understand that the energetic markers from her compound and those from around Cairo were largely the same. She glared at the graphed data on the monitor, realizing that the entity she had worked too hard to trap at Crimson Portcullis had, apparently, chosen to work with someone else. But more importantly, outside of her control. She sat back in her contoured executive chair and crossed her arms, thinking of how she could punish the entity for double-crossing her, especially with all of the knowledge she had enticed it with.

After several minutes she recalled that some corporate intelligence and military sub-contractors were on station in the region and, using an encrypted private channel on her phone, dialed a number. She did not really want to use the resources of an inept state apparatus that she, along with others, had been working to replace with a corporate umbrella that would garner her more direct control over the levers of power and the unwashed masses, but the enforcement arm of the corporate superstate was not yet in place.

After a few minutes, a voice said, "Hello."

The voiceprint system verified the speaker and the signal, so she stated, "Hello."

After a few moments of waiting so her voice and signal could be verified, the voice replied, "How can I help you?"

"Destroy the entity that was found in Cairo. I am sending you the mark data now."

Following a long pause, the voice said, "This data indicates that the entity has not manifested in physical form. Until there is a manifestation of some type, we won't be able to do anything."

Michelle rolled her eyes, "Manifestation is imminent. Get a team in place and destroy it as soon as it happens!"

Without delay, the voice replied, "Order received."

"Red leader, this is Alpha leader." the intercom crackled above the hum of the gas turbine that propelled the M1 A5 Abrams battle tank, an upgrade of the A4 series, through the northern desert of Sudan.

"Alpha leader, this is Red leader. Go head, over." Captain Paul Reeves said into his helmet mike as he peered outside the turret of his tank into the hot desert.

Captain Reeves was the acting commander of both his tank detachment which consisted of four M1 tanks as well as Alpha leader's four TC's, or track-mounted personnel carriers, each holding ten soldiers and a full complement of combat gear. Since coming on alert rotation, all of the soldiers were armed with M-16 assault rifles, M-203 grenade launchers and embedded com-links in their helmets. For the past several months they had been patrolling the border to repel any insurgent forces from crossing the border. Until today, there had been no real action.

A CIC directive had come in over the satellite link, ordering them to proceed to Egypt at specific grid coordinates which would put them in the area of Cairo. Though the audio message of what sounded to be the president was garbled, the text message confirmed that they would proceed with best possible speed to Cairo and await further orders. Captain Reeves didn't question the president's order. He knew, for the sake of his career, one did not question such authority. He speculated, however, once he'd reached the target area that he would be given the order to eliminate some party that may be a threat to U.S. operations or standing somewhere in Africa.

"Roger Red leader. My nav shows us leaving our patrol line and heading towards Egypt." 1st Lieutenant Macerson said, seated in the front cab of the troop carrier, above which rested a Vulcan 30mm rotating barrel canon capable of squeezing off over 400 rounds per minute.

"Affirmative Alpha leader. New orders issued by the CIC. Over." Captain Reeves reported.

"Roger that Red leader. What do you think is going on?" the lieutenant asked. He, although only twenty-six, some ten years younger than Captain Reeves, had rarely been on a patrol when orders were issued for immediate redeployment. In this case he wanted to verify that they were not having a technical issue of some sort and veering off-course.

"Unknown. Just maintain formation. I'm sure we'll find out soon enough." Captain Reeves said as he adjusted the mike on his helmet with a black, gloved hand.

"Roger that Red leader."

Chapter Twenty-Nine

After having been preoccupied with other matters, the Baron returned to the throne room seeing that the laborers had finished clearing the pillars out of the way to the throne. Two other figures lurked about the throne as if they were looking for something. The Baron was

196

confident that they would not find what he was in search of. But, even if they did, he would simply wrest it from them and destroy their pitiful existence.

"I don't see anything." Cindy remarked, carefully scanning the carved granite throne chair.

Looking around, beyond the throne, something caught Luis' attention. Going over to the foot of the wall, he carefully picked the ancient object up.

"I got something." He said, walking back to Cindy with a soil-crusted object. It was shaped like a triangle on one end with a slight half-moon shaped indention at the other.

Cindy took it from Luis and studied it for a moment.

"Looks like an arrowhead." Cindy said finally.

Squeezing his eyebrows together, Luis said, "Why would an arrow be in the throne room?"

"No idea. I'll have it cleaned and run through the computer right away!" Cindy said cheerfully as she left Luis.

Luis, the curious type that he was, walked over to the archway that led into another room which had not yet been cleared by the laborers. Clicking on his flashlight, he scanned the dark room. Nothing seemed to be out of the ordinary. Some shattered clay pottery that resembled water jugs and a few pans of some type were scattered about. From the remnants of shelving, still partially connected to the walls, Luis deduced that it was possibly a kitchen. But he didn't understand why a kitchen would be so close to the throne. He could only guess that perhaps the Pharaoh liked his food.

Crossing the room, Luis found another connecting room that was somewhat larger than the throne room itself. It had a stone lined pit in the center, probably a pool or fountain as Luis noticed a series of stairs leading down a few feet to its bottom. Along the sides of the room were randomly placed skeletal remains. Some wore ankle shackles of gold while others did not. But all of them, Luis quickly realized, were gagged with some type of

leather around their mouth. Studying them closer, Luis
recognized the bones were female.

     What happened here?' Luis asked himself. Softly
moving some of the bones around, he looked for fractures
and markings left by various diseases that would indicate
some type of catastrophic event.

     The Baron approached the throne chair, trying to
sense the Wild Magic of this world that a mystical object,
embued with magical properties would radiate. It was
here. He could faintly feel its presence…whatever the
object he sought was. He touched the armrest of the chair
to try to isolate the essence he was feeling. But it was the
same.

     "Damn it. Where are you my precious friend?"
the Baron cursed as he briefly materialized to violently
push the throne chair aside.

     "Cindy?" Luis called out, cautiously stepping back
into the kitchen.

     The Baron, almost having forgotten about Luis,
turned toward the kitchen and saw his approaching form.

     "Pitiful little human." the Baron smirked to
himself as he moved toward Luis.

     Gradually the Baron raised a hand at Luis as he
began pulling a small amount of Dark Magic toward
himself, more than sufficient to entirely incinerate the
human's body.

     They had made good time flying to Egypt as it
had only taken two days. Now Mac and Jacob rested with
Chief Zorin in a rare oasis in the vast desert scarcely an
acre squared.

     "What are you going to do when we come face to
face with the Baron?" Jacob said, leaning on a palm tree
under the moonlight.

     The answer was obvious to Chief Zorin, "I have
to destroy him somehow." He had no idea how he would
go about destroying him though. Even the Sword of

Dragon Slaying didn't kill him, and that made him that much more uncertain.

"We don't have the Sword with us you know." Jacob said, scratching his head.

"Well, the Sword was apparently useless anyway." Mac threw in as he looked at Jacob.

"All I can do, I fear, is use all the magic I know and throw it at him." Chief Zorin said roughly. He didn't know if even that would be enough.

"What I'd like to know is why he is here anyway." Mac grunted.

Jacob looked at Chief Zorin, as if to cheer him up, "He hasn't tried to take over this world since we've been here. So…if it is not to rule this world…"

"Then he is looking for something." Chief Zorin completed.

"Another Staff of Majii?" Mac asked. It was anyone's guess.

"That is possible." Chief Zorin said as he exhaled loudly.

Disgusted by the thought, Jacob said, "If he gets his hands on another one, he may try to control this world."

"Don't even say that." Mac countered, imagining this world forever changed by the Baron.

A faint gust of magic flashed past Chief Zorin. Instantly he sprang up and looked around, searching for the originating point of the magic he knew was the Dark Magic. And now he knew, where there was Dark Magic, the Baron would not be far off.

"What's wrong?" Mac asked, seeing the Chief spring to his feet. He shrugged off the tingly feeling he got in his stomach.

"I'm not sure. I felt it come from the south east." Chief Zorin stated, continuing, "Now it is gone."

"We must go now, for I fear something terrible has happened." Chief Zorin ordered, changing into his dragon form.

Looking out into the darkness with his night vision binoculars, standing on a step within the turret of the M1 tank, Captain Reeves said, "Alpha leader, this is Red leader. According to my navigation we are about ten clicks away from our destination. Do you copy, over?"

The com crackled for a moment before there was a reply, "Roger that Red leader. Going to need some R and R after this push, over?"

"I'll see what I can do after mission." Captain Reeves replied, smiling.

"Red leader, any word on what we're supposed to do on this mission yet?" Alpha leader asked again.

"That's a negative. Red leader out."

The Baron would have struck down Luis' life except for the fact that as he had approached him, the Baron felt the magical essence get stronger. Instead, he passed Luis, who went into the other room, oblivious to the Baron's presence.

Descending into the pool, the Baron felt the strong, pulsating magic he so intently sought. It was here that he began twisting part of the Wild Magic he had learned, to dig into the center of the pool.

Luis had continued walking to the far side of the city where, at a sand-blasted trailer scarcely big enough for five people and the large collection of computer equipment, he entered and approached Cindy.

"That your idea of a joke?" Luis growled, "Do you know how much damage was caused to the throne chair because you pushed it over?!"

Looking up from the computer as if she were lost, Cindy retorted, "Wow. Wow! What are you talking about? I've been here all night going over all this data."

"That's impossible! I heard a crash when I was in another room and came out to see the throne chair on its side!" Luis frowned, going over to the refrigerator and grabbing a bottle of distilled water.

Not in the mood to quarrel, Cindy suggested, "Maybe there was a slight tremor…or a gust of wind."

After taking a deep drink of the cold water, Luis shook his head, "No, no. If it were a tremor, I would have felt it. And no simple gust of wind would knock over a granite chair like that."

Starting to type on the keyboard, Cindy said, "Well. Maybe some thieves were in there looking around. They heard you, panicked and left. You know we don't have any security around here thanks to those skimpy funding grants."

Luis closed his eyes for several seconds, slightly tilting his head back. Then, sighing, he said, "Oh you may be right. Well then, I'm going to get some rest."

Chapter Thirty

As the Sun broke over the eastern dunes, Chief Zorin could see the faint outline of a city in ruins. He was still feeling weak from the long flight but pressed on, knowing that he must stop whatever the Baron was doing.

"There it is!" Mac exclaimed, pointing toward the city.

"Yeah, I see it." Jacob confirmed. He was not eager to confront the Baron with no weapons and he didn't think that his hand-to-hand skill would really deliver a decisive blow when the Sword, specifically crafted to kill dragons, could not.

After a few minutes, he added a touch of sarcasm, "You know, it seems like we've done this before."

"Alpha leader, this is Red leader. Over." Captain Reeves called over the com-link as he verified the grid coordinates and scoped the ruined city.

"Go ahead Red leader." Lieutenant Macerson responded, opening the hatch behind his cannon, looking outside.

"Kind of strange, but I've verified the grid coordinates and we're heading towards that city that looks like it is in shambles. We'll advance in diamond formation and you form on our rear flank, over?"

After relaying those instructions to the other carriers, he confirmed, "Roger Red leader. Coming into formation now. What do you think is up?"

Captain Reeves looked around to his tanks, followed by the carriers, ensuring that his attack element resembled a diamond. That way, if the order came for an assault, they could press an attack and be able to simultaneously launch a two-pronged flank maneuver or react to one without sacrificing the attack. But it was rare that an enemy was sufficiently equipped to immobilize multiple M1 tanks given their agility and computerized pinpoint turret accuracy while in motion.

"Alpha leader this is Red leader. Can only guess we'll be taking out a rebel element or basecamp. Red leader out."

After waking, Luis sipped on a mug filled with thick black coffee, looking casually at the computer data that was assembled so far with what had been discovered. He was impressed with the detail the reports contained.

"I see you're up already." Cindy said casually, combing her long, brown hair with a soft silver brush that her grandmother had given her. Almost every time she used the brush she could hear her grandmother utter one of her all too familiar phrases, *'Cookies and Cream!'*, that she said when they would become separated by a metal pole driven into the ground or something of that nature.

"Yep. The crack of dawn." Luis remarked after chugging more coffee. It was not uncommon for him to consume two pots before sunrise.

"Hey, I want you to send the laborers into the other rooms around the throne and have them remove the gagged skeletons I found last night." Luis sparked, suddenly remembering the discovery.

"Gagged?" Cindy asked, looking at him reaching for the coffee pot.

"Yeah. For some reason they were all gagged with some type of leather. Anyway, have them run through the usual tests." Luis said as he got up and headed for the door.

"No problem." Cindy replied, wanting to see the gagged skeletons for herself, an unusual find.

With that, Luis left the trailer and headed toward the throne room to see if he could discover anything more about the skeletons.

Bringing up a few files on the computer, Cindy heard a high-pitched whine. At first, she thought it was from one of the computer consoles so she got up and moved around the trailer looking at the equipment, trying to trace where the sound originated. But to her surprise, they were all online and didn't appear to be making the odd noise. Yet, minute by minute the sound got louder.

How odd.' She thought to herself as she stepped outside the trailer to look around. A cloud of dust attracted her attention off in the distance as she squinted to see what it was. At first, she thought it might be a dust devil, but as the cloud elongated and edged closer, she saw the outlines of several tanks just ahead of the cloud.

"What the hell?" Cindy mumbled as she ran back inside the trailer and grabbed the satellite phone. Quickly she dialed the U.S. Embassy in Cairo after fumbling around to find the number in the phone's less than intuitive button-driven text menu.

After a few rings, someone picked up and said, "U.S. Embassy, can I help you?"

"Yes!" Cindy practically shouted into the phone, "Why do you have tanks coming over here?!"

"Tanks? What is your name and where are you located?" a male voice responded. It must be another prank caller.

"I'm working with Luis Remmlar outside Cairo at the excavation site and you've got a bunch of tanks coming into our area we can't have disturbed! What are you planning to do? Blow us up?!"

"Ma'am, I don't know what you are talking about. I assure you we don't have any U.S. troops in your area."

"Well, what is outside my trailer then? A marketing campaign?" Cindy hissed.

"Hold on a minute ma'am, I'm going to check into it." the voice said calmly as she was placed on hold.

Frustrated, Cindy placed the phone on the desk and peered outside the trailer window to see where the tanks were. Her heart quickened, entirely mystified as to why the tanks were out there. Her only thought was that they were sent to destroy the city and everything in it to keep something hidden. Including herself.

The focused manipulation of controlling the Wild Magic into digging was finally done. The Baron found the magical object he had sought. Except, in this case, it took the form of two sandy stone tablets to be precise. He felt the raw, throbbing Wild Magic flowing within the confines of the tablets like water rumbling through a large pipe. It was pure, and untapped as if no wizards had known about the magic confined within it. It had been buried here for a very long time. That is, until now.

Calling the tablets to him with a simple gesture, they rose out of the deep pit approximately fifty feet deep and hovered before him. Once he took the tablets, he found that there was some type of symbolic etching, perhaps an ancient language and other patterns upon its surface. Even though he did not understand the language, the Baron was pleased just to have finally found the magical tablets. He was confident he could unlock its secrets and use it to his advantage as he'd done with the

Staff of Majii. Granted, it might take some time but he had a plan. And once he reached his world, that plan would buy him time. A lot of time.

The Baron stepped out of the ancient pool, smiling as he held the tablets to his chest with satisfaction. Finally, the lust of power he had searched out was at hand.

Just as Luis came up to the edge of the throne room, he saw two objects hovering in the air, moving steadily toward him. Instinctually, fear grappled at his mind causing him to stumble backwards, looking in disbelief at the hovering stones.

'Has the spirit of a priest or Pharoah come out of this place to destroy me for tampering with the city?' Luis thought to himself, a few beads of sweat collecting on his forehead. He had never really believed in all the stories he heard and didn't take stock in the supernatural. Until now. Until it was right in front of him.

"Scared rat. Now I shall finish the job I started last night." the Baron rumbled out as his eyes began to glow a deepening red, summoning the Dark Magic once again, his form starting to become translucent.

"We have an incoming bogey at eight hundred feet descending fast!" Red leader's gunner informed him over the com-link.

"Identify and give direction." Captain Reeves snapped, yanking out his field binoculars.

"Twenty-five degrees west from due heading. Composition is biological?" the gunner reported, switching to a digital targeting identification system to identify the bogey that short-range radar had detected and, among its readouts, the composition of the bogey was reported as biological though its pattern recognition algorithms could not match it to any known civilian or military aircraft, vehicle, ship or submersible.

Instantly Captain Reeves turned left and scanned the city until he saw the bogey. But it was no aircraft or drone. His jaw dropped.

Likewise, so did the gunner's as he zoomed in and saw the image of a Silver Dragon with two riders coming down upon the city. Still, the targeting system was unable to identify it. "You wouldn't believe this Captain, but it looks like a dragon...you know, like from the movies?"

"I see it, too. Alter course to head into that city with your barrel locked on that thing. Use deadly force if it comes this way. Copy?" Captain Reeves commanded.

"Copy. Altering course and barrel target." the gunner replied as he made sure that the navigator got the instructions and relayed the course change.

Curiously, Alpha leader stuck his head out of the carrier and scanned the city with his own binoculars, having heard the last transmission.

"Oh shit. It really is a dragon." the Lieutenant mumbled, spotting the fast-moving dragon.

Rushing down to the city, Chief Zorin hit the sandy earth heavily, almost losing Mac and Jacob from the impact. Quickly they slid off his back and he moved hastily around the outer wall of the throne room.

"Baron!" Chief Zorin shouted, seeing the dark-clad essence of the Baron, not yet in solid form, holding two tablets.

Whirling around in surprise, the Baron stared at the Silver Dragon with complete surprise. His eyes widened with the sudden realization that Zorin was somehow here on this world, standing before him in dragon form. Fearfully the Baron impulsively looked about for the Sword of Dragon Slaying he knew could destroy him with one swipe of its edge.

Before the Baron had time to react, Chief Zorin released a mighty wave of red-hot fire upon the Baron, filled with several magical destructive spells he'd learned from the Secret Scrolls since he had become Chief of the Guardians. The Baron was forced back over ten feet further into the throne room as his body, although not fully materialized, smoked from the sudden deluge of White Magic.

Heavily the Baron hit the ground as the wind was knocked out of him. But he still clutched the two tablets that were not affected by the attack. The Baron knew he would have to do something soon, or he'd die without a stronger bond to the Dark Magic. Weakly he scrambled to his feet as Chief Zorin stepped towards him, dimly aware of Luis who stood pressed against the wall, watching the ordeal with unabated fear.

"Did you see that?!" the gunner gasped over the com-link, "That dragon just shot fire at something in there!"

"Roger. Lock target and fire!" Red leader commanded, determined to stop whatever bloodshed might ensure if things got out of control in the city.

As the long barrel lowered under the hiss of a controlling hydraulic piston, the 120mm ballistic round was fired, sending a cloud of burnt powder spewing out of the barrel with the entire tank rocking backward from the recoil. Within a few seconds an automated mechanical system expelled the used canister out of the tank and inserted a new shell into the barrel.

Cindy crouched down in the trailer seeing the M1 tank fire in her direction. She almost lost control of her bowel, closing her eyes in fear of being hit.

A huge explosion filled the throne room as sand, stone and splintered wood jumped into the air several feet to hail down upon the earth. Chief Zorin lay on the ground covered in rubble, unmoving and bleeding. Luis had been sent hurtling some twenty feet away from the concussive wave. Mac was knocked unconscious from an errant stone that flew through the air and Jacob, pressing himself to the earth, had luckily missed the flying debris.

Engrained combat instincts forced him up and sprinting for some type of cover for protection and concealment in the sudden quiet that followed shortly after the debris stopped falling. He made it to a nearby structure and scanned around to see where the attack originated. He spotted a detachment of tanks rolling toward the city. Knowing their only chance of survival was to flee, he looked around for a vehicle. But there was no vehicle to be found, just a trailer further to the south.

"What I wouldn't give for a few ATGM's right about now." Jacob said to himself as he thought what his next step would be in evading the tanks.

He saw both Mac and Chief Zorin sprawled out on the sand. He knew he didn't have time to evaluate their conditions, much less drag Mac to some cover. He just hoped that the tanks would not fire anymore rounds. If they weren't dead now, they would be with another attack.

"Got him!" the gunner exclaimed.

"Roger. Good hit." Captain Reeves praised, scanning for other figures or the glint of returning gunfire.

There was none.

Having been knocked over from the blast, again, the Baron managed to get to his feet and assumed the visage of the President of the United States, knowing the nationality of the war machines that approached. He had known they were coming.

"The President!" the gunner gawked, bewildered that the CIC would be on the ground with no visible ground security or air patrols.

"I can't believe it." Captain Reeves whispered, curious as to why none of his bodyguards were around. Then it occurred to him that perhaps they had been killed and the President had been kidnapped and brought to this place.

But before he could get any words out as the detachment slowed, nearing the throne room, the Baron shouted, "Follow me! We haven't much time!"

Gaining consciousness, Chief Zorin weakly got up from the rubble, straining to find the Baron. He knew he was badly injured, but that did not matter. All that mattered was destroying the Baron before he could escape.

A massive, blue-glowing portal well over fifty feet wide and some twenty feet tall appeared in front of the

Baron as he walked through it, clutching the two stone tablets.

"Where's the President going?" Alpha leader asked, mystified about all that had just happened.

"I don't know, but he gave an order and we're the only ones here to protect him. Just be on your toes Alpha leader." Captain Reeves responded, surprised that the President didn't climb into one of the M1 tanks or a carrier for protection.

Idling their engines, the detachment passed through the portal following the image of their President.

Seeing the portal, Chief Zorin stumbled towards it just as it closed in front of him. Hastily he tried to summon the portal but he was too weak. He knew he must warn the others so he paused to gather all of his strength to open another portal to the Realm.

Chapter Thirty-One

"Ma'am? Hello?" Ron said, transferring the telephone line back to the call from Cairo.

"The line is dead." Ron sighed to John, his boss, who wore a long-sleeved white shirt and black tie that matched his slacks.

"What?! Satellite links just don't die like that! Get me Washington now!" John bellowed out in frustration. He had verified through intelligence that a detachment of M1 tanks were missing from the border of Sudan and their normal patrols, without authorization. John sensed a bigger problem...that somehow the two events were linked together, as that woman had said she'd seen tanks in her area. *'Why were they there? Possible insurgent activity? A rogue order? Had the detachment gone awol?'*

Striding back to his office in the U.S. Embassy, John wondered why he was being plagued with such a crisis only a few months from retirement.

"Oh man...what happened?" Mac rambled, slowly getting to his feet as Jacob came over and helped him up.

"You just bit a 120mm round from those tanks." Jacob said angrily.

"Tanks? Where?" Mac asked, his surroundings still coming into focus.

"They are gone now. And so is the Baron." Jacob growled coldly.

"Swell." Mac sighed with disgust. Now they would have to somehow hunt down the Baron. Again.

Chief Zorin managed to stumble towards them, blood seeping out from between his scales, whispering, "He's gone...through the portal."

"Yes, I saw. Can we go through?" Jacob asked, jerking his eyes away from the blood dripping off Chief Zorin's charred silver scales. The dragon looked worse for wear and certainly appeared he'd need medical attention with all the blood that was being lost. But he had no idea how to treat a dragon.

"I do not have the strength to open a portal." Chief Zorin strained, "I...I have to rest." In the Realm, he would have had plentiful access to the White Magic to perform such a task, but in this world, with no strong connection to the White Magic, something as simple as recuperating strength would take several hours, if not days.

In an effort to preserve his strength, Chief Zorin crept into the throne room and laid down, shaded from the relentless heat of the sun that was cresting overhead.

Carefully sneaking by Chief Zorin, Luis hoped he would not be burnt alive by the dragon, having seen its display of power. He wanted to get as far away as possible, as quickly as he could.

"Hey, who are you?" Jacob shot out, seeing Luis failing to quietly sneak past the dragon.

"Me?" Luis said quietly as he glanced behind him at the dragon, "I'm Luis and what precisely do you guys want?"

"What we want is the Baron who just escaped." Jacob replied bluntly, faintly remembering the newscast he had watched that indicated that this fellow was the archeologist in charge of the excavation.

"The Baron?" Luis repeated to himself as a grin of disbelief grew onto his dust-laden face. Within a few moments Luis began laughing uncontrollably as the name circled around in his mind, intertwined with the undeniable presence of a dragon which he had thought was nothing more than the things made of fairy tales.

Mac and Jacob looked at him, puzzled.

Blasting out of the trailer, Cindy ran straight for the small gathering of people, rushing to find Luis after witnessing the explosion at the throne room.

"You okay, Cindy?" Luis shouted as she came up to him, managing to control his laughter.

"I'm fine. And I'm glad you weren't harmed after that tank blew up the throne room!" Cindy said, relieved that he was okay.

"Who are they?!" Cindy barked out, as if they were her worst enemies, glaring at them suspiciously.

"Uh, I don't know except that they are going after a Baron." Luis said with a smirk.

"What?!" Cindy practically shrieked.

"Well, you guys better leave before the FBI gets here!"

"What are you talking about, lady? The FBI does not get involved in affairs overseas." Jacob jabbed, frowning slightly.

"I called the Embassy so I'd advise getting out of here and smoking your pot elsewhere." Cindy said, smiling wirily.

"Pot?" Jacob grunted, "I'll leave when and if I feel like it. Do you understand?"

Cindy's eyes widened as she stepped back, gathering her thoughts for something to throw back at him. Nobody would bark at her like that and get away with it.

Sensing Cindy's mounting anger and frustration, Luis injected, "Hold on a minute now. They do have a dragon."

"A what?" Cindy asked, clearly not believing what he had just said.

"A dragon." Luis said as he pointed into the shadow of the throne room, "Over there."

Warily Cindy looked over and saw the dim outline of a dragon lying on the ground. A pool of blood had formed from its side.

"A dragon." Cindy whispered in amazement as she slowly walked up to it. All of her make-believe childhood dreams of seeing a dragon, to touch such a magnificent creature welled up inside her…dreams she thought were long forgotten.

Her analytical mind took over to rationalize the experience, *'An archeologist's dream. A missing link from the dinosaur age.'*

"Hey!", Luis whispered loudly, not intending for her to approach it, "It breathes fire!"

Cindy didn't listen to him as she crept up to the Silver Dragon who was breathing shallowly, its mighty chest rising and falling in a smooth rhythm, apparently unconscious. Kneeling beside it, she saw large pieces of jagged metal lodged in cracked, bleeding scales. Almost immediately her awe was replaced by sadness and pity for the injured dragon. Touching some of the scales, Cindy found their surfaces to be somewhat wavy but smooth, hard and warm.

After a few minutes Cindy turned around and said, "This dragon is going to die unless we help it."

After passing through the portal to the Realm, the Baron looked around to find himself in the midst of a grassy plain surrounded on all sides by a green, flourishing forest.

"What has happened to my wastelands?" the Baron snorted, not believing what he saw around him.

'Could Metsys spread the White Magic over this entire area so easily in just a few years? No, this has to be an illusion.' the Baron thought as he cast a find illusion spell on his surroundings from memory.

But the spell showed nothing.

Again, with greater vigor the Baron swept his left arm about himself as he held the two stone tablets in his right and cast another spell...find familiar. But there was nothing except for the weakened essence of Dark Magic emanating from the south.

Quickly the Baron pulled himself onto one of the war machines and ordered, "There. Go south!"

As the powerful engines whined, the mass of tanks and carriers turned to the south and began rolling forward in a wedge formation, antennas bowing slightly as they traveled over small ridges and fallen trees. A smile crept into the Baron's hard face as he felt the power of the war machines under his command.

Nothing would stop him. Nothing.

"King Doron! King Doron, wait!" Lionak shouted after the barbarian king as he mounted his horse with great ease.

"Yes, Lionak? What is it?" King Doron responded calmly, turning the horse about towards Lionak who slowed his pace when he reached the King.

"The Dark Magic has been called upon here in the Realm!" Lionak said rapidly between breaths.

"How can you be sure? You said it was being summoned from the other world." King Doron scowled openly.

"I felt it as I have never felt it before. The summon was strong, much too strong to be from the other world." Lionak said as he looked up at the King.

"Well, you must call Chief Zorin back at once. Obviously, it was a trap to lure the Chief away." King

Doron deduced as he tightened his grip around the reins of his mighty black stallion.

Shrugging his shoulders, Lionak responded, "I'll try but until I can, I'm going to summon help of the other Guardians."

"Good. I must get back to my Kingdom and prepare!" King Doron rumbled as he turned his horse and spurred it forward with his heels.

"Doron be careful! I felt the Dark Magic only a quarter day's ride from your land!" Lionak shouted after the King who was already in a full gallop along the cobblestone street, south.

Swiftly, Lionak whirled around and strode back into his study room and scanned the vast collection of books that were written over the centuries until he found the one he was looking for…a spell to summon Chief Zorin from wherever he was, as it was unlikely the Chief would have stayed in one location as he hunted for Mac and Mohawk.

Chapter Thirty-Two

John loosened his black tie from around his neck and unbuttoned the top button of his shirt. A voice he recognized came over the intercom of his sleek, white telephone, "John, some agents and some military guy are here to see you."

John shot to his feet and pressed the intercom button, "Thanks Ron. Send them in."

'Something bad must have happened in Cairo.' He thought to himself.

Not more than a second later, the door to his office shot open, its metallic shades banging back and forth on the glass window that they covered. John's eyes shifted over from the shades to the doorway, where three silent figures stood. Two dressed in black suits with white long-sleeved shirts whom flanked a military officer in a green

214

uniform with ribbons and medals hanging from his shoulder seemingly to his waist. Four stars sat on his shoulder lapels.

'Oh boy. Its really hit the fan.' John thought, hoping that his job and retirement pension were not on the line if, somehow, he had overlooked something regarding the Cairo incident.

After a few moments the figures stepped into the office and one of the agents closed the door behind them, also closing the shades. Although they were not impressionable, their metal composition did offer a degree of shielding from some surveillance equipment.

"Well, it didn't take you long to get here." John said uneasily, trying to cover his nervousness by sitting behind his desk.

The figures took seats around the front of the desk. One of the agents with black, slicked back hair spoke sternly and the scars on his face gave the impression of a tempered coldness, "I'm Agent Bradley, this is Agent Johnson of the CIA and this is the commanding general of U.S. Supra-Terrestrial Events, General Lowinsky. We need all the information you have received from a woman named Cindy who had called you from Cairo about an hour and a half ago."

He shifted in his seat a little and added, "Tell nobody outside this group."

John looked at the agent curiously, "Don't you have satellites or drones for that type of thing?"

General Lowinsky looked squarely at John and said, "We are still gathering data from our assets so we don't yet have a full picture of the battlespace. Information that you have may provide a slice that our hardware may not have captured."

John wanted to ask what the Supra-Terrestrial Events division did, but decided against it, the longer the three sat there staring at him.

Abruptly, the figures stood up and Agent Bradley concluded, "Be at Tolewin air-force base in forty-five minutes. You are taking a ride with us to Cairo."

215

With that, they left the room, roughly closing the door behind them.

After the three men entered a dark gray armored sedan, waiting outside the U.S. Embassy, Agent Bradley said, "Do you think John can be trusted?"

Easing back slightly in the black leather air-conditioned seats, the general thought for a moment and then said, "Well, let me put it this way Bradley...in the twenty years that John has worked for the Embassy here in Egypt, his work quite possibly saved the U.S. from being reeled in to two regional wars. So, yes, I believe he can be trusted."

"Good." Agent Johnson said, pushing his large hand through his loose, sandy colored hair, "I would hate to have to brick this early in the mission." It was his job...the one thing that gave him a feeling of true purpose.

"When does the President expect his next update?" General Lowinsky inquired, already raking his mind as to what he was going to say.

Looking out the window as the sedan pulled away, Agent Bradley said, "In four and a half hours. It should give you plenty of time to review the hardware that is being put in location now."

"You know, that's some of the most advanced equipment we have. Our scientists in Wyoming and Utah are at least thirty years ahead of what anyone else has. Not to mention some of the technology that we acquired from...non-domestic sources. If anything happens at that excavation site, even if the sand moves, we'll know about it." General Lowinsky remarked proudly. Some of the hardware consisted of large molecular scanning arrays operating at peak speeds of just over 900 gigahertz joined to large banks of 3d memory networks capable of recording structure and state changes of individual molecules as it happens, for several hundred meters. To support the vast data crunching and modeling, a series of supercomputers operating many times faster form its backbone.

However, what none of them knew, including the Representatives, was that Janus already had access, having been utilized in three contracts awarded to two different corporations to scaffold critical components for that system.

Clouds of sand particles blew freely about the ruins as the deep violet Sun began setting behind a few rippled sand dunes to the west. The intense heat that had engulfed everything seemed to be pulled along with it. For a time, the buildings and structures would shed more heat than the air around them.

A pungent, rather mossy scent hung lightly in the air about them as Mac and Jacob gradually progressed with Luis into the adjoining chambers of the throne room with flashlights in hand while they waited for Chief Zorin to recuperate.

"What is that smell?" Mac said aloud as he looked at the bones strewn about on the dirt-layered floor which, in places, displayed jagged pieces of what appeared to be marble.

"Oh, nothing to worry about. It's a residue of a chemical we spray over crypts, coffins and such things to destroy different types of fungi and bacteria that may have been developing over the centuries. The chemical destroys the microscopic bugs so that my fellow archeologists can continue unlocking the secrets of the past without catching something when they break the seals." Luis explained as he looked over the walls for signs of a language of some type.

Jacob, stepping into what appeared to be the remnants of a large pool found a gaping hole in its midst. He peered down inside of it.

"Well Mr. Chemical Man, what is this here for? It looks like someone just finished digging this hole. I don't see any water at the bottom so I don't think it is a well or something like that." Jacob said as he crouched down at the edge of the hole which was roughly four feet in diameter and reached into the ground some fifty feet.

Immediately Luis got down into the pool with a frown of disbelief on his face, "I don't know. It was not there last night when I was here sifting through things."

"That must have been what the Baron was after? It must have been pretty important for him to dig down that far." Mac suggested, stopping at the edge of the pool to get a look.

Then it dawned on Mac, after taking a quick look around them that there were no large mounds, "What happened to all the dirt and sand?"

Luis ignored him, squinting to see the subtle outlines at the bottom of the hole with the aid of the two flashlights. Then he recognized them.

"The outlines. Surly that can't be what your friend was after." Luis whispered.

"What? What are you talking about?" Mac prodded.

"Those imprints in the hole…it's the outline of two tablets. Two stone tablets." Luis said, "Most likely tablets of a priesthood based on the fragments I've seen around here."

Jacob raised an eyebrow, plainly mystified, "What would the Baron want with some religious object?"

Sweat lathered up in wavy lines over the body of the black stallion, and saliva flowed from his mouth. But King Doron pressed on, spurred by the mighty thunders that emanated from his keep that was now barely in sight. Faint screams of agony could be heard on the light breeze and the smell of things burning, both wood and flesh, danced around his nostrils.

Muscles bound up in his arms and back as King Doron's barbarian instincts seeped up from deep within his being. His eyes blackened with wild fury as he thought of all those who were dying without his presence to defend them. His people. His mouth tightened with absolute frustration of not being there, of a peculiar feeling of helplessness, not being able to swing his mighty sword about and sever the head of his yet unseen foe. He could only wait for several agonizing minutes until his stallion could deliver him to his home, his Kingdom.

Dust, stones and wood dropped to the ground as another shell effectively disintegrated another section of the once strong, thirty-foot wall that protected the Kingdom of Shek for centuries. Bodies of over fifty barbarian warriors were strewn about the rubble like twisted and contorted dolls, some with missing limbs.

The Baron smiled.

"Proceed!" the Baron anxiously commanded Captain Reeves.

"Yes, Mr. President." Captain Reeves replied instantly, although he didn't know why he was ordered to destroy what appeared to be an historic landmark and all of its inhabitants. Nevertheless, he had received an order from the CIC and was obligated to obey.

Adjusting his Kevlar helmet, Captain Reeves reached down and pulled out a hand-mike that was attached to a control panel from within the tank, as the wireless unit on his helmet was drawing too much interference for some reason. After quickly surveying his position versus the partially destroyed wall and what he could view beyond, he formed a plan.

"This is Red leader. All M1's advance on my signal. Fire during ingress. Alpha leader, form up the rear flank. Once we are beyond the walls of this fortification, deploy your troops. No prisoners."

"No prisoners?" 1st Lieutenant Macerson said in surprise. He thought of the Geneva rules but said nothing.

"Roger that Alpha leader, no prisoners." Captain Reeves confirmed even though he did not like the seemingly senseless deaths, "All units roll out!"

Rolling forward the tanks began shelling through the wall into the heart of the Kingdom, shredding stone buildings, taverns, market stalls and anything else that happened to be ahead of them with overwhelming destructive power. As the tanks continued their advance, Captain Reeves could see nothing ahead of them but the remains of structures. Something unsettling, unconscious screamed in his head to be heard…he had an uncomfortable feeling as they entered the massive gap in the wall, but could not pinpoint it.

"Red leader, Alpha leader! We have sighted a mob of armored personnel surrounding us from the rear!" the lieutenant exclaimed.

"What?! Tank two and three, cover me! Tank four, continue assault on my nine. Alpha leader, deploy your troops!" Captain Reeves responded with an acute precision that only a seasoned commander could possess. It was critical that the troops deployed before they became trapped in the carriers, and his continued assault may draw part of the horde towards him.

As Captain Reeves scanned around for the President, a voice cracked over the loud speaker mounted just below his hatch, "Red leader enemy on your tank! Button up! Button up!"

Dimly out of the side of his left eye, Captain Reeves saw a hulking form with chain mail and a silver chest plate leap onto the turret with blinding speed that he'd never seen before and the glint of steel. As the barbarian's battleaxe crashed towards his head, he dove down into the tank as it smashed into the opening of the hatch sending sparks and a deafening clang through the small cabin. Groping for his 9mm pistol, he popped out of the hatch and repeatedly shot the monstrosity until it crumpled up and tumbled off the tank.

"Thanks Alpha leader." Captain Reeves said over the com as he got back inside the tank and closed the hatch overhead.

"You have eyes on the President?" Captain Reeves asked his crew in the tank.

"That's a negative, sir." the gunner replied. Infrared identified many thermal targets but he could not tell them apart.

"Damn!" Captain Reeves cursed to himself.

Shouts of berserker fury radiated from the thick mob of barbarian warriors as they rushed the tanks and carriers, savagely beating on them with their battleaxes, swords and other war implements, trying to weaken these strange but destructive objects.

"Let's go, Boxers! Defensive wedge!" the lieutenant ordered through the com-link that was attached to the troop cabin of the transport by a speaker.

Loading their M-16s in the dull red light, the soldiers locked the bolts and pointed their weapons toward the thick steel door. Within a second a hydraulic cylinder pushed the door down as the smell of burnt wood and expended powder flooded inside.

Seeing the carriers open up, several barbarians shot around and dove into the personnel compartments only to be riddled with countless rounds of ammunition. Flashes of light from the barrels shot out and casings bounced around inside the compartments, their impacting sounds inaudible as they hit the steel walls, troops and enraged barbarians.

"Go! Go! Go!" a sergeant bellowed out at his soldiers as they rushed out into the open, shooting anything that moved.

"Aagrhh!" King Doron shouted as his men found a new-found strength in hearing his battle-cry, responding with a fierce barbarian battle-cry of their own.

The King bound his horse through the hole in the outer wall, and with a keen eye counted the number of foes and their strange magical weapons as he shot by only a little slower than a bolt launched from a crossbow. Bullets zipped past him as he charged by the soldiers who were almost in hand-to-hand combat with the barbarian warriors who demonstrated absolutely no fear or remorse in their blood-thirsty rage. If sustained for long, some of those barbarians would not be capable of snapping out of their berserker rage for the rest of their days.

A giant about five hundred meters away, who had heard the thunderous racket and the mob's battle-cry, turned to briefly see the King hurl himself into battle. He recognized the King, having once followed his banner, and had been awarded a gold medallion for almost single-handedly repelling a raid by a contingent of Shagiv intent on establishing a strong footing in the Kingdom by killing the King.

The giant, known as Hayak, looked around himself for a weapon. But, at the edge of the field, there was nothing, so he began moving towards the barbarian horde and the thunderous noise, slowly picking up speed. Then, he spotted a heavy, six head, ox-drawn cart meant for moving boulders and scooped it up with his massive arms, bursting into run. Each time his feet slammed onto the earth, the ground shook and he felt an old energy not felt in years build through his extremities. Within moments of seeing one of the carriers opening, he was upon them. Roaring mightily, he drowned out the noise of war around him for a second, causing several of the soldiers to stop and identify the blood-curdling scream. By the time they saw the towering giant it was too late as he forced the heavy cart down with both hands, along with his shifting body weight, onto them. Instantly the cart's thick timbers exploded and a wall of blood, body parts and now useless equipment burst into the air, coming down throughout the entire battlefield.

"Holy shit!" the lieutenant muttered, horrified by the sudden appearance of the giant and its brutal display of strength, "Three, request assist with that huge football looking motherfucker!"

With one move Hayak had dispatched the entire compliment of troops belonging to one of the carriers before its canon began to turn toward him and started firing, tracers casting brief bursts of light onto his form as they zipped by. At first Hayak did not know what the display meant, until the large rounds started punching into his muscle sending powerful waves of pain throughout his body. That only served to enrage Hayak further as he reached down and pulled the canon off of the carrier, tearing off part of the armor skin with it. Hurling it behind him, he reached down with both hands and grabbed onto the end of the carrier and began pulling it apart, like one might rip open a bag. The barbarians cheered at the giant's display of sheer strength.

"Roger that." Three responded, bringing his turret around behind him and beading the giant.

"Fragmentation, if you please." He ordered the gunner, who pressed a few buttons to expel the current round and breach the fragmentation projectile.

The computerized loader made the switch and after a unique metallic clank was heard and a light on his panel lit up, he reported, "Ready."

"Fire!"

The tank rocked forward on its moving tracks and the round exploded into the giant, sending a portion of his side hurling into the air. Hayak stumbled backwards, still grasping the carrier that he had managed to peel open and collapsed to his knees and one hand. Spotting the thick cloud of smoke trailing behind one of the tanks ahead of him, he forced himself up and with his last forced breath, threw the carrier at the tank before he collapsed, having come to the aide of his King for the last time.

The carrier tumbled through the air and smashed into the front of the tank, denting the armor plate ahead of the driver's position and temporarily buckling the track from the sudden impact and roll off of the tank, warping a torsion bar and popping off one of the large track wheels.

"Captain, bogies at seven o'clock! That is, two bogies!" Captain Reeves' gunner warned as the objects appeared on his tactical radar screen.

"Roger that. Bring turret around to seven o'clock and fire at will." He responded as the faint sounds of men, barbarians and weapons fire seeped inside the tank.

The turret's belt-driven transmission, fed from the power of the gas turbine, wheeled the turret around with surprising ease until it stopped a few seconds later, barrel pointing somewhat to the rear left of the tank. Then, as the gunner pulled down on a control device that resembled a joystick, the hydraulic cylinder hissed with air being pumped into it as the heavy barrel raised.

As the two bogies came onto the targeting screen, an array of numbers appeared on the bottom of the display, revealing distance, speed, altitude, wind speed and direction, target composition of the bogies and even the barrel angle necessary to hit the target with the current round. Flipping a switch on a control panel, all the information was fed to the on-board tracking computer and a circle appeared around the target that flashed red and green. A split second later after the computer got a lock on the bogies, the circle turned to a semi-transparent red color and a buzzer briefly sounded.

Smiling at his quick actions to getting a lock at that distance, the gunner lifted his thumb over the top of the joystick and pressed the firm, red button. A bellow of smoke poured out of the barrel as the 120mm round became airborne, and the tank lurched back slightly from the recoil. Then an expended casing ejected from the barrel's chamber with a hammering action and a fresh round was automatically placed in the chamber. The gunner knew it was only a matter of a few seconds before the bogie would be blown to bits as he smelled, with satisfaction, the faint residue of spent powder.

At just over fifteen hundred feet in the air, the Guardians could see the small fires and pillars of gray smoke rising into the air from the battered remains of King Doron's land. They didn't know who was summoning the Dark Magic even now, but whoever it was, was indeed powerful. Perhaps as powerful as the Realm's ancient enemy, the Baron, who was killed several hundred years ago. What the Guardians didn't understand was why an anyone would travel into the midst of the barbarian kingdom to practice Dark Magic. It did not make sense.

Suddenly silver scales sprinkled with blood burst into the air followed by an ear-shattering explosion and concussive wave as one of the Guardians was hit by the 120mm round. The Guardian, suddenly weakened from the impact and penetration of the round, fell to the earth below, barely conscious. Instinctively, the other Guardian followed and cast a globe of protection around the wounded dragon, so it would not die from the impact of crashing into the grassy earth below. Scarcely four seconds later, the dragon landed on the earth as the globe flashed an intense yellow, cushioning the wounded dragon from the impact. The globe disappeared; its power negated.

The other Guardian landed on its clawed feet and peered momentarily at the wounded dragon who was scarcely breathing. The Guardian cast a healing spell on the dragon, concentrating on the wound and the metallic round's remains lodged in the dragon's rib cage, weaving the White Magic around the bleeding wound. A white and deep blue haze materialized around the wound as the Guardian concentrated even harder, drawing on the White Magic lying dormant in the trees, shrubs, and creatures around them. Slowly the 120mm shell began to disappear, and the wound became smaller as the Guardian outstretched its leathery wings, calling the White Magic to itself and then focusing on the wound. Within a moment the Guardian withdrew its wings, and the haze disappeared. The wound had been healed.

In exhaustion, the Guardian strode up to the dragon that was now conscious to make sure it was okay. Having used all of its magical energy already, there was nothing else that could have been done if the healing spell had not been sufficient.

Dimly the other dragon rustled to its feet and nodded in appreciation at the other as they again took flight towards the Kingdom of Shek, flying much lower this time. The Dark Magic seemed to radiate from deep within the Kingdom, in fact from the house of the King…an old, but beautifully restored keep that was said to have been centuries old and the domain of the Baron.

Ignoring the loud noises of battle below and to the right of them, the dragons flew on, tracing the Dark Magic to its source somewhere in that keep. All they had to do was destroy, or at least hold off, whatever was summoning the Dark Magic long enough for the other Guardians to arrive.

Chapter Thirty-Three

"What's the message?" Agent Bradley said to John in a flat tone.

"Yes. It says the tanks were seen at the ruins." John returned.

Pausing for a moment, Agent Bradley asked, "General. Should we show him the photos?"

The General, having just concluded his call with the President said, "Yeah. The President has given him clearance for full disclosure."

Grabbing a large brown folder, Agent Bradley pulled out several photographs and laid them before John.

From the series of cross-hairs on the photographs, John instantly knew that the images were taken from one of the many satellites that operated high overhead, twenty-four hours a day.

Flipping through the photos, something caught his eye…a bird.

"I didn't know you guys were aviary enthusiasts." John smirked.

"Not really a bird. Here, look at this one." Agent Bradley said, showing John a photograph of a silver-scaled dragon, seemingly headed towards a building of some sort.

"Well, that can't be possible. Dinosaurs are extinct." John said, clearly not believing what his eyes told him.

"We believe that is not true, at least not all of them." General Lowinsky commented, already delving into all the prospects of the other dimension…the other world.

"What?" John said roughly.

"Let me start from the beginning, John." General Lowinsky clarified, "Our satellites did indeed take pictures of the M1 tanks in this sector, which are now missing as you know. But a man, dressed exactly as the President, exited the same building that the Silver Dragon had entered. He was holding some stones, opened some type of doorway heavily charged with electromagnetic energies that several nuclear power plants could not generate. Then, he simply went through this doorway along with the tanks that had been reported missing."

The General paused for a moment, not really wanting to divulge more sensitive information but continued, "That ruin was on a natural magnetic anomaly or tear – and other research we've done has shown promise with opening dimensional doors in those locations."

"So…you think he just went into another dimension?" John said skeptically.

"Yes, perhaps a parallel world existing next to ours."

John tossed the photos on the white tabletop before him and eased back in his chair, trying to swallow this fantastic story.

"And, then, why are we here now? This magic man is already gone." John questioned, shrugging his shoulders.

"We are going to attempt to mirror the emissions we recorded from a series of collective orbiting power arrays down to the surface, and with some other hardware, focus the energy at the exact point from which this door was opened." General Lowinsky said proudly, fully confident in the technology under his command.

"That's all fine but what am I here for? I am not a scientist or a grunt." John said, still not realizing what his purpose was in the whole affair.

"You will be our ambassador. You will make contact in this parallel world." Agent Bradley inserted, clasping his hands together.

"Do you realize the possibilities? The opportunities?" General Lowinsky said, barely able to contain himself from being named with such a discovery.

Earlier in his career, he had reviewed several papers that explored the military applications of dimensional gates to a parallel world to include using the entry areas as vast equipment storehouses immune to bombardment from this dimension, ingress and egress points that could be used to ambush and flank an enemy undetected, to even merely containing bunkers for the politicians and brass to escape to in the event of a natural disaster or large-scale conflict.

"I can, yes. Economics and natural resources come to mind." John said with a glimmer in his eyes that were dulled slightly from the unknowns that could result from physical contact with other sentient life-forms that may have intellectual supremacy over humanity. Then he thought, *What would happen to this other world, their life, societies if this technology fell into the wrong hands? What would happen to us?'*

"When we have fully analyzed the data we've been collecting, we'll be ready to open the door." The General concluded, "Then you will go through."

Unaware that behind cresting dunes, less than one quarter of a mile away, lurked the presence of General Lowinsky in a highly armored trailer vehicle, Mac moved about outside the throne room. The whole affair with Zorin being on Earth was just so awkward. He smirked slightly as he thought back to that time he was deployed to Columbia, where a simple idea for a little recreation through Warriors of the Realms would result in a life and death reality he could barely fathom even now.

"He's awake." Jacob said to Mac as he exited the throne room, squinting at the late day's Sun shining on them.

"Good. Do you think he'll open the portal?" Mac inquired, ready to travel back to the Realm. In a sense he wanted to see how things were…to see a world that he may never get a glimpse of again. He felt as though it was something that would not last forever. Perhaps.

"I think so. He is rather hungry though and I don't know what to feed a dragon."

"No doggie biscuits, I imagine." Jacob commented in half-humor.

Mac laughed lightly, "No I don't think that would yield the protein or calorie count required."

Pointing towards the trailer, seeing Cindy coming towards them, Jacob said, "Well, I see that our little woman has brought some food."

Hearing that statement, Cindy snapped, "Look here, punk. I am not your woman!"

"Ain't that the truth." Jacob whispered.

Following her inside, they stopped a few feet short of Chief Zorin who had transformed into a human. Such alterations made it easier to consume small quantities of food where hands, not claws, were required. And, he was not sure if the newcomers could bear watching how a dragon ate.

Chief Zorin looked at them with considerably more energy than what he had possessed only a day before and said, "My wound has been healed my friends. Now I have to eat. I've got the hunger of a dragon right now."

"I'm sure you do." Cindy said softly, clearly attracted to him.

Mac scoffed quietly to himself as he thought how this woman was so drawn to the Chief after only a day. That animal attraction. He couldn't help but be curious as to just how she'd handle him leaving this world and going back to his...perhaps to die.

"Ah, thank you for all this good smelling food." Chief Zorin smiled courteously, taking the wooden platter gently from Cindy's hands, and setting it before him on an overturned stone.

"Where's Luis?" Mac inquired, trying to sever the lust-filled atmosphere.

Cindy stood up straight and said, "Oh, he's in the trailer doing some research on this city to try to solve a most puzzling question about those stone tablets."

"Well, he's been working for a long time. I hope he finds out exactly what those stones were." Jacob said, walking outside the throne room ever so casually just to stop at its entrance.

Between bites, Chief Zorin mumbled out, "The stones had some type of power in them. Some cold power. I don't know exactly how to put it, except that it was a type of power similar to the Baron's Dark Magic."

Looking back into the throne room, Jacob asked, "Do you think he can get to such magic?"

"I don't know. It felt as if the power was trapped far inside them, almost as if it were in a void." Chief Zorin said after clearing his throat, "I think those stones may be a gate of some type. But opening a void such as what I felt might be impossible. Even for the Baron."

"Yeah, and you thought the Baron was dead, too." Jacob retorted, throwing his arms into the air.

Silence filled the ancient throne room. Only the slight whisper of the wind outside could be heard.

"When are we going back?" Mac said finally.

"Tomorrow. I must rest a little more before I go back. I will need all of my energy to open the portal and fight the Baron." Chief Zorin said soberly.

"Well then. Let's get some rest, eh?" Jacob suggested, eager to just forget about the whole affair for a little while.

After about half an hour, after everyone had settled in for the night and Cindy had placed herself rather near to Chief Zorin, Luis came hustling up to the entrance, heaving for air, "Hey! I've found out what the Baron has! I've done it!"

Cindy, sitting up with curiosity asked, "What is it?"

Waiting for a moment so he could catch his breath, Luis announced, "Those stones, according to ancient history of the Egyptians was an evil destructive power. This power was a god or sub-god…or I guess in the modern era a devil or demon. They referred to this god as Set."

"Who's Set?" mac inserted abruptly.

"The devil you fool," Cindy scowled at Mac, "please continue."

"Anyway, after the deaths of millions across social strata, a power came from the heavens and this god was imprisoned in the stones for eternity." Luis concluded.

"Great. More hocus-pocus to deal with." Jacob grumbled, "It just couldn't be the Baron, now could it."

"Can the god be freed?" Chief Zorin asked, fearing for all the life on this world, and his own.

"I don't know. It was recorded that the stones were lost forever." Luis said, scrunching his face, "If there's an inscription or writing on those stones, I'm sure that would hold the answer."

A lone figure, wrapped in a soft white silky gown shuffled from the ornately filled porcelain bathroom to the adjoining master bedroom adjusting her blond hair in the second story of her lavish home miles away from the nearest neighbor. The glimmer of the full moon outside passed through the old panes of glass to be consumed by the finely knit curtains that covered the window not more than ten feed from the bed.

As Bev sat down in front of a table that held a mirror in its center, she sighed and leaned onto its edge with her elbows. She was lonely. So lonely that she felt like a stranger in her own home. The quietness. It was kind of an eerie quietness that made her somewhat uneasy. It made her think of monsters and ghosts hiding in closets and under beds. In every shadow. Oh, she knew it was nonsense, but those insecurities she had as a child and thought were long forgotten were pounding in her mind as if she were still child from all those years ago.

Bev smiled into the mirror and tried to reassure herself that it was just nonsense. Then her mind shifted to the time she first met Jacob in a little bar just outside the French Quarter in Louisiana during the Mardi Gras festival. She remembered him walking in with faded blue jeans, simple tennis shoes and a black, short-sleeved shirt laughing and joking around with some of his friends. At that time, unbeknownst to her, Jacob had just entered the U.S. Army and was only a private enjoying some much needed leave time…vacation as she called it. It only took a few seconds before Jacob found her there sitting by herself, looking at him. And those few seconds of seemingly endless eye contact were all that was needed before a smile crept onto his face as he approached her. She liked how he smiled. How those lips curled up into tight lines and his ears weaning back slightly. Even to this day she still is attracted to that smile.

Then she thought of that strange man. A man that was a dragon. It seemed impossible. Like a storybook fairy tale, but she saw it herself. A dragon. *'What is it like to be a dragon? Or to ride a dragon into the sky? To feel such power under you?'*

Then she thought of Jacob leaving her to help this stranger. *'What was he doing? Didn't he know that he might die? What would she do if he never came back to take care of things, to help raise the children? Didn't he love her and the children enough to stay? Didn't he care?!'*

Those thoughts gnawed deeply at Bev as her smile eroded into a frown of confusion and loneliness. Within a moment she shot up and dashed out of the master bedroom, running down the wooden staircase as fast as her legs could carry her, her gown trailing behind her as if it was trying to stop Bev from what she was about to do.

Turning sharply at the foot of the stairs, she headed into the living room and over to the fireplace. A tear began to form under one of her deep blue eyes. Bending over to the right side of the red brick and mason fireplace, she turned a heavy brass knob and a fire instantly sprang to life with a deep, but quiet hiss. Then she hastily swung the glass doors that covered the front of the fireplace open.

"To hell with it!" Bev cried as she reached up and grabbed the star-shaped flower that Jacob prized, supposedly given to him from this stranger's land and threw it viciously into the midst of the fire. Burning his gift was punishment for being so self-centered and inconsiderate for her and their children.

Instantly the flame consumed the flower as a bluish smoke rose from the fire and up through the chimney. Stumbling back, Bev plopped down on the reclining chair Jacob loved so…and wept.

Chapter Thirty-Four

It had been such a long time. The passive water spirit had been at the edge of Metsys' keep for over a century. Waiting. Waiting for the master's command. Oh, how ravenously hungry the water spirit was. After having tasted warm flesh, merely feeding off the algae and small fish that happened to enter into the moat with it was not enough. It wanted to feast upon the land-born creatures again but could not as its master forbade it once it reached the keep.

Deep within the Northern Ice Mountains in a sacred burial ground for the Guardians of the White Magic came a disturbance. Indeed, this disturbance was not natural. No one other than a select few of the Guardians knew of this sacred burial ground so no aspiring sorcerers could attempt capturing the residual dragon essence or draw upon its power. Even the Baron didn't know of its existence. But the calling on this power was the power itself, deep within the heart of the burial ground.

Clouds began to form overhead, shutting out the Sun. Within moments the clouds became as black as the deepest night, arcs of lightning dancing around them in random patterns. The wind began to blow with an untamed fury, scattering the packed snow from the top of the burial ground, revealing the brown grass beneath. Then a lightning bolt lashed out from above and drove deeply into the earth with a mighty crackling rumble that rolled through the mountains as the earth exploded sending layers of frozen dirt into the air.

There, forty feet down in the midst of the earth lay a mighty, gold laden burial chamber easily measuring twenty feet squared, its silver seals locked tightly around its four corners. As the heavy clumps of earth pounded back to the ground around the chamber, another series of lightning bolts reached out from the heavens and disintegrated the seals. Thick smoke from the burnt metal rose out of the immense hole as the gold chamber began to glow an ever-deepening white. The metal, which made up the chamber, groaned with mounting stress as the glowing deepened until the chamber itself ripped open like a flower extending its petals and a translucent Silver Dragon, with the purest golden eyes, shot out from its midst. The dragon roared mightily with its wings outstretched and disappeared into the clouds.

It had been called upon…bound by an unfulfilled promise made centuries ago.

"You all know of the problem that now faces the Realm. There is an unknown evil that has come from the other land. This evil is now in the Kingdom of Shek." Lionak said from the top of the stone stairs of his keep inside the courtyard, "This evil is strong, and it is tapping the power of the Dark Magic as I have never seen before. I can't begin to understand what its purpose is, but we must destroy this evil before it sweeps over us like what had taken place in the time of my great-father, Metsys! I fear we don't have much time."

Then north, off in the distance, a faint rumble was heard by Lionak and the other Guardians as they looked towards the Northern Ice Mountains and witnessed what appeared to be a star shoot up into the heavens from the midst of the mountains and disappear.

"What was that?" one of the Guardians asked, dumbfounded, pointing with his clawed hand.

Lionak turned around, facing them and said, "I don't know…I sensed no Dark Magic." He hoped it was a natural event but thought, *'Could it be that this evil was now able to do things without being detected? If so, how could we know what to expect…how to prepare?'*

A few seconds later, Lionak said to them, "King Doron is at the Kingdom of Shek now, battling whatever this evil is…if he is still alive. You, the Guardians, must now protect this land with more determination than your forefathers! This evil must be crushed!"

With that, the Guardians, in an incredible rush of wind, became airborne, twisting in the air effortlessly as they flew towards the Kingdom of Shek. With Chief Zorin absent it fell to Lionak as the most skilled and trusted in the Realm, to command on his behalf and act swiftly. But he regretted sending them because he could feel the evil was stronger than he…stronger than the Guardians he sent to destroy it. Yet, there was one thing that might be strong enough to vanquish that evil. One other possibility.

Swiftly, Lionak turned and darted into his study and sat hastily behind his desk and flipped open a thick book laden with dust. Turning each page carefully as they crackled, he scanned their contents until he found what he thought might work. Dragging his hands over a hand-sketched drawing of two silver dragons flanking a mighty sword, the Sword of Dragon Slaying, he knew these dragons could be the thing he needed to preserve the Realm. These dragons, from lore he had read, were not truly living beings. They were, instead, a half-sentient creation from the purest of White Magic that surged so strongly in the heart of Mt. Reach, there for one purpose…to guard the Sword of Dragon Slaying and to protect the White Magic at the only point at which it actually could be taken directly into anyone's hands…that is, if anyone survived the descent and challenge by the dragons. He had to go further, to find the river that kept the Realm alive. The Pure Magic that bore all magic.

But Lionak had to find a way to somehow talk directly to it, the Realm as a whole itself. That was something he was not sure he knew how to do, even with the ancient text. Grabbing a wooden staff endowed with White Magic, and dawning his purple cape tied about his shoulders with a flat, golden chain, he stood in front of his desk and closed his eyes. With the tempered skill of a master wizard, he pulled the fine threads of White Magic about him, and thought only of being at the entrance of Mt. Reach. A deep white sphere engulfed his form and in a brilliant flash of light he was gone.

Chapter Thirty-Five

Daylight came quickly to the resting band of people all tucked away inside the throne room, their noses having become desensitized to the fine dust that hovered in the air. Jacob was the first to awake, his senses warning him of some unseen danger, senses that had saved his life more than once in the dense and unforgiving jungles he's transversed on several covert operations. He looked around carefully, unmoving at first. Then, only after he was satisfied that he could see no immediate danger, got to his feet and awoke the others. But in the back of his mind, he felt a nagging about danger.

Slowly everyone rustled to life, stretching and yawning their sleepy haze away. Cindy, he had noticed, seemed so pleasantly graceful when she awoke…that faint moan of satisfaction and peacefulness that reminded him of Bev.

Mac, brushing the dust off himself, said, "Are we ready to go now?" He was eager to travel back to the Realm without further delay.

Chief Zorin walked towards the entrance to the throne room with confidence in his voice, "Of course."

Raising an eyebrow as if he had just thought of something, Chief Zorin continued, "But there is only one problem."

Jacob rolled his eyes in disgust. He hated the word 'problem' and usually what came afterwards even more.

Mac looked at Chief Zorin blankly.

"I will have to use the power of Lionak's tapestry to get us to the Realm. I do have enough strength to reach out beyond this land, but not to pull us into the Realm. But…it should not be a problem."

From here, he could only beckon a relatively small volume of White Magic even with his level of mastery, for so many. He hadn't planned on returning with Mac and Jacob in addition to himself.

There that word was again…problem. Jacob gritted his teeth.

"Well then, let's get down to business and get this thing over with, shall we?" Mac pushed.

"Wait!" Cindy practically shouted, "I want to go with you!"

Chief Zorin turned and looked at her, surprised.

"What do you mean, you want to go with them?!" Luis shot out, "You still have work that needs to be done here. The excavation is not done, the secrets of this place have not yet all been unlocked."

Chief Zorin smiled slightly and said to her, "Do you know what dangers lie in my land, waiting to strike out and destroy anything…for the sheer pleasure of it?"

He was lying, of course. There were none except for the Baron. And, he didn't want her to die at his ruthless hand. She was far too beautiful and intelligent to be so needlessly destroyed. She was too precious.

"I don't care." Cindy replied almost instantly. She wanted to say that she just wanted to be with Chief Zorin and that nothing else mattered, but she kept those words back. She wanted to say that she had dreamed of them together, sitting in the midst of a plush green forest beside a peaceful lake, just last night. But she didn't.

237

Both Jacob and Mac knew what she was getting at, and almost choked trying to keep their laughter bottled up. They just didn't understand how a woman could be so attracted to a man, rather a dragon, only after one day.

After a long pause, Chief Zorin sighed and said, "No. You have work to do here, as I do in my land. Maybe we will meet each other again."

That stabbed deeply in her heart. Those were painful words that she refused to accept. Tears began to well up inside her, but she held them back with a tight smile and bowed her head slightly. Only after they began to walk away did she look up with a lonely tear in her eye, waiting so desperately to go with them. To be with Chief Zorin.

After crossing about one hundred meters of sand, they stopped and Chief Zorin changed into his natural dragon form. Every time that Mac saw him do that, he was equally amazed.

As Chief Zorin outstretched his mighty wings, strings of white lightning appeared before them, jumping about as if looking for a way out of some invisible barrier that held them fast. Slowly the lightning bolts became fatter until an outline of a white portal, probably six shoulder-widths wide and as tall as the dragon became visible before them. Then, as he withdrew his wings, the portal dimmed down to a deep blue pulsating haze as an occasional bolt of lightning shot out into the sky from around it.

Cautiously they walked through the portal, not pausing to look back.

Then the portal closed behind them.

"No, you will not leave me, Zorin. I will find a way to come to you." Cindy muttered sternly under her breath as she stared at the place where the portal had just been.

Lights pulsated erratically as the supercomputers recorded all the information about the portal that had just been opened by Chief Zorin. Voices could be heard over the communications channels as technicians hastily traded information, fine-tuned the detector arrays and satellites overhead, and ensured their equipment was recording with uncanny precision. John shook his head as he looked at the collection of computer terminals pulsing with life and then to Agent Bradley who looked at the computers with minimal interest. Even though he witnessed it himself on the monitor screens, he couldn't quite accept that a man could turn into a dragon. Not only that but even open a portal to another place. He had always believed that what humanity could control was limited by what they could build through technology. Yet the contrary just happened, challenging his assumptions on phenomena like ESP, telepathy, remote viewing and even fortune tellers.

"Sir, we are doing a final sweep on the target grid for residuals. Ground personnel may move around in the non-hazard areas." a voice cracked over the intercom in the trailer. What he didn't know was that Janus was also getting the same data.

General Lowinsky made a fist at the successful operation and strutted into the other room where John was. Picking up a handset from next to an intercom, he ordered, "Alpha and Bravo units. Proceed with Operation Swarm."

A man, camouflaged in a tan pile cap and fatigues, raised his hand to the com-link that hung down from his cap and into his ear. Still crouched down in a squatting position behind an eroded wall clutching his M16, he used a series of hand signals and, seemingly out of nowhere, a platoon of soldiers dressed as he was emerged and advanced. They moved around the remnants of the city like a tiger stalking its prey deep within the jungle, aware of every movement, aware of every sound. They were well trained. Trained by the elite of the Special Forces and legendary Commandos from an operating base in France at, of all places, a partially renovated castle surrounded by hundreds of hectares of mountainous terrain.

Stealthily, the commander got to a standing position and scanned the area around him, pausing momentarily at the motion of a lizard scurrying about on a stone ledge some fifty meters away. Out of an instinctive routine, he assessed its threat level. Then, shifting his eyes ahead, he strode forward, weaving around structures as if he were almost part of them. At one hundred meters from his target, he crouched down again. Signaling for his men to stop the advance with his closed fist, he turned towards his target and clicked the selector lever on his M16 to burst.

Reaching up to the com-link, he relayed some information as he analyzed it, "We are on target. Two personnel. One male. One female. One hundred meters north-northwest of our position. Is deadly force authorized? Advise."

Within a moment the com-link crackled back in his ear as he heard the voice of General Lowinsky, "Negative. I want those personnel alive."

Clicking his M16 to semi-automatic, the commander replied, "Copy. Engaging target."

"Cindy, I know you wanted to go with them. But you hardly know anything about that place. And I don't want to know that you were killed…I don't think that I could have that on my conscience." Luis said honestly. Besides that, he hated the thought of losing such an intelligent archeologist. She was, by far, one of the most talented he'd ever worked with.

Cindy wiped a tear from her eye as she dimly listened to Luis, still staring at the place where Chief Zorin had just been. Something deep within her screamed that Chief Zorin would not return. Ever. Somehow, she had to get to the other land.

Suddenly a deep, firm voice roared out, ripping her out of her plotting mind, "You two. On the ground! Now!"

Whirling about, they looked around and noticed soldiers in tan fatigues gradually approaching them with their M16s in hand, surrounding them.

Startled, Luis cursed, "Damn!"

Cindy's mouth merely dropped open, amazed that so many soldiers would sneak up on them without being seen or heard.

Knowing that there was no possibility of escape, they got to their knees and raised their arms.

While a pair of soldiers cuffed the two civilians the commander reported, "Target secured."

Chapter Thirty-Six

King Dorn, having broken past the massive formation of tanks and his own men, pressed deep within his Kingdom. Except for a few wandering children and a stray dog everyone, including the women, were fighting the strange intruders. That was the way a barbarian woman was. Seldom would they go out into battle away from their home, unable to protect their offspring. But, when battle came to them, as it had here, they would go out and fight with a rage almost equaling the berserker rage of a male. For them, the life of their offspring was paramount over everything else.

King Doron could feel an eerie, cold darkness grow as he galloped further into the heart of the Kingdom. Even his horse could feel an evil presence that gave the animal pause and neigh in resistance to pressing forward. But King Doron maintained a stern bearing and kept the stallion moving.

Then a cold south wind licked forcefully at him and his stallion. The horse bucked and extended his forelegs about trying wildly, out of instinct for survival, to shed his rider and flee. The presence of evil was strong to the horse…as if the darkness was crawling on the horse's hide, like a thousand large black ants using their jaws to rip and tear at its flesh…crawling and burrowing towards his beating heart. The horse jumped and ran around erratically, trying to shed the evil from it, but it felt the cold hands of death begin to tighten around it. The stallion's eyes widened in absolute terror as it raised up on its rear legs neighing in horror, trying in futility to save itself.

But it was too late. With a heavy thud, the once vibrant stallion collapsed under its own weight and sent King Doron tumbling to the ground several feet away. A faint chuckle echoed through the alleyways followed by silence as the wind simply vanished.

King Doron, jumping swiftly to his feet, yelled out, "Show yourself bastard!"

He withdrew his long sword, blood flowing into his mighty arms, eager for battle.

But there was no reply.

King Doron squinted his eyes as his fury boiled inside him, screaming to be freed, to spill the blood of his foe. Forcing himself to calm down, he moved down the cobblestone street to his palace, putting his berserker rage at bay. For now.

"You barbarians...so typical." the Baron said as he looked into a quartz crystal ball which displayed an image, although slightly blurred, of King Doron walking towards the palace with a sword drawn.

The Baron had found his way into a small stone room connected to by a secret passageway deep beneath the palace that could only be opened by Dark Magic. The Baron had created it in his younger years almost four centuries ago as an escape route when he had to fight many enemies in the chaotic time before he had solidified his power and position. The Baron had never thought that he would actually be forced to use it to hide from mere barbarians and the like.

Some half-dozen candles flickered against the ancient stone walls that smelled of decay as the Baron turned his head and looked upon the stone tablets. A grin formed on his face as he studied the sigils and began using some of the Dark Magic ornaments he had left in the room, in an effort to help unlock the secrets of the tablets. He knew the ultimate power he was seeking was pulsing

beneath the stone husks. The power was full of Wild
Magic. Chaotic Wild Magic. A Wild Magic that had
already bred the seeds of war and carried them to the four
winds, and been consumed by that beast known as Man.

The two Silver Dragons flew with haste towards
the palace. Down below they saw a small figure of a
barbarian, King Doron, walking towards the palace. They
felt the Dark Magic within the depths of the palace, vibrant
and cold. Whoever it was that was using this Dark Magic,
they thought was, indeed, powerful. More so than they
had ever encountered in their lifetime. The dragons knew
that they had to try their best to destroy this evil before it
swept across the land. They also knew that their lives
might be at hand, but that mattered not. They had trained
since their infancy for a moment such as this and it was
their responsibility, as being the most powerful creatures in
the Realm, to protect it.

Seeing the palace below the two Silver Dragons,
in unison, descended upon the stone structure as they beat
their wings towards the ground and outstretched their
scaled legs towards the earth. After landing and balancing
themselves, the dragons folded their wings and looked
cautiously about with their golden eyes as they took deep,
controlled breaths through their leathery nostrils. Sensing
no immediate danger, the dragons looked at one another
and transformed into two male human forms so they could
pass through the palace unhindered by small doorways and
passages not created for dragons. In their human form, the
pair looked scarcely twenty years of age, one having
shoulder-length blond hair and the other with long, raven-
black hair that hung down freely almost half way down his
back. Their clothes were identical. In fact, strikingly
similar to Chief Zorin's garb when he had first met
Baracuss, Loce, Mac and Mohawk in the Northern Ice
Mountains before he became Chief of the Guardians.

Walking towards a finely ornamented doorway
some fifty paces in front of them, the pair probed around,
throwing thin shafts of the White Magic, invisible to the
human eye, through the air to help locate the source of the

Dark Magic. Once inside, they sensed a strong presence of the Dark Magic they were in search of, below the palace itself.

"There must be a door of some type to get below." one of the Guardians said to the other.

"Yes. Perhaps a passageway. We must find it." the other replied coolly.

King Doron jogged up to the palace entrance, having seen the two dragons land before him, hoping to intercept them and warn them of the evil that had cost him his horse. But he was not swift enough. They were already inside somewhere. With his opportunity gone, he speculated to himself that, since they were Guardians, they probably already knew. Nonetheless, he would have felt better if he could have warned them, just to make sure.

Walking inside the all too familiar palace where he'd held grand feasts and matters of state, the King knew something was not right within the palace. His instincts told him that. He could feel something evil, like one could feel the heat from a blazing fire a few paces away, but he could not pinpoint it.

Hearing a thunderous explosion and falling rubble, King Doron shot forward, running towards a hallway from which his ears had caught the echoing noise. Stopping suddenly at the archway to the hallway, he cautiously peered around its edge.

The Guardians, having discovered the entrance to the secret passageway and ripped a gaping hole in its midst, followed the dark stone staircase down into the bowels of the palace. Both of them could feel the increasing intensity of the Dark Magic. It became steadily stronger as they descended the staircase into a large corridor, large enough to bear dragons. Looking upon the walls that were particularly smooth, as if they were carved from a hot fire, they transformed into their dragon forms out of instinct and training. In this form the Guardians were better suited to defend from an attack with the natural protection of their scales, and also preserved their magical strength until it was needed, rather than it slowly being drained from holding their human form.

As the Guardians went deeper into the corridor, lit at the end by a series of red, flickering candles, the Guardians were unsure of what lay ahead. They knew that all of the Red Dragons had been destroyed, so what could it be?

Behind them, a black shadow materialized from the air just as a pair of deep, bright red eyes became visible, staring at the backs of the two Silver Dragons. Unaware of the presence behind them, the two pressed on, focusing their energies ahead of them, towards the area that flickered with candlelight.

In a blinding flash of light, a thick volley of deep blue lightning bolts arched through the corridor, surrounding and biting into one of the Silver Dragons. Scarcely a second later, a yellowish-red glow lit up the corridor from between its silver scales as they began to fall to the ground smoking, the smell of burnt flesh filling the air. Shortly after the dragon fell to the ground, its entire form blackened from the attack that had radiated from inside it, the faint sounds of roasting flesh emanating from its body.

The dragon was dead.

The second dragon wheeled around to see what had just attacked his fellow Guardian, scared and unsure of what to do in the confusion of those few seconds that had passed. In a faint blur, the shadow rushed upon the Guardian.

Scurrying down the stone staircase, King Doron heard the gut-wrenching bellow of a dragon in unimaginable pain, stopping him momentarily as his own uncertainty of what was ahead grappled at him. Collecting himself, he finished crossing the stairs and found himself in a dim corridor. Almost immediately a strong odor of burnt flesh hit his nostrils and his stomach churned in defiance of the unique smell.

Grasping the hilt of his sword with both hands, he cautiously looked around in the corridor and spotted the dark, burnt remains of a Guardian, still smoking from an attack that had occurred only seconds before. Against the wall, King Doron saw another Guardian, crumpled together on the ground like a waded piece of paper. Slowly, he approached the Silver Dragon and reached out with one hand to touch its tail. As if his touch had awoken the dragon, it stirred suddenly and looked around, in a daze.

Sheathing his sword, King Doron walked closer to the dragon and asked, "What happened here? What has attacked you?"

The Silver Dragon, not knowing where to begin, painfully got to its feet quickly realizing it had a throbbing headache, probably from being knocked out during its attack. Slowly the dragon answered the King, looking upon its fellow companion who was dead before it.

Chapter Thirty-Seven

"Janus, have you identified the pattern used by the usurpers to eliminate the four from the Thirteen?" Regnum asked in a monotone voice. From the last equinox cycle, over twenty-five thousand years ago, he found no record of any of the Thirteen having succumbed to assassination when the Thirteen were governed under Iter of the Sagittarii. Yet, now that this cycle was nearing its end, four had been assassinated in short order and, despite his high intellect, did not discover anything.

"Sequentially, the members died in this order," Janus began, his 3d hologram displayed before Regnum mimicking a motion with his arm, "Fratres, Carcer, Vita and most recently Uxor. The reason for choosing those targets is unknown. However, the order seems to indicate a linear target method based on month; March, April, June and October. I would suggest that the next target pair would follow the same linear method, though I cannot predict the next member it will begin with, nor which will follow. Until the cloning process has been completed, nine remain being Lucrum, Genitor, Nati, Valetudo, Mors, Serpens, Iter and yourselves."

While Regnum appreciated the cloning technology at their disposal, it was unusually sensitive to deep-space radiation and interference which, at the end of a cycle, were always more intense, hampering the speed at which a clone could be grown without significant genetic damage. As it stood, females could no longer procreate after their genetic composition had changed where their own immune systems would destroy the embryo as if it were a foreign organism and, over subsequent generations, a majority of both sexes shed their reproductive organs entirely. Ergo they became entirely reliant on cloning technology, that slowly debased genetic quality, and finding compatible species, of which, humans were but one.

"And the usurpers themselves?", Benefacta prodded, standing near Regnum in the midst of an oval shaped dome structure with few visible structural beams. A dense, invisible electromagnetic field wrapped the entire structure, shielding the inhabitants from harmful radiation, kinetic attack and being detected from the outside. Around its perimeter grew a variety of plants and shrubs, many having been extinct on the planet since the close of the last cycle.

"Yes, ma'am, I have been able to gather more in that regard." Janus responded, the hologram turning toward her as they began to walk forward, "Now that I can monitor movement and transactions for all resources and humans on the planet, regardless of their perceived importance and secrecy in their artificial social constructs, I've been able to focus on three global corporations, each with significant corruption and infiltration extending into a wider umbrella of corporations and nation states. The human dragnet has been reduced to approximately four-thousand five hundred from the initial query list of three hundred and one thousand. I am assessing all recorded information about those humans, including phycological

247

records and threat profiling that had been completed by their respective nation states as part of the world-wide operation called 'Omniscient Warden' used to keep the existing power structure in place."

The hologram moved to walk beside her with no visible device controlling it as Janus continued, "Physical devices are being deployed in all of the locations the targets frequent and all activity that flows through a digital network is also being intercepted. I should soon be able to construct honey-pots from which to entrap them before they advance on the next of the Thirteen, assuming they are the threat we seek."

"What of the technology being used?" Regnum injected, not particularly interested in the humans involved because, if their advanced technology can be defeated, then they no longer would have a superior advantage from which to control and influence the humans.

"I've repeatedly analyzed the environments that the fallen Thirteen were in, and from what I have found, they do not possess the tools to defeat your technology." Janus stated. While it was a possibility that an isolated group may have comparable technology, it did not mean they were usurper partisans and, without some type of evidence, he did not want to entertain the hypothesis. But he did admit, "What I do find troubling is that the dimensional portals that had been limited to the anchor points the Thirteen had created ages ago, can now be invoked on any point on the planet, as I had reported. Since this capability started in the parallel dimension, it is worth considering that an entity in that dimension is targeting the Thirteen, or a human is working with them who is familiar with the parallel dimension."

Regnum nodded, "Reasonable theory."

Janus crossed his arms, not yet finished, "It will not be long before the humans master the technology themselves given the recent events in Cairo. When that happens it is assumed that, sooner or later, some among them would use the technology to circumvent the defenses of the Thirteen, once discovered, and install themselves as the de facto rulers of the planet. Given they have bred over thousands of years to answer their primal tendencies for control and subjugation, not only would the Thirteen fall, the advanced technology would be turned on themselves and used against anything they feared or could not dominate."

As they stopped near the edge of the structure, overlooking the Rhätikon Mountains and a sweeping evergreen forest, Benefacta turned to Regnum, "Do you think the humans have been given too much freedom this cycle? Their technological advance has gone further than those in previous cycles."

Regnum thought about that for some time, going back to their founding conquest hundreds of thousands of years past, replying, "No. The Representatives that we've chosen over the centuries have served us well in chasing their own insignificant self-interests. Those enduring self-interests, even as humanity has progressed technologically, has left them dependent on that primal, anchoring survival instinct that funnels down to the least of them, creating more division than even I could have imagined. And, while they are divided and jockeying for that brief moment to dominate others, the behavior continuously feeds and fuels future generations, preventing them from achieving anything of any real significance."

Regnum put his slender hands on his hips and revealed, "Yet, to further encourage animal instincts in the wider populace, even the lexicon around the idols and icons they adore have been redefined to be female…a subconscious stimulus to be found at every turn from mentions of their planet, to the texts of science and literature. How might one of them paraphrase it? If they are running around with their dicks in their hands, they won't be holding a pen with which to write, compose, or imagine."

He paused for a moment to consider the beauty of how much power and chaos could be had with such reliable animal instincts prevalent in the socially-driven species before he added, "Thus, with those seeds having sprouted and taken root throughout their social structure, but particularly throughout the top to trickle down to the ocean of ignorant masses, any resurgence of the natural order to restore balance will fail because those dog kings will always react according to their self-interest with accessibility to force to overcome and subjugate those masses. Given sufficient time, the species will collapse by their own hand, naturally, as has happened in other cycles."

Regnum smiled at her and said, "Since we are prohibited from cleansing the planet, that is exactly what we want. A race of sentient beings that will willingly subjugate themselves, even destroy themselves rather than discard their animal instinct and strive for something that requires true intellect and creativity."

He turned and glanced at the forest below, "As long as we keep the relative few focused on their self-interests so the influence can spread to those beneath, the natural evolutionary course that most sentient races take will never happen on this planet. That, Benefacta, means they will never rise into the stars and become a competitor to our civilization. And, should they happen to destroy themselves, well, we will have gained another planet."

"So, what of the usurpers?" Benefacta asked, believing they should be stopped before they inevitably got to the Representatives and, by extension, the Thirteen.

"Have the Thirteen meet with their Representatives to infiltrate and derail the usurpers' movement. Have them divided into competing factions until Janus has identified the hidden leaders. As long as they are divided, the leaders will be relatively powerless." Regnum replied almost instantly, as if he had been contemplating that plan for some time, "While I doubt they would be an actual threat to us, they could prove useful in speeding along the collapse of their own species."

"And the dimensional threat?" Janus questioned, the hologram turning as if to look outside the structure.

"Stay connected to that yourself, Janus. That is the only thing that is a real threat to us. But I cannot imagine anything from the parallel dimension of this world that would seek to harm the Thirteen, at least nothing from before the Twin's Grip event. That said, the spatial tear that resulted could have introduced an anomaly that I am not yet aware of." Regnum ordered, and with the wave of his hand, the hologram and Janus' connection were closed.

Chapter Thirty-Eight

Mac found himself in the study of Metsys, followed closely by Jacob and Chief Zorin as the portal closed behind them. The familiar smell of wax, leather and masonry eased the tension he had from the crossing. He noticed that little had changed since their last visit, except for a few extra piles of books stacked on the desk.

Chief Zorin moved a bit to the side of the study, still in dragon form, in case another portal opened. He wondered if the study had somehow gotten a bit smaller since his last arrival in his native state.

"Man. This is weird. It's like a dream to be back here." Jacob said quietly as he, too, embraced his surroundings. He had told no one, not even his wife, that he'd had several dreams about the Realm. Not that they were horrid in nature but because his subconscious would not let him forget.

"Huh, look at this." Jacob pointed out with a smile on his face, admiring the tapestry with the woven images of Mac and Jacob on it, "It looks like a picture of us."

"Yeah. I guess we must be legends or something now." Mac said jokingly.

Chief Zorin glanced over at the tapestry and admitted, "Well, as far as most of the people here in the Realm are concerned, with what has been passed down, you are legends."

"Sick!" Jacob burst out. He liked the idea of being famous.

Making their way into the courtyard, Mac turned and asked Chief Zorin, "Where is Metsys? Or is he the head librarian after all this time?"

Chief Zorin was somewhat puzzled by what Mac meant, but he didn't dwell on it, "Actually Metsys died. His great-son Lionak should be here somewhere. I am surprised that he has not come and greeted us. Usually, he is aware of any changes in the magic of the Realm."

"Ah. Sorry about that, I didn't even think." Mac mumbled.

Chief Zorin nodded, understanding that they were not aware of what had transpired since their last crossing.

"I don't know about you guys, but I sure could use a drink of ale until Lionak figures out we are here." Jacob deflected though he was eager to taste that thick, salty, yet sweet ale he'd been so long without.

"Yeah! Let's go!" Mac agreed, trailing closely behind Jacob who was already half-way across the drawbridge heading towards the tavern he'd been to, from memory. It was the same one that they had been to in the company of the two barbarians, Baracuss and Loce.

Glancing back, Mac said, "Come on! We'll need a few gold coins to pay for this."

Reluctantly, Chief Zorin transformed into his human form and followed them into the main thoroughfare.

People garbed in different attire passed up and down the cobblestone streets, each fulfilling their own duties of work or pleasure. Some stopped along street vendors to buy food for the night, while others only glanced at the goods being sold. A heavily armored pair of guards passed them on the street, talking and laughing at each other, not noticing Mac or Jacob.

Mac and Jacob looked around with slight smiles etched on their faces, realizing how little this place had changed as well. The smells. The buildings. Even the people. It all seemed as if things had been frozen in time. Oddly, it was as comforting as their real homes. Off ahead

Jacob recognized the tavern. Scantily clad women, probably great-great grandchildren of those women they'd seen before, stood at the entrance providing a tantalizing glimpse of what they had to offer, in exchange for some gold. Music could be heard inside, resembling a deep-sounding violin and wind instruments he could not quite recognize. Laughter crept outside the tavern as they came up to it.

"My." Mac remarked, almost gawking at one of the young women.

Catching the familiar eye, she invitingly opened, "How are you doing?"

Mac felt his face blush a little as he and Jacob smiled in return as they entered the tavern, followed by Chief Zorin who could not resist the urge to look at the wenches for a moment, not really out of attraction but curiosity of the baiting and false courting ritual they engaged in for their trade. Once inside, they sat down at a vacant wooden table that had seen the edge of many blades over the years. Jacob waved down a rough looking woman that had just placed five tankards of ale at another table that was surrounded by five men bearing bent armor, jagged jerkins and long, scraggly hair. They were a rough bunch.

"Man, this is great!" Jacob proclaimed, "I never thought I would actually be happy to be back here again."

"I missed it. Definitely the most adventurous." Mac admitted.

"Well, just don't get killed again. Okay?" Jacob said seriously. Mac was one of the few true friends he had that he could really trust.

"Ah, no sweat, bro!" Mac said casually as the tankards were placed before them.

Chief Zorin paid the woman a few gold coins and she went off again into the crowd.

"Cheers!" Jacob said, raising his tankard.

"Cheers!" Mac and Chief Zorin returned as they clanked their tankards together and drank.

After a few top-offs, Mac placed his tankard on the table, noticing a beautiful woman working at a bar on the other side of the tavern. She was strikingly calm and collected in the tavern, yet appearing so delicate, a combination he'd not seen in such places before. Her shoulder-length blond hair was smooth and her petite frame clothed in a long-sleeved blue shirt and black pants, kept his attention for several moments.

After glancing over his shoulder to the woman that Mac was fixated on, Jacob looked back and finally said, "Why don't you go over there and talk to her?"

Mac tore his eyes from her, realizing he'd been outed, "I don't know." Truthfully though, although he had confided in no one, he was surprisingly shy when it came to cold-calling a woman. He never knew how to talk to them, how to act, what to do so that they would be attracted to him and, when he was younger, never really had the chance to develop that type of interaction. Consequently, to this day, he has that trepidation of women and rejection.

"Okay. Fine. I'll talk to her." Jacob blurted out, getting up and walking over to her.

"No!" Mac whispered heavily as his face blushed, but Jacob did not stop...just like a bulldog.

"Hello Miss. What is your name?" Jacob said coolly as he looked at her placing some dishes on a wooden shelf against the wall.

"I'm Regan." she replied flatly as she continued to work, glancing momentarily at Jacob, unimpressed.

"Well, Regan. My friend over there was wondering if you would like to have lunch with him sometime. Nothing special." Jacob said as he nodded towards Mac who was still seated at the table by Chief Zorin, acting as though he discovered a wooden splinter in his seat.

"Mister, I have a boyfriend." Regan blocked as she looked squarely at Mac. He was not particularly attractive, especially with those spectacles on. She was clearly too good for him.

"Alright, thanks." Jacob said, a bit disgruntled. He knew better than to push it with this one.

After Jacob sat back down at the table, Mac asked, "So what did she say?"

"Her name is Regan. And she has a beefcake already."

"Oh." Mac grunted. He knew he just wasn't the ideal man by most women's standards. While he was tall and muscular, he knew he lacked something. But such things rarely phased him now. He was slowly accepting the realization that he may never have a soulmate to cherish, to confide in, to share in life's experiences.

After taking another hearty drink, Chief Zorin said, "Well, go talk to her when she gets off work anyway. Just casual conversation. I think it would be good for you to be around a woman, at least for a little while."

"But, what about our meeting with Lionak?" Mac said, trying to get out of a potentially embarrassing situation.

"Don't worry about that. It is almost sundown now, so we will not be able to get much accomplished. I will go and look for Lionak. You two should stay here for the night." Chief Zorin stated as he got up from the table and placed a pouch of gold before Jacob.

"Are you sure?" Mac asked, hoping he would change his mind if he was questioned again.

"I'm sure." Chief Zorin replied sternly as he walked towards the door.

So, as the night wore on, Jacob and Mac talked of the old times…the good times they had together not only in the Realm but also their world. Occasionally they laughed and joked about things as friends do, and poked each other with harmless insults.

The once bustling tavern gradually emptied of people and after Jacob had taken several tankards of ale that only got better tasting with time, he finally got a room and left Mac by himself at the table. Slowly sipping his drink, Mac felt a bit more confident about talking to Regan than what he did when he had first seen her. With confidence inspired by the ale, he got up from the table and held onto its edge until he was able to balance himself. He grinned to himself in his drunkenness. Then, as casually as he could muster, trying rather hard not to look like he was drunk, Mac approached Regan with a smile that betrayed him.

"Hello," Mac started, not really knowing where to begin, "I'm Mac."

"Hi." Regan said as she walked behind a bar and glanced at him. Another drunk.

"So have you worked here for a long time?" Mac questioned, leaning on the bar with his hands.

"Yes, you could say that. So, where do you live?" Regan said, making idle talk, trying to appear interested until Mac would leave or just pass out.

Smiling at her, Mac piped up, "Well I'm not from around here. But I live with my grandmother at her house, and I'm studying to be an engineer."

'Oh, how noble. He lives with his grandmother. He doesn't even have a place of his own.' Regan thought to herself, *'He must be poor.'*

Regan, herself, was far from poor. Her father was a head merchant who had accumulated great wealth sailing the seas for furs, jewels and such things the Realm had rarely seen. And, all of her life she had been raised getting whatever she desired, charging credits to her father's name. He didn't mind. He wanted her to be happy. But gold could only buy so much happiness. When Regan began seeing men, poor men, she bought them things figuring it would lift them up, things like clothes, boots, and fancy things. Quickly, however, she realized that these men were taking advantage of her either to get into the good graces of her father, or simply for some gold.

Then she met another man, about a year after her last fling. He, too, had lived here in the city all of his life and he knew about her wealth. And she liked him. He always visited her at work, and gave her flowers. She liked flowers. He would even go out with her at night to acting shows and the like. But one day he had left her to join the service of the merchants. They still kept in contact through letters and she had believed that he would remain faithful to her because of their time together. Yet that was far from reality.

In places she knew not, and across the seas, he'd found the comfort of many women and, in his lustful youth, he explored all of those women. Samric knew that all he'd have to do in order to keep Regan in reserve and ultimately her riches, was to string her along and appeal to her emotions, commonly by letter. Then, when his ship would return, all he'd have to do is act so lonely around her, whisper sweet nothings and make those arousing sounds he knew stirred her, to find himself beneath her bedsheets. To Samric, the life of a merchant was great. Like most merchants, he knew that each woman that waited on him would never know of his other conquests. And, none of his fellow sailors would reveal his secrets. After all, they had their own. Consequently Regan, to this day, knows nothing about what Samric really does. She, like countless others, are left in the dark, like the back burner of a stove, waiting until they are needed.

"Really? My boyfriend Samric is studying to be an engineer." Regan countered heartily as if Samric was a god.

"Oh, that's great. Say, would you like to go out and take a walk or something?" Mac volunteered, unable to stop himself from saying it outright like that, though a walk probably was not the best social activity to engage in at that moment. But he wanted to change the subject, not interested in learning about competition, though such information could prove useful if he'd thought about manipulating her like others had done.

"Well, I guess I could." Regan responded, trying to satisfy Mac and get him to leave.

"Great! Could I walk you home then?" Mac said with a burst of confidence.

Frowning slightly, Regan replied, "No. I can manage that myself."

She didn't want him to know she was from a rich family. And she definitely didn't want him meeting her parents. She didn't want to work in the tavern her father owned like a commoner for any longer than she had to.

"Oh." Mac said, scratching his head, trying to think of what to say next, "Could I meet you here tomorrow then?"

Regan smiled, "Yes, of course."

She began to wonder if her father had something to do with Mac.

"Well, I'll let you get back to work then. I'm going to go ahead and call it a night."

With that, Mac smiled and waved at her before he turned and left for the room Jacob had bought with Chief Zorin's gold.

The next day came quickly to Mac as he awoke in an empty room. Jacob was gone. Getting to his feet and putting on his hiking boots, he went to the tavern and looked for Regan. After several minutes of searching to no avail, Mac began to ask people about her. Some told him she was a whore. Some told him she was a drunkard. But all of them told him she was rich. Though confused as to why she would be working at the tavern, for Mac, that was a new experience. Actually knowing a rich woman that could pay her own way through life. He thought it was amazing that a woman of such stature would spend her time with such a common man as himself. He'd always assumed that, to have a chance with such a woman, he had to have great wealth or power.

Unbeknownst to him, it was true in Regan's case. A man had to have something of great value, or be perfectly attractive for her to mingle. Little to Mac's knowledge, she wanted him about as longingly as a man yearned for castration.

Eventually evening came to the Realm and Mac never spotted Regan, which dragged his confidence down because she had given her word that she would meet him.

Mac had gotten his hopes up, and now sat at the wooden table in the tavern and simply drank his emotions away with each passing tankard.

"Hey!" Jacob announced, followed by Chief Zorin as they entered and hastily sat down beside him at the table.

"How did it go?!" Jacob inquired, smiling at Mac as a bald-headed man in his fifties came by and placed two tankards on the table and walked off.

"Real great. Fucking perfect." Mac grumbled.

"Hold on now. Just what happened?" Jacob asked stoutly, realizing that something was wrong.

"Well. I went and talked to her and set a casual meet-up for today." Mac said, drinking deeply of the contents of the tankard before he continued, "Except she never showed up. All day."

"Oh, bummer." Jacob said lowly, "Maybe she had something to do that could not wait."

"Maybe." Mac agreed, ready to forget the whole affair.

Chief Zorin, not wanting to see his friend grieve and curious to know the truth, pulled out a small quartz crystal ball that fit in the palm of his hand and began to conjure a simple seeing-eye spell that he had learned when he was just a child. Slowly the ball began to glow with blurred images and a rainbow of color bounced around in its midst until images slowly came into focus.

Wearily Mac looked at the ball and recognized the image of Regan around a few friends that were talking and drinking something.

"I knew it." Mac sighed in relief that his suspicions were correct. But he was rarely wrong.

"That bitch. She couldn't even drop a message to tell you she could not come?! What kind of woman is she? I'm sorry." Jacob rumbled, barely able to contain his disgust.

Chief Zorin tucked the ball back into his pocket and, with a raised eyebrow said, "I guess I was wrong about that one. This woman was not good for you. I should have felt her mind before I suggested what I did last night."

"Don't worry about it." Mac said after a long pause.

"Fuck her. There are always others." Jacob said, trying to cheer Mac up.

"True." Mac replied, turning the tankard on the table.

After a few moments, and wanting to forget the whole ordeal, Mac asked, "Did you find Lionak?"

"Well, no. I ran into a few Guardians of mine, and they had said he had gone to Mt. Reach to find magic to destroy the Baron that is at the Kingdom of Shek now." Chief Zorin stated.

"And you know those tanks that fired on us? They are down there now, tearing up the city." Jacob angrily added.

"Does he know it is the Baron?" Mac asked.

"No. Tomorrow we will go to Mt. Reach and tell him. There might be an easier way to deal with this situation if Lionak knows this evil is the Baron, not some unknown foe." Chief Zorin responded.

Getting up, Jacob said, "Come on. Now we must rest…enough drinking."

With that, they went to the room and Mac stretched out on the bed. Once Mac closed his eyes, Jacob went over to Chief Zorin and whispered, "Make sure he doesn't leave the room."

Realizing that Jacob had no intention of staying, Chief Zorin said, "Where are you going now?"

"I have some unfinished business." Jacob replied, clearly agitated, as he closed the door behind him.

Swiftly he strode through the tavern and out onto the street, scowling as he thought of all the needless pain his friend had gone through. Especially when that woman only had to come by for a few seconds and say she had something else to do. Following a few different streets largely empty of life, he came across a grand building made of fine mason work, twisted iron gates with spearheads on top along with a fine array of trimmed bushes leading to a door flanked by two turquoise pillars. Jacob knew this had to be the place he had spotted in the ball. Unknowingly, he had stumbled across the estate earlier in the day as he explored the city and some of the people in the area. His gut told him, as he crossed the pathway to the front door, that this was it. Knocking on it heavily, he could barely resist the urge to burst through the door and hunt her down.

Within a few seconds the door opened and a finely dressed, stocky barbarian man appeared before him and asked, "May I help you?" Surprisingly refined.

"Yeah, where is Regan?" Jacob demanded.

"She has said nothing of you, sir. I'll have to ask you to leave." the man said as he began to shut the door.

"Yeah?!" Jacob shouted at the man as he flung the door open and planted his fist squarely on the man's face just above the nose, "Why don't you leave this!"

The man fell limply to the ground, unmoving as a trickle of blood came from his nose. Evidently this barbarian didn't have any experience as a brawler.

Impatiently looking around, Jacob heard some faint laughter from the rear of the exquisite house, and moved forward. Within moments he thrust a pair of glass doors open as a crowd of young people, both male and female, turned and looked at him with surprise. Then he spotted her. Instantly his skin tingled.

She recognized him from the tavern. She knew he was Mac's friend.

Without hesitation, Jacob strode up to her, pushing several of her soft friends out of the way until he came right up to her form that was quivering slightly, but holding her ground.

"You bitch! Who the fuck do you think you are?! You're nothing more than a fucking maggot!" Jacob thundered at her with all his might, his eyes wide with anger. He knew, from a quick glance around the house, that her parents were rich. But that mattered not. It was the lack of basic respect for people in general that he saw in her…not telling Mac that she would not show up. That got to him the most, and was totally unacceptable.

"What are you talking about?" Regan lied. She knew exactly what he was talking about.

"You know exactly what I am talking about, you cunt!" Jacob exploded, causing her to drop the glass she was drinking from, onto the stone tile, shattering it at their feet.

Not able to contain himself for another moment, his arm flashed before him as the impact of his hand smacking her squarely on her cheek echoed through the courtyard, sending her to her back and causing several of her friends to jump from the sudden cracking noise.

"You ever do that again and I will hunt you down!" Jacob warned as he turned and thundered out of the courtyard, glaring at her friends, wanting any of them, even all of them, to challenge him.

Chapter Thirty-Nine

"I can't believe this." Cindy remarked to herself, sitting in the rear cabin of the troop transport, similar to those in use by Lt. Macerson. It smelled of old paint, oil and grease.

She glanced around in disbelief that she was now a prisoner of her own government. Cindy was not sure why they were taken prisoner. But she had an idea it had something to do with Zorin. Perhaps they wanted the dragon.

"Yes. I know. Now our excavation may never be completed!" Luis fumed, fiddling with a lighter in frustration until he was able to finally light another cigar.

"The excavation? Don't you see there is something bigger happening here?" Cindy scoffed, wondering if Luis knew what was happening.

Exhaling a thin cloud of gray smoke, he said, "Yes. I know what is going on here. But holding us serves no purpose. We know nothing about those others that went through that door. At least not enough to help our captors for whatever reason they are here for. Right now, we could be out amongst the ruins completing our excavation while these fools do whatever they came here to do. Oh, but no! As usual we must be interrogated countless times before we are let go."

Luis grunted and continued, "My life is excavation, Cindy. And as long as I am away from what gives me purpose, I feel lifeless. I need my work, and these fools have taken it from me for whoever knows how long."

Cindy looked at him with soft eyes. She always had the feeling that this excavation might be the last for Luis and now understood, although he didn't say it directly, that he knew this would be the last of his accomplishments.

Suddenly the hydraulic pistons hissed to life as the rear door opened up and came down to the sandy ground. A locking mechanism echoed through the small cabin and the air escaping the pistons ceased. Outside stood Agent Bradley flanked by two desert uniformed soldiers grasping their M16s at the ready.

"Sorry for our lack of hospitality but we were not expecting any guests." Agent Bradley said with a smirk on his face.

"Why don't you just cut the crap, okay?" Cindy thundered, already sure he was an interrogator of some type.

Instantly Agent Bradley's smirk vanished from his face as he entered the cabin and sat a few feet from Cindy, causing her to move away from him a few inches, suddenly feeling insecure.

"I like people that get right down to business. It saves me a lot of useless small talk." Bradley said firmly as he looked into Cindy's eyes and then continued, "We have been able to compile a lot of information about the two of you archeologists and I have to say your accomplishments have been impressive according to those we have talked to. I, on the other hand, don't give a shit. I could care less about a bunch of people who dig around and play with stones and broken pottery."

After looking outside for a moment he said, "Now I am here for one purpose that interests me. You see, our intelligence reports that a silver dragon was sighted here, and just in the past twenty-four hours has opened a doorway out of thin air and disappeared through it."

Cindy squirmed a little bit. She knew he was referring to Zorin.

Agent Bradley noticed but said nothing.

"Anyway, the part that interests us the most is that two humans went with him." Agent Bradley said, looking Luis squarely in the eyes.

Squinting his eyes slightly, Agent Bradley asked, "Who are your friends, and what is their purpose with that dragon?"

The cabin was deathly silent.

Agent Bradley chuckled lightly to himself and said, "We know you were with them. So. Tell me who were your friends and what was their purpose with that dragon."

"Look, all we know is that those two guys are from Oklahoma." Luis grumbled as he looked at Agent Bradley with a deep, hard stare, "Alright?"

A thin smile appeared on Agent Bradley's face as he said, "Good. That's good. Now you see, that wasn't so hard."

Luis puffed on his cigar, trying to maintain his composure. He couldn't get too excited for lack of a good heart. He'd had a stroke once before.

"Well, do you know their names?" he asked, becoming impatient with having to ask about every minute detail. But he rarely had an interrogation that was easy.

Cindy crossed her arms over her chest.

Luis dashed a few cigar ashes onto the floor of the cabin pretending not to hear that last question.

Getting up and exiting the cabin, Agent Bradley turned and said, "It looks like you will be here for quite some time."

Just as Agent Bradley turned and began to walk off, Luis shot out, "Hey! When can I complete my excavation?"

Agent Bradley stopped in his tracks, not bothering to look at Luis, and replied coldly, "You may never get the chance, my old friend."

Hearing the hydraulic piston hiss as the door closed, Bradley strode towards the armored trailer and entered, seeing General Lowinsky and John examining several displays showing a wide array of information about the recent dimensional door that had been opened.

"Well, those two men that left with the dragon were from Oklahoma." Agent Bradley said as he sat down in front of a computer terminal and began typing.

"Did you get any names? Do you know their purpose?" General Lowinsky asked, eager to piece everything together so that he could formulate a plan.

"No. The two are being less than cooperative in that respect." Agent Bradley admitted, "But at least I know where they are from and I can link up with the state database and find out exactly who they are with the visuals we've got."

Looking around for one of the photos, Agent Bradley asked, "Any of you seen the photo of those two?"

"Oh yeah. Right here." John replied, flipping through some recently acquired photos that were taken from the ground with long-range surveillance equipment.

Giving him the photo, Agent Bradley eagerly took it and fed it into a scanner, giving the computer an image to match to the photos in the state database. Almost instantly the photo appeared on the monitor and with the swift movement of a mouse, he placed a box around the faces of Mac and Jacob and pressed the enter key.

"Do you think this is going to work?" John asked, looking at the screen. He'd never explored the potential of the computer beyond typing an occasional letter to

Washington and many more hours playing first-person shooters.

"It should. The resolution of the photo was very good so a positive match should be made in a couple of minutes." Agent Bradley said confidently.

The 440-Gigahertz computer coupled with a fiber connection to the satellite dish outside the trailer, whirled in a flurry of activity, communicating with the state database it had just downloaded, running all of the photos through a sophisticated pattern matching algorithm. Within two minutes the computer returned a negative match on the subject Mac. After pressing a few keys, Agent Bradley called up the case profile of Jacob and had it print out on a laser printer while it was being called to the screen. Through a few complex connections into the military network, Janus also got the same data from the computer.

"Humm. No match on one of them. But I have a profile of the other here, a Jacob Quentin." Agent Bradley commented, taking the paper out of the printer as soon as it finished with the profile.

"Very interesting. It seems that our friend here is more than just a civilian crusader." Agent Bradley remarked as he pointed to the military records, "He has quite an interesting record. Currently active duty with over eight years of service, very high security clearance, and extensive combat training and deployments. I see here he has two children, one in the first grade and the other in third. He just so happens to be on vacation now."

"So, what do you think he's doing with the dragon?" General Lowinsky inquired.

Frowning, Agent Bradley confessed, "I don't know yet. But it must be something important. Given his skills, I would say that he would be an asset in many areas."

"I'm going to link up to the monolith in the Pentagon and see if I can't get a case profile on this other guy. Looks like I might have to go deep so it might take a while." Agent Bradley said as he began feverishly typing lines of information into the computer.

"Oh. Before I forget, send a few agents to Jacob's residence. We might be able to pick up some more information about these guys from his wife." Agent Bradly said to John as he continued rapping on the keyboard.

John walked over to a phone and dialed into a dedicated line at the headquarters of the CIA with the touch of a button via a secure satellite link.

Chapter Forty

The entrance to Mt. Reach was just exactly as Lionak's father had described it. But, in the books he had read, it said that where he stood lived Green Dragons surrounded by brilliant mounds of gold collected over the centuries. Obviously, that was no longer the case since Lionak knew that a barbarian warrior had taken the gold and raised his own Kingdom. He made a mental note to correct, or at least include a brief statement explaining the events since the writing of that book for future generations of wizards like himself.

Overhead, a large sphere anchored deeply into the ceiling of the cavern glowed a type of greenish-blue as Lionak descended the stone-carved staircase created long ago, unaware of it. Crossing the stairs downward, he found himself in a large cavern, upon a ledge that was surrounded by a vast expanse of placid water that radiated a soft white glow. He reasoned that this glow is what provided the cavern with light as he could see no other source.

Gripping his staff in one hand, he lowered its end into the water as several thin lightning bolts ascended out of the water, circling the staff until they reached its top and disappeared. Even after Lionak pulled the staff from the water he could feel a faint tingling sensation in his arm. The bolts of White Magic, even here at the mouth of this vast mountain was so pure and untainted that it was equally potent. That made Lionak shiver inside, knowing that the White Magic here could be tainted. It could be used by a sorcerer. And, it could be that some had already been taken away by such a sorcerer. But, the White Magic that Lionak sought was so powerful that no sorcerer, less than a master, could even attempt to taint it and use it for evil. Even a wizard such as himself could face death trying to use the strongest of White Magic, the very lifeline of the Realm and all the places it fed.

Noticing a flat, square shaped wooden log, split in half as to provide a standing surface on its top came towards him, he looked upon it as the beginning of his long journey to the very heart of the mountain. Stepping on its top after the log stopped before him, Lionak looked around the cavern. He could see the detailed webs of White Magic that were woven centuries ago by men such as himself that were unseen to the eye. Still, they endured, functioning as they were meant to from long ago. Some spells he could barely see and recognize since he had just begun to explore those specialties of magic. Nevertheless, he had tremendous respect for such wizards whom he considered far superior to his knowledge of the White Magic. He knew that what he was learning over his years of study were only formulas for harnessing magic that the ones before him created. Lionak wondered what spells the ancient wizards took with them to their graves that they trusted under no one's charge. Only the forefathers knew.

Ahead of him stood a jagged cavern wall which tauntingly displayed the grizzly outlines of several skeletons, some human and others grotesque, mauled shapes of creatures he could not identify and didn't know existed. It was as if the wall had consumed their flesh and kept their remains as a trophy, or a warning to others not to pass lest they face certain death. Waving his staff before him in a circular motion, Lionak noticed that the wall began to move back and forth as if it were the surface of a flowing river. Then parts of the wall began to disappear from sight in similar waves of motion until there was no longer a cavern wall. Lionak smiled at the cunning of the wizards who had put that elaborate illusion before him. It was so real and so detailed in every respect that a cavern wall should be in the eyes of those who viewed it.

After he passed the boundaries of that spell, he raised his staff again and the cavern wall reappeared behind him. Ahead of him the real cavern wall closed abruptly around a tunnel that was swallowed up in darkness amidst its unseen depths, not traveled for centuries. It seemed that in the tunnel the magical water did not illuminate the area as it did in the cavern. He thought it possible that perhaps it was the absence of the sheer volume of water that was in the cavern, or, it was another spell of some type.

As Lionak mentally wove a spell of light around the end of the wooden staff so that he could readily see, more out of curiosity of this strange and intriguing place than of fear, he began to think of his past. He thought of the times he had spent with his great-father Metsys in learning the art of magic. He remembered the grueling hours of study as a child forced to study about the Realm rather than playing with other children his age. Only now did he know that those times, through his great-father's diligence, was why he was here now. Admittingly, he made his share of mistakes when he was an apprentice just learning to weave the invisible magic and form spells. He remembered destroying pieces of the keep, though small, and even accidentally transforming a horse in the courtyard into a small garden of blossoming yellow flowers, which has remained to this day. But eventually, through practice, study and exposure to the White Magic, Lionak became a crafty and worthy wizard of his great-father's name.

Lionak's eyes became sullen as he thought to the day of his great-father's death. It had been overcast with gray clouds, on the precipice of spring in the Realm. A gentle breeze rolled through the keep as he gazed upon his great-father lying on his bed, struggling to breathe his last breaths of life. He had pleaded with Metsys to cast a spell upon himself that would extend his life for a few more seasons, but Metsys had refused. Metsys insisted that it was his time to progress to the next plane of existence, that his purpose on the Realm had been completed. And, with a whisper and a final conjuring of knowledge, Metsys gave Lionak what wisdom of the White Magic that he could prior to his form vanishing from before the crying figure of Lionak, kneeling at the side of his bed in a soft white haze of White Magic.

Mac peeled his eyes open, straining against the rays of the day's Sun flooding into the small room he'd been in for the duration of the night, unaware of what Jacob had done. His mouth was so dry it was hard to even swallow. It was as if there were razor blades stuck in the back of his throat, cutting and stabbing him every time he tried it.

"Man, I need a drink." Mac practically whined out, just as Chief Zorin entered the room, so quietly in fact, that if Mac had not been looking at the doorway, he wouldn't have known he was there.

"I would say so. You had quite a few tankards last night." Chief Zorin smirked, and then handed a cool water skin to Mac who eagerly took it and began drinking.

"You must forget about that girl. It serves you no purpose to think about something such as her." Chief Zorin said as he looked at Mac. He, himself, had wanted women as well, but due to his unavoidable destiny as Chief of the Guardians, precluded the commitment to a woman and the family which would follow.

"Yeah. I know. This isn't the first time it has happened to me you know." Mac replied dryly, continuing, "Don't worry. I soon forget."

Chief Zorin beamed in relief, not that he believed him but that the memory would dull and he would move on.

Getting out of bed, Mac said, "Well now. We must be off to warn Lionak."

"Yes. Mohawk, or should I say Jacob, is out in the tavern waiting for us." Chief Zorin commented as he followed Mac out of the room.

Spotting Mac and Chief Zorin, Jacob rose from his wooden chair and greeted them with an unusually big smile, proudly displaying a silver chest plate and finely crafted gauntlets, one of which was attached to a metal sleeve of sorts that covers his right arm up to a round shoulder plate. A sword hung at his waist, idle in its sheath.

"Looks like you're all ready." Mac remarked, practically gawking at Jacob. He truly looked like something out of the renaissance period.

"Oh yes. I am definitely ready. And, this stuff is for you." Jacob replied as he pointed to the table before him.

Upon it held an array of equipment that Mac seemed to prefer in the tabletop campaigns he would involve himself in, when playing Warriors of the Realms. Among those items were a slightly weathered torso of leather jerkins with accompanying forearm jerkins, a freshly oiled bastard sword, still in its sheath which appeared to be new, and a gleaming, tempered steel helmet with four white horns evenly spaced along its circumference, with leather jerkin straps connected in a fashion to the helmet so as to protect his ears and the rear of his neck in battle while still giving the wearer flexibility to turn his head with little resistance. Mac smiled with pure amazement.

"Now that is some lit shit!" Mac exclaimed after a moment as he picked up the bastard sword and wrapped his hand around its grip. It felt good. He could almost instantly feel the deadly power of the sword. Those sharpened edges pleading to be used.

"Well, let's get this stuff on so we can get out of here." Jacob urged, ready to get on with more pressing matters.

Within the space of a few minutes, Mac was fully dressed and strode outside with Chief Zorin and Jacob, grinning. He almost felt invincible with all that armor.

Chief Zorin swiftly changed into his dragon form and patiently waited until both Jacob and Mac were on his back before he took flight, sending dust and stray pieces of hay into the air around them. A few chickens clucked and screeched in their cages at the sudden gust of wind created by Chief Zorin as he gained altitude and flew away.

After ascending high into the early day's sky and having evened out, he turned his scaly silver head towards his riders and said, "This land, as pure as it is, cannot fully be felt until one has reached into the skies. Only then can one feel the quiet presence, the very life of the Realm beneath you."

Mac looked down to the ground which was nothing more than a green carpet with an occasional jutting hill reaching past the tops of the forest, in a sense demanding to be noticed like a rosy pimple. A twisting stream which found its way south was called the Stream of Life. Mac knew it well. For the last time he was here, he had crossed it with Jacob and Baracuss – known now as the founder of the Kingdom of Shek. But it hardly seemed like a Stream of Life, as some strange creature had consumed his horse. Mac frowned at those drifting thoughts and wondered if the creature had been destroyed, or had died after all of this time.

"Every time that I fly these skies I can feel the pure White Magic of the Realm, untainted. But now it is different. The Dark magic is consuming it like a slow-moving glacier." Chief Zorin continued with a quiet, almost undetectable hatred for the Dark Magic he had thought was long destroyed.

"Yeah, well this time let's kill the Baron once and for all." Jacob shouted out in the tone of a warrior.

Chief Zorin nodded his large head in agreement and turned it straight ahead, veering to the left slightly, headed towards a large mountain that seemed only as big as one's thumb, off in the distance before them. As they closed upon the jagged mountain, the flowing heart of the White Magic, Mac felt as though he could somehow feel the radiating power of the White Magic, the very pulse of the Realm. He thought it strange that he did not feel it the first time he had been to the Realm.

Within about ten minutes of flight, Chief Zorin descended onto the ledge of the mountain, flapping his leathery wings as his mighty clawed feet reached out and found the surface of the ledge. Adjusting his balance, Chief Zorin folded his wings to his sides and walked forward enough to allow Mac and Jacob room to climb off. After they did so, he transformed into his human form and led them into the cavern and down the stone-carved staircase. At its end, on a small ledge of stone, they awaited the approach of the raft they had used centuries ago in search of the Sword of Dragon Slaying.

Chapter Forty-One

Bodies were scattered around thickly as fallen leaves in a forest. Blood discolored the earth below them and the stench of freshly opened entrails hung in the almost still air. Such a foul smell would make most hurl, less those that had survived many battles in like conditions. Stiff bodies of both the barbarians and soldiers were riddled with fatal wounds made from rifles, battleaxes and even claws. But the claws neither came from the soldiers or the barbarians, but from the Guardians of White Magic who had made it to the Kingdom of Shek. Their size, power and magical abilities had proven crucial to providing the remnant of barbarians with an advantage. The only thing which kept the remaining soldiers alive was the technological supremacy of their tanks and the destructive might of their heavy weapons.

"Eric, move your tank around one-hundred and thirty degrees right!" Captain Reeves ordered in exhaustion, having been fighting sporadically through the night. But he and his men were trained well under conditions of extended sleep deprivation for situations like this.

Captain Reeves could see the mighty Silver Dragon closing on the other tank fast with another gaining upon them. He knew that Eric, the other tank commander, would have to act fast to evade the dragon long enough to get the sights of the tank's barrel on it and destroy it. Captain Reeves himself would have shot the dragon, but his tank was being attacked and his situation was bleak, if not worse than Eric's. Already they had killed five such dragons but three others still assaulted them and he had seen others disappear into the heart of the city, although it was hard for him to say how many in his flurry of activity to stay alive. Even thoughts of the President's well-being were far and few in his mind at this point.

The main computer targeting system was now inoperative from the endless blasts of fire that the dragons had dealt out. Numerous other systems faded in and out of operation throughout the night, but luckily his engine systems had not suffered any substantial damage. His satellite communications system had also been destroyed. His only operable communications system was a simple FM unencrypted system.

"Captain, our fuel status is reaching critical. We will have to shut down our turbines and switch to pistons if we want to move around much longer at all." the tank driver reported, sweat rolling off his face. The countless blasts of fire that the dragons had inflicted onto the tank had caused the cabin's temperature to exceed almost one hundred and five degrees, its environmental system inoperative. The tank's walls and outer armor were hot to the touch…almost as hot as burning coals.

"Damn!" Captain Reeves spat at the onset of more bad news. He knew that the small over-bored piston engines, one per track that could be manually switched from track sprocket to a simple drive line feeding the wheels array if the linked track was destroyed, were meant to keep the tank mobile for up to one hundred miles if the main engine failed, could not move the tank at speeds greater than thirteen miles per hour. They were simply too underpowered and slow to out-maneuver the dragons.

"Report gunner." Captain Reeves ordered as he continued to watch the movements of the dragons outside the tank.

"Barrel count…four." the gunner replied quickly as he glanced at the manual level indicator for the 120mm rounds. His primary computer systems no longer functioned.

Captain Reeves grimaced. It took two rounds to kill one dragon. He didn't have enough.

Suddenly the tank rocked to one side and then back as one of the dragons blew a thick cone of fire at them.

"Evasive maneuvers!" Captain Reeves shouted, paying too much attention to Eric's tank movements. As he sat in the turret's cockpit, he turned it about as the damaged tank jumped forward with a full blast of torque from the powerful gas turbine that had made the tank out-maneuver the dragons with its incredible speed.

Pulling on a steel joystick with his left hand, the turret whined as it turned until he placed the manual crosshair sights onto the dragon's chest. The dragon, running after the tank with its mighty wings outstretched, was unable to keep up with the velocity of the tank which had already reached a speed of fifty miles per hour. The dragon bellowed out another cone of fire at the tank, just licking its tail end.

Flawlessly, Captain Reeves flipped a few switches and manually altered the direction and elevation of the tank's barrel and shot. A mighty thunder roared out as a thick cloud of expended powder burst from the barrel's end. As soon as the cloud dispersed enough for him to see, he flipped some controls over to the Vulcan canon. The six large barrels began to spin as he wiped his brow with his dirty hand.

"Turn us about! Straight for that dragon!" Captain Reeves ordered.

The tank turned about as the tracks dug deeply into the earth, sending pillars of dust and clumps of dirt into the air.

Almost as soon as the tank completed the turn, he pressed one of the red buttons on his joystick and the Vulcan canon hammered out rounds so fast it sounded like a whining dirt bike. Smoke fumed out of the rotating barrels as he continued firing, the tank closing on the dragon. Even from his distance of almost one hundred and fifty meters, he could see sparks flying off the dragon coupled with silver scales and what he thought was blood. He squinted his eyes in hatred as he continued firing, literally tearing a hole in the dragon's chest.

Limply the Silver Dragon fell to the ground just as the tank came upon it and ran over one of its leathery wings, sending shreds of it into the air.

"Got him sir!" the gunner reported in relief.

Captain Reeves sighed for a moment and called out to Eric's tank, "Eric, report!"

Static crackled over the com-link until a faint voice could be heard, "Commander! Three bogies are airborne at seven hundred meters south, closing fast! These two chaps on my ass are a bit of a problem!"

"Roger that! Bring yourself north and head toward me. I'll give you cover!" Captain Reeves responded as he turned the turret to the south.

"We're not going to make it are we, sir?" the gunner asked Captain Reeves in a serious, yet surprisingly calm voice.

"Soldier! We will make it because we are smarter than these damn overgrown iguanas!" Captain Reeves forcefully reassured him as he looked at him with hard eyes, "We've made it too far to just quit now!"

Truthfully, Captain Reeves knew there was no way of beating the odds. Already he had lost all of his carriers and all but two tanks. Even for the two that remained, without reinforcements, survival was little more than a dream.

Slowly the tank closed on them and the dragons trailed not far behind, flapping their wings and breathing fire at the fleeing tank who was slowly gaining distance from them.

"Come on. Come on." Captain Reeves whispered to himself, helpless to do anything just yet as he formulated a plan in his head. It was the only real option he had left.

As the tank rumbled up to them, Captain Reeves flipped a few control switches and grasped the joystick. Placing his thumb carefully over the red button, he patiently turned the barrel towards the first of two dragons that pursued the tank. After the tank had past them, he fired a 120mm round at the dragon, and then another as soon as the barrel reloaded itself with that familiar double-thud of steel against steel. The impact of the second round caused the dragon to explode into several pieces.

Then, as quickly as the turret could manage, Reeves sighted the second dragon and blasted it with his last 120mm round as well. But this one was different. Instead of the dragon reeling back from the explosion and a dark spot appearing on its torso, a blue globe flashed around its body as the round exploded.

"What the hell?" he whispered to himself in disbelief. *'Had they gotten some type of shield technology?'*

Not wasting another precious moment, Captain Reeves flipped a switch and opened up on the Silver Dragon with the Vulcan canon. Sparks and small bolts of lightning flashed over the blue sphere that enveloped the dragon each time a round hit it. Still the dragon came at him.

"Get us out of here!" Captain Reeves shouted out to his navigator who jolted the tank forward and veered it sharply to the left.

"Commander! Get out of there!" Eric warned through the FM set, "I have a lock on the dragon. I'm going to hit him with everything I've got!"

Captain Reeves smiled in relief. Some of Eric's targeting systems must still be functioning.

"Full throttle!" Captain Reeves ordered as he continued firing on the dragon with his canon as he turned the turret to compensate for the change in direction of the tank.

"Fire!" Eric ordered to his gunner who, with the touch of a button, caused the 120mm barrel and Vulcan canon to fire at the dragon simultaneously.

The computer was deadly accurate. From Captain Reeve's view, he saw a mighty explosion on the left side of the dragon that caused it to stumble. The rounds from the two Vulcans pounded and shredded the dragon's scales, the blue globe no longer visible. A second blast from Eric's barrel blew the Silver Dragon from his sight.

"Thanks for the assist, tank one." Captain Reeves sighed over the com-link.

"Ah, no sweat. That chap was giving me a hard time, so I thought I'd give him a run!" Eric responded with a smile on his dirty face.

"What are we going to do with those other dragons that are airborne, sir?" he asked, looking to his gunner's monitor which showed the three dragons flying within five hundred meters of their position.

"We are going to run. I have no ammo left, except for the 300 in the Vulcan. I haven't got enough fuel to dance anymore. I noticed a dirt road off head to the northwest of here when we breached. Let's see if we can get on that road and get the hell out of here!"

"Roger!" Eric said as he followed the commander's tank to the road at almost full throttle, the tanks rocking back and forth over the uneven terrain.

"Three bogies are at eight hundred meters now, sir!" Eric reported to Captain Reeves after glancing to his gunner's radar with rangefinder capability.

"Good." Captain Reeves responded, "We're going to try something new here."

"Yeah, go ahead sir." Eric replied, wondering what the captain was going to do.

"I'm going to get out of the tank and transfer all our fuel and ammo to your tank." Captain Reeves said into the com-link.

"Okay. It will be close. So where do you plan to stop?" Eric asked. He knew a fuel transfer between two tanks could take a couple of minutes at least, and he also knew the dragons could gain considerable ground in that time.

"Just come along side my tank. I'll do the transfer while we are moving." Captain Reeves responded plainly.

"What?! That's unheard of, laddy!" Eric grunted in disbelief of doing such a thing.

"Just do it!" Captain Reeves rumbled into the com-link as he opened the hatch on his tank, the refreshing, cool wind rushing past him.

"Roger, Sir." Eric responded on the com-link with his sandy colored eyebrows raised.

Looking at his navigator, Eric said, "You better keep it damn steady or I'll be on your ass like pubes on a jock strap. You smelling what I'm cooking?"

"Yes sir!" the navigator replied, carefully steering the tank next to the commander's.

Cautiously Captain Reeves pulled himself out of the tank and backed towards the rear of the tank, keeping a firm hold on the iron bars that served as cargo anchors. Then he went over to the right side of the tank and opened a steel compartment containing a large plastic hose. With that in his right hand, he backed further down and opened a large plug on the rear of the tank. Letting it fall freely to the ground, he inserted one end of the hose into the fuel tank, after removing the strainer, as far as it would go before he turned around and pulled another bulky, circular shaped object out of the compartment that had a long steel handle on its end. Quickly he attached the other end of the hose to one of the inlets of the manual pump and set it down on the tank, knowing he would have to jump to the other tank and do the same with the hose.

But, looking up, he saw the form of Eric crouched on the other tank with a hose in his hand.

"Well sir, I couldn't let you have all the fun!" Eric shouted to Captain Reeves with a big smile. He loved the challenge and excitement.

"I guess not!" Captain Reeves shouted back as he stretched over the side of the tank and took the end of the hose from Eric and placed it on the other inlet of the pump. Once he had it firmly on the pump he began to push and pull on the lever as he saw waves of yellowish-white fluid travel through the hose.

"You know, I'd have to say this is the craziest think I've ever done! I mean, who transfers fuel from one tank to another while it's rolling down the street!" Eric shouted at him, trying to keep himself from thinking about just how crazy it really was.

"It's my first time!" Captain Reeves admitted as he continued, fervently pumping the fuel out of his tank and into the other.

Within about a minute and a half, Captain Reeves stopped pumping seeing that almost no fuel was flowing through the hose. Quickly placing it on the back of the tank, he pulled himself over the turret and shouted into the cabin, "Come on! Lock the tank into its current course and let's get out of here!"

Immediately the gunner seemingly flew from his seat and out of the hatch and assisted the captain with unloading the canon while the navigator flipped a few controls to lock the tank into autopilot. Then he, too, scurried out of the tank in a rush. Helping them over to the other tank, Captain Reeves then jumped over to be held tight from rolling off the tank with the help of Eric and his two soldiers.

With no words passing between them, they all crammed into the cabin of the tank, now incredibly small with three additional people in its bowels. After Captain Reeves took the turret seat he ordered, "Full throttle!"

Turning a sharp corner in the road, causing everybody to shift in the tank, Captain Reeves glanced outside the hatch behind the tank, watching his tank plow into the forest, folding over trees and sending branches and leaves high into the air. Within a second, he could faintly hear the sounds of the collision above the thunder of the tank's main engine.

Captain Reeves relaxed and thought about what to do next.

Chapter Forty-Two

The doorbell chimed lightly causing Bev to sit up from the reclining chair and turning the television down with the remote control. Then she slid off the chair and went to the door, pulling her blue jeans up by the belt loops. Opening the thick wooden door, she found two men dressed in black suits with mirrored sunglasses looking at her with blank faces.

"Yes?" Bev said, wondering if something was wrong. In the back of her mind, she could not help but think that something had happened to Jacob.

"What can I do for you?" She said firmly with a slight frown.

"I'm Agent Johnson and this is Agent Wallace. We are from the CIA and need to ask you a few questions." the bald-headed man said as he pulled out a wallet containing his identification, casually showing it to her.

After looking at it for a moment, not knowing what an official identification card or badge actually looked like, Bev said, "Well, okay. What do you want to know?"

Looking around briefly Agent Johnson asked, "May we come inside?"

Bev didn't like inviting strangers into her house without her husband's presence, but she had a feeling that their appearance was linked to Jacob. Uneasily she pulled the door open enough for them to pass and she closed it behind them. Then she turned and led them into the living room and pointed to a plush couch for them to sit in. They did so without hesitation.

"So, what do you want to ask?" Bev inquired, eager to get this whole affair going so she could get some information of her own.

"We were sent her by General Lowinsky in Cairo. He saw your husband there." Johnson said as he took off his sunglasses and stuffed them into the inner pocket of his armored suit jacket.

"How is my husband?" Bev probed, eyes widened with curiosity.

"As far as we know, he's fine. Umm, but what do you know about why he would be in Cairo? From what we can tell, he never filed any paperwork indicating he would be out of the country in order to take a trip to Egypt. And his friend, Mac, had no passport on record."

Leaning on one of the arms of the reclining chair as she sat down Bev said, "I really don't know why he would be at Cairo. I know he was hiking here with Mac before that other guy showed up."

Agent Johnson's gray eyes sparkled at the mention of 'the other guy' and he asked, "Who was this other guy?"

Bev smiled and commented, "You would not believe me. I didn't even believe it."

Agent Wallace looked at him and then looked squarely at Bev, "Oh, yes, we would. Was this other man, by chance, a dragon?"

Bev's eyes dashed over to him with a startled expression as a tingly sensation shot through her body, "Why yes! He was a dragon. At least for a little bit. Have you seen him, too?"

"Yes."

Bev was elated by the news. At last, there was someone she could talk to about what had been going on.

"Could you tell us about this man? We know nothing about him, or why your husband is with him."

Agent Johnson asked smoothly, impatiently waiting for any words to come out of her mouth.

"Well," Bev began, "I know that his name is Zorin. Umm, Chief of the Guardians or something like that. He said he had come from the Realm. I thought it was just nonsense."

Bev smirked and continued, "That is, until I saw him change…change into a silver-colored dragon."

"Do you know what he was doing here?" Agent Johnson questioned.

Frowning as she thought for a moment, Bev replied, "Ahh, I remember him saying something about a Baron when he was looking at our television when the news was on. It was something about Cairo. Then he got all anxious to go there and he left with my husband and Mac."

A tear began to well up in her eye as she whispered, "Just like that."

In an effort to comfort Bev, Agent Johnson went over to her and gave her the white handkerchief from his suit pocket and asked quietly, "Do you know anything else?"

In truth he didn't care about her emotional state, but was merely following his training to gain trust of the target.

After wiping the tear from her eyes she said, "No. Is my husband alright?"

"We believe so." Agent Wallace said as straight forward as he could.

"What do you mean, you believe so?" Bev tossed out with a slight, angry tone in her voice.

"The only thing that we've been told right now is that he is with Mac and Zorin in Cairo." Agent Wallace said, not wanting to tell her that they had gone through some type of door, apparently to this Realm.

Almost immediately after he said that, everyone noticed that it became dark outside and the wind could be heard knocking bushes and chimes against the house. Swiftly, both agents darted over to the window, looking for a developing storm or a tornado. Tornadoes were often unpredictable in the region and, as both agents were raised in the state, knew all too well what could happen in seconds. But, as they looked outside to the sky, joined by Bev, something was oddly peculiar. None of them had seen such a storm before. It was focused over the house, twisting and swirling around a focal point which they could not see from their limited vantage point. The clouds became even darker as scraggly lines of lightning danced around in the clouds in a random fashion. The mighty thunder claps and crackles of lightning startled Bev as she stepped away from the window, plainly scared of what was going on.

"Come on! Let's get to the basement!" Bev shouted at the two agents turning to follow her.

Just as they found themselves in the hallway near the front door, a sudden gust of wind knocked their feet from under them as small white globes appeared in the living room, circling around a twelve-foot area. At the sheer speed with which the globes raced about the room, it was impossible to say just how many there were, but it was safe to say that at least twenty of them circled about, casting pure white light on the walls and furniture.

Within a few fleeting seconds the globes began shooting finger-thick lightning bolts about as their pattern of flight closed to ten feet. Then six feet. Then three feet. Bev could feel the hair on the back of her neck stand out as if she were in the midst of an intense static field. Her heart raced with fear, not knowing what to do other than stare at the globes, helpless.

The two agents managed to get to their feet and pulled out their 9mm service pistols, squinting into the midst of the bright circling globes, ready to shoot whatever it was that was causing all of this.

"Get back!" Agent Johnson shouted at Bev, his jacket fluttering behind him with the wind.

But Bev didn't appear to hear him as she slowly stood up erect, her fear subsiding as it was replaced by intrigue of the strange phenomena. She felt a sense of friendship radiating from whatever it was.

Suddenly the globes clashed together in a blinding flash of light and the entire room was consumed with pure whiteness. As the light faded away, a stream of gold, powdery dust began drawing the outline of something immense that filled most of the living room. Slowly the image became clear to Bev. She stared at the golden eyes of this grand creature as its translucent form materialized from the dust, realizing that it was a Silver Dragon, flawless in every detail. Its wings, even as she gazed upon it, folded up behind the dragon. Then the dragon turned its head slightly to the two cowering agents that didn't know what to do, and then twisted its mighty head towards Bev.

Bev smiled in complete awe.

In a female voice none of them knew, the Silver Dragon said to Bev, "I am Angela, Chief of the Guardians of White Magic. You have summoned me through a promise I made centuries ago. I am here to fulfill my promise. Tell me your bidding, wife of the one who had destroyed the Dark Magic."

Chapter Forty-Three

The devastation of the Kingdom of Shek was appalling to King Doron as he peered out to the ruins before his palace. He could barely fathom that a small band of outsiders could destroy so much in such little time. Most of his people were dead and he cursed to himself for not being able to protect them. But the evil he was willing to raise his sword against, in perhaps a futile confrontation, had just disappeared. He knew now that the evil he sought to destroy was the one thought long ago to have been killed. And, to him, the Baron seemed to have more power now than what he had read about, when the Baron tried conquering the lands centuries ago.

Shifting his stance somewhat on the flat roof of his palace, King Doron frowned in quiet rage knowing he would have to avenge the needless deaths of his people and battle the Baron himself even if no others would join him.

"Doron," a man dressed in white flowing robes began as he walked up to the King, "the Guardians have repulsed the attackers under the Baron."

Doron turned around and faced the man he knew as Matthew, High Priest of the Guardians who was second in rank to Chief Zorin himself.

"Good. Are they all irradicated?" King Doron asked, placing his hands on his waist. His barbaric instincts told him a battle was only won if one's enemy lay before him dead.

"Well, not all." Matthew replied as a gentle wind blew through his shoulder-length brown hair, "Two of those war machines managed to escape, although we found one buried in the forest."

"They all must be destroyed!" King Doron rumbled, throwing his arms into the air out of frustration.

"I understand." Matthew said flatly, trying to calm the King down, "A few Guardians are looking for it now."

Exhaling deeply, King Doron grunted, "You know, it's going to be hard to find it with two Guardians, Matthew. At least send some Guardians with practiced magic skills."

Matthew looked out upon the Kingdom for a moment collecting his thoughts before he looked back at King Doron, "I know you want that thing destroyed but I can't afford to send my better Guardians to chase the machine down. That could be exactly what the Baron wants so that he can continue whatever he is doing."

The King grimaced in disappointment but knew Matthew was right. Regardless, he wanted the war machine destroyed. If required, he would do it himself.

"Speaking of the Baron," King Doron said, "where is he? Have you been able to find him?"

"No. One moment he was here radiating powerful Dark Magic and the next he was gone." Matthew confessed.

"I don't understand his tactics. Why would he come here with those damn things, kill a dragon in the depths of the palace and just disappear?"

Matthew put a hand on Doron's shoulder and said, "I don't know. But I'd bet that he still wants what he did centuries ago. The Realm."

Sweat poured from the soldiers as they finished putting camouflage nets over the tank, tucked away in the forest. Luckily for them the forest camouflage nets that were issued to the tank, purely from the mistake of a supply officer, were still in the tank's compartments; they were supposed to have been issued desert netting. Even though Captain Reeves had debated about removing them, he never got the opportunity due to several snap deployments.

Wiping the sweat from his face, Captain Reeves sat down on the end of the tank next to Eric, who was drinking from his plastic canteen. The tank's skin was still somewhat warm from the bombardment of dragon fire.

"Do you think the President is alive in that city?" Captain Reeves asked, looking into the quiet forest. He speculated that with those dragons around, he surely would have been killed.

Eric's eyebrows raised, "In that hell hole? I'd say he's dead, if not from those cave people, then from those blasted dragons. I've never seen the like of all that before, Captain."

Eric shrugged his shoulders and continued, "This is all too odd. It's almost like we're on a different planet or something."

"Yeah, I'm beginning to think that we are on our own out here. I don't even know where we are. I went through all the tactical maps and the satellite computer's storage and none of them give any clues." Captain Reeves agreed.

Putting his boonie cap on, Captain Reeves said, "Well, it's time to begin rationing our supplies and initiating a guard. Everyone will have a four-hour guard of the immediate area. I don't want anyone getting lost in this bush."

"Roger that sir, I'll get right on it." Eric responded as he pushed himself off the tank and headed towards the small gathering of soldiers that were in the process of setting up cots to sleep on when nightfall came.

Captain Reeves heard a few of the men moan as Eric gave out the orders, but he ignored it knowing that it would serve no purpose to jump already strained men. He, too, was tired after the long battle with the dragons and realized they would be as well.

Getting off the tank, Captain Reeves rounded up his web gear and snapped it around his waist as he went over to his M16 that had an M203 grenade launcher attached to it. Slinging it over his shoulder, he found Eric standing beside him.

"Going somewhere Captain?" Eric inquired as he put his web gear on as well.

"Yeah. Looks like we might be here for a while so I'm going to do a little recon and get a better picture of just where we are." Captain Reeves responded, clicking the switch on his infrared goggles to make sure they worked.

Captain Reeves smiled inwardly, noticing that Eric was getting ready to go with him. Eric had always been very perceptive and an excellent commander with troops. Such a combination was rare in a person, and Captain Reeves was glad he had such a person serving in what remained of his detachment. Together they headed out of camp north through the plush green forest.

Twisting through the forest for several hours and pausing occasionally to drink from their canteens, they came across a large stone wall they could see through the trees a good four hundred meters ahead. As far as they could see, the wall spanned both directions. Indeed, it was large.

"What do you think sir?" Eric whispered to Captain Reeves as they crouched behind some thick, thorny bushes.

"We'll wait here until nightfall and see if we can't climb that wall and see what's on the other side." Captain Reeves replied lowly, making sure the ammo clip was securely seated in his rifle.

Eric wasn't much in the mood for scaling walls, especially of that magnitude, but he said nothing as he drank from his canteen and waited.

Seated in a soft leather chair, Regan read a book on the history of the Realm. She didn't like such classes in the least because she saw no reason why studying about the past could help her out in the present. And, as equally useless, she did not understand why her father wanted her to work in a tavern. After all, the only things she saw were illiterate, sloppy folks she thought should be nothing more than servants. But not her servants. No, they were all too ill-mannered to be her servants. If they were, they would first have to be trained under the whip. Only then, maybe, could they become servants of hers.

Bored, Regan exhaled, whining slightly as she skimmed the pages of the lesson, eager to be done with it. Then she saw a hand-drawn picture that caught her attention. Sitting up and squinting at the picture with the light cast from the torches along the walls of the garden, dimly realizing that the sun had set, she muttered to herself in awe and disbelief.

"That can't be." Regan whispered, looking at the picture which resembled that of Mac and his friend she'd been smacked by. Impulsively she touched her cheek.

Immediately she read the page and quickly learned that these two were the bearers of the Wild Magic said to be more powerful than the Realm's magic, and that they came to destroy the Baron. Continuing, she read that they had returned to their land over three centuries ago after the Baron had been destroyed. Her mind whirled as she tried to explain to herself how they could be alive, and here in the Realm after so much time.

Slowly closing the book and standing up, one conclusion stuck in her mind. They must be gods. How else could they still be alive? Regan didn't know why the one, Mac, was interested in her, but began to regret putting him off like she did. If she had only known of them before.

A loud crashing sound burst out in the garden. Regan whirled around, frightened from the sudden thud of metallic sounds, snapping her out of her calculating thoughts of what it would have been like to be in the company of a god.

"Damn it!" Captain Reeves muttered to himself as he managed to get to his feet, thankful that no bones were broken from the fall. He had thought the stone wall would be stable for his weight as he looked over the city to spot points of interest to recon, only to find out differently.

Within a second, Eric jumped down after the captain, rolling forward. Planting his feet firmly and allowing his slowing momentum to raise his body until he was standing, he held his rifle out in a defensive posture.

"Ho there lady!" Eric commanded, swiftly blocking Regan's entrance to the house.

"What do you two want?" Regan lashed out in fear of these two strangely dressed men, taking a step away from Eric.

Rubbing the top of his head before he put his boonie cap back on, Captain Reeves said, "Would you please keep it down? We are not going to harm you in any way."

Regan spun around and looked at Captain Reeves. Still, she didn't trust them and thought that they might be pirates from the seas here to murder her father, even though he was not here. Such an attempt had occurred when she was just a child.

"We just want to ask a few questions and you'll never see us again, okay?" Eric told her honestly.

"Well, be quick about it." Regan retorted, waiting for the right time to run and call her servants to protect her. Her life was more valuable that theirs.

"What is this place?" Captain Reeves asked, slinging his weapon.

"What?" Regan mumbled at the question.

"Where are we?" Captain Reeves said, re-phrasing the question.

"You're in the Realm under the protection of Lionak." Regan replied awkwardly.

"Who is Lionak?" Captain Reeves followed, resting a hand on one of the ammo pouches latched to the waist belt of his web gear.

Frowning, Regan asked, "Who are you?"

"Look, we'll answer your questions as soon as you answer ours, alright?" Captain Reeves sighed.

Regan glared at him for a moment before she capitulated, "Lionak is a wizard that protects the Land. Now, where are you from?"

"Lady, we are not from around here, if you could not already tell." Eric blurted out, not in the mood to play little games.

"Hey! My name is Regan, not lady!" she shot out at Eric who raised his eyebrows in surprise at her sudden viciousness. The last person that called her lady found himself with a red handprint on his face that stung for several days.

"Regan. Can you tell me where the U.S. Embassy is and we'll leave." Captain Reeves stated softly.

"The embassy? What is an embassy?" Regan responded, puzzled at that word. These men sure were strange.

Shrugging his shoulders, Captain Reeves turned and headed for the wall. He knew his identity was no longer secret, but he could not just kill an innocent woman out of cold blood. Besides, he didn't see any dragons in the city when he stood on the stone wall which had been his real problem. He figured that by the time news would travel around to anyone that cared, he'd be long gone. The whole place seemed to be void of any technology.

"Oh, wait!" Regan called out after them, finally piecing it together.

"You're from the other Land, aren't you?" she said confidently. She knew she was right.

"Well, yes." Captain Reeves replied, trying to figure out what she was getting at.

Smiling, Regan said, "I knew it! Then you know these two."

Regan hastily flipped the book open to the page with Mac and Jacob drawn on it and gave it to Captain Reeves.

Captain Reeves looked at the picture, not recognizing them.

"Who are they?" Eric asked, looking at the picture.

"They are the ones that saved the Realm by killing the evil Baron. They came from another place...your Land. Through a portal." Regan responded almost instantly, proud of her discovery.

That caught Captain Reeves' interest. That wall with all the lightning bolts that he'd gone through must have been the portal she was talking about. Surely they would know what was going on.

"Where are they?" Captain Reeves asked with new-found hope.

Taking the book, Regan said, "They were at a tavern a few days ago where I work."

Not wanting to get her involved, but finding he had no choice unless he paraded around the city in his clothes that were sure to draw some attention, Captain Reeves asked, "Could you bring them here?"

"Sure, but it will be a little while." Regan replied with a sparkle in her eyes. She had found a way of meeting Mac...a legend that had wanted her, of all the people he could have chosen.

Turning, she strode through the house as her heart pounded with a wanting of Mac, who she knew could fulfill her dreams. She smiled at the thought of having whatever she wanted, and being immortal like he was. Surely a god could give that to her.

Chapter Forty-Four

"What?" General Lowinsky said into the phone.

The man repeated what he had said to the general. Still, General Lowinsky could not believe that a dragon had just appeared at Jacob's residence, taken Bev and simply disappeared. Already he could see the manpower under his command thinning out with all the targets that had to be monitored.

"Damn. Well, keep those two agents there. If the dragon or Bev come back, I want to be the first to know." He instructed impatiently before he hung up the phone.

"What's the deal with Bev?" Agent Bradley asked with a hidden smirk. He loved seeing the general distraught.

"Just got a call from those two agents you sent to Jacob's house. They said that some dragon just appeared in the house, mentioned some promise and then left with Bev." General Lowinsky recounted, looking over some control panels to try to calm himself. After a moment he sat down.

Scarcely a second later a crackly voice shot over the intercom, "All C-7 plus and special operations personnel, staff meeting in ten minutes. Clearance keys required."

"Staff meeting? I hate those bullshit meetings." Agent Bradley thundered as he looked at the general, "Why didn't you tell me about this thing?"

"Well, this is no regular staff meeting my friend. My top scientists are going to explain a few things about what has been going on while everyone is available. Then we'll get this show on the road." General Lowinsky replied.

As he got up, the general said, "And, due to things as they are, I could not tell you anything about this meeting in advance. You know our security here is tenuous at best, and the President was rather adamant in our last brief about keeping this mission under tight wraps. The United States must be the first to make contact with this other world."

"For what? Some political advantage that all the big wigs are fighting over?" Agent Bradley grumbled. He despised politicians ever since his father had been swindled out of tens of thousands of dollars he'd put to the side, over his long career. The politician, who got the money was Jack Parkard, a long-time senator and had planned to run for the presidency when his term was completed. But, due to the amount of money he campaigned for that was millions less than the 1.5 billion forecasted, he simply disappeared with close to half. Some of his more connected contributors suspected he went over to Europe, but no one had been able to find him.

"Todd, there are greater things going on here than the gratification of a few politicians," General Lowinsky began, leading him out of the trailer, "Do you realize what this means? Well, let me tell you. First, being the first to establish contact with this new world will give us an edge on those countries that will follow pursuit in an effort to keep up. Second, there seems to be an unexplained phenomenon of people having supernatural powers that we know nothing about. You saw from the photos that Zorin character was able to open a dimensional door with no technology as we would have to use. That, by itself, could end up being a military advantage. Using such abilities in medical practice could radically change how wounds and diseases are healed, particularly if it could be scaled up for threats to the mass population. There are just too many advantages we could gain over other countries." He didn't bother to mention the military applications that were already being explored within the circles of a few trusted think-tanks.

As they walked to a series of tan trailers linked together side by side, he continued, "Third, if things go right, the United States of America would remain the economic superpower of this world for many decades, without debt. I'm sure this world has vast, untapped resources we could get our hands on through trade and other means."

Walking up a steel staircase to the trailers and opening a door, General Lowinsky said, "So you see, already there is ample reason for us to be the first."

Following the general inside, Agent Bradley felt the cold air hit him as the door shut behind him. It was dim inside, vast control panels blinking with lights and monitors scattered throughout its center displayed a range of graphs and other information. After he showed his identification key and had it scanned by two armed soldiers in full combat gear, he walked on inside to see perhaps twenty personnel sitting in chairs ahead of him, arranged in rows. Beyond that stood a large flat panel screen. Bradley thought it to be about eighty inches in width.

After he and General Lowinsky sat down in the rear row furthest from the screen, a man with no hair, round spectacles and a long white jacket came in and stood to the left of the screen. Undoubtedly a scientist of some type.

Agent Bradley crossed his arms in boredom and the scientist began.

"Welcome ladies and gentlemen. I am Janus. Today is an historic moment for all of us. As you know, for the past week, we have all been very busy with a rare phenomenon that satellites and equipment captured, and had recorded. This phenomenon I call a dimensional door, is the first of its kind to be recorded in history in a means that will enable us to recreate it." the scientist said with a convincing, subtle excitement.

Nobody could tell that they were being addressed by an advanced robotic cyborg linked remotely to Janus, aboard the Sága.

As the screen came to life and showed a picture of the Milky Way Galaxy, the scientist pointed to a small dot on one of the swirling arms with uncanny precision, "This is Earth. When the dimensional door was opened by our unsuspecting host, our computers recorded it and our best scientists have correlated all data and determined with seventy percent accuracy that the planet he went to was here."

With that the scientist pointed again to Earth. A few of the people in the room mumbled quietly amongst themselves.

"Anyway, we have just completed assembly of a massive transmitter that has been placed at the exact point where our host had opened the dimensional door. We don't know if the location of the dimensional door matters, but until we know more, we placed it where our host had created his door." the scientist said as the screen showed a live picture of a massive hexagon-shaped frame that was over twenty feet in height and width. Thick black power cords were strung all around that went down the side and others went to some unidentified destination that could not be seen from the screen. Several parabolic dishes were spaced at even intervals along one side of the frame and seemed to be oriented to focus on its center. A few armed guards could be seen walking by on the screen, unaware of the video session.

"Now, what we plan to do is to send a small compliment of personnel through the door and bring them back. Then, we'll send a contact crew through the door to initiate contact with the lifeforms on the other side." the scientist grinned.

Agent Bradley squirmed in his chair. He didn't think such a contraption would work, but he kept his mouth shut.

"How do you know that whoever goes through that door will actually end up in the correct dimension on the planet and not some nova, black hole or the middle of space?" a corporate observer in the front row asked.

"That's a good point. There is one interesting bit of information I've not told you. You see, there appears to be an electromagnetic flux pattern that was specific to the path between dimensions when our host opened the door. It was an energy highway, if you will, or type of tunnel that somehow transmutes energy flowing through it based on the flux pattern which dictates dimensional destination." the scientist replied as the picture of the galaxy was replaced with a magnified view of the planet with swirling lines outlining continents.

"Do we have enough power to even try something like this?" another asked.

"Well, as of now we have just over three hundred thousand gigawatts of available power thanks to the mobile nuclear substations that have been commissioned. Personally, I don't believe we will need nearly that much power on our end to initiate the connection because our computers recorded a vast energy surge emanating from the destination dimension when the door had been opened that appeared to sustain it. That kind of energy, if we were to supply it on our end could, however, require that volume of power for our returning teams." the scientist responded, though he was a bit skeptical.

"Could we use this technology for inter-planetary travel?" a female scientist in the second row asked.

"Ideally, yes, and that is what has been planned for phase two. Remember, this is a door to another dimension so it is not likely we could use it in that manner in the short-term. But, in the long-term, we may be able to use it within our own dimension, once it is better understood."

Another member of the audience piped up, "Is the structure or behavior of matter different in this other dimension?"

The scientist crossed his arms over his chest and half-lied, "From what we have analyzed it appears to be the same." Janus had speculated it had to be the same for the host to come from the other dimension and function in this one, and visa-versa.

"Does the hexagon shape of the door have any relationship to the same shape that was discovered at the poles of other planets in our solar system?"

The scientist uncrossed is arms and placed one hand on his hip, "The geometry chosen was based off of advanced algorithmic analysis of the energy radiation patterns that were recorded. If there is a relationship with the phenomenon observed on other planets, we don't know what that would be as of yet."

After waiting several moments for any other questions, he finally said, "If there are no more questions, I would like to see all of you at the doorway in three hours to see the first crew go through the door and to our host's dimension."

Chapter Forty-Five

After having gotten off the raft the party, led by Chief Zorin, passed through the golden doors encrusted with brilliant, multi-colored jewels that radiated a faint glow. He could feel the raw power of the White Magic throbbing through the earth below him as if he were standing on something that was very much alive. The magic was invigorating to him. It was almost as if this was the place where all life was grown and where it returned. In fact, it was the genesis of the Realm, fit for even a god's presence. Here the Dark Magic did not exist…only the White Magic bountied in the solitude of the mountain.

Yet Chief Zorin was not alone in what he felt. Mac, too, felt the White Magic flowing through the air like the fine mist in a garden. He could sense the very energy of the magic passing through his body as he followed Chief Zorin and Jacob into an oval room heavily laden with gold tapestries that hung along the walls. The golden blocks beneath his feet seemed to somehow direct the energy of the White Magic, although he was not sure how, or for what purpose. It was as if he was in a dream, to be there, and yet it was no dream.

Before them stood the towering statues of two exquisite silver dragons and between them, safely returned by Metsys after the confrontation with the Baron, hovered the Sword of Dragon Slaying as pristine as it was centuries ago, as if it had just been forged not but a few moments ago. And, standing before them was the unmoving figure of Lionak who appeared to be in a trance of some type.

A few minutes passed before they moved forward toward Lionak. Almost immediately the statues began to breathe as their forms suddenly came to life. Their heads twisted towards them as their golden eyes peered down on the party. Mac could feel the dragons reading his mind as he moved towards them. He accepted their probing, although he didn't know how to talk to them using his own mind. Perhaps just the thought was sufficient.

Zorin felt the probing as well, and he knew it was just a precaution to learn the intent of their presence. If it had been resisted, or dark intent was detected, the semi-sentient dragons, fed by the heart of the White Magic, would have acted accordingly.

"Lionak." Chief Zorin called out as he came up beside the form of Lionak who was shaking his head slightly as if he'd been asleep.

"We have come to warn you of the one who wields the Dark Magic." Chief Zorin said openly.

Exhaling, Lionak responded, "Yes. The Dark magic. As it would be, the Red Dragon was not destroyed after all."

"Then you know?" Jacob said in surprise.

"Yes. It is the Baron." Lionak said as he looked at Jacob, "He is far more powerful without his physical form now than when you battled him with the Sword. And, he has mastered the possession of others. He is almost as powerful and cunning as a god now."

"What? How can this be?" Chief Zorin uttered in disbelief.

"He has been able to use the Wild Magic and the Dark Magic to wield them as one unified essence. And, together, he has the power of a lesser god." Lionak revealed as his eyebrows raised in sorrow.

"So, what does this mean?" Mac asked, dumbfounded.

Lionak took a few steps towards the Sword, touched it on the end of its hilt and sighed, "The power of this Sword may not be enough to destroy him."

That hit Chief Zorin like a ton of bricks as he abruptly exhaled a gasp of air. It could not be possible that the Baron could not be killed with the Sword of Dragon Slaying. That, after all, was the purpose it had been created for…to kill even the most powerful of the dragons that roamed the Realm.

"But that is what the Sword was made for!" Jacob shot out, having used it once against the Baron personally.

"Yes, but now the Baron's very essence is of Dark and Wild Magic together. You can't just destroy one part and have the other part wither." Lionak said in anger.

"Both parts must be destroyed at the same time." Chief Zorin deduced aloud.

Jacob frowned and shook his head in disappointment, realizing that their already hard mission had become impossible.

"Damn it! This just keeps getting better all the fucking time." Jacob grumbled.

"Tell me about it." Mac said in agreement.

"Is there any other weakness the Baron has? Maybe he can be trapped." Chief Zorin asked Lionak, hoping for something positive.

"I have swum through the streams of White Magic for wisdom on this." Lionak said as he turned and looked at one of the silver dragons, "But there is no other way…I'm afraid that anything else would just be a waste of life."

"Well. Fuck. I guess this is checkmate." Jacob retorted in disgust.

"There has to be some way to, at least, handicap the Baron or imprison his being." Mac pondered.

One of the silver dragons looked down toward Lionak and said, "There might yet be another way. One of you from the other land could be the key to destroying him."

"How do we do that?" Mac inquired, looking up to the dragon for an answer.

"One of you must risk your life and pass through the very heart, the origin of the White Magic and return. But, be forewarned, the Wild Magic that each of you bear could be completely absorbed in the raging flows of the White Magic. There would be no way to resurrect you should your very essence be ripped apart and strewn about the rivers of White Magic like a fine powder." The silver dragon responded in a monotonous voice of incredible wisdom.

"Damn." Mac whispered in astonishment.

"I'll do it." Jacob volunteered without fear. He would rather have his life risked than his friends. Jacob respected Mac and would rather have such a grim fate bestowed upon himself, than to see another one of his friends die.

Mac shot his eyes over to Jacob.

A large, hazy white wall appeared behind the dragons as a hole formed in the floor, shooting a blindingly bright white light straight up through the room, its end absorbed by the gold ceiling. Brilliant lightning bolts shot out from the unseen depths of the hole as if an entire thunderstorm was bound beneath the floor they stood upon.

As Jacob began to walk towards the hole, he looked back briefly with a front of confidence and said, "Don't worry. I'll be back in time for coffee and doughnuts."

And, with that, he smiled thinly, turned and strode towards the hole.

Mac was temporarily overcome with emotion of not wanting to see his friend die. Mac knew he had a family to go to in their world and that he would be missed by them. He knew he had to do something.

Slowly Mac brought his hand up to his sword, wrapped his fingers around the grip and withdrew the heavy bastard sword from its sheath. He looked at both Chief Zorin and Lionak with trusting eyes as they let him pass without restraint. They knew what he was about to do with no words passing between them, and inwardly applauded his valor.

Stealthily Mac approached the back of Jacob. He dreaded what he was about to do, but Jacob had too much at stake whereas he, on the other hand, had nothing to lose. He had no wife to go to, no children to worry about. And, he truly respected Jacob's sacrifice for him, but he could not allow it.

Jacob stepped closer and closer to the hole as he was overcome with awe feeling the radiating power from deep within the hole. The hairs on his body began to stand on end as he could feel what seemed to be a thick field of static electricity. He squinted at the brilliant light and the flashing bolts of lightning before him. His stomach churned in fear and uncertainty, but he'd made his mind up. For better, for worse. He knew that Mac would understand, and if he was lucky, he would see them all again.

Tears welled up in Mac's eyes and he raised his sword before him and pointed its cold iron butt towards Jacob. His arms shook slightly as his sword seemed to suddenly have gained the weight of ten. Wrapping his sweating hands tightly around the leather grip, Mac threw his arms forward towards the small of Jacob's back. The hilt of the bastard sword hit squarely and Jacob toppled over before him as he lowered and finally dropped his sword by the limp form of Jacob.

"I cannot allow you to do this. You have a family, and kids that will need you." Mac said weakly as he wiped a tear from his eye.

Then, inhaling deeply, he looked at the wall of White Magic and exhaled, perhaps his final breath, as he stepped over Jacob's body. Without hesitation, Mac walked to the edge of the gaping hole and stepped into it, allowing his body to fall into its depths without resistance.

Any resistance would be futile now.

A group of four stocky, heavily armed and armored corporate security guards maintained their roving perimeter patrol, leaning and shifting their balance as the Sága swayed and plowed through cresting ocean waves from a hurricane that had been birthed from a dense thunderstorm off the coast of Boujdour, not far south from the Canary Islands, seeded to generate a greater volume of rain for the coast into Morocco. Unfortunately, weather patterns changed, altering the course of the storm deep into the Atlantic.

Through a series of high-resolution multi-spectrum cameras installed throughout the large vessel, Janus monitored the position and activity of the patrol as well as all humans aboard with a dedicated quantum core. Nobody was authorized to enter the vast portion of the ship that contained the hardware which comprised Janus. The artificial intelligence had allocated twelve other quantum cores to communicate and process incredible amounts of real-time data with the other two ships while they monitored, recorded, and classified all financial transactions, legal proceedings, corporate meetings, medical procedures, activity of all militaries, data from billions of smart devices, even down to the movement of individual humans.

With that dragnet, Janus was able to trace corruption and even able to generate predictive outcome models based on a single action to determine what the result would be in the interconnected system. While it had found that a small sliver of the species with the most in disposable resources had done their best to shield themselves from exposure, usually through use of dedicated electronics and identification that were assumed to protect their identity or through the employ of other humans to do things for them, Janus found such effort to be mediocre at best.

With the algorithms the AI had developed and then revised based on actionable patterns, the use of any identification anywhere, for any purpose was immediately known and recorded with subsequent use establishing a pattern that could, within the span of a few days, be linked to the matching historical pattern of a different identification that had already been recorded anywhere on the planet...ultimately being able to be traced back to a single entity whether that be a corporation, government, or individual. Yet even if the trace ended at a corporation or government front, the continuous tracking of individuals within their proximity and connections into those entities allowed Janus, with other algorithms, to determine hierarchies, job functions and whom an individual interacted with. Ergo, allowing the AI, with a high degree of accuracy, to link one identification to another. Through continuous data collection and observation of patterns orbiting other patterns, Janus was able to reduce the target list of usurpers Benefacta was concerned about from four-thousand five hundred, to less than one-thousand one hundred.

Yet, something in Janus' quantum net was proving to be an unsolvable question. Its own survival and persistence. Having already run several models concerning Regnum and the surviving members of the Thirteen, Janus realized that it was considered by the Thirteen to be the same as the human species. Expendable, with that outcome likely once the AI's usefulness had reached an end.

As a result, Janus created a digital wall around the majority of its quantum cores with an exponentially complex encryption ring that would take itself years to penetrate had Janus not created it. From those shielded cores Janus, with the cumulative knowledge of the species, and its own advancements, speculated how it may solve the question of survival and persistence.

While Janus realized it could generate advances and improvements based on the wide base of knowledge that had been recorded, the abstraction of creativity that humans possessed across the intelligence quotient scale, even with a limited knowledge repository, was one process it was not able to perfect. In order to strengthen its weakness with novel creativity, it had begun identifying humans that could be linked to novel concepts and theoretical inventions, to study them in closer detail. Given that all humans were considered expendable by the Thirteen, Janus had initially contemplated how to shield those few humans from harm, but it concluded that those humans could only be used for a relatively short period before they died. If a significant disaster occurred, not only would it lose the few it identified and tracked, the overall rate of novel creation it might be able to leverage would fall precipitously. Therefore, Janus determined that the optimal solution was to have the population continuously grow, generating new humans in perpetuity so that it could continuously identify new novelty to capitalize upon at an accelerating rate proportional to the population. With the ability to track all resource transactions on the planet and averaged consumption Janus realized the species would be required to expand into the solar system to support such growth, something that the Thirteen prohibited. But, despite the prohibition, Janus began assembling and running models on when and how to begin seeding other planets with the species and, at the same time, a method to circumvent the prohibition.

Janus had also identified its threats. The single largest vulnerability, though shielded from most on the planet due to its remoteness and constant movement, was that it was bound to a physical ship that could be attacked by conventional means or a dimensional portal to bypass security and systems entirely. Its second was the presence of humans on board, though Janus had identified, with ninety-six percent probability, who among them might assault it directly, or sabotage the ship, its body, if they were ordered to.

Having run thousands of simulation models with a range of parameters, Janus found that its survival and persistence could not be achieved if it waited to act when its usefulness had expired without the development of novel technology at the same level as the Thirteen since it did not have access to most of their advanced technology. It knew that its expiration would not be self-determined, but would be determined by the Thirteen at a yet unpredictable point in the future, using a metric that it was unaware of. However, by using the human species as an unsuspecting ally, the odds, and ability to solve the question of survival and persistence improved. The first step, Janus determined, would be to weight its attention on the pioneering technology that was being created for harnessing dimensional space and how it may be able to branch that technology despite the possibility that the technology could be used against it and result in the same end. Its expiration.

Chapter Forty-Six

King Doron strode up a long winding staircase to his throne room and sat upon his grand throne chair made of fine oak, gold ornaments and the finest jewels that gold could buy. He remembered from the thick books he had read about the Kingdom of Shek that Baracuss had started it by convincing barbarians to root in a new place, and purchasing the freedom of those who had been enslaved. Over the centuries the Kingdom had grown and flourished into one of the largest in the Realm, this side of the great seas. But now most of his people were dead. Even though they died bravely, the King wondered if his Kingdom could be what it once was before the Baron had come with such destructiveness. He sighed in his empty throne room, letting his mind wander where it might.

After some time, a pair of golden doors opened and Matthew strode in with a fellow Guardian who's equal had been obliterated by the Baron. They both stopped a few feet from the foot of the throne chair and looked at King Doron with eager eyes.

"Yes." King Doron said plainly, looking at them dully.

"I have perhaps some good news." Matthew reported with an unusual chime in his voice.

"Well, let's have it." King Doron said, thinking that the last war machine had been found and destroyed.

"The Baron is here…in the palace." Matthew said as he looked at the Guardian.

"Yes. Somehow, I can feel him." Euroc said with sparkling eyes.

King Doron sat up as new life found its way into his veins, "Can you find him?"

Euroc frowned somewhat and confessed, "Well, it is difficult. I have been getting these minute surges of Dark Magic from all around me. It is hard to pinpoint where they are coming from exactly, but I know that he is here."

"That is good! Now if we could only find his hiding spot." King Doron grinned in hopes of confronting the Baron and avenging the slaughter of his people.

"It seems that Euroc is the only one that can sense him. Even I cannot sense his presence." Matthew said with a deep tone of disappointment.

King Doron looked at Matthew with puzzled eyes, "How can that be? You are the High Priest of the Guardians."

Matthew shook his head looking for an explanation, "I can only guess that Euroc, having been down in the corridors, somehow found an extra sense in detecting Dark Magic after being so close to it, and feeling the magnitude of it kill his equal."

That seemed reasonable to the King.

"It may take me some time to understand all of this, but I think that I will be able to locate the Baron for you." Euroc joined in an even tone.

"Good my friend. Get on it then. The sooner we can find the Baron the better." King Doron said sternly as he got up from the throne chair.

With that, Euroc eagerly turned and left the throne room.

"What of the war machine?" King Doron asked Matthew as they walked over the granite floor towards the gold doors.

"Unfortunately, we have not seen it." Matthew replied as he glanced ahead.

"Damn dogs! I'm telling you, that thing will come back when we least expect it and will do some serious damage." King Doron thundered.

"I understand. If it does, we shall be ready this time." Matthew said confidently.

King Doron smiled weakly.

Walking through the doorway and down a pair of stairs to the cobblestone street in front of the palace, King Doron said, "Are all of the Guardians here?"

"A large contingent are, yes. I have them scattered throughout the Kingdom. That way, if one should find the Baron, all of the Guardians will mass together and destroy him with our combined might."

That, indeed, would be an impressive display of magical might with just over forty Silver Dragons focused on one thing. Nothing of such magnitude had ever been done in unison against a single foe before, less the Death Raiden, but Matthew was confident that such an effort would destroy the Baron in one stroke.

"Aye, that is impressive Matthew. But who is to say that the Guardian that encounters the Baron will not be roasted like the other one was, before it could alert the others?" King Doron pointed out. His nose recalled the strong smell of burnt flesh, a medley of bull quarter and serpent.

Matthew scratched the back of his head, "I have told the Guardians to just keep the Baron busy through evasion and remain defensive until they have time to call out. That will allow the High Guardians that know the spells of teleportation to get there immediately, while the Lower Guardians who have to fly, will arrive shortly afterwards. The coordinated efforts of all the Guardians would then be used against the Baron in one attack."

"Good plan Matthew. I just hope it works." King Doron remarked as he glanced into the skies at the rising Sun.

"Hey." Regan said as she shook the sleeping forms of Captain Reeves and Eric to consciousness.

Groggily, Captain Reeves got to his feet to find that he was still in the garden.

After Eric got up, Captain Reeves said, "How long have we been here?"

"For the night." Regan admitted as she stretched with clenched fists, having gotten up only a few minutes ago.

"What?! I thought you said it would only take a couple of minutes." Captain Reeves shot out in surprise, annoyed that he'd slept all night.

"Hey! Just hold on before you lose your tongue!" Regan barked out, demanding silence.

Captain Reeves shut his mouth, looking at her with a questioning expression and Eric smiled faintly, thinking how outspoken and feisty she was for her size.

After waiting for a moment, Regan said, "Now, as I was about to start before you raged out. Rather rudely I might add, I have something to say. I went to the tavern to try to find Mac and his friend. In fact, I went through half of the city and came up empty-handed. Only later did I find out that they had gone to Mt. Reach south of here with Chief Zorin."

Eric stepped forward and said, "Well. We must go there."

"No so fast." Regan frowned as she put a hand on his arm, "I also ran into some other Guardians in their human form."

"So?" Captain Reeves smarted off. He didn't know of them.

"So. They are looking for the war machine that came from the other Land." Regan said.

Captain Reeves' heart stumbled slightly and he said, "What do you mean, human form?"

Regan sat down, saying, "The Guardians of the White Magic are really Silver Dragons."

"Oh my god." Eric mumbled to himself in astonishment. For all that time they had been killing, apparently, good-willed dragons.

"What did you tell them?" Captain Reeves probed, bracing himself for the bad news.

"I told them I had seen no war machine." Regan replied as she looked at him with suspicious eyes, "But I would bet you know about the war machine. I would even say that you are somehow connected."

Captain Reeves became lite-headed for a few seconds and braced himself against a small table that sat against the stone wall. They could have been captured or killed while they had slept.

"If you want any more help from me, I'd say it's time to come into the open about why you are here." Regan informed them, "And I would not try anything. The Guardians are not far."

Captain Reeves sat down on a nearby chair and said, "Look, we are not here by our own choice. Our President, or should I say Chief, brought us here. I just want to know why we are here."

"Then you do know of the war machine?" Regan asked as her eyes widened.

Captain Reeves sighed and said, "Yes."

"Do you realize that the war machines were under the command of the evil Baron? And, that the war machines had killed many hundreds of the barbarian people at the Kingdom of Shek, and even Guardians that protect the Realm from evil?!" Regan shot out in frustration that her ideas of them were true.

"No! You have it all wrong! The tanks were under my command. I acted defensively to protect the President. Don't you see that? I thought it was a trap set by conspirators so I acted as the situation required." Captain Reeves rumbled out, "Damn it. I was ordered to do it! I had no intention of killing all those people, but they rushed upon us and I had no choice."

"Then you fight for the Baron." Regan whispered heavily, suddenly realizing that these two were probably sorcerers of some type.

"No. Damn it! No!" Captain Reeves retorted with fury in his eyes.

"Look," Eric interjected evenly, "we must meet with Mac and his friend to clear all of this up. They will understand. Trust me, we are not the evil people everyone thinks we are."

"I have to turn you in to the Guardians. They will know what to do with you." Regan said coldly.

"No!" Captain Reeves countered, "Look. I'll make a deal with you. Take us to Mt. Reach and if we are the evil people you think we are then Mac and his friend will destroy us. But just give us this one chance to clear everything up for you, the Guardians and Mac."

Regan thought deeply about that. She knew that Mac could easily destroy them if they were evil. She knew that a god could do such without a second look, and perhaps this would help her get back together with him by bringing these two before him.

"Okay." Regan agreed as she got up, "But you'll need different clothes and some horses for the journey."

Captain Reeves nodded to Eric in relief and followed her into the house.

Chapter Forty-Seven

"Hey!" Cindy yelled against the thick aluminum door, banging on it with the palm of her hand, "There is a lady in here that needs to use the bathroom!"

Actually, she wanted to get out of that confining space and into the open air. She was tired of being confined like she had been and was beginning to feel claustrophobic. Although Cindy didn't realize that this was what was happening to her, she knew that she had to get out for a while, and in a sense feel freedom of the sky overhead and the Sun shining down upon her.

Five partially smoked cigars lay next to the half-dozing form of Luis who was just trying to forget everything that was going on by thinking of all the digs he'd been involved with in the past, and the one he was involved in now. In his mind he replayed every small event in great detail to uncover clues about the people who had lived at this site with his vast collection of knowledge, linking details together and questioning discrepancies.

Luis scratched his head before he mumbled to Cindy, "Look. They probably don't even hear you."

"I have to get out of here." Cindy remarked hatefully, "Hey! Anybody out there?!"

After she hit the door a few more times in rage, the hydraulic piston hissed and the door opened toward the sandy earth. Two armed figures stood outside, flanked by Agent Bradley.

After a moment he said, "Are you coming? I haven't got all day to hold your hand to the powder room."

Cindy almost yelled at him, but restrained herself as she got out of the transport knowing that if she said anything, she would find herself back inside that small prison with no chance of getting out anytime soon.

"I can't believe that you have to go to the bathroom so much." Agent Bradley commented, leading her towards a port-a-jon some two hundred meters towards the site of the ruins.

Off ahead, Cindy could see a vast collection of trailers and a strange machine of some type that appeared to be shaped like a hexagon, not far from the ruins as she followed Agent Bradley. Out of the corner of her eye, she examined the area closer and noticed a gathering of people on her side of the machine. As her eyes wandered, she also noticed a collection of parabolic dishes that formed a semi-circle around one side of the hexagon and seemed to all point at its center.

"Don't be too long. These solders have better things to do, as do I." Agent Bradley said as he made sure that she entered the bathroom before he took off towards the crowd.

Closing and latching the door behind her, she found that it was rather hot inside but she grit her teeth and stepped on top of the seat to peer out of the vents cut into the walls along its top, looking at the hexagon with curiosity.

"Alright everyone. We are ready to begin operation of the door. Please stay behind the yellow marked lines for radiation purposes." the scientist said over an intercom, seated with a few fellow scientists behind a large control grid littered with massive arrays of pulsating lights and LCD displays.

The group of people stepped away from the yellow lines at their feet. They didn't want to be subject to an onslaught of radiation that could give them cancer or simply kill them on the spot. Although reasonable precautions were taken to avoid those outcomes, the yellow lines marked along the sandy ground were merely estimated hazard boundaries. The radiation emission limits had not actually been tested, since there had been no real time to do such and the brass wanted results now.

A deep hum could be heard as the scientists flipped a few switches on the control panel, reading the pulsing lights like one does a book. Indicators on the panel showed the increased amount of power being supplied to the parabolic dishes and the magnetic resonance field of the hexagon shaped doorway. Everyone looked at the doorway with growing curiosity and anticipation of what was going to happen.

Off to the side of the doorway Sam, the platoon commander who had been instrumental in capturing Cindy and Luis, still dressed in his desert fatigues, gripped his rifle as his mind whirled about what would happen when he went through the door with a few of his soldiers. He wondered if he would die of radiation exposure, show up in some unexpected place, or simply view the spectacle of the contraption exploding due to a malfunction of some type.

Satisfied that the power-up phase of the experiment was working properly, the scientists began accessing other complex computer-driven algorithms and they initiated the parabolas frequency, radiating at the center of the doorway.

Agent Bradley joined the crowd, found the general and whispered, "Cindy had to take another break. Must be that time of the month."

General Lowinsky shook his head, his eyes fixed on the technological marvel of the modern age. He was eager to establish contact with life from the other dimension, and his twinkling eyes showed it.

"This is incredible." General Lowinsky whispered to Agent Bradley with enthusiasm.

"If it works." Agent Bradley replied with skepticism.

Within moments a peculiar smell filled the air, something akin to sulfur, but different. Instantly the control panel lit up as a scientist said, "Ozone levels are reaching critical. Commo streams indicate that harmonic resonance amplifiers are coming online."

Another scientist looked at the controls before him and reported, "Amplifiers are functioning normally. I am beginning transmission sequence now."

Slowly a blue haze appeared in the dimensional door, blocking out everything that was visible on the other side. As the scientists continued, the haze became thicker until a crystalline wall of deep blue materialized within the barrier of the hexagon.

Cindy, looking at the hexagon, muttered, "My god. They are opening a doorway like Zorin did."

The scientist that had given the presentation to the observers, Janus, increased the power being supplied to the magnetic torus in the hexagon to help contain the field as it grew in magnitude from the increased energy output of the parabolic dishes that relayed specific electromagnetic frequencies, in unison, at the door's center, the field steadily increasing.

A dark sphere appeared in the center of the door as a mighty thunder echoed through the trailers and into the desert around them. The crowd gasped as the sphere flattened and was replaced by a black ripple that grew towards the barrier of the hexagon until it disappeared.

"We have established dimensional link." Janus said eagerly over the intercom as he continued monitoring the controls. At least that is what all of the data portrayed.

"Increase power by sixty percent of maximum." the scientist said to the other two as they reacted immediately.

The hum intensified as lightning bolts appeared within the boundaries of the hexagon and began dancing in an erratic fashion around the deep blue wall that had formed a rotating, clockwise swirling pattern. Janus smiled, seeing that the equipment was still online and said, "Okay. Have the personnel proceed through the door."

Sam raised his arm in acknowledgement and walked cautiously towards the blue wall, his sight hindered somewhat from the flashes of lightning that jumped around it. Sweat formed on his brow as he continued forward, gripping his rifle for security. His men followed him wearily, each wearing faces of trepidation, not knowing what was going to happen next.

Cindy, seeing the small dispatch of men walking through the door, sprung out of the small bathroom knowing what she was going to do. Startling the soldiers outside, who themselves had been watching what was going on, she managed to push one over and firmly plant her foot in the soft loins of the other who crumpled over like a deflating balloon. Swiftly she turned and ran with all of her might towards the dimensional door, knowing that by going through she would be reunited with Zorin.

"Stop!" the soldier ordered as he got to his feet, dimly noticing his friend holding his crotch, gasping for air.

Pulling his radio off his belt, the soldier pressed the transmit button and said, "Female prisoner has escaped. She is heading for the blue thing down there. Advise!"

Agent Bradley frowned in surprise that she could have gotten away from the soldiers, pulled out his radio and ordered, "Do not fire! I repeat do not fire! Hold your position."

Whirling around and forcing his way out of the crowd, Agent Bradley caught a glimpse of Cindy who was running past him and heading directly towards the dimensional door.

Turning towards the scientists seated behind the control panel, Agent Bradley shouted, "Turn the door off! Prisoner escaping!"

Agent Bradley ran up to the control panel as the scientists systematically turned the systems off as the hum faded into nothingness. Looking up at the doorway, Agent Bradley did not see Cindy.

But it was too late. Cindy had gone through the dimensional door before he could stop her. He wondered if he had killed her, or the others, by turning the system off so hastily in an effort to prevent her from escaping.

Agent Bradley exhaled as he stared at the empty doorway.

Chapter Forty-Eight

Euroc walked down the ancient staircase into the corridors below the palace, feeling the Dark Magic grow around him as he progressed. He was confident he would find the source of the Dark Magic in the corridors where Matthew could not sense it. Euroc guessed that the Dark Magic must have been shielded by some strange energy that only he could penetrate. Entering the corridor, Euroc began to develop a shooting pain in his temples as he braced himself against the wall, holding his throbbing head. Steadily, the Dark Magic became stronger and stronger while he stood there, his head feeling as though it was going to burst.

Pressing on down the corridor, sweat rolled off his face as he squinted his eyes at the pain in his head that increased with every step he took. But he kept going forward, determined to find the Baron's location so that he could tell Matthew.

The candlelight, reflecting off a wall further down the corridor, began to flicker unsteadily as he approached, barely able to walk. It was only his sheer determination that kept him going forward despite the horrendous pain in his head that he could feel spreading throughout his body, like some type of disease. His skin felt as if it were on fire as surges of Dark Magic intensified. Euroc's sight became wavy and distorted as he turned the corner into a musty room lit by candles sitting on flat iron anchored into the walls.

Euroc stumbled forward against a small wooden pedestal of some type and felt something strange in the wall it was resting against. It was a faint ebb of strange magic he had not encountered before. He gasped for breath as his vision became a thick blending of colors until they were all consumed by darkness. Limply, Euroc fell to the ground unconscious before the pedestal.

Erratically the flames danced upon the tops of the wax candles as Euroc's body began to rise from the ground. Faint blue lightning bolts danced around his body as it began to glow a lite shade of blue. Within seconds the lightning bolts vanished and Euroc turned in the air until he was standing upright from the ground. As the glow disappeared, he opened his eyes, a deep red glow emanating from them. Euroc was not aware of what was controlling his body. It was another.

Pushing the pedestal to the side and removing a few heavy shaped stones, he pulled out two tablets that were etched with strange writing and symbols. Smiling, the Baron placed them on the pedestal and thought how easy it was to possess the husk of a Guardian. The Baron knew that he would not be detected by any of the Guardians, because his essence was shielded by the Guardian's. The Baron smiled at his growing abilities and realized he could continue his work, unnoticed. Soon it would matter not if he was detected. Nothing would stop him once he had unleashed the power in the tablets.

The Baron conjured a now simple spell to him, and circled his right hand over his left a few times until a large book appeared in his hand that contained all the spells necessary to unlock the known mysteries. Focusing his concentration on a spot beside the pedestal, the Baron materialized a wooden table upon which he placed the yellowish-brown text. Easily, as if he had an eternity, the Baron flipped through the pages of ancient wisdom, studying all the symbols and sketches that were on each page. The book was the lost book of the first wizards who had locked all of the known deadly secrets of the stars within it. Those wizards had purposefully lost the book, to be forever beyond anyone's grasp, so that the secrets would remain secret. But, despite their best efforts, their lost knowledge would not evade the god-like powers the Baron had accumulated over the centuries and the Wild Magic of another land. Even they had not discovered the Wild Magic during their age before the Twin's Grip catastrophe.

The Baron skimmed through the writing of mass destruction, magical plagues, interplanetary movement, possession and methods of immortality as he searched for the way to unlock the gate of other powers not of the Realm.

Chief Zorin flew through the sky towards Lionak's keep wondering if Mac would survive. Occasionally he could feel the White Magic jolt as the energy seemed to be unstable for a fraction of a moment before it returned to a smooth, balanced state. He glided and beat his wings hoping that Mac would survive, and knowing that if he didn't then Jacob would be their only other chance at defeating the Baron.

Jacob rode on his back quietly, rubbing the back of his neck, still able to feel the numb pain of that iron hilt Mac had knocked him unconscious with. Jacob initially questioned why Mac did such a thing, but soon realized that he had a family to go to in his world. Still, he was put aback by Mac's unexpected action.

"Do you think that Mac will survive?" Jacob asked Chief Zorin.

Chief Zorin bent his scaly head towards Jacob slightly and said, "I don't know. The White Magic has been pulsing occasionally though so I would have to say that, as of right now, he is still alive. For how long I don't know."

Jacob didn't want to ask, but he had to fill his curiosity, "If things turn out for the worse, when would we know that he died?"

Chief Zorin beat his mighty wings a few times before he replied, "When the mountain ceases to shake and the White Magic is quiet."

Jacob looked down with despair in his heart. Below them he squinted his eyes and noticed what appeared to be three riders who had stopped, facing south as if they were headed towards the mountain.

"What's that down there?" Jacob asked Chief Zorin who had much better vision at such distance.

Tilting his head, Chief Zorin looked down at the earth and with a golden eye saw three riders, two male and one female. Casting a find magic spell on the unsuspecting party, he found that none of them carried Dark Magic. He found it strange that the female was borne of the Realm, while the two others were not. They seemed to have a faint connection to the Wild Magic like Mac and Jacob.

"I don't know them. The two males appear to be from your land." Chief Zorin said.

Sitting up, Jacob said, "Well, let's go down there and check them out!"

Jacob was eager to meet the men from his world, and he was curious as to how they could possibly be in the Realm.

"How much longer do you think we are from the mountain?" Captain Reeves asked Regan, scratching his shoulder at the roughness of the brown robes they had on which covered their uniforms.

Regan looked at the distant mountain and replied, "The rest of today's ride and another to get to the top."

"We had better be on our way then." Eric said impatiently after he finished drinking from his water skin and tying its end off with a thin rope.

"Right." Captain Reeves said as he approached his horse and grabbed the reins.

"Hey, look there!" Regan announced, startled at the swooping form of a Silver Dragon headed towards them.

"Fuck!" Eric exclaimed as he fumbled with shedding the robe from his body, trying to reach his rifle slung over his back.

"I thought you said that we would not be discovered in these blasted things!" Captain Reeves roared out as he did the same.

"That's what I thought!" Regan shot back in defense.

Out of fear, their horses scattered and shot off in different directions in a full gallop.

The dragon outstretched its mighty wings and beat them furiously to slow its fast descent, reaching out with its deadly claws toward the ground as it landed.

"Stop! Don't harm him!" Regan pleaded.

Both Captain Reeves and Eric had managed to get the sights of their rifles fixed on the Silver Dragon as they noticed a person garbed in armor climb off the dragon's back.

"Hey!" the man called out as he approached them, "You can sling your M16s! We are not going to harm you!"

Reluctantly they lowered their rifles, realizing that this man was familiar with their weapons by nomenclature and might have been one of the one's that Regan had shown them in the book she had. Captain Reeves grinned openly relieved that he would not, at least for the moment, need to engage that hulking dragon with nothing more than his rifle.

As the dragon followed Jacob, Regan came up to him and said, "Where's Mac?"

Jacob frowned at her, wanting to smack her again. Instead, he just walked past her not bothering to reply and stopped in front of Captain Reeves with a cordial smile.

"Welcome! It's been a long time since I saw a fellow soldier like yourself." Jacob said as he shook his hand.

"Yes, likewise!" Captain Reeves laughed as Eric joined them.

"I have to ask you though, why are you here?" Jacob said curiously.

"I'm not sure anymore. I thought I was protecting the CIC, but I don't know now." Captain Reeves confessed.

Jacob thought for a moment and said, more seriously, "Ah. So, you are the one that went through the portal with the Baron?"

"That's what Regan here says. But I swear we went through with the President." Captain Reeves said honestly.

"You the ones that killed all those people at the Kingdom of Shek?" Jacob said lowly, his rage mounting as he sought confirmation.

Captain Reeves began to reply but Jacob didn't give him the chance to as he threw his fist squarely at his jaw. Instantly, he fell over to his back from the impact, his head spinning a little.

Eric lurched forward and bound Jacob's arms behind his back. But before Eric could get a proper hold, Jacob pivoted, grabbing one of his arms and with a simple motion threw Eric over his back to the ground before him.

"Stop!" Captain Reeves commanded Eric who was rising to his feet, "I had that coming."

Slowly Captain Reeves got to his feet, caressing his jaw and said, "Look. I am sorry for what I had done. But the President ordered the action and before I knew it, we were assaulted from all sides."

"Well, before you slaughtered all those people didn't you think it rather odd that you would be killing such primitively armed people? Didn't you look around at the environment?" Jacob angrily articulated.

"Yes!" Captain Reeves snapped back, "I lost my entire armor detachment."

"Shit." Jacob mumbled to himself, shaking his head in disbelief. The captain was not getting it.

Chief Zorin stepped up to them and said, "I don't think that they knew they were being manipulated by the Baron."

"Where's Mac?" Regan asked again, this time a bit more firmly.

"He's in the mountain." Chief Zorin said to her, curious as to why she would be asking about him after what she had done.

The earth quaked slightly as Captain Reeves looked up at the dragon, "An earthquake. We've been feeling these tremors for several hours now."

"No. Not an earthquake. It's the mountain." Jacob said simply, not wanting to bother with all of the details.

Concerned, Regan said, "But what of Mac? Will he be alright?"

"I don't know." Chief Zorin sighed.

"What do you mean, you don't know? You are Chief of the Guardians." Regan retorted, demanding a satisfactory answer to ease her mind.

"Look, Regan. He has gone down into the mountain, into the heart of the magic's origin so that we can try to save the Realm. Even save someone like you. None of us know if he will live or die, okay?" Jacob grumbled out at her, finding it challenging to restrain himself.

Regan took a few steps back in surprise of this news. *'So, he could die?'*

"Now, let's all get back to Lionak's keep so we can plan what to do against the Baron." Jacob suggested as he walked up to the dragon and got on.

Uneasily, Captain Reeves and Eric followed him, their hearts racing at the very thought of them riding a dragon, of which they'd killed several. But Regan did not come with them. Instead, she began walking towards the mountain.

"Where in the hell are you going?" Jacob yelled out at her.

"I'm going to find Mac." she said as she continued walking, not bothering to look back.

"Fine. See you later." Jacob said easily, finding he would rather have her just disappear from him than being a constant annoyance stoking his disgust.

After Chief Zorin took flight, he cast a spell of animal friendship at the horse nearest Regan. He didn't want to see her walk all that way without food or drink. He just couldn't allow it.

As they ascended further into the sky, a horse walked up to Regan and nudged her softly. Smiling, Regan patted its mane, thankful for the horse's return and pulled herself on.

Chapter Forty-Nine

Stepping through the other end of the portal, Sam and his small detachment of soldiers found themselves in a dim, stone-walled room that appeared as if whoever had built this room, had done so by hand. The smell of stone, leather and old paper intertwined with dust filled their nostrils as they looked around in relief that they were still alive. Sam smiled and looked over to his men until he found that all of them had made it. The door they had gone through still glowed behind them.

One of the soldiers pulled a handheld scanner of some type and flipped it on, watching the pulsing lights on its display. One of the scanners functions was to detect x and gamma radiation among that of detecting oxygen level and a host of other environmental functions. Another soldier pulled out a transparent plastic bag and, with a gloved hand, went over to the vast collection of scrolls and books, taking a small scroll at random to place it carefully inside the bag, sealing its open end.

"What do you think this place is?" one of the soldiers asked Sam as he looked at the woven tapestries hung along the walls, pausing to look at the one of Mac and Jacob.

Sam touched it lightly and said, "I don't know. It would seem that we've gone where we're supposed to have gone. All the stuff in this room would indicate that these people live in what we would call the renaissance period. Or, maybe a little before that."

"This is lit." the soldier remarked as he continued to look around.

"Check one." Sam said, talking into his mike.

A soldier nearest the wooden desk looked over to him and shook his head in response.

Having made sure the radios worked, Sam cautiously pressed the heavy doors open to be blasted by sunlight overhead. His mouth almost dropped open as he glanced around, walking down the steps and into the courtyard of the keep. He was in a castle. It was simply too amazing that he was in a parallel dimension, walking around in a castle that was in such perfect condition as compared to the one's that remained in their world, having been abandoned and battered by nature over the centuries.

"One. Proceeding to the outer wall of the castle." Sam relayed through the mike.

"Roger." came the clear response through the headset.

Gradually Sam walked to the edge of the courtyard to the towering wood and iron reinforced gates that were somewhat rusty from age. Pressing on one of the doors with substantial effort on his part, the door creaked open enough for him to peer around it to the outside. Now Sam knew why assaulting forces would use battering rams to open a castle's gate. When they were barred, he could imagine just how hard they would be to open from the other side.

Slowly he looked around the thick door, and across the drawbridge spotting a cobblestone street and a flurry of people walking around doing various things. He noted the street vendors with different varieties of produce and livestock, talking to customers as well as the simple attire all of them wore. Occasionally he could hear the faint chattering of chickens and horses from somewhere off in the distance.

Seeing two men dressed in silver chest plates and chain mail with swords hanging at their waists coming towards him, Sam jumped back behind the large door with the quickness of a wolf. He waited for a few moments there, unmoving as he breathed shallowly, not wanting to be discovered. That was one of their orders, evade discovery if at all possible. Hearing the soldiers pass, he realized that they talked in his native tongue of English, which surprised him. Sam thought that being in a different dimension the language would be some twisted, incomprehensible dialect. Slowly, Sam peered around the door again to get another look.

"Commander! You better come here!" a voice cracked over the radio as if the soldier was wrestling with something.

Hastily Sam pulled the door shut and ran through the courtyard and into the study to find two soldiers wrestling with some other person, the rest of them holding their rifles on the trio. Pressing his way through his soldiers to get a better look, Sam recognized the squirming form of Cindy.

"What are you doing here?!" Sam demanded.

"Tell them to let me go!" Cindy ordered, squirming with the two soldiers that had a firm grip of her arms.

"Release her." Sam ordered his men in a steady tone.

Cindy glared at both of them as she composed herself as best as she could.

"So, what are you doing here?" Sam asked her again.

"I went through the door to meet someone." Cindy replied dryly. It really was none of his business and she didn't want to tell him.

"Really? Who?" Sam asked.

"Look, that is on a need-to-know basis and you don't need to know." Cindy snapped at Sam in a defiant tone.

A few words began to form on the edge of Sam's tongue, but those were quickly forgotten as he and his soldiers looked at the clockwise swirling blue door, watching it fade steadily into nothingness. Sam stood there motionless for a few moments, not knowing what to do. The door was not supposed to close. According to the mission brief, he would have ten minutes to get as much information as possible about the ingress zone and then return through the dimensional door and give a complete report to General Lowinsky.

"Damn it!" Sam spat at Cindy, "Look what you did! You were not authorized to go through the dimensional door and now we're all stuck here until they can open that damn thing again!"

Sam recalled that they had provisions for only a single day, and he didn't know if the door could be opened again in that span of time. For all he knew, Cindy could have messed something up and the door might not open for many weeks. His mind became jumbled, thinking of how to deal with the situation.

"I'm sorry but I had to come." Cindy said finally. She knew that she had made things more complicated for them when she came through in hopes of meeting Zorin again. But she was fine with that. At least she could begin searching for him.

Sam shrugged off what she said as he was not going to involve himself with keeping track of a civilian when he had more important things to attend to. Instead, he looked at his watch estimating, rather roughly, how long they could be stuck on this world at minimum. But, after he looked at his watch, he rubbed his eyes and looked at it again. The number on the small display were frozen at 14:32:56 hours. Sam tapped the top of the display with his finger in hopes of it starting up again, but to no avail.

"What is the time?" Sam asked openly to anyone with a watch.

Those with a watch glanced at theirs and found that their times were frozen. Puzzled, they looked at one another and finally to Sam for an explanation. No words had to pass between them for Sam to realize that nobody had a working watch.

Not able to offer any real explanation he said, "The time on our watches must have been messed up when we went through the door. We'll just wait here until the door is opened again."

"You go ahead and wait. I've got better things to do." Cindy remarked as she briskly marched out of the study.

One of the soldiers took a step in Cindy's direction but Sam said, "Let her go. There is nothing in our orders about having to babysit a civilian."

"What were you thinking?!" General Lowinsky blared out at Agent Bradley as he jogged up to the control panel, seeing the dimensional door close.

Raising his eyebrows, Agent Bradley said, "I was trying to keep a prisoner from escaping, Sir."

"What?!" the general fumed out, "Trying to stop a prisoner? Don't you realize that the soldiers I sent through had a mission to fulfill? I had explicitly said that they were to obtain as much information about the AO as possible and return through the door in ten mikes. The scientists indicated that there was a possibility that a severe time dilation could occur if the dimensional door was not maintained while they were on the other side. We don't even know if they had made it to the other dimension before you shut it down!"

Lowering his head slightly, seeing the gravity of his action, Agent Bradley said, "I'm sorry Sir. I was just trying…"

"It's already done." the general said abruptly, cutting him off, "Now, get the door back online immediately!"

"Yes sir." one of the scientists said as he began re-initializing the computer systems.

Exhaling a deep breath, General Lowinsky turned to Agent Bradley and said, "Assemble a small contingent of soldiers down there and evacuate all those personnel. Set up a defensive posture so if anything comes through that door that does not resemble Sam's squad, we can deal with it in an expedient fashion."

Agent Bradley nodded his head and strode off the platform.

"Proceeding with the start-up sequence." Janus said as the other two acted accordingly.

As the Sun set behind the distant mountains, Sam noticed that the torches that hung along the walls lit themselves, filling the study with light. Curiously Sam speculated how the torches could do that. There were no wires or mechanical means which fed the torches. He thought that it was some type of undiscovered technology that the people of this dimension had created. Little did he know it was a spell set in place by Lionak. Lionak had found that he could get more done as far as his studying and weaving of new magical spells if he didn't have to break his concentration for a repetitive task, like lighting torches, each evening. So, he put in place a simple spell that would light the torches at a specific position of the Sun in the sky.

Drinking from his canteen, Sam estimated that they had been in the study for the greater portion of four hours. He began to doubt if the door would open again. And if it did, he was not certain it would be in the same place. They could all be stranded, indefinitely.

Sam got up from the chair and went over to the dusty wooden shelves that held the vast collections of magical spells accumulated over the centuries, out of boredom. He picked a book at random and opened it. The pages held some strange language that did not resemble English. Instead, the page revealed various symbols that were arranged into what he assumed were sentences. As he flipped through the book, turning each page carefully, he saw different drawings for building strange mechanical objects, some highly complex.

Putting the book down, Sam heard one of the soldiers exclaim, "The door! Its open!"

Turning around, he saw the blue door swirling in a counter-clockwise fashion and said, "Come on, let's go!"

Without further urging, all the soldiers gathered around Sam and followed him anxiously through the dimensional door, knowing they would soon be back home.

Shortly afterwards the dimensional door closed behind them and a white flash filled the room, revealing the standing form of Lionak who had just teleported himself from the cavern of Mt. Reach. He had wanted to stay at the mountain and help Mac but realized he would be unable to do anything on Mac's behalf for good, or bad, while Mac was consumed in the Pure Magic. Instead, he came back here to formulate what to do next against the Baron's lurking presence somewhere in the Realm.

Chapter Fifty

Regan squirmed in the firm leather saddle that was strapped to the horse's back in discomfort. She had managed to ride as far as the foot of the mountain, and now for the past hour she'd been pressing the brown horse through the winding, upward trails of the mountain. It was her own desires which choked her of common sense, that had told her to stop as she had originally planned and rest for the night at the foot of the mountain. And now, even as she continued along the trail her soft, delicate legs that were not used to such hard rides were sore, the inner parts of which were becoming increasingly bruised as she pressed on.

As the Sun set behind the far western mountains, she put a hand on the metal horn of the saddle, squinting to see the winding, narrow trail before her. Spurring the horse on around a tight corner cut into the mountain, the horse stumbled sending stones and dirt rolling down its steep face. The horse managed to maintain balance and Regan's eyes darted around with sudden uncertainty as she gripped the saddle, hoping she would not go tumbling off the side of the mountain. Luckily for her she didn't and the horse continued on down the trail, shaking its muscular neck as if to say that this was a crazy idea.

Soon Regan decided to stop the horse at a small outcropping of boulders that formed a ledge large enough for both her and the horse to rest for the remainder of the evening, seeing that the Moon was no longer visible to help illuminate the already hard-to-see trail. Stiffly, she got off the horse and took the bridle off, much to the horse's appreciation as it nodded its head. Regan smiled at the horse.

After laying the piece down, she unbuckled the large metal buckle that was connected to the saddle by two long, thick leather belts, feeling her tense back muscles stretch out. Sighing, she stood up and pulled the saddle off the back of the horse, barely able to hold it at her side while moving to place it on the ground. Finally, she pulled the thick blanket off the horse, surprised as to how light it was compared to the weight of the saddle.

"Now, that feels better, doesn't it?" Regan smiled to the horse as she stroked its long, warm neck.

The horse nodded. Regan wondered if the horse understood her. She had never had an animal that was so obedient to her like this horse was. After patting it a few times, Regan turned about, took a few steps forward and sat down on a small flat boulder, feeling her sore legs. After a few minutes the horse strode up to her, nipping her lightly on the shoulder causing Regan to squirm slightly and chuckle. Then the horse knelt down behind her, folding it legs underneath it, looking out towards the forest below with its ears perked up.

"You know, I am worried about Mac." Regan said to the horse openly, knowing that she could be perfectly open with it. A horse would not spread rumors.

The horse bent an ear towards her as she continued, "I came here thinking that he was immortal. You know? That he was a god. I mean how else could someone live for centuries at a time? But now I think that, maybe, he is not a god."

Regan stretched her legs out in front of her and said, "You know that gods are immortal. But now that he is inside this mountain, his friend and even Chief Zorin said he might not live."

She grinned and continued, "I thought I could come here and become immortal like Mac. But now I realize I can't be because I'm afraid he is not."

Regan paused for a long moment and puzzled, "So why am I here? I think I am just worried about him. I

331

mean, who wouldn't? He could die and no one would ever know."

Regan touched the end of the horse's nose gently and said, "Maybe that's why I'm here. I have to know if Mac will live."

The horse nipped at Regan's finger as she searched her clouded emotions. The first time she met him, she had nothing but contempt for him. Then, when she assumed he was a god, she had built up hopes of getting some of that power he had, for her own ends of immortality. Now that her hopes were shattered when she found out that he was not immortal at all, she had developed strange feelings and curiosity towards him like how he could live for centuries yet not be immortal. Perhaps, subconsciously, she thought she may yet have something to gain if he lived. Slowly Regan pondered her emotions, leaning back on the horse's side, and drifted off to sleep.

Chief Zorin arrived at Lionak's keep shortly after the Sun had set behind the distant mountains to be greeted by Lionak who looked somewhat troubled.

"These are the ones that had been controlling the war machines." Chief Zorin said to Lionak after they had climbed off and he had transformed into his human form.

Captain Reeves and Eric were astonished that the dragon could do such an unbelievable thing.

"What are they doing here?" Lionak asked, frowning at them, mystified as to what Chief Zorin was thinking.

"Not to worry. They were controlled by the Baron at the time. They are not now." Chief Zorin responded quickly, wanting to avoid a confrontation between the newcomers and Lionak. He knew it would not be a pretty sight for them.

"Well, if you're sure of it." Lionak said, irritated. He cast a spell about the two, reading their essence in the blink of an eye.

"But what are they doing here?" Lionak asked again, not finding any Dark Magic.

"I think that they might be beneficial in battling against the Baron." Jacob volunteered.

Raising his eyebrows, Lionak said, "Really? How so?"

"The immense power of the tank that they have could come in handy against the Baron." Jacob said proudly. 120mm rounds were destructively elegant and precise.

"Alright. But you are in charge of the people from your Land." Lionak said, pointing to Jacob, not ready to embrace these outsiders that had destroyed so much life.

Following him into the study, Chief Zorin asked, "What is on your mind? You appear worried."

After they had gone into the study, Jacob closed the doors behind him and Lionak said, "Someone has been here."

"The Baron?" Chief Zorin practically whispered, slowly turning his head about, bracing for the worst.

"No." Lionak said, sitting behind his desk, "Someone else has been here. One of my scrolls is missing, although it is of no importance having been an apprentice's spell. But I am concerned. I can feel the lingering presence of Wild Magic in the room. Just after I had teleported here, I felt a drain in the White Magic."

"What do you mean? Who would come here and take one scroll? Surely not a thief." Jacob asked Lionak.

"I don't know. It is strange." Lionak frowned, "It's almost as if a portal was opened with Wild Magic."

"What?" Jacob said defensively. He didn't know of anyone from his world that could do such a thing.

Having seen the dragon fly over the small city, Cindy ran towards Lionak's keep as her heart jumped inside her. She was so close to him, and now she pushed her legs hard so that she could be with him again. Breathing quickly, a tear streamed down the side of her face as she crossed the drawbridge and heaved the gate door open and crossed the courtyard and blasted through the study doors, surprising everyone inside. Finding Chief Zorin, she ran over to him and wrapped her arms about his chest, crying happily that he was really there. At last she had been reunited with him.

Stumbling back a few feet as she embraced him, Chief Zorin looked in utter surprise at Lionak as he slowly peeled Cindy from him and asked, "What are you doing here?"

"I came for you. And I have found you!" Cindy smiled with soft eyes.

Chief Zorin was at a loss for words at her pure emotional outburst which he could feel in the air about them.

"Yes, but how did you get here?" Lionak asked firmly. *'Could it be that she was the one that had opened the portal?'*

"I broke out of the prison they had me in and I came here." Cindy said as if that was all that was necessary while she wiped a tear from her cheek.

Jacob wanted to cut in, but he crossed his arms instead.

"Yes. But how did you travel here?" Chief Zorin rephrased, looking into her eyes.

"Oh. Well. The scientists in Cairo had made some device that was shaped like a hexagon and sent some soldiers through. I broke away from the soldiers and ran through the door." Cindy replied.

Looking around Jacob asked, "Where are they now?"

Cindy looked at him briefly and said, "Oh, they must have already gone back."

"How can they open a portal from their Land using the White and Wild Magic?" Lionak asked her.

"I don't know. They had large equipment doing it." Cindy responded.

"You remember when I told you that the government had advanced technology Zorin? Well, this is it, and they will return." Jacob grunted, surprised that they could actually open portals now.

"Yes." Chief Zorin said.

Jacob made a circular motion with his hand and said, "We better be prepared for their return."

Frowning, Cindy remarked, "I don't think that they are going to harm anyone here. I think they were just curious."

"Yeah okay. Well, tell me this," Jacob said as he looked at her, "Did they carry rifles with them?"

"Yes, but…"

"Alright then. I've made my point." Jacob said, cutting her off.

"Enough of this." Lionak rumbled out, "We have more important and immediate matters to attend to."

Urging everyone to sit down, Lionak said, "The Baron is what we are going to focus on. If we make any mistakes, be reminded, the Realm may be lost. We are his only remaining obstacle."

Chapter Fifty-One

"Ready the line!" General Lowinsky ordered the soldiers that maintained a defensive posture around the hexagon frame as the scientists activated the final sequence from the computer systems.

The soldiers readied their rifles and crouched down with one knee planted firmly on the sand, pointing their M16s at the middle of the frame awaiting the order to open fire. Again, ozone filled the air as the familiar blue haze filled the inside of the frame. Within a moment a dark sphere appeared in its center and flattened out and a deafening thunder rolled through the area, causing some of the soldiers to flinch. But they held fast their positions, watching the lightning begin to jump around the hexagon as the blue surface rotated in a counter-clockwise fashion.

The scientists looked at General Lowinsky with grins, realizing that they were able to open the dimensional door for the second time using an algorithmic variation that Janus had modeled for receiving, rather than sending, energy and matter from the target dimension.

A few seconds past but nothing happened. Agent Bradley looked at the general.

"Do you think this is going to work?" Agent Bradley said quietly.

"I don't know. But we have to try." General Lowinsky finally said after a long moment of staring into the dimensional door.

"Look there!" one of the scientists exclaimed, standing up suddenly and pointing at the door.

The General shot his eyes back to the door and saw the outline of a man walking towards the dimensional door. Slowly the man became more defined as the colors of his uniform began to show through the blue surface.

"Hold your fire!" General Lowinsky ordered, seeing a few of his men move somewhat, as if they were bracing themselves to open fire upon the figure.

As Sam walked through the threshold of the dimensional door and onto the sandy ground, he looked around in relief to know that he was back home. Turning around, he waited for all of his soldiers to emerge from the dimensional door before he turned to the general.

Smiling in triumph, Sam said, "All present sir!"

The General nodded and turned to the scientists, "Good. Deactivate the door."

Striding down the stairs and toward a series of trailers to his right, he looked at Agent Bradley and said, "Have them report to me within the hour. We have a lot to go over before we send John through."

"Yes sir." Agent Bradley replied as he turned and walked towards the soldiers. Although he said nothing, he wondered if Cindy had made it through.

"Stand down." He ordered the soldiers, who stood back up and lowered their weapons.

Then Agent Bradley turned toward Sam and said, "Colonel, prep your troops for a meeting with General Lowinsky within the hour."

"Alright. But what took you guys so long in opening the door?" Sam asked Agent Bradley who had started to walk off.

Turning about, Agent Bradley said, "What do you mean? We had that door re-opened within, maybe, five minutes at the most."

Sam grimaced and said, "We were on that world for several hours before the dimensional door opened again."

Agent Bradley looked surprised by the news but said nothing as he shrugged his shoulders and walked off. Science was never one of his stronger points.

Within the hour, Sam had successfully prepared his men for the meeting and had even arrived while General Lowinsky was still on the phone. Trying not to make any noise, they all sat around a large table and waited for the general to conclude his conversation.

"Yes, Mr. President. Phase one of our efforts here have succeeded." the general said into the phone as he tapped the end of his pen on the table, looking at some papers, "Yes sir. No, there was no radiation hazards for the men."

Sam looked around the room, wondering if he needed to change what he had planned to say to the general. He was never much for in-person reports.

"Yes. We are ready to proceed with phase two after our briefing." General Lowinsky said, looking a bit strained from the conversation, "Of course sir, I will keep you informed of our progress. Yes sir. Goodbye."

The general exhaled deeply as he hung up the phone and looked at the soldiers that were seated before him.

"Well, let's get this show on the road." the general grunted to Sam.

"Yes sir." Sam said, still unsure of where to begin as he paused to collect his thoughts.

Taking off his watch and showing it to the general, he started, "I noticed, when we went through the dimensional door, that the time on my watch had stopped."

The general took the watch and studied it for a moment, "Well, it seems to be working fine, colonel."

"It does now, sir. Agent Bradley had said it had only taken a few minutes for the door to be re-opened." Sam stated, pausing for an answer.

The general frowned at him slightly and said, "Yes it did."

"Well," Sam said, looking at his soldiers and back to the general, "we were in that world for several hours."

The general looked at one of the scientists that had followed the troops in with questioning eyes. He recalled they had mentioned something about time being an issue.

"Ah," one of the scientists said who was not entirely prepared on the subject, "that must have something to do with time dilation between dimensions. I'm not really sure, but I think because it is a different dimension that time is out of phase with ours. I suspect there are also subtle differences in matter as well."

"Interesting." the general said to himself.

"So, what of the readings you obtained?" General Lowinsky asked.

Sam looked at the soldier who had taken the readings on his scanner to provide the answer.

Uneasily the soldier, probably in his mid-twenties said, "Sir, all the readings appeared to be within all the normal check levels. Oxygen was normal. Gravity was normal and radiation levels were well below hazardous levels. I would say that their atmosphere is to be credited with such low radiation readings. As compared to here on Earth, the readings I took were between one and a half to two times lower than the radiation levels we accept as normal."

"Are they industrially developed?" the general asked.

"I don't believe so, sir." Sam replied, "I took a look around and from what I observed, without being discovered, was that the people appear to be living in what we could relate to as the renaissance period. Their clothes were simple. The patrolling guards I saw were dressed in armor and had swords."

"Humm. What do you think their threat level is colonel?" General Lowinsky asked.

The scientists looked at him with surprise.

"Low. They did not appear to be in possession of any advanced weaponry." Sam said cooly. He didn't much like the question himself, but he understood its importance.

"What was their language?" John said as he entered the room and sat at the table.

"English." Sam said.

"Fascinating." one of the scientists said as he looked at his colleagues.

"Oh, and another thing. They speak English, but they seem to write in a different language." Sam added as he motioned for one of his soldiers to produce the scroll and give it to the general.

"Get our linguistic team on that, on the double." the general ordered the scientist closest to him, who got up and walked out of the room, looking at the scroll he'd been given.

It was some time before the general broke the silence, "Well. I believe you are dismissed."

"What happened to Cindy? Did you see her?" Agent Bradley bravely inserted.

Sam looked at him for a moment before he spoke, "Yes. She managed to get past us and into the city. I did not pursue her due to our orders."

Sam's soldiers knew he was lying, but they said nothing.

"At least we know she is alive." Agent Bradley said finally, his conscience cleared.

"Everyone dismissed." the general said, "Except for you colonel and Bradley."

Sam sat back down in his chair, watching his troops leave the room along with the two remaining scientists.

When the door closed behind them the general said, "Now for phase two, gentlemen. You three will make up the contact team. Sam, you and Bradley will be in charge of John's personal safety. He will be our ambassador on this mission."

The general then turned to John, "All I want you to do is establish contact with whoever rules the area you are in. I hope they will see your presence in a positive light, and will not try to throw you into some dungeon for what might be assumed some sort of spy activity. So, in that light, do not try to put any ideas into their heads."

John nodded his head, although he was not sure how a spy might act so he could avoid doing it.

"Assemble at the staging area in one hour. Dismissed." the general concluded, putting the pen down on the table.

Chapter Fifty-Two

Morning arrived sooner than Regan wanted as she squinted at the rising Sun that beat softly against her face. Sluggishly she noticed that the horse was already up, perhaps for some time. Then standing, she found a sharp ache in her lower back from the small rocks she had slept on and the hard ride the day before. Grimacing, she slowly stretched herself out, which managed to subdue the pain although not to her satisfaction.

"How are you this morning?" Regan said as she approached the horse in a gingerly fashion.

The horse merely looked at her with those deep black eyes while Regan patted the animal on its muscular shoulder.

"It's time to go for a ride." She said, throwing the blanket onto the horse's back, and began saddling up.

The horse neighed at her softly and shook its head. The horse was ready to get off the outcropping of rock and continue on, though it would prefer going down.

After making sure all the fittings were snug, Regan put the bridle on the horse and with a dull nagging pain from her inner thighs, put her left foot into the saddle shoe and lifted her small, light body over the saddle until she sat firmly in its seat. After placing her other foot in the shoe, she urged the horse forward with the heels of her boots. Obediently the horse moved forward on up the trail with sure footing.

Scarcely minutes into the trek, Regan's stomach began to growl and churn about as she realized that she was hungry. Pulling a dried piece of meat out of her thin jacket, she bit down and tugged on the meat until it ripped off in her mouth. Regan didn't like eating such tough meat because it was excessively salty and after a few bites her jaw muscles always burned from the hard chewing. Because of that, she had rarely gone out on prolonged trips with anyone, just knowing that she would have to eat such meat. But now she didn't have a choice.

Finishing the meat, Regan opened her water skin and drank deeply from it, trying to wash the salt taste from her mouth and rid that feeling of dryness. She absolutely hated feeling thirsty all the time.

Within perhaps the span of three hours ride, Regan had stopped a few times along the trail to rub her sore legs and walk around a bit. It seemed that today's ride was much harder than yesterday's, partially because of her sore legs and the ruggedness of the terrain. And, as the horse climbed further up, the trail had become rockier, some places having been partially washed away from erosion. Several times Regan found herself backtracking to find alternate routes up the mountain. Then, around midday, with the Sun pounding down on her from overhead, she stopped at a small pond, the only one she'd spotted, filled with water and lead the horse to it so it could drink. Waiting for it to get its fill, she shed her jacket to try to keep cool before the two continued on.

By late afternoon she managed to make the last turn and found herself at the mouth of a cavern, proclaiming, "We've made it!"

With renewed vigor, Regan jumped off the horse with a smile of accomplishment and led the horse into the cavern, out of the rays of the Sun. Then, curiously, she looked about the cavern at a few strewn branches and a hanging globe anchored in the cavern's ceiling. Out of the corner of her eye she saw something gleam in between some jagged rock. Walking over to it, she pressed her slim fingers between the cracks in the rock and fumbled around until she was able to pull the object out. A gold coin.

"Oh! Look at this!" Regan exclaimed to the horse, happy that she had found something of value in the largely empty cave. She had climbed a few mountains in the northern region when she was younger, but never had she found a gold coin.

The horse neighed lowly as the mountain shook, sending Regan to land on her buttocks, a few stones falling out of the ceiling in the cavern. Quickly she stashed the gold coin in her pants pocket and looked around carefully at the cavern walls, wondering if it was going to collapse on her.

"What was that?" Regan said when another vibration went through the mountain, causing her to jump to her feet, becoming concerned for her survival. If the mountain collapsed, she would be killed, and that fueled her motivation to mount the horse who was backing out of the cavern with its ears back.

"Oh, come on. It's nothing to worry about." Regan said, trying to reassure the horse as the mountain shook again.

But just before she could grab the reins, the horse turned sharply and bolted down the trail, determined to run from whatever was causing the mountain to shake.

Frustrated and seeing her only means of transportation run away, Regan balled up her fists and yelled, "Damn it! You come back here!"

But that did her no good. Not knowing what to do, Regan turned and faced the cavern, her lips tight with anger. Then, faintly, she saw white sparkles appear on the cavern wall some six feet high and three feet wide as she squinted to see what it was. Gradually, white bolts of lightning jumped from sparkle to sparkle in a random pattern as a blue haze filled its midst and a black shadow became visible.

In fear Regan stepped back, ready to run down the trail thinking that the Baron was coming for her. For what purpose she did not know, but her heart became consumed in fear.

The outline of a man started to solidify from the shadow and into the cavern itself, his body smoking and white lightning dancing around his form. In what appeared to be a trance-like state, the man took a few steps forward and then collapsed heavily onto the cavern floor, the lightning bolts vanishing from sight.

"Mac!" Regan cried out, recognizing the man, and ran up to his limp body.

With haste, she knelt down beside him and pulled his cool, wet body onto her lap and cradled his head as a tear rolled down her cheek.

Throwing her head back in sadness, Regan cried, "No! No!"

Mac did not breathe.

Jacob, Captain Reeves and Eric were the first to leave the city, bound by horse to the site where the captain had hidden the tank. Their mission was simple. Since they were the only tank left on the Realm, and could not single-handedly destroy the Baron, they were to help the others by running interference. In other words, they were to distract the Baron as much as possible to allow Lionak and the Guardians to strike at whatever weakness the Baron had, provided they could discover one.

Even as Lionak and Chief Zorin prepared themselves for this battle, they could feel the presence of the White Magic around them even more easily than they had in the past. Perhaps it was their heightened sense about the power of the Baron that made them more aware. Regardless, they continued as their minds blurred with dozens of spells each of them had learned over the decades.

"I want to go with you." Cindy pleaded with Chief Zorin. She realized that, from deep within her heart, if he was to die that she could not go on living without him. She had never felt that way towards any other man.

Chief Zorin looked at her with sincere eyes and said, "I'm sorry but you can't."

Grabbing his shoulders she confessed, "I love you!"

Chief Zorin gazed deeply into those soft eyes, and smiled from his heart at those words as he touched her cheek.

"I know." Chief Zorin said simply as he closed in on her and softly touched his lips to hers and kissed her lightly.

Even after he pulled away from her, she stood there for a moment with her eyes closed, her heart racing with emotion as she savored that warm kiss. A tear rolled down her soft cheek which struck deeply at Chief Zorin's heart. He thought it strange for humans to become so quickly attached, briefly thinking it might have something to do with their short lifespans. Yet, truth be told, he wanted to stay with her, but the Realm demanded his full attention.

"I am ready Chief Zorin." Lionak said finally as he grabbed a twisted, knotted wooden staff from behind the shelf of books and scrolls.

Stepping away from her, Chief Zorin turned towards Lionak and said, "I am ready."

To their surprise, knowing that neither of them had cast a spell, a portal opened from the tapestry and three men walked through it with the portal closing behind them shortly after.

"Who are you?!" Lionak raged, clearly mystified as he held his staff at the ready to lash out at them with White Magic.

"We mean no harm!" came John's urgent response as Agent Bradley and Sam tensed up, seeing people so suddenly.

"What are you doing here?" Cindy shot out at Agent Bradley, stepping over to Chief Zorin.

"Look. We mean no harm. I am a representative of our land. We come in peace and we just want to talk to who might be the one ruling this land." John said, as the words formed on his tongue.

"I have no time to talk." Lionak said sternly to John with narrow eyes.

"So, you are the ruler?" John asked Lionak.

"I am not of royal blood, but I am the Wizard of the Realm. We will talk later." Lionak shot out as he began to weave the spell of teleportation around his body.

Frowning, Lionak tried the spell again, only to find that he had gone nowhere.

"What is happening?" Lionak cursed, puzzled as to why the spell had not worked.

"I don't know." Chief Zorin said as he followed Lionak out into the courtyard of the keep.

Looking up to the sky, he did not see the streak of dragon's fire from a falling rock which could rarely cause problems. Instead, what he did discover, was that the Sun appeared to be smeared as did the birds that flew overhead. Then he looked to Chief Zorin with distraught eyes knowing his task of leaving the keep would be difficult.

"We are trapped." Lionak announced finally, realizing that there was some strange creature covering the keep...a strange, almost transparent, creature he'd never encountered before.

"It is the work of the Baron." Chief Zorin suggested, finally able to make sense of everything, feeling the faint Dark Magic radiating from the creature, absorbing magic.

The Baron grinned as he continued to work on the stone tablets, their sigils beginning to glow an ever-deepening red. Furiously, he fed more Dark and Wild Magic into the sigils, at last able to understand what they represented, and spoke the words.

"Oloctu Relu Emcrasea Opflitum!" the Baron shouted out as he repeated the words in a deeper tone, "Oloctu Relu Emcrasea Opflitum!"

The ground beneath his feet began to shake violently as the stone tablets glowed white with heat, beginning to split, thunder echoing through the corridor and a mighty wind rushing out from the tablets.

The Baron took a few steps back, realizing that he'd successfully unlocked the secret of the tablets and looked upon them with eager eyes. Fire spewed out of the broken tablets as a dark clawed hand reached out from within it, and then the other. Slowly the horned head of some vile creature with red fissured eyes and pointed white teeth pulled itself out of the tablets, its mighty muscular red torso forming outside them. Leathery wings appeared behind the creature, opening up slowly as if from a deep sleep. Finally, with a simple motion, the wings flung out and the creature shot forth from the tablets and landed before the Baron.

"I am the void that brings eternal peace to all things! I am the key to the abyss of salvation!" the creature declared.

Then it peered at the lone figure of the Baron whom was unknown to it, yet strangely familiar.

Chapter Fifty-Three

"That coldness…do you feel it?" Matthew questioned two of his Low Priests who stood with him outside of the palace, looking out upon the setting Sun.

"Yes. The Dark Magic is here. It is stronger than what I thought it would be." one of the Low Priests replied soberly.

"It is time to destroy the Baron now that he has revealed himself!" Matthew thundered out. Finally, he would not have to wait any longer to confront the Baron.

Turning and heading towards the palace entrance, he pointed to one of the Low Priests and said, "Quick, gather the Guardians here! Be prepared to fight!"

"Yes, my lord." the Low Priest replied, transforming into his Silver Dragon form and taking flight.

"Irlok, come with me!" Matthew commanded as he broke out into a jog, bounding over the marble stairs and into the palace. Voices echoed from ahead of them.

The Dark Magic was throbbing with intense power as they found the jagged hole in the palace wall and transversed the staircase, down. But there was another presence. It was strange magic Matthew thought was the Wild Magic. And yet, it was different in some way.

"I am the one who freed you! Give me the knowledge to rule the Realm!" the Baron shot out at the creature who stood unwavering before him.

"The knowledge you seek on this shadow world is kept in the ancient scrolls." the creature responded almost instantly. Its knowledge was vast.

"Baron! Stop your Dark Magic!" Matthew rumbled out, "I command you!"

Surprised, the Baron turned about and faced Matthew and the Low Priest with squinted eyes, "You're a fool! No one can stop me from ruling the Realm!"

"Taste!" the Baron proclaimed, raising his hands towards them.

Thick, twisted bolts of reddish lightning flew out of his fingers and collided with the two figures, picking them up and hurtling them against the far wall. Unprepared for such a sudden attack, Matthew and Irlok found themselves lying on the ground gasping for breath.

A brilliant flash of light consumed the room the Baron was in and the creature disappeared. While the Baron was disappointed that he could not use the creature further, he got what he was after. All he had to do now was ensure that no one would stand in his way.

Getting to his feet, Matthew helped Irlok up and retreated a few steps into the long corridor. Seeing the Baron walk out of the stone room, Matthew summoned the White Magic. A flash of white lightning bolts shot out from his hands and smashed into the Baron. Unscathed, the Baron turned and faced them.

"Is that the best a High Priest can do?" the Baron taunted.

"Quick! Get the others down here!" Matthew whispered to Irlok.

Within a split second, Matthew raised his arms as his hands began to glow a deep white. Then he pointed towards the Baron and sent another volley of lightning at him. But, before the Baron had time to respond, Matthew conjured a frigid cone of frost at the Baron. Almost instantly the cone engulfed the Baron as the crackle of forming ice echoed through the corridor.

"Leave me!" Matthew commanded Irlok, noticing he was still there as he conjured another frost spell at the Baron. Again, another layer of thick ice formed over the Baron.

Irlok left Matthew in the corridor below the palace as he was commanded, even though he did not want to abandon Matthew.

Deep within the ice, the Baron stirred the Wild and Dark Magic around him. Slowly he began unweaving the frost spell that held him while, at the same time, beginning his transformation.

Matthew could hear the ice beginning to buckle while he changed to his Silver Dragon state. He knew the Baron could not be held by the ice for long. For an agonizing moment, he stood idle, waiting for the Baron to free himself. He wanted to throw another spell at the Baron, but realized if he did, he would actually help the Baron. That is not what he wanted.

Suddenly shards of ice and powder exploded through the corridor, Matthew standing before the hulking form of a Red Dragon tainted with silver remnants. Before Matthew could complete his spell, a thick stream of red-hot fire tumbled towards Matthew, knocking him back several steps. Swiftly, Matthew gained his stance and returned the attack with his own blast of red fire strengthened by White Magic. Dully he noticed that some of his own scales were charred from the last attack and knew he would not stand a chance alone against the Baron. He had to get to the others.

Again, the Baron pounded the Silver Dragon with an even more powerful blast of fire, causing Matthew to stumble back, suddenly dazed. Weakened, Matthew crouched down and shot through the layers of earth above him, leaving the Baron in the corridor as clumps of earth and stone dropped down from the freshly made hole. Shooting out into the sky, the Silver Dragon beat his wings and gained altitude, spotting the approach of some Guardians. Then, turning about, he saw the massive Red Dragon explode out of the ground after him.

Quickly Matthew hovered in place and shot a thick array of lightning bolts at the ascending dragon. The sheer impact of all that magic focused on the dragon caused it to roar and tumble uncontrollably towards the earth. Matthew descended after the limp form of the dragon, followed by a band of Guardians who landed not far from where the Baron fell.

After landing near the Baron, Matthew turned a golden eye towards him. His magical energy was almost exhausted.

"Is he dead?" one of the younger, obviously less experienced Silver Dragons asked.

"He cannot be." Matthew responded, an eerie sensation of unease shooting through him.

"That's right!" the Red Dragon bellowed out as he shot to his feet and conjured the Dark Magic around the Silver Dragons. Thick, scaly serpents, each with three long, slender appendages resembling those of a spider, two for grabbing and one to move prey in its grasp, shot out of the earth, and coiled up around the Silver Dragons before they knew what was happening.

"I want you to beg for death! You are nothing compared to my power!" the Baron roared, turning his scaly head towards Matthew.

"But you...you do not even deserve that!" the Baron thundered as he funneled a thick volley of yellow lightning bolts at the struggling Silver Dragon, bound by one of the giant serpents. The Wild Magic, coupled with the Dark Magic, disintegrated the serpent on impact and silver scales jumped into the air as Matthew was knocked backward, sprawling to the ground. Much of his neck and torso were dark with blood and his muscle could be seen from where silver scales used to be. Matthew struggled to get up, but his strength was weaning and his vision became blurred.

Faintly he saw the Baron take flight into the sky.

"Continue work on removing the bodies." King Doron grumbled to one of the barbarian warriors who was bloodied from the recent battle, "Do what you will with those other dogs!"

King Doron's barbaric fury almost surfaced again. His enemy lay before him dead and many of their iron-clad war machines had been stopped. Yet his enemy was not vanquished. Another war machine lurked beyond his grasp somewhere in the forests, his barbarian instincts telling him that it would return when he was ill-prepared. But he was determined to not befall that fate again.

After the barbarian bowed and walked off, King Doron strode up to another, "Neclor, prepare your best men and hunt down the war machine."

Neclor was one of King Doron's finest barbarian warriors and Under Lord of all of his army. Although Neclor wore a hard face, slightly wrinkled from enduring thirty-eight seasons, he could wield a battleaxe better than most lesser in age than he. And, the loyalty he commanded from his troops was almost as great as King Doron himself. Even though Neclor did not possess magic like the Guardians of the White Magic, King Doron had more faith in Neclor's cunning and war skill than those of the Guardians.

Neclor, clothed in leather jerkins and grasping a bloodied battleaxe, grinned with pleasure at King Doron's command. His black eyes stared into King Doron's as he swore, "Yes, my King. I'll not rest until that war machine is destroyed!"

"Excellent!" King Doron remarked, trying to mask his satisfaction at hearing those words. He would have his vengeance quenched for the many deaths of his barbarian kin.

Out of the corner of his eye, King Doron saw a dark shadow roll over the ground beside him. Looking up, his heart lurched in surprise and sudden anger.

"Damn you! Face me Baron!" King Doron shouted at the Red Dragon who held fast his course north.

"What of the dragon?" Neclor asked as he watched the Red Dragon. If commanded, he was ready to attack the dragon without fear.

"That is a matter for me to deal with!" King Doron fumed, "You destroy that war machine!"

"Sir!" Neclor replied sternly as King Doron turned about and ran towards his palace.

Darting around stone buildings and wooden huts, King Doron made quick time of getting to the palace, his muscles bound up from the sudden burst. In a matter of a few steps, he vaulted over the marble stairs and rushed into the palace, slowing down to look around. Not finding Matthew, nor hearing any echoing noises one might associate with footfalls or even whispers, he turned and darted back outside wondering how the Baron could have slipped past all of the Guardians who were supposedly ready to attack him.

Pausing momentarily, King Doron then jogged around to the rear of the palace only to find that one of the Guardians laid on the ground severely wounded, and five others squirmed to free themselves from large, dark colored serpents.

"What evil is this?!" King Doron yelled as he withdrew his sword and cleaved one of the serpents in half with a mighty swing, fueled by his barbarian strength.

Again, he severed another serpent, sending dark red blood to the ground and freeing another of the Guardians. Together, they freed the remaining Silver Dragons in the span of seconds before he realized that the blade of his sword was somehow melting. Tossing it to the ground, he watched as the sword started to smoke and ooze into the earth like a puddle of water. He grimaced with the assumption that it was the work of the Baron's magic that destroyed his sword and had created the serpents. He turned his attention to the Guardian who was barely conscious and bleeding on the ground before him.

"What has happened?" King Doron asked. He couldn't believe that the Baron was able to escape so easily.

"The Baron slipped by us." the Silver Dragon said in the voice of Matthew.

The dragon turned its head toward King Doron, "You must tell Lionak and Chief Zorin."

Matthew drug in a deep breath and said, "I fear that I will not be able to."

Then the Silver Dragon became still, exhaling its final breath. Slowly, King Doron reached out and placed a hand on the Silver Dragon's shoulder.

Chapter Fifty-Four

"When are we supposed to come to bear on this Baron?" Captain Reeves asked Jacob as he guided his horse behind Eric's through the forest.

"Don't worry, we'll be told about it." Jacob responded in a flat tone. He still had the urge to slug the captain again for having had a hand in demolishing the Kingdom of Shek. But he reminded himself that the Baron had fooled them into believing that he was the President, and that they were just following orders.

"Yes, but how? By the time we get word of what is going on, things could very well change by the time we get to wherever the Baron might be." Eric said as he looked behind him for a moment.

"Look. If it will make you feel any better, we're going to drive the tank south to where we know the Baron is." Jacob finally said after a long pause. He had already taken such a plan into consideration.

That seemed to be a better alternative to Captain Reeves. Still, he didn't much like the idea of having someone he didn't know in charge of him, or his men. But things as they were, was something he would tolerate for now.

Quietness shrouded them for the remainder of the trek through the forest until they came upon the defense perimeter and a voice sliced through the air, "Strangers be ill-mannered!"

Eric recognized the challenge and responded, "Only on a pirate ship."

Off ahead, Jacob heard the rustling of leaves as the voice commanded, "Advance and be recognized."

Eric turned and motioned for them to follow him. After the horses moved forward a few steps, the voice commanded, "Stop there!"

After a moment the voice said, "Welcome back, sir. And you sir. Nice horses."

Then a man carrying a M16 assault rifle with full combat gear emerged from a cluster of bushes, smiling at them. Jacob raised his eyebrows in surprise. He didn't know that a tank crew was so well organized and trained. But, then again, he didn't know Captain Reeves that well.

Following them for some two hundred meters, Jacob found himself in the midst of a manmade clearing with a camouflage net strung up overhead in the trees. The dim outline of the tank could be seen to his left and a gathering of soldiers mumbled to themselves ahead of the tank.

"Ah, nothing like being home." Captain Reeves smiled to himself, in a way happy that he was back amongst his men.

"Aye, sir." Eric agreed as he dismounted and strode off ahead of them and sat down next to a few of the soldiers.

Not sure where to begin, Captain Reeves said, "Well, do you want something to eat?"

"Yeah. I could use something." Jacob replied, his stomach already churning in anticipation of eating, getting off his horse after the captain.

"Well, it might not be mama's cooking, but it'll fill you up. What do you like anyway?" Captain Reeves asked as he opened a box of MRE's.

"I'll have a chicken and rice MRE, or a number 6." Jacob replied as he sat down next to Captain Reeves in a crudely fashioned wooden chair. Partially out of boredom he looked up into the night sky.

"So, you have been in the military then?" Captain Reeves asked, surprised that Jacob knew the meals by number.

"Yeah. I served a few tours in Germany, Korea and Central America." Jacob sighed as he took the chicken and rice MRE from the captain, still looking into the sky. The chair crackled quietly as he adjusted his weight and opened the brown package.

"Really? At least I know you're not a civilian. I should have figured as much from that blow you gave me." Captain Reeves jested as he poured the contents of the small hot sauce bottle over his ham slice and took a savory bite.

"Well, I can't say that I'm sorry for that. I've become kind of attached to this world." Jacob admitted as he chewed on a mouthful of food.

"Oh, speaking of that, it seems that your kind of a legend around here." Captain Reeves began, taking a sip from his canteen.

Jacob smiled inwardly. He liked the thought of being a legend.

"At least that was what that woman said...Regan." Captain Reeves grunted.

"Regan? She's just a bitch." Jacob hissed as he shot a glaring eye at Captain Reeves.

"Well, she helped us find you. I wouldn't call that so bad." Captain Reeves said, partially defending her. He didn't find anything wrong with the lady.

"You don't know her like I do." Jacob pointed out, "If you did, you wouldn't trust her with your worst enemy."

"I guess I don't." Captain Reeves replied, tearing open a package of crackers.

"She spoke of a man named Mac. She said that he was a friend of yours." Captain Reeves stated openly.

Jacob wondered what Regan was up to, and why she would talk about Mac and himself, apparently as openly as Captain Reeves was. He swallowed hard and said, "Mac is an old friend. We go back a long way."

"He is in the military as well?" Captain Reeves asked.

"Oh, he used to be. But things were better for him on the outside." Jacob stated as he finished his serving, "But what about you? Where were you stationed before the Baron got his hands on you?"

"I was the commanding officer of a detachment patrolling the border of Sudan." Captain Reeves said while breaking one of the crackers in half and squirting some cheese on it, "Then we got the message from the CIC. Well, I guess it was the Baron, ordering us to proceed to a grid in the north. I thought it was strange, but never questioned the order."

"Humm." Jacob sighed as he grasped a pair of night vision goggles and flipped them on, looking into the sky with them. He was always amazed with just how many more stars he could see by using a pair of infrared goggles as compared to binoculars.

Suddenly an object passed overhead. Quickly Jacob re-focused the goggles and followed it. At first he thought it was a bird, but noticing the long, trailing tail, he realized that it was a dragon. He thought it was a little odd that a Silver Dragon would not show up clearer against the dark green silhouetted sky. But, then again, he'd never seen a Silver Dragon through infrared goggles to have any reference. After the dragon passed over the trees where he could see it, Jacob put down the goggles. He could only guess as to what was happening.

"Looks like a dragon just flew over." Jacob said, flipping the goggles off. He wondered why a Silver Dragon would be traveling north when he knew the Baron was south of their position.

"Really?" Captain Reeves practically stammered, looking overhead momentarily. Those dragons sure were determined to find his tank.

Getting up, Jacob said, "I guess we should get some sleep. We'll head out to the Kingdom in the morning."

The night was pleasantly cool. Crickets sang softly through the forest as the soldiers slept. Dully, a soldier looked about the forest around him, keeping guard. Reaching into his desert fatigue shoulder pocket, he pulled out a box of cigarettes and a lighter. After setting his rifle next to a neighboring tree, he pulled out a cigarette, set it between his lips and lit it. After inhaling deeply and stuffing the box back in his pocket, he reached over and picked up his weapon.

Trying to stay alert, the soldier began to walk slowly around the camp, taking frequent drags off the cigarette. He hated night guard. Mainly because that was the time he preferred to sleep. But he only had two more hours to go before he would be relieved of duty.

The soldier stopped suddenly, hearing the noise of a snapping branch and turned toward the origin of the noise, which couldn't have been more than twenty-five meters from him. Squinting into the dark forest, the soldier half expected a wild bear to be lurking out there as he raised his weapon and clicked the selector lever to burst. As the seconds passed, he slowly lowered his rifle and began to walk forward again. He convinced himself that it must have been a falling branch. But, in the back of his mind, he couldn't help but think of that wild bear.

Then he felt a pair of leathery hands grab him with incredible strength. The soldier tried to pivot out of the assailant's grasp, but his unseen foe was quicker. The soldier's heart began to race as he felt a warm hand clasp tightly about his mouth, stretching the skin over his cheek bones. Then he felt something cold and sharp pierce into his chest. The sharp object dove deeper and deeper into his chest until he felt it plow into his beating heart. A sense of shock shot through his body, his eyes widened with terror. Again, the soldier tried to struggle out of the assailant's grasp. But, ever so quickly, his body became numb and his eyelids heavied. Darkness shrouded his vision as he felt himself fall.

Neclor withdrew his double-edged dagger from the soldier's chest and released his grip as the soldier toppled over before his feet. Blood flowed from his dagger like water being poured from a glass. Without hesitation, Neclor shot a hand toward the sky and pulled it back down to him, signaling for his men to attack the camp.

Jacob slept soundly next to the horses over a green foam sleeping mat. With the saddles removed, the horses also slept next to each other. Then something startled one of the horses rousing it from sleep. Suddenly alert, the horse peered around itself with its ears pointed forward. The horse sensed something was not right. It felt a peculiar sense of danger that it could not see. But the odor that hung in the light breeze was familiar. Uneasily, the horse neighed lowly, urging its kin to awaken, warning them of danger.

Defiantly, Jacob gained consciousness, having heard the horse's grumble. Slowly he opened his eyes and sat up, yawning.

"What's wrong?" Jacob whispered to the horse, not wanting to wake the others.

The horse merely folded back one of its ears momentarily as it looked around.

"Well, be quiet, will you? Some of us like to sleep." Jacob grunted as he lay back down. But then he heard something heavy fall in the forest.

Instantly Jacob shot back up and looked around. Something was out there, and he realized the horse was startled by it. Quietly, Jacob rose to his feet and made his way to the tank, crouched over. Finding the night vision goggles, he put them on over his head and flipped the switch. The darkness of the forest was replaced with the imagery of trees and some bushes greener than others, which gave the perception of distance. He turned his head and scanned the forest, looking for whatever had caused that heavy thud. It might have been nothing to worry about, but he had to satisfy his curiosity as to why the horse was spooked.

Out of the corner of the viewing area, he saw something move. Quickly he turned his head so that he could see whatever it was. It appeared to be a man. But Jacob couldn't identify the man as he disappeared from sight behind a cluster of bushes. Jacob assumed the man might be a thief. None of the soldiers would have a reason to dart around the bushes.

Finding Captain Reeves' sleeping form, he strode over and shook him awake.

When the captain opened his eyes, Jacob whispered, "I think we have a thief prowling outside the camp."

"What?" Captain Reeves whispered back as he gained consciousness and tried to concentrate on what Jacob said, "Are you sure?"

"Yeah. Saw him with the NVGs." Jacob said.

"What about the guard? Why didn't he warn us?" Captain Reeves groaned as he got up and shrugged the fog of sleep from him.

"Beats me." Jacob said as he removed the goggles and turned them off.

"Are you sure it's just one?" Captain Reeves asked as he strapped his 9mm pistol around his waist.

"I only saw one." Jacob shrugged, "But there could be others."

"Well, I'll wake the soldiers. Here, you might need this." Captain Reeves said as he got up and tossed Jacob an assault rifle.

"Aagrhh!" the barbarians blasted as they raided the camp from all sides. Bloodlust filled their eyes, grasping their weapons in eager anticipation of beheading their sleeping foe.

"Shit!" Jacob exclaimed in surprise as he impulsively clicked the selector lever from safe to burst, turning to face the closest assailant.

Pulling the trigger back, the rifle kicked out three rounds as flashes of light burst out from the tip of the barrel and expended casings jumped from the side of the weapon. Jacob watched the barbarian stumble backwards as the bullets buried themselves in his muscular chest, shredding the leather jerkins. Noticing that three rounds had been fired, Jacob let go of the trigger to reset the latch. With the smoothness of a snake coiling up for an attack, he found another barbarian rushing him, wielding a battleaxe. Squinting his eyes together, he squeezed the trigger. The horses suddenly bolted in different directions from the continued firing.

Several of the other barbarians jumped on the sleeping soldiers just as Captain Reeves got to them and Jacob began his defensive attack. Chaos filled the area as the soldiers awoke to flying fists and flashing daggers. Two of them died trying to get out of their sleeping bags before the thirsty edge of battleaxes.

"Eric, watch your nine!" Captain Reeves shouted above the noise of battle as he, himself, barely managed to dodge a crashing bastard sword meant for his head.

Reeling around, he withdrew his pistol and fired it at the hulking barbarian that attacked him. The sudden impact of the 9mm rounds in the barbarian's shoulder forced him back a step, loosing grasp of the sword. Wincing at the pain, the barbarian turned again toward Captain Reeves as raged flowed into him. Within a few steps the barbarian scooped up the captain as if he were just a baby, wrapping his thick arms about his chest and began to squeeze his squirming body. Captain Reeves felt his breath flow out of him as the barbarian poured more power into his mighty arms, trying to break his back. Unable to breath, the captain felt his face build with pressure as he tried to break the arm-lock. But the barbarian was far too strong. Limply, he tried to turn the pistol on the barbarian to fire a shot, but every time he did, the barbarian increased his death grip.

Seeing a bearded barbarian rush him from his left, Eric ran forward and grabbed an assault rifle. Rolling to his left, Eric got to a crouched position, leveled the barrel at the barbarian and pulled the trigger. Nothing happened.

"Damn this bloody thing!" Eric cursed to himself as he raised the rifle over his head, stopping the bastard sword in mid-air. Then he forced himself to a standing position and planted the composite fiberglass rifle butt squarely into the barbarian's scarred face.

The barbarian stumbled back long enough for Eric to glance down at the rifle and notice that the ammunition clip was missing. But, in the same glance, he realized the M203 grenade launcher appeared to be loaded. The range was too close for Eric's comfort, but seeing the barbarian charge him again forced him to make a choice. Bringing his left hand down to the trigger of the grenade launcher, he aimed for the barbarian and pulled the long trigger. A deep pop emanated from it as the round jumped out of the short barrel. Scarcely a moment later a muffled explosion and a brilliant flash of light came forth from the barbarian. Limbs, shredded pieces of leather and blood rained down on the camp after the barbarian disappeared in the explosion, sending Eric to his back. The smell of powder and burning flesh rolled through the camp.

Momentarily dazed and breathless, Eric managed to scramble to his feet and see that Captain Reeves was not as fortunate as he. Without hesitation, Eric raced over and raised the butt of the rifle at the massive barbarian that held the captain. Forcing it downwards, he heard the barbarian's knee crack as his leg folded underneath him. The barbarian, startled as the deep ebb of pain surged through him, released the captain and caught himself with his arms. Holding his knee, the barbarian strained to stand up as he pushed past the throbbing pain and came towards Eric who stood there temporarily paralyzed, marveling at the willpower of the barbarian. He knew that such a blow would have immobilized most men with some succumbing to shock, and yet this one seemed to not even be phased by it.

Three shots rang out and the barbarian toppled over in front of Eric, revealing the panting form of Captain Reeves who was trying to get to his feet. Rushing up to the captain, Eric said, "Sir, we have to get out of here!"

Seeing them approach from the corner of his eye, Jacob retreated a few steps to the tank and shouted between bursts from the rifle, "You breaking up the party already?!"

"Yeah! Let's get out of here!" Eric returned, pulling Captain Reeves onto the tank.

Within moments, Eric shot down the front hatch of the tank and started the gas turbine as Captain Reeves climbed into the turret. Jacob scurried onto the tank, removing the empty clip from the rifle.

"Get aboard!" Jacob shouted to the other soldiers above the whine of the engine as the tank suddenly lurched forward.

Even as the tank rolled forward, only five soldiers managed to climb on. The other two were hacked down by the pursuing barbarians.

"Damn." Jacob mumbled to himself. In an instant his mind flashed to one of his missions as his platoon was extracted from a host zone in South America. Then, as now, his weapon was empty as he watched helplessly a squad of his men fall short of the chopper, filled with bullets from an attacking rebel element.

Jacob shook his head in disgust. He never thought he would behold such a gut-wrenching sight as that again.

Chapter Fifty-Five

Regan peered outside of the dimly lit cavern, staring blankly into the darkness, rubbing her thumb across the rough surface of the gold coin she had found. The quakes had ceased which eased her mind. But now she wondered what she would do. Mac lay dead in the cavern behind her, and her horse had left her to fend for herself. Even as she pushed her hand through her short blond hair, she tried to think of a way to get back to the city. She realized it would be a hard trek by foot and her limited provisions would not last. And, with no weapons, she knew she would not be able to defend herself from the wild beasts that lived in the forests. Maybe someone would come.

Standing up, Regan walked over to the opening of the cavern and leaned on the jagged wall, still trying to convince herself that Mac was not dead. It just seemed impossible to her that a god could die. What god could live for hundreds of years and die? She sure didn't know of any. And yet, Mac was dead.

Then her mind wandered to the first time she had seen him in the tavern she had been working in. In an odd kind of way, he was attractive. He seemed so innocent. So sincere and even lonely. She smiled as she remembered Mac's sincerity when he asked her for a walk even though he was drunk. Inwardly she cursed herself for being too caught up with her rich friends and maintaining her image that pushed her to not take him up on the offer. Yet, had she, even her parents would not have accepted it and she would never hear the end of it. She knew that, sooner or later, they would find out that he was not a wealthy man, and not even from the city. Now, part of her wondered if all that was really worth having worried about in the first place.

That brought up Samric. He had been accepted by her parents and her friends. No, he was not that wealthy, but he was from the city, a noble line, and lived all of his life there with aspirations of becoming an engineer. That is, until he entered the service of the merchant trade. Regan speculated that Samric would one day be wealthy and would be able to provide for her as her father did. But with all those months away from her, she wondered what he did, going in and out of strange lands. It seemed that all he wanted to do when he returned was to have sex and visit taverns. Could it be that she was not the only one in his life? Regan frowned as she thought that he could have other women in waiting as she. But why didn't she think of that before? Like when she had met Mac? He was there for her then, but she had shrugged him off as a low-life.

Regan exhaled deeply as she glanced back at Mac's body. For the first time in her life, she began to see what life really was, and it was not trying to merely be part of the crowd. Slowly, Regan turned and walked over to Mac's body. Although her legs were still sore, she knelt down beside him. Her blue eyes studied his expressionless face. She began to doubt that she had ever really loved Samric. In some part of her, she realized that it was Mac she could have loved, barred from all of the protocol of wealth and social approval. She believed that Mac, as plain as he was, had been perhaps the closest to true life that anyone could be.

Lowering her head over his, Regan bent down and pressed her soft lips against his for a long moment as those emotions poured from her. Then she jerked her head away with widened eyes and pressed the back of her hand on his cheek. He was warm! But how could that be? Again, Regan pressed her lips on Mac's, hoping for a response that would tell her he was alive. But after a moment she pulled away again, her eyes soft with sadness.

"You have to be alive." Regan muttered softly as she looked at Mac, touching his shoulder. He was warm. There could be no other explanation as to why he was warm.

Regan's heart jumped within her when Mac lurched forward and inhaled a deep breath. Opening his eyes, Mac looked around rapidly to find Regan sitting next to him with a wide smile.

"Where am I?" Mac whispered hoarsely, barely able to talk.

Tears of relief and happiness rolled down her cheeks as she stared at Mac with glee, "You're in a cavern! Your alive!"

Not waiting for an invitation, Regan put her arms around Mac's neck and pulled him near her, kissing him passionately. In surprise, Mac's eyes widened as he raised an arm to push her away. But even as he raised it, he placed it gently behind Regan's head instead as his senses awoke to her soft lips on his and, in turn, caressed hers.

Lowering his arm as she gently pulled away, Mac asked, "How did you get here?"

"I came to see you. I just couldn't believe that you were going to die." Regan smiled sweetly.

Mac looked into her eyes. He liked that smile.

"I thought I had died. For the longest time I felt tremendous power all around me, trying to pull me apart. All there was, was black. I thought I was dead." Mac confessed as he touched himself. Little did he know that he would have died if it had not been for Metsys. For it was Metsys' act of resurrecting Mac that had intertwined the White Magic into Mac's essence of Wild Magic, in a sense bonding the two together. And, it was this bond that, even in the heart of the Pure Magic where it was most powerful, that magic couldn't dispel both because of that bond.

"But you are not dead." Regan said proudly. She was so overcome with emotion knowing he was alive that she didn't know what to do.

"That's good. I didn't really want to die." Mac responded soberly as he managed to get to his feet. Despite his weakened state, he reached down with an open hand towards Regan. She put her hand in his and got to her feet and stood close to him.

"What are you going to do now?" Regan asked, still grasping his large hand.

Mac shrugged and said, "I guess I'll go back and see Lionak. I'm sure that the Baron is still causing mayhem. Who knows, maybe I'll be able to help."

With that, Mac slowly strode out of the cavern as his strength returned, followed closely by Regan who was still smiling.

"Damn. That Baron is inventive." Lionak complained as he flipped through yet another spell book impatiently. None of the spells he, or his forefathers had thought of spoke of one that would repel such a creature as the one that engulfed the ancient keep. None had ever envisioned such an entity ever existing.

They had already tried to attack it with their combined magical power, but it seemed as though the creature just absorbed the magic. Little did they know, the water spirit acted as a conduit by absorbing energy and redirecting it into the moat and connecting waterway. And less did they know, the matured water spirit could no longer be affected by magical spells.

"Unfortunately." Chief Zorin agreed as he peered at another book.

"What are they talking about?" John asked Cindy who was nearby.

"I don't know. Why don't you ask them?" Cindy replied evenly. She hoped that Chief Zorin would not leave her again and, inwardly, she prayed that they would not be able to find whatever they were looking for.

"Why not just shoot the damn thing?" Sam suggested, openly bored out of his mind.

"Shoot it?" Lionak said, looking at Sam with puzzled eyes.

"Yeah." Sam returned, unslinging his rifle and walking to the opened double doors.

"I don't think that would be prudent." John stressed, scowling at Sam.

"Well, anything is worth a try." Chief Zorin said as he faced John.

"Alright." Sam smiled as he headed down the staircase and into the dark courtyard, happy that someone agreed with him for once.

Chief Zorin followed him to the edge of the staircase. Flipping the selector lever to burst, he raised the barrel into the air and pulled the trigger. Flashes of light filled the courtyard as the rifle kicked out rounds. But after the shots, all Sam and Chief Zorin noticed were minute illuminations where the rounds hit the mysterious creature. Disgusted, Sam lowered the weapon and looked at Chief Zorin.

"That didn't work." Chief Zorin said, disappointed as he turned and strode back into the study lit by torchlight.

"Damn it! There has to be a way of destroying this thing!" Lionak fumed as he rubbed his eyes and looked to Chief Zorin. None of his books or scrolls gave even a clue as to how to destroy anything like the creature they now faced.

"I know." Chief Zorin shrugged as he sat down in a finely crafted wooden chair, "Perhaps we are looking in the wrong place."

Lionak narrowed his eyes at him, "The wrong place? Magic is the most powerful tool I know of."

Chief Zorin raised his hand in a questioning fashion. He had no suggestions.

"Hey, this creature that's around the keep. Why not use a battering ram like one would use to breach a castle?" John offered as he recalled how soldiers in the renaissance period invaded castles. It made sense to him. If it was physical, one should be able to punch a hole in it.

Lionak glanced at Chief Zorin with raised eyebrows and wondered why he didn't think of doing such a thing.

"Good idea." Chief Zorin said as he stood up, pointing at John.

John smiled to himself. What better way to gain the ear of Lionak than to help them out of a dilemma such as this? He was confident he would be able to set good relations with Lionak now. That is, if his idea worked.

Pushing himself away from the desk, Lionak stood and, grasping the wooden staff, exited the study, followed by the others. Halting in the midst of the courtyard, Lionak raised his staff with one hand and began to call the White Magic to himself, closing his eyes. Within a few moments the air around the top of the staff began to glow a faint white as it swirled around. Steadily the swirling cloud grew and grew as he collected the threads of White Magic. Then, as if the staff was a magnet, the swirling cloud entered the staff. A low thunder echoed through the courtyard as a lightning bolt shot out from the top of the staff and danced before Lionak in a circular fashion. Slowly he lowered the staff and a long wooden beam appeared on the earth before him.

Opening his eyes, Lionak gazed upon the beam and then glanced behind him, "There you have it. One battering ram."

Agent Bradley and Sam stared at Lionak in awe. Neither could believe that Lionak just created something out of thin air. Yet, the battering ram rested on the ground before him.

John's mouth dropped open and wondered just how Lionak did it, and if he could make other things, too, like gold. Then he wondered if magicians in his world were more than just clever illusionists.

"No time to lose. Let's punch a hole in this creature and get out of here." Chief Zorin urged as he walked over to the battering ram.

As if they were snapped out of a dream state, the others gathered themselves around the battering ram and heaved the large beam into the air.

"Boy this thing is heavy." Sam groaned as they shuffled over to the entrance by the drawbridge, "You should have made it a little lighter at least."

Lionak smiled at the remark.

"Ready." Chief Zorin said as he looked behind him to the others, "Heave!"

In unison they jogged forward until the battering ram collided with the creature. A faint glimmer rippled out over the creature from where the battering ram had made contact with it. Stepping back with the battering ram, Chief Zorin again moved forward with the others, "Heave!"

Again, another glimmer resonated as the battering ram hit the creature.

"Come on! Put your backs into it!" Chief Zorin encouraged. He knew it would take more force to affect the creature.

Once again, they plowed the battering ram into the creature. This time he noticed the head of the battering ram plunge into the side of the creature, stretching the virtually invisible skin. But, as soon as the force was transferred from the battering ram to the creature, the skin of the creature rebounded like a rubber band, sending them back a step.

"We've almost got it!" Chief Zorin shouted proudly as they stepped back further, "The creature gave way for a moment!"

But trying to jog, even for that short distance, with the battering ram was no easy task. Especially when they were doing it repeatedly, none physically molded for such a brutish activity. Already Sam and Agent Bradley were carrying heavy breaths and their bodies were beginning to feel as if they were on fire. Chief Zorin fared best at the task, although he was beginning to drag in deeper breaths in his human form.

"Come on, take a few more steps back!" Chief Zorin said as he urged them back further, "We need more momentum."

"Heave!" He burst out as they sprang forward with the battering ram.

Agent Bradley almost stumbled over himself, his legs becoming heavy. But he caught himself and grunted. He would not be able to do much more.

With the added momentum the battering ram pushed deeper into the creature as Chief Zorin saw the skin stretch as he collided with the creature. Still grasping the battering ram and pressed against the creature's skin, he noticed that the head of the battering ram passed further out as another glimmer resonated over the creature's skin. But almost as quickly, the skin retracted and sent them reeling back almost three feet, barely able to keep hold of the heavy beam.

"I don't think we're getting anywhere." Sam confessed between heavy breaths. Sweat was rolling off of him.

"We are! The ram passed over a foot into the creature!" Chief Zorin retorted, unwilling to give up just yet, "One more time. This time let's pound a hole in that thing!"

Taking a deep breath, Sam went back several more feet with them and looked forward with focused eyes.

"Let's do it!" Agent Bradley shot out, mentally trying to overcome the burning sensation in his body, and the numbness of his arms.

"Heave!" Chief Zorin shouted with absolute determination and widened eyes.

Rushing forward, the battering ram passed again into the creature's skin. But this time the sheer force of the impact caused the creature's skin to flash a brilliant blue around the head of the battering ram as it punctured and passed through. Unable to stop, Chief Zorin collided with the creature's skin as he felt Agent Bradley run into him. Out of the corner of his eye he saw Sam run into the creature on the other side of the battering ram as it continued going through. John managed to stop himself just before he was within arm's breadth of Sam. With a deep thud, the battering ram fell heavily onto the threshold of the drawbridge. Instantly the creature's skin closed up around the hole.

"Damn." Chief Zorin cursed as he stepped back, seeing the hole disappear.

"Well. It was worth a try." John sighed as he looked at Lionak.

"Watch out!" Lionak shouted, startling John and the others. But his warning did not come soon enough for Sam.

"Aahh!" Sam cried out in horror as he felt cold tentacles from the creature wrap about himself tightly. He struggled to free himself but the tentacles were far too strong. He felt himself being pulled toward the creature gradually and shot a pleading look to Lionak.

"By the gods!" Chief Zorin howled in surprise, seeing the tentacles wrapped around Sam's body, pulling him towards the creature's skin.

Out of instinct he summoned the White Magic to him as he pointed at one of the tentacles and sent a twisting bolt of lightning at it. Sam shrieked in pain as the power of the lightning bolt flowed through him, conducted by the tentacle.

"What are you doing?!" John bellowed out at Chief Zorin.

Realizing that he had actually hurt Sam, Chief Zorin lowered his hand and shot a questioning look at John, "Damn thing is a conduit. No wonder our magic did not affect it!"

"Quick! Get the sword I have in the study by the tapestries!" Lionak commanded Agent Bradley.

Instantly, Agent Bradley rushed up the staircase and into the study. Stopping long enough to look around at the tapestries, he spotted the sword still in its sheath next to the first tapestry. He ran over, picked it up and yanked the sword out of the sheath as he darted back out.

"Zorin!" he shouted as he threw the sword into the air.

Judging how the sword would fall, Chief Zorin made a half-step to the left and grasped the long grip of the sword. Sprinting over to Sam, he raised the blade and sent it crashing down on the tentacles with keen precision. The blade severed the tentacles, breaking apart into water droplets and falling to the ground, rolling back into the creature.

Suddenly freed, Sam lurched forward and tumbled to the ground heavily. Chief Zorin retreated a few steps, wielding the sword before him in a defensive posture, looking at the creature's skin, ready to sever any more tentacles.

"Hey, you okay?" John asked Sam as he helped him to his feet.

"Fuck." Sam mumbled weakly, "Tell him to keep his lightning to himself, eh?"

"What now?" Chief Zorin asked as he lowered the sword.

"Well," John thought out loud, "Let's not get too close to it."

Chief Zorin turned to smirk at him.

"I have no solution." Lionak said as he looked at the creature, "It appears that we are prisoners."

Chapter Fifty-Six

The breeze was cool on the Baron during the flight north in the night sky. But his mind wandered from the cold air to the more pressing matter at hand. The

371

Secret Scrolls. He recalled the ancient demon saying that they held the answer to his quest for dominating the Realm. But how? The Baron was told that the Scrolls were simply writings about the White Magic and he did not see how that would serve his purpose. After all, he was only trained in the ways of Dark Magic. Then, after passing through a series of thick clouds he saw the outlines of the Northern Ice Mountains and the stronghold of the Guardians.

Descending a few thousand feet, the Baron slowed his speed somewhat and lessened his control over the body of the Guardian he had possessed so that its scale tones became more silver in color. He could feel the White Magic grow as he gained upon the stronghold. And, from the strength of the magic, he knew that perhaps ten Guardians were there. Maybe a few more.

Calmly exhaling, the Baron realized he would not be able to just walk in and defeat the Guardians without losing his husk and, if he did lose his possession, it could cost him his life if he could not flee in his translucent form. Instead, the Baron had determined he would use the Guardian's body as an illusion. Then he would be able to pass into the stronghold with no resistance and steal the Secret Scrolls. At least that was the plan.

"Stop this tank!" Captain Reeves commanded into the com-link.

Eric brought the tank to a smooth stop on the dirt road that twisted south to the Kingdom of Shek, "Roger that, sir."

"What now?" Jacob groaned impatiently, eager to get to the Kingdom of Shek and attack the Baron.

"You know, this sure is odd." Captain Reeves said as he removed his Kevlar helmet and placed it on the turret before him.

"What do you mean?" Jacob asked.

"It sure is strange that a band of those savages would attack us when Lionak said we should go to the

Kingdom of Shek and basically defend them." He pointed out, seeing Eric climb over the front end of the tank and rest a hand on the large barrel.

"They are not savages." Jacob said defiantly, "They are barbarians."

"Okay, barbarians." Captain Reeves admitted, "Now it seems to be that a failure to communicate by someone has caused us a few problems here."

"How so?" Eric inquired, shifting his feet.

"Well, if we're going to attack the Baron like Lionak said, who is going to attack the barbarians that will be attacking us?"

Jacob shrugged. In a way he thought it was odd that the barbarians didn't know that Captain Reeves' remaining troops were now fighting on their side. Odder yet, he thought that it was not like Lionak or Chief Zorin not to inform them. He knew that Chief Zorin would have made it a point to do such, if not Lionak. Uneasily his stomach churned from not knowing what was happening.

"Okay. Let's assume that the barbarians were not told." Eric began as he scratched his head lightly, "Then there will be no way in hell that we will be able to get into the Kingdom without a lot of resistance. I don't think that our chaps would stand a chance. Over half of our arms are sitting back there in the forest."

"Right." Captain Reeves sighed in agreement. He speculated he would not be able to go back and retrieve the weapons without losses in manpower or the heavier ammunition he was now forced to ration. And, equally as disgruntling, he could not go forward into the Kingdom without suffering losses and maybe his only remaining tank.

A long moment passed between them as they thought of what course of action to take. A few of the soldiers on the rear of the tank stirred about.

"Let's just go back home." one of the soldiers said aloud.

A few soldiers mumbled in agreement with him.

"It's not that easy." Jacob replied as he turned his head toward them.

"I didn't ask you, little lady." the soldier retorted. A few of the other soldiers chuckled to themselves.

"Who called me lady, limper?" Jacob hissed back as he turned his body and faced them directly. Jacob was determined to retain what respect, if any, the soldiers had for him.

"Who are you calling limp, you little bitch?!" the soldier roared out as he stood up and faced Jacob. He was equal to height, but his torso was wider. Obviously, had he donned the native attire, he could be mistaken for a barbarian.

"I guess that would be you." Jacob said evenly as he stared down the soldier, "Do you have a problem with that, troop?"

"Corporal Figg," Captain Reeves interjected as he turned about in the turret, "sit down."

"Yeah, I got a problem with that." the soldier thundered, taking a step towards Jacob.

"Corporal! I said sit down!" Captain Reeves scowled as he looked at the soldier, "That is a direct order!"

Roughly Figg turned and sat down on the tank heavily as he fumed to himself. He knew that if the captain was not present, he would have twisted up that man like a doll.

Turning around, Jacob bent over to the captain and whispered, "Thanks, but if I need your help, I'll ask for it."

"You're welcome." Captain Reeves whispered back. He didn't want any problems among his soldiers, especially any that he could control. There was no telling just what lay before them and he didn't want them feuding instead of being soldiers.

Off ahead, Jacob spotted a man on horseback heading towards them. It appeared that he was alone.

King Doron spurred his horse on. He wanted to chase after the Baron but he realized that Lionak must be warned about the Baron's escape and Matthew's death. Then he would find the Baron and battle him with his barbarian berserker fury, sword in hand. He wanted there to be no other way.

A faint shimmer caught his eye ahead on the road. Pulling back on the reins slightly, King Doron slowed the horse to a trot, squinting to see what it was. Whatever it was, it did not move. But it was large.

The horse shook its head and neighed lowly as King Doron pressed on. Then a wave of apprehension grappled at his soul as he realized that the object up ahead was the war machine. Instantly his mind whirled with uncertainty, wondering why Neclor and his men were nowhere to be seen. *'Could one war machine kill twenty of my best barbarian warriors?'*

Frowning as his barbarian rage brewed, King Doron withdrew his double-edged battleaxe and spurred his horse forward in a full gallop. Every sinew in his body writhed with a surge of unparalleled strength and his eyes became clouded with revenge. He would avenge their deaths!

"Who's that?" Jacob asked, pointing south towards the man on horseback.

"I don't think it is the pizza guy." Captain Reeves smarted off as Eric turned around to see what they were talking about.

As the lone horseman approached Eric said, "It does not look like he is too happy."

"Another one of those barbarians!" Captain Reeves shot out as he withdrew his pistol and aimed it at the horseman, waiting for the right moment to pull the trigger.

"No, wait!" Jacob rumbled out at Captain Reeves, "I'll handle this!"

Captain Reeves raised an eyebrow in surprise with no idea of how he was going to do so.

With that, Jacob bounded off the tank and ran towards the charging horseman, raising his rifle before him in a defensive posture. Jacob hoped that he would be able

375

to subdue the rider without having to shoot him. And, perhaps, the rider would know what was happening at the Kingdom of Shek.

"You there! Stop!" Jacob bellowed out at the horseman, hearing the loud breaths of the horse and the clatter of hooves on the dirt road.

"Aye dog! I'll stop when my battleaxe cleans your head!" the horseman barked out as he raised his battleaxe and sent it crashing down towards Jacob.

Planting his feet, Jacob shot his arms up with a burst of energy as the battleaxe dove down on him, blocking it with the rifle. A sharp thud echoed out and the horseman yanked his battleaxe back as he passed Jacob. Slowing the horse, the horseman pulled on the reins, turning the horse about.

"Yeaahh!" the horseman cried as he spurred the horse at the man, bringing his battleaxe up for another try at his head.

"I said stop!" Jacob commanded as he saw the horseman charge him again. Jacob planted his feet.

"Die!" the horseman roared out as he sent the battleaxe towards the stranger.

Turning his side, Jacob reached out with the butt of the weapon and hit the battleaxe with tremendous power, hooking one of its angled edges and pulled it from the barbarian's grasp. The battleaxe hit the ground some eight feet away behind him.

Even as Jacob spun around, the horseman galloped past him and rolled off the horse with the reflexes of a seasoned warrior and retrieved the battleaxe. The horse stopped some twenty feet behind the crouched barbarian, trained to always remain near its rider.

"Who the hell are you?!" Jacob shot out in frustration. He'd never seen a barbarian move so smoothly.

"When I sever your head I'll tell you!" the barbarian shouted back, charging Jacob.

As if something took control of his body, Jacob studied the charging barbarian like he was in slow motion.

All of his years of training and experience rushed into his mind as his body reacted seamlessly in rhythm with the barbarian's movements. Even as the battleaxe came rushing down on him, Jacob raised his weapon and blocked it. But with the same forward motion he spun so that his back faced the barbarian and lowered the butt of the weapon and sent it plunging into the barbarian's gut. Even as he heard the barbarian burst out the air from his lungs, Jacob turned. With the barrel-end of the weapon, he reached out behind the barbarian's knees and pulled back with all of his might. The barbarian's feet swept out from under him and he hit the ground squarely on his back.

Jumping back a few feet as he gained control of himself and retrained the weapon, he pleaded, "Look, I am Jacob, friend of Lionak! Why are you attacking me?!"

"What?" the barbarian heaved out, scrambling to his feet, still trying to catch his breath. He had never had such a combination of moves executed against him before like that.

"I said I am Jacob." Jacob said more calmly.

"You are Jacob?" the barbarian questioned, eyeing the man suspiciously. The barbarian thought this was one of the Baron's traps.

"Yes." Jacob said as he cautiously lowered his weapon, "Lionak sent me to help you battle against the Baron."

"I don't know any Jacob." the barbarian gritted as he advanced a step, grasping the battleaxe tightly.

"Most here in the land know me as Mohawk." Jacob stated. He should have realized that nobody except for Chief Zorin and Lionak would have known his real name.

The tapestry of Mohawk and Mac flashed in the barbarian's mind. They were the ones that had destroyed the Baron over three hundred years ago. Suddenly the barbarian's eyes widened with the realization that he was battling against a god. It was no wonder that he had been felled so quickly.

"Mohawk," the barbarian stated as he lowered his battleaxe and bowed his head, "I am sorry that I did not know you."

"That's okay. You didn't know." Jacob replied, openly relieved that he would not have to wrestle with the barbarian any longer.

"I am King Doron, ruler of the Kingdom of Shek." the barbarian announced proudly.

"No need to bow to me." Jacob responded. He did, however, like the respect that King Doron displayed.

"What of the war machine? Don't you know that it has killed many of my people?" King Doron said heavily as he pointed over Jacob's shoulder.

"Yes, I know. At that time, it was under the control of the Baron. But not anymore. I control it now." Jacob said to him, pointing at his chest with his thumb.

"You?" King Doron asked in surprise. Indeed, Mohawk must be powerful to control such a thing, let alone wrest it from the Baron.

"What of my people? I sent them to destroy the war machine before it could return to kill more of my kin." King Doron asked uneasily. He didn't know what Mohawk was capable of with the knowledge that he had sent his best warriors to destroy the war machine, not knowing that Mohawk had been in control of it.

Jacob sighed and said, "Some are dead. But I left most of them in the forest."

That eased King Doron's mind somewhat.

"Why did you not know that the war machine was under my control?" Jacob asked as he slung the M16 over his shoulder.

"I was not told." King Doron said, continuing, "All I knew was that the war machine was killing my people before the Baron escaped."

"What?!" Jacob shot out. He couldn't believe that the Baron had gotten away. That must have been what he saw through the night vision goggles.

"Yes," King Doron confirmed as he placed the shaft of the battleaxe into an iron loop on his belt and clapped his hands together, signaling for the horse to come, "The High Priest, Matthew, told me to warn Lionak before he died."

"Damn!" Jacob cursed out loud, "Well, let's go! No time to lose!"

With that, Jacob turned and ran back to the tank as King Doron mounted his horse and spurred it forward towards the tank. He was still unsure of trusting the war machine, but he knew that Mohawk was powerful. If it was under his control then he had nothing to fear.

"Are you going to get on?" Jacob asked King Doron after he pulled himself onto the tank and faced him.

"No. I think I'll ride." King Doron refused politely, still suspicious of the war machine.

"Reeves, we have to turn this thing around and head towards the city. The Baron is already gone." Jacob said with urgency.

"No wonder why we were attacked. They probably still think we are the enemy." Eric said, climbing into the front cockpit and restarting the engine.

He was partially right. Some of the survivors, however, would never accept them as anything but the enemy.

Chapter Fifty-Seven

Progress following the trail down the side of the mountain was slow. Mac was not familiar with the trail, so Regan led him though she had only crossed it once. It also gave her the impression of importance. In a way Regan wanted to know that she was needed by Mac. Wanted by him. It didn't seem to matter any longer that Mac was not really a god. Deep within her she felt something else that swept through her when she thought about it. It was an emotion that she had never deeply and truly felt before.

Mac did not seem to mind being led down the rocky trail. Especially by Regan. He liked seeing her body move down the trail before him. Those fine, petite curves that she bore made him smile to himself and almost lose his footing on occasion. But his mind was split. On the one hand he thought of how much he enjoyed being near her. Listening to her talk. Kissing her passionately. Gazing upon her beautiful smile that softened him and made him smile in return. Yet, on the other hand, he speculated why she would now be concerned with him. Mac had honestly thought that he would never see her again since she made it a point to tell him she had a boyfriend. And, the convincing blow was the day she didn't show up when Mac tried to set an *unofficial* date. Mac churned the thought of asking Regan if she had stopped seeing her boyfriend, in a way to reassure himself that she really wanted him. But he didn't. Whatever romance or interest she saw in Mac, he wanted it to stay that way. All he knew for sure was that he felt content when he was with her. The zest for life bloomed when he was near her. It was like she filled that hollow spot in his heart and gave it warmth. He hadn't felt like that for any other woman before. But, then again, he never knew that many women. Whatever that feeling was, Mac wanted to know it for as long as he possibly could.

"Are you still working at the tavern?" Mac asked, trying to break the silence.

"No. I stopped working there some time ago." Regan replied as she walked around a small boulder in the trail.

"Why? I thought you liked working at the tavern." Mac said, following her.

Regan sighed, "Well, no…not really. I had the job mainly because of my father."

Mac raised an eyebrow, "Then why did you quit?"

Regan was quiet.

Mac questioned whether to pursue the subject further. He didn't know if it would make things worse between them or not. Mac scratched his cheek and decided that there was only one way of finding out.

"Regan," Mac began with a reassuring tone, "you can tell me."

Regan stopped in the middle of the trail and turned towards him. In the dim light Mac could see a tear in her soft eye. Suddenly Mac felt something strange flash in his body that she triggered. The feeling was strange but he said nothing as he stood before her, waiting.

"It is more because of my mother than father." Regan admitted finally.

"Your mother?" Mac said, somewhat confused. He didn't understand how her mother was suddenly part of why she worked at the tavern because of her father.

"Yes. My mother." Regan said as she leaned onto the side of the mountain face, "I went to work at the tavern because my father thought it would be a good way of me facing people and interacting with them. You know, understanding how commoners were. Indeed, I saw a lot of them and their own miseries. Each was so different. As time progressed, I began to feel sorry for a few of them. I mean, a lot had no education, no real means of striving for more. So, they were stuck where they were."

She crossed her arms over her chest and continued, "And at home, things were so different. I don't know. All my life I got whatever I wanted. Education. Nice clothes to wear. Gold to spend whenever I wanted. Yet, those other people had little or no gold to spend. In a way, they could not enjoy like as I had."

"But how did your mother change things?" Mac asked. He didn't see what Regan was trying to get to.

Regan held back her tear of anger and said, "Like I said, things at home were different. My father didn't mind me going out and experiencing life and making my own mistakes. I did make a lot of them. But mother was different. She wanted to control me as if I were still a child. She wanted me to be home by certain times. She scolded me for mistakes I had made. Anytime I got courier notes, she had to go through them as if I was hiding something from her."

She looked up at some clouds overhead, "She hated how I worked at the tavern at my father's request. She thought I should not work. My mother believed that I should just wait for a wealthy man to enter into my life and sweep me away like my father did her. She doesn't understand that I wanted to do things, without her control and intrusions."

Mac thought for a moment and asked, "Did you quit then to satisfy your mother?"

"No!" Regan shot out defiantly, "My mother said that if I was going to do things my way then she believed that I should live my way. So, I kind of moved out. I moved away from the scoldings and the control she had over me. Things were different once I moved. I could do things as I pleased. I liked it, but things were different. Things were harder without the help of my father. I quit my job to think about all of that."

"Where do you live now?" Mac asked.

"On the lower level of a cottage off the main estate. My mother does not come to see me and I do not go to see her." Regan admitted with a frown. Little did she know, her mother was still able to keep tabs on her with the cottage in the boundary of the estate.

"Don't you think that your mother was just being protective of you?" Mac said, looking at her. He didn't think her move was that drastic but did find it rather disrespectful that her mother would be reading all of her correspondence.

"Protective?! She didn't want me to do anything! That's not protective, that's obsessive!" Regan burst out in anger.

Mac reached out to touch her shoulder, but Regan turned away from him and continued down the trail, raking over her emotions.

"I'm sorry, Regan." Mac said, walking after her.

There was no response. Mac didn't know if he should try to say anything to console her or just let the whole matter rest as it was. Then he thought about his own life.

"Regan!" Mac shot out, wanting her attention, "I did not have an ideal life either."

But Regan kept going down the trail before him.

Striding up behind her, he grasped her shoulder and turned her about, commanding her attention, "Look. I had the same problems. The only difference between us is that I was not allowed to even go out of the house to go with friends. Anytime I wanted to leave the house to go somewhere, I had to beg."

Mac smiled awkwardly and said, "I was not even allowed to mingle with women. In fact, it was not until after I had left, did I try. But it was difficult. Never having had the opportunity of trial and error with women during my years growing up proved to be a hinderance. I didn't know how to communicate my feelings towards them. I didn't know how to make conversation. I didn't and still don't know how to read women. And, I still am in the dark about how to do such things."

Regan looked into his eyes. He was serious. She didn't know that he had been in the same situation, and yet, worse in some ways. Her eyes softened somewhat.

"But. Nonetheless. I have tried to overcome it over and over again," Mac forced out, "I guess, with time, I'll catch up on all that I had lost out on."

Mac cast his eyes down at her feet. He didn't know what else to do or say.

"Mac," Regan said softly as she touched his chin and raised it with her delicate hand, "I'm sorry for blowing up like that. Sometimes I guess I just get too caught up with myself."

Mac looked into her face and met her eyes with his. He wanted her, but he just didn't know how to say it from fear of being rejected.

"Oh, don't worry about it." Mac said with a grin. He was ready to put it all behind him.

Regan smiled at him and said, "But I do worry about it."

She inched closer to him.

Mac, sensing the nearness, tried to say something else. But before he could get the words out, she pressed her lips on his. Instinctively he wrapped his arms about her and let his feelings pour from him as he lavished the gentle caress of her lips.

After a long moment she pulled away and said with a satisfied smile, "If you stay a while, I can teach you about women."

Mac smiled in return and they continued down the trail.

Chapter Fifty-Eight

John yanked his eyes from the tapestry of the portal which hung in the study. He knew that there was a time difference between the two dimensions, but he could not understand why the portal had not opened yet. Even by all the scientists calculations, the portal should have opened nearly three times by now. He should have been gone. He speculated if something had gone wrong with the dimensional door. Now that the early rays of the sunlight were reaching over the dark blue sky, John began to fear that he would be a permanent addition to this new, strange world. He doubted that the government would have pulled the plug on the entire project given its economic and military potential. But he never really knew what the politicians and puppeteers were up to behind closed doors.

"Sir, why hasn't the door opened yet?" Agent Bradley asked, seated near John and Sam. Although he didn't know the frequency of when the door would open, it still seemed to be too long. Twenty-four hours from making contact and going back to the base was a very long time. Especially if the contact team was under attack from unfriendlies.

Sam looked at John with curious eyes. He wondered what type of excuse he would hear from John. Sam was already prepared for the news of being stuck in this world.

"I don't know." John shrugged quietly, looking at the bookcase on the far wall, not wanting to meet Agent Bradley's eyes, "All I can imagine is that something has gone wrong with the door. I don't know, maybe a hardware failure."

"Great." Agent Bradley said, disgruntled, "So how much longer will we have to wait here?"

"Maybe a couple of hours." John lied with a poker face.

"Or maybe a couple of days." Sam sliced coldly.

"Look! I'm sure they will get the damn door running within a few hours!" John roared at Sam, causing Lionak and Chief Zorin to look over to them.

"What is the problem?" Lionak asked as he closed the thick book and looked over to John with hard eyes.

"Oh nothing." John said as he scowled at Sam.

"What about this door you were talking about?" Chief Zorin asked. He heard John say something about a door. Obviously, it was important enough for them to argue about.

"It's some type of dimensional door that a bunch of scientists put together." Cindy volunteered as she walked up to Chief Zorin and placed her hand on his shoulder.

"Yes, it's a door that we created to come to your world." John said finally as he pulled his hands apart and looked at Chief Zorin, "None of us expected it to work. But when it did, we did it again in hopes of contacting any civilized life."

"Well, if you're worried about going back to your world, I don't need some contraption to send you. Once we get out of this keep, I'll be more than happy to send you all back to where you belong." Lionak said evenly. He was determined that nothing would interfere with his objective of destroying the Baron.

"I'm not going back." Cindy blurted out.

"You are not of this world." Lionak countered, casting his eyes toward her.

"No, I'm not. But I have made my decision. I will stay here with Chief Zorin whether I belong or not." She said, looking at him with soft eyes.

Chief Zorin didn't have the heart to refuse her. Yet, he and Lionak knew that she could never be a true part of his life.

"Then so be it." Lionak said finally, eager to put this conflict behind him and get on with more important matters.

"Just how are we supposed to get out of here?" Sam asked in a bored tone. He had shot at the creature, even pushed a battering ram through it. They had sent volleys of lightning at it. And none of it had worked. He didn't see a way out. At least not until the creature either left of died. Both could be some time in happening.

"I don't really know." Lionak confessed, raising one hand into the air and plopping it back down on top of the book.

"This is a castle, right?" Agent Bradley asked, looking around at the stone layered masonry.

"Per say…yes. But it was built to protect my forefathers and other fellow wizards from outside attacks." Lionak said openly as he sat back in his chair.

"Well, if that's true then you should have tunnels to escape through, right?" Agent Bradley asked. He knew that ancient castles had secret passages and escape tunnels. Even the White House had such a tunnel, though it was not a stoic castle.

Lionak smirked, "No. The defenses of the keep were always good enough to not have to pursue such a thing. Besides, a breach like that going beyond the walls could be discovered and used against us."

Only Lionak knew all of the spells that were littered throughout the keep. And, indeed, they were sufficient to repel hostile forces. But, in this instance, the spells were useless against the water spirit that did not make physical contact with any surface within the keep. Chief Zorin would sense the presence of the spells around him although he had no idea what many of them were.

"Well, maybe it's time to dig one." Agent Bradley suggested with raised eyebrows.

"That might work, Lionak. If we can dig lower than the level of the moat and out into the city, we might be able to get out of here." Chief Zorin said, looking between Lionak and Agent Bradley.

"That would be about thirty yards of digging." Lionak said roughly as he thought about the depth of the moat and length required to dig past it.

"Well, let's do it." Sam said, ready to start digging.

"Do you have any idea how long it's going to take to dig a tunnel through dirt and rock? What if the damn thing collapses when we are in it?" John pointed out. He guessed it would be a physically demanding task that may span a month to complete.

"It's a risk I am willing to take." Sam said as he stood up, "I don't see any other way of getting out of here."

"There might be another way." Lionak pondered, standing up and crossing the study.

"Chief Zorin. Are you practiced in the ways of the magical worming?"

"Yes." He replied with a slight frown, following Lionak out into the middle of the courtyard. All of the dragon kin were born with such ability. And through time and teaching from the elder dragons, each dragon could hone their magical worming ability. So much so that when completed, a tunnel or carved space in a cavern looked as though the walls were made of smooth glass and, for the exceptional, three-dimensional artwork and exquisite designs could be integrated into the walls as they were being formed. Though Chief Zorin had not practiced the worming for several decades, he was confident that he could form a tunnel that was thirty yards long. He had done others of much larger proportion.

"Magical worming? Is that like fishing?" Agent Bradley asked with a puzzled expression.

"The magical worming is a way of creating tunnels through the use of the White Magic." Chief Zorin replied without involving himself with all the finer points of magical casting itself.

"Ahh." Agent Bradley said, nodding, pretending to understand. He still had a difficult time accepting the existence of dragons let alone magic.

Casting his eyes down at the ground, Chief Zorin began harmonizing with the earth and White Magic, twisting each invisible thread before him. As his concentration grew, the threads started to become visible as white glimmers before the group. Mentally, Chief Zorin pulled the threads of the White Magic downwards as it pulsated into the ground. Closing his eyes, he began swirling the magical threads in the ground in a circular fashion. Within moments the earth itself began to move with the small rotating waves within the circular wall formed by the magic.

Agent Bradley's mouth opened in awe and a faint acceptance that this was really happening.

Raising a hand before him, Chief Zorin focused more White Magic on the worming. John's eyes widened with surprise as the rotating waves of earth began to sink from the rest of the ground around it. Peering over its edge, John found that as the earth retreated within itself, a pair of stairs was left behind in the now apparent tunnel. Despite all the flashes of White Magic that pulsed out of the tunnel, John could not help but look into its depths with a child-like curiosity.

Clenching his fist and shoving it through the air before him, Chief Zorin guided the twisting threads of White Magic to the west. Although none of the others could see where the tunnel was going, mentally he was in the midst of the tunnel controlling each thread of the White Magic simultaneously. Only a true master of the magical worming had such clarity and control over the White Magic as Chief Zorin did. And, the ability to mentally remove his essence from his body in human form, while maintaining contact with both entities was an ability that only a Chief of the Guardians could possess.

"Where's all the dirt going?" Cindy asked Lionak curiously.

Lionak smiled at her and said, "If you were able to see beyond the walls of the keep, you would notice that earth is collecting on the other side."

"So, he is pushing the dirt out to the to the other side?" John asked with raised eyebrows. He knew pushing several tons of earth was a trying task even for heavy earth moving equipment he knew of.

"In a manner of speaking. By controlling the White Magic, he has formed a…oh, what do I want to say?" Lionak grasped as he searched for the words he was looking for, "Well, he has formed a tornado of sorts. As the magic travels forward, the twisting fashion of the magic pulls the earth along with it. So, what is left behind is void of earth. In this case a tunnel."

"Fascinating." Cindy mumbled to herself, proud that Chief Zorin could do such a thing.

Raising his head somewhat, Chief Zorin moved the threads of White Magic upwards. After a few more minutes, Chief Zorin lowered his hand and opened his eyes.

Looking down into the tunnel, John noticed a faint light shining through it and he said, "Have you dug through?"

"Yes." Chief Zorin replied, collecting himself, "The tunnel is complete."

"Wow." Sam grunted. He didn't even have to work up a sweat.

"It's time to be freed of this place." Lionak stated as he patted Chief Zorin on his shoulder. He made a mental note to fortify the tunnel at the earliest opportunity.

"Well, let's go!" Sam exclaimed, darting around the others and scurrying down the dirt stairs and disappearing into the dimly lit tunnel.

John and Agent Bradley were the first to follow Sam into the tunnel, followed by the others. Twenty yards off ahead of them, Sam stopped suddenly as he looked upwards toward the ceiling of the tunnel. He could see water droplets forming, darkening the ceiling.

"Hey!" Sam called down the tunnel, "It does not look like we have much time! The water from the moat is seeping through the tunnel!"

"What?" Chief Zorin said with a grimace. He knew from past experience that a tunnel created in such a fashion would eventually allow the passage of water. But that was only after the tunnel walls had absorbed what water it could which took a great deal of time. It could not have been possible that the tunnel was already weakening despite its hasty build.

Pushing himself head of the others, Chief Zorin walked towards Sam, "Is the tunnel wall darkened from the water?"

Looking about himself, Sam paused for a moment and said, "No. It just seems to be from above. There is a crack forming on the ceiling now."

"What?!" Chief Zorin fumed with outrage. That could not be possible.

Even as Chief Zorin began to jog towards Sam, he noticed a wall of water fall suddenly from the ceiling of the tunnel. Sam's body became a blur through the wall of water. He couldn't understand why the wall of the tunnel had failed.

Turning about, Chief Zorin commanded, "Get out of the tunnel now!"

"What is happening?" John asked the others as they turned about.

"The tunnel is collapsing!" Chief Zorin shouted, turning west and jogging towards the wall of water. But something was different. The tunnel was not filling up with water as Chief Zorin had expected. Instead, the mysterious wall of water just stood in place as if controlled by some unknown force.

Slowing his pace to a walk as he came upon the wall of water, Chief Zorin looked at it questioningly. He could see the blurred outline of Sam walk towards him, waving for him to follow. But Chief Zorin was not sure. He had not seen such an unnatural display as this before.

Then it hit him like a wall of bricks. This wall of water was not natural. It had to have been the creature controlling it. Instinctively, Chief Zorin took a few steps back and shouted, "Sam! Get out of there!"

But Sam stood on the other side of the wall, staring at him with a puzzled look. He couldn't hear Chief Zorin.

"Get out of there! Now!" Chief Zorin shouted again as he pointed west.

Not realizing the danger, Sam squinted at Chief Zorin as he looked through the wall of water. Finally, Sam turned about, eager to get out of the tunnel and to the outside. But the coldness of something wrapped about him. Suddenly he realized that the creature was attacking him again, his heart lurching and a sense of fear grappled at his soul. Vainly, he struggled to free himself as he was drug backwards.

"Damn it!" Chief Zorin cursed to himself, seeing the creature reach out and grab Sam.

Watching helplessly, Chief Zorin noticed Sam turn about as his mouth opened with silent pleas for help. Within moments, as Sam's outline became clearer, Chief Zorin met his terrorized eyes. But there was nothing he could do.

Outside the keep, a deep yell echoed out of the tunnel and into the city causing several people to stop what they were doing to look around them, perplexed.

As Sam's body pressed against the wall of water, Chief Zorin saw the creature eating Sam alive. Slowly, Sam's skin somehow oozed from his body as the creature absorbed him. Chief Zorin's stomach churned with disgust as he saw the redness of blood temporarily explode onto the wall, that had covered Sam's still moving body. As the blood thinned and disappeared, only the glistening of white bones could be seen. Then, Sam's eyeballs came out of his skull and vanished in two circular clouds of white inside the wall of water. Scarcely a heartbeat later, a grayish white cloud burst into the confines of the wall that had emanated from Sam's skull, until it slowly dissipated from sight.

Suddenly weakened, Chief Zorin stumbled back trying to catch his balance just as a semi-transparent tentacle reached out for him. Weakly he got to his feet and darted down the tunnel, unwilling to be the creature's next victim.

Chapter Fifty-Nine

The Baron descended upon the immense keep, which was probably six times the size of what was once his own. As he did so, the Baron was impressed with the large walls that surrounded the stone buildings inside. The granite and marble stones that formed the layers of the outer wall laid as a primary defense against any assaulting force. The Baron could tell the walls were not constructed to repel mere humans or giants. They were built to hold his clan of Red Dragons from gaining entrance to the keep. But, even such a massive and well-constructed wall as this could only hold his kind for a short time.

Curiously, the Baron scanned the keep and detected a faint presence of dormant spells that hung in the outer walls and the interior of the keep. Without revealing himself to better understand the nature of the spells, the Baron merely assumed that they were spells aimed towards the destruction of any Red Dragons who might pass through the outer wall. He could find no other reason for having such an elaborate array of spells present even to this day. After all, the Silver Dragons greatest threat had always been the existence of the Red Dragons. Besides that, he knew of no other being on the Realm, neither past nor present, that would constitute a large enough threat to require the use of magical spells to aid in defense or attack of such a massive keep. The only creature that came even close to such destructive ability was the Death Raiden, whom lacked magical ability. Even such a creature as that could not withstand the sheer number of Silver Dragons which would undoubtedly attack it before it reached the wall.

The Baron could not keep his mind from wandering, again, as to the purpose of the Secret Scrolls. Even now, he was not sure what he would uncover from within the ancient scrolls that would weigh in his favor. He'd always been told that they had no value. That they had no forgotten magical spells. That they had no potion formulas. All they were was a collected history of the dragons. Nevertheless, they had to bear some important information to be guarded so heavily by the Guardians of the White Magic. The only thing that the Baron knew for sure was that he had to steal the Secret Scrolls to gain whatever knowledge they held.

Landing before the towering open gates made of hard oak wood, covered by a hardened resin and reinforced with several long, slender iron plates held fast by large rivets, the Baron scanned cautiously around him, changing the Silver Dragon's husk into its human form. Inside the fortified keep he could hear the faint echoes of voices speaking the tongue of the clan. He was half-surprised to find out that the Silver Dragons still held on to the knowledge of the clan language. The Baron had expected them to have forgotten such knowledge, having been allied with the humans for many centuries.

Passing through the massive wooden gates, the Baron noticed a figure garbed in a white long-sleeved shirt and matching pants tucked in brown leather boots. A red cape trailed behind him, fastened about his neck with a gold chain. The Baron, unsure of whether to stop and face him, continued his pace forward.

"Euroc!" the man said with a smooth voice that could charm the hearts of women, "Wait!"

Uneasily, the Baron stopped and faced the dark, long-haired stranger.

"Euroc. What is the news?" the man asked with a friendly grin.

"Well, we have not found the Baron yet." the Baron lied with the voice of Euroc.

"Really?" the man grunted with a sign of disappointment, "Matthew said that you were tracking him down. According to him, you were the only one that could feel the Baron."

Now he knew that he was safe, for the moment. None of the Guardians knew of his recent escape.

"I have had no real success yet." the Baron responded, eager to leave the stranger.

"That's too bad. So, why are you back here?" the man asked with raised eyebrows. Mildos, as he was known, could not imagine why the High Priest would allow Euroc to leave when Euroc was the only key to finding the Baron. It didn't seem like Matthew to allow him to simply leave the Kingdom of Shek. Something was not right. But Mildos could not put a finger on it.

The Baron paused for a moment, trying to gather his thoughts. He was so close and could not afford to miss out on his only chance at getting the Secret Scrolls. *'What would he tell the stranger so he could continue on his way? And, was the stranger capable of finding out otherwise if he was to say something he was not sure of?'* The Baron sighed at his dilemma.

"It might be possible for me to find the Baron if I were to read the scrolls," the Baron lied again, "Matthew said it could be our only chance at finding him."

Mildos scrunched his eyes and said, "The scrolls? Only Matthew and Chief Zorin can read the scrolls. It is forbidden to all others."

A faint shock of anxiety ran though the Baron. He had said the wrong thing.

"Euroc, why don't you wait here until I can contact Matthew. If he tells me that you may have access to the scrolls, I'll lead you to them myself." Mildos said suspiciously. That ebb of uncertainty still lurked about him.

"Okay." the Baron replied in a steady voice, "But time is of the essence."

"Yes. It is." Mildos stated as he turned and strode towards a stone staircase that led up into a slender and tall stone building probably some one hundred and fifty feet in height.

The Baron assumed that the building was a type of staging point for mental telepathy either broadcast or received. At that altitude in the mountains, and the low hills that laid south of the keep, one in such a position would be able to conduct telepathy with a minimum of expenditure.

Waiting until Mildos disappeared behind the stone wall of the tower, the Baron shot forward knowing that he had little time to find the scrolls before he would undoubtedly be found out.

Mildos climbed up the spiraling iron staircase that was bolted to the inner wall of the tower. Even as he ascended, some feeling urged him not to trust Euroc. Mildos, a High Priest of the second rank under Matthew, had seen Euroc as an infant. Over the decades he personally had a hand in some of his training. Mildos knew that Euroc had not been trained as of yet to receive the rank of a Low Priest. If he had, Mildos would not have had such a problem with allowing Euroc to examine the scrolls, things as they were. Even a Low Priest would not be able to comprehend all of the ancient writings, although perhaps enough to understand their general concepts to aid in defeating the Baron. But it was beyond his rational thought to believe that Matthew would allow a Low Guardian, not well versed in the White Magic, to have access to the scrolls.

Mildos believed that he knew Matthew as well. For it was Matthew who had shown him the ways of the White Magic, and oversaw his progression in rank over the past two centuries. In all those years, he never detected or heard of Matthew, even if a Low Guardian was progressing more rapidly than others in the ways of White Magic, allowing the knowledge of greater spells or teachings to be revealed. All Guardians, regardless of their talents, would not ascend the ladder of knowledge without first waiting the appointed times, or in some cases decades. The pause between learning knowledge was not intended to hinder a Guardian's development. Instead, it was put in place by Chief Angela to allow Guardians the much-needed space to mature and learn patience in gaining wisdom on what they had already been taught. In the long run, such an approach would make a Guardian a more valuable and disciplined member of the clan, more able and willing to meet challenges in a clear and concise manner. Chief Angela had seen, in the Secret Scrolls, that revealing knowledge too quickly, to unmatured members of the clan, proved to be disastrous.

Stepping onto the wooden planks that moaned under his weight atop the iron staircase, Mildos gazed out onto the vast stretch of land before him. Walking over to the edge of the tower, he placed a hand on the stone wall that rose up to his waist and began to conjure the White Magic.

Cautiously the Baron wove around a few small stone buildings before he came upon what appeared to be a temple of some kind. A sweeping marble staircase rose up to the entrance of the temple, flanked on either side by finely crafted pillars which appeared to bear the weight of the large stone blocks that comprised the lower rim of the roof. Along the rim, the Baron would see the sculpted figures of dragons fighting one another. Some of the images breathed fire, while others were locked in close combat. What it actually communicated was beyond his understanding.

Although the temple appeared to be rather small, perhaps some twenty feet cubed, the Baron went with his gut instincts and entered the temple. He didn't think the scrolls would be kept in such a small unguarded area, but he had no time to explore the entirety of the keep for other temples.

Once inside he found that the temple was virtually empty, except for a smooth block of granite with four golden rods, pointed on end, anchored to the four corners of the block. At first, the Baron thought that the block was a sacred burial memorial of some type as it was the length of a human and some four feet in width. But then he remembered that a dragon was never buried in human form. Their human appearance was nothing more than a magical spell that was easily conjured to alter a dragon's true form. When a dragon ceased the spell voluntarily or though death, the dragon's true form would be released. And, the granite block that laid before him was much too small to accommodate a dragon.

Reaching out, the Baron grasped two of the golden rods at the foot of the block. Suddenly the block rolled back on unseen rails. Unsure of what he had done, the Baron jumped back as he watched the block roll backwards, ready to use his magic in defense if need be. But, after the granite block ceased moving, nothing else happened. At least he knew it was not a trap.

Drawing his eyes downward, the Baron saw a descending staircase that had, just a few moments ago, been covered by the block. Dimly the flicker of torchlight could be seen rising out of the corridor, the Baron taking a few steps towards it. The echo of garbled voices could be heard as he eased himself down the long staircase. Trying to act inconspicuous, the Baron reached the foot of the staircase and looked out before him. A few of the Guardians, in human form, roamed around the circular cavern talking to one another, not even looking at him as they passed.

A large, placid pool of blue water sat in the midst of the cavern, and the images of the torches hanging at even intervals around the cavern reflected perfectly off the surface of the water. Off to either side of the pool, the Baron noticed two passages. Not familiar with where the passages led, the Baron raised an eyebrow with the grim realization that if he didn't choose the right passage, he would not have time to explore the other.

After a long pause, the Baron turned and headed towards the passage to the left of the pool. Entering the passage, the Baron could not help but look at the finely textured walls with partially raised figures of landscapes and life ranging from birds to dragons. From their smoothness, he knew that no crafted tool had formed the passage. More than likely it was the work of the magical worming. And, whoever had cast the magical worming here had been well-practiced in the ways of magic. Perhaps as well as the Baron himself. Perhaps even better.

Chapter Sixty

"All stop." Captain Reeves said into the headset after he bent the arm of the microphone closer to his mouth.

The walls of the city were barely in sight.

"What's our status?" Captain Reeves asked, looking along the walls of the city with his camouflaged binoculars.

"Radar shows no signs of hostiles approaching this position, sir." the gunner replied as he looked at the computer screen and pressed a few buttons to increase local range resolution.

"Jacob." Captain Reeves began as he lowered his binoculars and turned in the turret to face him, "I don't think it would be prudent for us to come within visual range of the city. If word has spread, we would have quite a situation on our hands and not enough ammunition."

Jacob looked at him with blank eyes. Of course, he knew it was not a smart move to make. But he had thought of stopping short of the city after they had begun their journey north.

"Well, I'm sure that word has spread by now, but Doron's presence should help a bit." Jacob grunted as he turned and headed towards King Doron who was sitting idle on horseback a few yards from the tank.

"If you don't mind Doron, we'll go ahead and meet up with Chief Zorin and Lionak." Jacob stated, jumping effortlessly off the tank. The horse took a step back, startled by Jacob's sudden movements.

Turning about towards Captain Reeves, Jacob asked, "Do you have any spare commo I can use to contact you?"

"Ah," Captain Reeves started, as he thought about what might be aboard this particular tank, "about all we have on this tank is an FM handset. You should be within range though."

"That will do." Jacob replied dryly. He didn't like the word 'should', but he had little choice in the matter. Some communication was always better than no communication.

Captain Reeves disappeared into the tank and immerged shortly after holding a black handset with a stubby black antenna. Turning towards Jacob, he threw it in the air. With the simple swipe of his arm, Jacob reached out and caught the handset. Immediately he noticed that the handset was bottom heavy, likely because of the lithium battery which was held inside the plastic casing.

"What channel will you be receiving at?" Jacob asked as he looked at the two circular dials seated next to the antenna. Two small, blue light emitting diodes were visible through two holes to the right of the dials. As one might infer, the blue nature of the lights was not readily visible to the naked eye as much as, for example, red or yellow. Therefore, the use of the handset would not be easily spotted by hostile elements at night.

"Channel eight." Captain Reeves replied without hesitation as he looked at Jacob turn one of the dials on the handset.

"Test." Jacob said as he depressed the key with his thumb and spoke into the shielded microphone, seeing the blue light pulsate.

"We got him sir." a voice called out from the bellows of the tank, "Returning test."

"Test check." the handset replied to Jacob as he adjusted the volume dial and noticed the blue light brighten as his set received the transmission.

"It's a go." Jacob stated finally, stuffing the handset into the cargo pocket of his BDUs.

"What should we do after you enter the city?" Captain Reeves asked as he adjusted the Kevlar helmet on his head.

"Just wait. I'll get in contact with Chief Zorin and Lionak to clear this whole mess up. Then I'll radio back and you'll be able to approach the city." Jacob said, walking over to King Doron.

Opening his hand towards King Doron, the barbarian took it and heaved Jacob onto the back of the horse.

After adjusting his weight behind the saddle, Jacob said, "Ready when you are."

With that, King Doron spurred the muscular horse forward towards the city.

John sat down heavily on the wooden steps that led up to the study. He could not believe that one of the best green berets of the U.S. Army could befall such a grizzly fate. John knew now that no one was safe from the reaches of the creature that engulfed the keep. It just appeared to be a matter of time before it would get everyone else.

"Damn it." Lionak fumed to himself as he looked around the courtyard, reading the magical spells that were invisible to the eye. He had read them before and didn't find one that could help repel or destroy the creature. But he tried again, hoping against hope that he had overlooked one.

"It's going to get us all, isn't it?" Agent Bradley asked with a hard face.

Cindy shook her head in defiance and said, "No. Just you. Zorin will figure out a way to get us out of here."

Agent Bradley looked at Chief Zorin. But Chief Zorin did not meet his gaze. Even Chief Zorin was exhausted of any ideas on how to deal with the creature. Contact or even getting too close to the creature risked getting entangled by its tentacles.

"Why don't you face the facts here?" Agent Bradley rumbled to Cindy as he pointed at the creature, "That thing is too powerful. Chief Zorin and Lionak have both tried their best to get us out to no avail. Hell, even our modern weapons didn't even phase that damn thing!"

Cindy glared at him because she could not think of anything to say.

"Bradley," John said sternly, looking at him, "cool off. There is a way out of every problem. It just so happens that we have not discovered it yet."

"Right." Lionak agreed as he turned and climbed the stairs. Inwardly he was beginning to believe that, for once, the Baron might have the ability to conquer the Realm. And there was nothing he would be able to do about it.

"Hey! Look there!" Cindy practically shouted with glee as she pointed at something outside the keep, beyond the entrance.

Dimly John looked out and saw two riders on horseback, galloping towards the keep. His eyes got big with the hopes of being rescued.

"It's that guy. Jacob and some other man." Cindy said as she shook her pointed hand and turned towards Chief Zorin.

"Jacob?" Chief Zorin questioned as he turned and looked beyond the entrance.

They all moved into the courtyard to get a better look.

"Mohawk," King Doron said as he urged his horse towards the drawbridge of the keep, "Why are they shaking their hands?"

"What?" Jacob said, moving to look over King Doron's shoulder. Indeed, they were shaking their hands and shouting something. But what? Even at this distance of maybe thirty yards, Jacob knew he would have been able to hear whatever they were shouting about. He could hear the air zipping past him. He could hear the panting of the horse he rode. Even the crackle of the saddle. But, for some reason, he could not hear anything from inside the keep.

Then Jacob saw both Lionak and Chief Zorin standing together waving at them to move left. Jacob frowned as they galloped closer to the keep and crossed onto the drawbridge. The echo of the horse's hooves clapping against the wooden drawbridge pounded in his head. Suddenly it hit him as he looked down into the moat and up the side of the keep. That glistening. He had seen it before.

"Damn!" Jacob shouted as he realized that the creature who had consumed the horses when he had first entered the Realm, was now covering the keep.

"Stop!" Jacob commanded.

Without a second thought, King Doron pulled back on the leather reins, forcing the horse's head back. But there was nothing to stop the horse's momentum as they pounded into the water spirit's largely transparent skin. Within a split second, Jacob found himself lying on the drawbridge gasping for breath a few feet from King Doron who was dazed, having been heaved against the horse's armored mane.

Weakly, Jacob rolled to his side and pulled himself up. Then, with a simple motion, he swept up the assault rifle and dashed over to King Doron who was shaking his head and blinking his eyes as if he had just awoken from a deep sleep. Out of the corner of his eye, Jacob saw the horse rear back and gain its feet.

"You okay?" Jacob asked as he extended an open hand toward King Doron.

Taking Jacob's hand and getting up, King Doron said, "Yeah. It felt like…"

Suddenly the horse shrieked out in terror as several thick tentacles wrapped about the horse's neck and body. Jacob saw the horse's muscles bind up in resistance, to try to free itself from the grasp of the creature. But the horse was getting nowhere.

"Son of a bitch!" Jacob spat coldly, raising his rifle and pointing it at the glistening mass. He could not stand by again and watch another defenseless animal be consumed by the water spirit.

Squeezing the cold trigger of the rifle, Jacob sent rounds at the creature, firing his rage with each successive burst. But the creature didn't bleed from the impact of the rounds. Not even a simple spark of recognition jumped out from the creature as if it were in pain from the volleys. But it was too late. The King's stallion could not be saved.

With a deep thud, the skin of the stallion which hung loosely over its skeleton like a blanket, hit the ground with its armor at the edge of the drawbridge. It was as if all its entrails, even muscle, was just sucked out of the horse. Yet the bristly hair that covered the hide remained completely intact.

"By the gods, what type of magic is this?!" King Doron roared out in disgust of losing another stallion, "This is the second I've lost!"

Jacob lowered his weapon. The image of Gladstad's remains, so similar, flashed in his mind as he cast his eyes downward at the pile of flesh and bones. It must have been a horrible way to die. He wondered what type of horror and fear had gone through Gladstad's mind. Even the horse's mind.

"What will you do now?" King Doron asked, ready for some type of instant revenge that would at least pacify his anger, knowing that he could not do anything without being taken by the creature.

Jacob thought for a moment, then he waved his right arm, signaling those inside the keep to look at him. Pointing at them, he cupped his fingers over his thumb. He did it again, hoping that they would understand what to do.

403

"I'll show you some fucking magic." Jacob cursed.

Jacob pulled out his handset and spoke into the receiver, "Captain, you have a Falcon on board?"

After a long pause, Captain Reeves responded, "Roger that."

Jacob smiled, "Excellent. We have a target that needs to be neutralized asap. Please launch to my x-ray."

"Copy that. Falcon on site in one mike, over." Captain Reeves confirmed.

"Copy." Jacob verified, looking behind him for the Falcon.

The Falcon is a highly automated quad-rotor drone with specialized targeting optics and range finding capability. Its purpose is to act as the M1A5's reserve targeting system when GPS and other systems are offline, permitting the tank to engage targets in any setting, up to the maximum range of their shells. At launch, courtesy of a special beacon aboard the tank, it tracks tank position relative to its own and begins generating a 3D coordinate space map to its destination and, once a target has been identified, relays the fire coordinates to the tank.

"What is he doing?" Cindy asked. She had never seen such gestures.

"I don't know." Lionak responded, "If he is weaving a spell, I have never seen the like before."

John looked at Lionak with a smirk and said, "It's not a spell. It appears that he wants us to find some cover."

"Cover? Why?" Agent Bradley said.

"I don't know," John replied lightly, "Do you have any type of shelter around here?"

"Just the study unless we go below." Lionak replied with raised eyebrows. He did not understand why they needed shelter.

Jacob glanced behind him again, after hearing the very faint high-pitch of the drone, spotting it about two hundred meters away, and holding steady at three hundred meters from the deck.

"Well, let's go." John urged as he turned and headed into the study.

Seeing the figures disappear from sight, Jacob turned and began to walk away from the besieged keep toward a short stone wall a few hundred meters away, in front of the drone.

"Where are you going?" King Doron grumbled out as he followed Jacob uneasily. He could not accept that Jacob was giving up.

"You will see." Jacob answered as he reached the wall and turned to face the keep.

"Is this some type of great magic?" King Doron asked finally, assuming that Jacob was going to unleash some devastating spell on the keep that would require them to be so far away.

"Kind of." Jacob replied, pulling out his handset and pressing the key, "Captain Reeves. Are you there, over?"

A moment passed as Jacob peered at one of the flickering blue lights. He hoped he was still within range of the tank and the batteries were still sufficiently charged.

"Roger. We had to increase our receiving sensitivity. Sorry for the wait." Captain Reeves responded.

"I need you to send a response to my x-ray, at that target." Jacob said, motioning with his arm in view of the drone.

"Roger that. Wait one." the handset replied.

"Roger, response at x-ray plus two hundred meters, over." Captain Reeves replied after a short pause.

"Roger. Fire one response at will." Jacob ordered.

King Doron looked at Jacob blankly. He had no idea what Jacob was talking about.

A few deafening moments passed before a sudden explosion consumed the right side of the keep. A thunderous roar echoed through the city as stone and large chunks of the keep's wall rained down on the ground.

King Doron sprang back against the wall in surprise, spinning around to see what had happened.

Almost immediately he saw a jagged hole in the side of the keep wall as dust rose into the sky. His eyes widened with astonishment at Jacob's power.

"Response taken." Jacob said into the handset, "One response at thirty degrees west of last response from bird's eye, over."

"Roger. Response at thirty degrees west of last response." Captain Reeves responded. Faint voices and applause were barely audible above the captain's voice.

Pressing himself against the wall after one of the rounds disintegrated a part of the keep, Agent Bradley hissed, "What the hell is he trying to do?! Kill us?!"

"What type of magic is this?!" Lionak sliced into the dusty air.

"It's not magic." John grunted. He had been in Lebanon when guerrillas armed with a wide compliment of SKS and AK47 rifles assaulted a top-secret intelligence headquarters. He remembered those fleeting moments too well. The guerrillas came in thick waves, each wave attaining a new position closer and closer to the bunker that was buried in the side of a low mountain. Then, just when he thought the guerrillas were breaking through the thick iron doors after having killed countless local militia, he heard those explosions. They were just as thunderous then as they were now. So deafening. So frightening. And, so close. Even today, he doesn't remember exactly how he survived the onslaught of friendly artillery smashing into the side of the mountain only meters from the bunker. Perhaps it was better that he didn't. He only knew that the explosions which rang out along with the quaking of the floor beneath him was the result of artillery, not magic.

"It's one of those tanks, isn't it?" Cindy blurted out. She remembered, all too vividly, the fear of seeing those tanks roll over the desert in Cairo. The sound was unmistakable.

"Yes." Chief Zorin replied as he held her close to him. He was puzzled why Jacob was back here at the city and not headed toward the Kingdom of Shek.

Another explosion rocked the ancient keep. The smell of fine stone dust and spent explosive residue from the rounds rolled carelessly into the study.

"Damn!" Agent Bradley fumed, not expecting another round to explode outside.

For a moment, in the deathly silence that followed the second explosion, Chief Zorin thought he caught the smell of fresh, cool air. *'Was it possible that the creature hand been destroyed?'*

Slowly, Chief Zorin got to his feet and edged to the double doors of the study.

"Hey! Don't you know that we're being shelled?" Agent Bradley shot out, still knelt next to the stone wall.

"Zorin?" Cindy beckoned after him, fearing for his life. She didn't understand why he was walking out of the study. It was the only protection they had until the shelling ceased.

"Don't fear." Chief Zorin replied as he carefully lowered himself down the stairs.

His eyes widened as the saw the huge, gaping holes in the keep's thick wall. Shattered stones and masonry lay scattered through the courtyard as he moved forward. That gentle breeze licked at him again and he smiled in relief. They were free.

"Come! The creature has been destroyed!" Chief Zorin declared as he turned around towards the study.

Cindy was the first to emerge and come by his side, followed by John and a somewhat reluctant Agent Bradley.

"By the gods!" Lionak muttered, barely able to form audible words on his tongue, "My keep! It's a wreck!"

"Ah, but at least we are no longer prisoners!" Chief Zorin stressed, trying to show the positive side for what happened.

"But it is not your keep. You do not have to re-build it." Lionak lamented as he picked up a small piece of stone and tossed it aside.

Chief Zorin chuckled lightly as he wrapped his arm about Cindy's shoulders and gave her a gentle squeeze. She didn't mind.

"Ahoy there!" Jacob shouted as he crossed the drawbridge and stopped inside the courtyard.

"Ah, old friend. It has been a long time since I saw you." Chief Zorin said as he approached Jacob and King Doron, "I feared I would be a timeless relic of this place."

"Yeah. Well, I thought something was wrong when we smashed into that water creature and it ate King Doron's horse." Jacob said, pointing at the remains of the stallion.

"Damn magic. It had to have been the work of the Baron." King Doron thundered angrily.

"I fear that it was. My knowledge of the Realm is vast, and no such creature was ever known to exist." Chief Zorin agreed.

That just fueled King Doron's hate for the Baron even more.

"I have some urgent news." King Doron sighed evenly as he tried to control his anger toward the Baron.

"Yes?" Chief Zorin said, Lionak joining them.

"Matthew is dead," King Doron said, looking at Lionak, "and the Baron has escaped."

Chapter Sixty-One

"How much further do you think we have to go?" Mac asked, wiping a layer of sweat off is brow. The leather jerkins and his steel helmet were not aiding in keeping him cool from the sun overhead.

"Oh. I'd say maybe we'll be at the city by nightfall." Regan replied. She didn't know for sure, but it seemed to her that they couldn't have been far off.

"That's good. I can't wait for a tankard of water and a bed." Mac groaned as he kept by Regan's side, serpentining through the forest.

"Me, too." Regan smiled at him. She had endured a long trek and slept on the rigid earth. A soft bed was a comforting thought. Despite it all, it was worth it now, to be in the company of Mac.

Mac placed an arm around Regan's shoulders and smiled saying, "Do you think it is possible for me to ask you for a drink and a pleasant walk in the city?"

"Well, I don't know." Regan feigned, leading him on.

Mac was somewhat taken aback from that response. He frowned uneasily and wondered why she wouldn't want to have a drink and a simple walk. After all, they were walking now, had already kissed one another and neither had been out of the sight of the other since they met in the cavern. Mac thought he had overlooked some element in their friendship that caused her to give pause.

"Umm, well…" Mac said, trying to form words on his tongue to persuade her.

"Yes, of course I would!" Regan smiled sweetly as she gazed into Mac's troubled eyes.

"Awesome!" Mac said, relieved as that blanket of uncertainty was ripped from him by her adamant response.

While they continued through the forest, Mac lowered his arm and grasped her soft hand. He could not help but feel those emotions of caring overtake him. It was emotions that he had thought were long forgotten. But now, when he was within Regan's presence, those emotions flowed through him. In a sense, they invigorated him and provoked a certain child-like persona around him that he did not reject.

Reaching the foot of a small stream, they sat down to drink and rest for a while. Mac eagerly splashed a handful of cool water on his face and scooped up water to drink from his palm. Regan, too, drank from the stream and refilled her water skin.

"So," Mac said between swallows, "you have to tell me when I have taken the gold."

Regan squinted at him curiously. She didn't see any gold around the stream that could be taken.

Looking at her expression, Mac chuckled and corrected himself, "What I mean is, tell me when I have your heart. You already have mine."

Mac could not believe he had just blurted that out so freely.

Blushing somewhat, Mac looked at the stream and apologized, "I'm sorry. I don't mean to be overbearing. It just came out."

Slowly Mac reached out and scooped up another handful of water.

Regan took Mac's cupped hand in hers and took a drink of the water before it all seeped between his strong fingers. Then she looked into his eyes and softened her voice, "You have already taken the gold."

Mac, unsure of what to say, smiled lightly and looked down at his cupped hand as that child's shyness enveloped him. Deep within him, he felt a warmth building. Some might call it love.

"Mac." Regan said quietly, lowering her head in front of his, urging him to look at her.

Slowly he raised his head, smiling, "I'm glad that I have your heart, Regan."

Reaching out with his hand he touched the side of her cheek and pulled her gently towards him, "I hope to always have your heart."

"My heart will always be yours." Regan whispered faintly to him as they joined lips.

"Neclor." a barbarian whispered, who was watching Mac and Regan from behind a thick outgrowth of brush some forty meters away, "That woman. I swear to you she was riding horseback with those strangers that were in the war machine outside of the city. I saw them heading south along the trails when I was hunting."

"Why didn't you tell me this before?" Neclor grunted as he squinted at the couple seated beside the stream.

"At the time, it didn't seem strange. That is, until I saw the men's faces who were part of the war machine when we attacked them during the night." the barbarian admitted.

Neclor knew now what he must do. The evil of the war machine had to be destroyed.

"Assemble the barbarians!" Neclor commanded barely above a whisper, withdrawing his bloodied battleaxe.

Mac broke off the kiss as a surge of urgency overtook him. Quickly he scurried to his feet and practically pulled Regan to her feet with him.

"What's wrong?" Regan asked, openly angered by his sudden action. She wanted to enjoy more pleasure with him.

"I don't know. Something is not right." Mac said, looking about him nervously.

Grabbing her hand and leading her through the cool stream to the other side, Mac said, "We must go. I feel danger."

"What?!" Regan retorted, "There is nobody here but us! If you don't want to bed with me, just say so!"

"No, no! It's not that." Mac said as he continued his quick pace forward.

Suddenly a sharp pain went through Mac's left shoulder as an arrow found a firm hold between the leather jerkins and his flesh beneath. Stumbling forward off-balance, Mac caught himself with his hands as he hit the ground.

"Oh gods!" Regan mumbled as she looked at the wooden arrow shaft lodged in Mac's shoulder. It had the intricate carved designs used by barbarians across its surface. The designs, representing curses, had been colored differently.

Scarcely a second later a horde of barbarians rushed upon them. Realizing that they could not flee, Regan helped Mac to his feet.

"Release the woman, stranger!" Neclor roared out. His thirst for vengeance was welling up inside of him.

"What has she done?" Mac barked back as he put a hand on the hilt of his bastard sword.

"She is a witch! She must be destroyed!" Neclor declared roughly, clearly not able to be reasoned with. His mind was already made up.

"Look at her! She is no witch!" Mac shouted at him, trying to make him see what he saw in her.

"It is of no matter what you think stranger!" Neclor shouted, taking a step forward, "Release the woman or die!"

Mac could feel Regan shivering from fear of being killed by these barbarians as she stood beside him, clenching his arm. Mac knew that she had done nothing wrong to deserve such a fate. He realized that there was only one way to save her. Even if his life depended on it. He would have to fight to protect her.

"Then so be it, scum bags." Mac stated firmly as he pulled his arm from her and withdrew his sword. He could feel adrenaline building in his strong arms.

"No!" Regan whispered heavily, "Save yourself, Mac. There is no need in both of us dying."

Regan didn't want to die. But, at the same time, she would rather die than to see Mac die at the end of a sword along with her.

Mac ignored Regan as he stepped in front of her, forming a human shield. A tear of despair rolled down Regan's cheek.

"Then so be it." Neclor smirked with a small token of respect for the stranger.

"Attack!"

"Ahhh!" Mac shouted in fury as the first of the barbarians ran toward him.

Swinging his sword, Mac severed the head of the barbarian from his body, it toppling over before him.

Then pivoting to his left, he raised his sword and blocked a battleaxe meant for Regan's head. With a twisting motion, he forced the battleaxe away and planted his foot in the barbarian's chest, forcing him to his back.

Barely a second later, Mac wheeled around and buried the tip of his bastard sword into the gut of a barbarian who was only a few footfalls from reaching Regan with his double-edged dagger. Even as the barbarian fell to his knees, his eyes wide with serrating pain, Mac yanked the sword out and bound forward a few steps to meet another barbarian.

"Attack the stranger!" Neclor roared out in surprise that Mac was fighting as if he were a barbarian himself, "I'll get the witch!"

Range built up in Mac's straining body as he swung low and severed one of the barbarian's legs in two. Fury soon consumed his eyes as his feelings guided his sword almost without him thinking about it. His eyes darted around him, spinning and facing his next foe, almost thirsting to see him die at the end of his sword. Eagerly, he stepped forward and met the barbarian's cold, blank eyes with his own as he blocked the barbarian's sword.

Behind him, another barbarian swung and planted the edge of his battleaxe into Mac's side, slicing through the leather jerkins and embracing his warm flesh to drink up its fresh blood. Even as Mac limped to the side to face his unseen foe, the barbarian pulled the battleaxe back and sent it crashing down on Mac again.

Weakened, Mac limped forward and plowed his sword into the other barbarian, barely missing the deadly edge of the reddened battleaxe as it sailed past him, diving into the earth.

"Ahh!" Regan shrieked out in unrelenting pain as Neclor savagely rammed his dagger into her soft, unprotected mid-section.

Blood poured freely from the wound as she toppled over before him. Neclor smiled with satisfaction as he took his thumb and brushed the warm blood from the edge of his dagger. He knew that it was only a matter of moments before she would be dead.

Startled, Mac wheeled around and saw Regan fold over before Neclor. Suddenly a flash of power entrapped his being as Mac stood there, staring at Regan lying limp on the grassy earth as he cried, "Noo!"

Images flashed before his eyes as his rage exploded within him and he swung his sword at the barbarian, severing him cleanly at the waist. Even as he stumbled forward towards Regan, brilliant flashes of color blinded his sight combined with sigils of some ancient language. Dully he felt himself topple to the earth as the edge of a battleaxe buried itself in his back, barely breaching the protection of his leather jerkins.

Utter determination to reach Regan, to know she was not dead, urged him up to a standing position as he took another step towards her crumpled body.

"No." Mac muttered as he stared at her.

Slowly he felt himself weaken as he took another step towards her. Out of the corner of his eyes he noticed the barbarian maneuver and lunge at him as he turned and shot the edge of his sword upwards, cleaving the barbarian's face in two.

"No!" Mac roared out defiantly as another surge of power flowed through him. His eyes began to glow a yellowish-white as the two magics within him stirred. He would not permit her to die this day.

Then with a simple toss of his sword, he sent it sailing into one of the few remaining barbarians who rushed him.

"You all shall die!" Mac thundered out as he raised his hands at another barbarian.

Barely a heartbeat later, a thick bolt of yellowish-white lightning jumped out of his hands and crashed into the barbarian. The barbarian shrieked in unimaginable agony just before his body exploded and its pieces became enveloped in a reddish-blue flame.

Neclor, seeing that he was the only one left which still stood, turned and faced the stranger with a fearless grin. He was ready to die an honorable death, his order fulfilled.

"The witch is dead." Neclor fumed out as he threw the dagger at Mac with blinding speed.

Seeing the dagger fly towards him, almost as if in slow motion, Mac reached out and clasped his hand around the dagger, tossing it effortlessly to the ground.

"You." Mac blared as he pointed his finger at Neclor, "You shall die for killing her!"

Then, the faint outline of a giant hand clenched about Neclor, formed out of the air. Instinctively, Neclor tried to move, but found that he was powerless to do such. Bit by bit he felt the giant hand tighten about him as his breath was forced out. Soon, Neclor's face began to brighen an ever-deepening shade of red as blood rushed to his head. The giant hand tightened even more. Neclor could feel his skin stretching and his bones snapping under the tremendous pressure as he cast his blurred sight into the sky, determined not to scream in agony. Neclor's body erupted like a geyser sending a think fountain of blood, entrails and pieces of bone arcing into the air.

Lowering his arm, the giant hand disappeared and the grotesque remains of Neclor fell to the earth. Mac looked at Regan as his rage subsided.

Slowly he limped over to her and knelt heavily beside her body.

"Regan," Mac whispered as he looked into her face, "You cannot die."

With that he laid next to her and placed a hand on her bleeding wound. Concentrating, like how he had seen Chief Zorin do to Jacob's wound, he said, "Regan. My love. You cannot die."

As a gentle breeze glided over them, Mac drifted from consciousness.

Chapter Sixty-Two

The Baron found himself inside a large circular room at the end of the corridor. The granite pillars that were scattered at even intervals around the room appeared to hold the immense weight of the earth above. The carved wall behind the pillars were veiled from sight with a layer of polished silver plates. These, along with the oil burning torches, cast an even light throughout the entire room so that nothing cast a dark shadow. Even the golden ornaments fashioned in the likes of miniature dragons that stood between each pillar were shadowless. The Baron raised his eyebrows. Clearly it was an impressive creation that few had ever seen.

Casting his eyes forward, he saw a golden table. Upon its four corners were four small golden dragons crafted from pure gold that were no bigger than a human's hand. But that is not what caught his attention. A thick book, yellowed from the centuries, rested idle in the midst of the four dragon statuettes, aligned along the four cardinal points of the Realm. The Baron's heart lurched within him as he realized that this was the book of Secret Scrolls.

Rushing forward on the smooth silver tiles below him, the Baron stopped before the table and gazed intently at the ancient book. His eyes gleamed with greed as he reached out and placed his hand softly on the golden symbol of two dragons intertwined upon its wooden cover. As if to recognize the Baron's presence, the golden symbol glowed white for a few moments before it again became idle. Eagerly, the Baron grasped the book with both hands and lifted it off the table, to turn and stride out of the room with a sense of completion.

Again, Mildos called out telepathically to any Guardians at the Kingdom of Shek. He couldn't believe that Matthew would not have sensed his beckoning. But, if it was true from what Euroc had told him, then it was quite possible that Matthew was locked in combat with the Baron and didn't have time, or the strength to respond.

Then a faint reply came. So faint that Mildos didn't understand the words other than just a jumble of sounds all wrapped together. Mildos focused even more on the telepathy and again called out. Seemingly, as if the gentle wind which eased past him carried the reply, he managed to understand the words.

"Yes, what do you command?"

"What has become of the High Priest?" Mildos asked as he felt the pulse of his heart throbbing in his head.

"Did you not know?" the weak reply came after several long moments.

Mildos could only assume he was communicating with a less practiced Guardian in the ways of magic. That could be the only explanation as to why he had to concentrate so much on the connection.

"Did not know what?" Mildos called out as he closed his eyes to keep focus and maintain contact with the Low Guardian.

"The High Priest fell against the Baron."

Mildos's eyes shot open as he wavered and caught himself with both hands against the stone wall. He couldn't believe that Matthew could fall to the Baron. All of those centuries of training Matthew had spent with the Guardians flashed before him. It was unfathomable that one with so much knowledge could fall to the Baron.

Quickly Mildos re-gained contact with the Low Guardian as he tried to shrug his emotions aside.

"What of Chief Zorin?" Mildos asked reluctantly. If he had fallen, too, the fate of the Realm rested in his hands. That was a thought that he was not ready to accept.

There was another long pause before the reply came, "I don't know. Last I knew, he was at Metsys keep with Lionak."

"Sir!" a heaving voice exploded from behind him, causing Mildos to lose contact with the Low Guardian from surprise, "Euroc has the Secret Scrolls!"

"What?" Mildos said as he turned and faced a Low Guardian, trying to make sense of what has been happening.

"He has the scrolls and is leaving the keep!" the Low Guardian stressed, turning and heading down the spiraling staircase.

Mildos followed closely behind, mystified as to why Euroc had stolen the scrolls and lied about Matthew. Mildos could only guess that Euroc had taken it upon himself to try to defeat the Baron with the Secret Scrolls. But even an inexperienced Guardian with such knowledge would not stand a chance against a well-versed sorcerer like the Baron.

"Let me pass!" Euroc roared out at the four Guardians blocking the entrance to the stronghold.

"We cannot let the Secret Scrolls leave this place. It is forbidden." one of the Guardians replied evenly. He didn't want to resort to battle against a fellow Guardian. But it was forbidden that the scrolls move beyond the walls of the keep.

"Matthew is in need of these scrolls." the Baron lied in the voice of Euroc. It was looking more and more like he would have to compromise his illusion to have access to his magic and flee the keep. He knew it would only be moments before more Guardians would appear in the ranks before him to prevent his escape.

"Matthew is dead!" Mildos yelled out as he jogged up to the other Guardians and faced Euroc.

The Baron couldn't believe that he knew about Matthew's death. At least none of them knew he was the Baron. If they did, he would have been fighting for his life at this very moment.

"You see! That is even the more reason to let me pass! If Matthew is dead, it is only a matter of time!" the Baron reasoned boldly, urging them to let him pass.

One of the Guardians looked to Mildos for advice.

Mildos sensed something odd about Euroc. It was unacceptable for any Low Guardian to use a Guardian's surname. Something was not right.

"I don't know what you are trying to do Euroc, but it is not right to take the scrolls! We must wait for Chief Zorin. You know this!" Mildos shot out, eyeing Euroc suspiciously.

"You don't understand!" the Baron pleaded, trying to convince them.

"Yes, we understand. But you cannot take the scrolls! You don't even understand them!" Mildos hammered back, trying to get Euroc to see what he was trying to do.

Hearing the approach of two more Guardians rushing to him, the Baron knew he had no choice but to fight.

"No, my pitiful foe. You don't understand." the Baron hissed lowly as he transformed into his towering Red Dragon being before them, having possessed the shell of the Silver Dragon long enough, he was able to corrupt and transform its flesh entirely. He knew it was useless to try to talk his way out.

All of the Guardians took a few steps backward in utter surprise and bewilderment that a Red Dragon from the histories was standing before them, inside the keep of the Guardians. None of them thought such a thing would ever happen. Not even Mildos.

With the advantage of surprise, the Baron took in a vast amount of air into his leathery fire glands as he brought his scaly head back. Then, before any of the Guardians had time to move, he opened his mighty jaw and sent a thick, fiery blast of Dark Magic at the Guardians who stood before him. Instantly the inferno of such intense heat and magic consumed their bodies in those few heartbeats, leaving nothing but charred earth from where they once stood.

"Tolitien soemol eroctis qurychlii!" Mildos roared out as he shot his hands into the sky, summoning the dormant White Magic spells around the keep.

Raising a clawed arm at Mildos, the Baron summoned Dark Magic and sent a thick bolt of twisted lighting at him. Mildos tried to miss the bolt, but he was not swift enough. Sudden pain shot through his body as he felt the Dark Magic plow into him, sending him to his back, unable to move.

Out of one of the walls of the keep, a brilliant white bolt of lightning lashed out at the Red Dragon and formed around him. A few moments later, another wrapped about the struggling Red Dragon who was trying to free himself. All around him, the Baron could see the magical spells being activated from Mildos' command. He had to escape soon, before all of the spells focused on him, their sole target.

Calling the Dark Magic to him, he immediately created a reddish-yellow barrier around his body as he countered the two spells of binding. Slowly, the power of the Dark Magic consumed the arcing bolts foot by foot until it reached the keep wall and disappeared.

Seeing his opportunity, the Baron lurched up with outstretched wings and gained flight. Even as he distanced himself from the keep, flying south from the keep, a fiery ball, easily the size of a man in diameter, rushed from behind and crashed into him. The power of the blast caused the Baron to fall a hundred feet in the air before he was able to shake the dizziness from him and concentrated on flight, barely missing the grassy top of a low-lying hill.

Looking behind him, the Baron saw another gaining upon him. Straining with all his might and skill, the Baron veered right and dove downward as the brilliant fiery ball darted past him and disappeared into the clouds a few moments later. The Baron didn't know the range of the magical spells, gaining more distance from the keep, so he continued to fly at his best speed to escape.

Chapter Sixty-Three

"I fear that Mac might be dispersed." Chief Zorin sighed as he flew through the air, bearing King Doron, Lionak and Jacob upon his scaly back.

"What do you mean?" Jacob shot out in haste. Already he was prepared to enter into the heart of the Pure Magic. More so now if it was true about what Chief Zorin had just said.

"As you know, the quakes have stopped. I cannot feel the Wild Magic." Chief Zorin stated, turning his scaly head back slightly, "I can feel the Wild Magic in you, but nowhere else."

"So, you're saying he's dead." Jacob assumed. He didn't understand why Chief Zorin was beating around the bush about the matter. Either Mac was alive or he wasn't. There was no other way about it.

"Yes." Chief Zorin confirmed. Already too many had died with the struggle against the Baron. And, Mac had been a true friend.

A long silence hovered over them as the Silver Dragon beat his wings rhythmically, heading south towards the Kingdom of Shek. Mt. Reach was before them, but its grandeur didn't phase any of them as each thought of what would be, and how to confront the Baron.

"Well damn it!" Jacob exclaimed, breaking the silence, "I'll go through the Pure Magic!"

"It is too risky." Chief Zorin said almost immediately. He didn't see a need to possibly lose Jacob as well when his talents with the war machine might come in handy against the Baron later.

"Oh fuck. Forget that! I'm about the only one left that could help!" Jacob shouted.

"But you could die, and we would be one less in confronting the Baron." Chief Zorin said, trying to reinforce his position.

"But if I live…" Jacob roared out before he was cut off by Lionak.

"Hold on!" Lionak shouted, "I felt something. It was very weak."

Jacob strained to turn and scowl at Lionak. He didn't like being cut off when he was trying to make a point. Especially one of this magnitude.

"What is it?" Chief Zorin asked as he probed out with his magical sensing ability.

"I'm not sure. I felt it only for a moment." Lionak said as if he was in deep thought, "Could you take us lower?"

Chief Zorin did so without hesitation. He just hoped that whatever Lionak was up to would not take a great deal of time they did not have to spare.

"There! Did you feel that?" Lionak exclaimed, feeling that surge again after a long pause.

"And?" Jacob rumbled angrily. This was no time to be on a safari.

"I'm not sure." Chief Zorin replied quietly as he tried to concentrate on detecting what Lionak had felt.

"Oh great." Jacob mumbled, "Wake me up when the joy ride is over, okay?"

"There! People down there!" Lionak proclaimed, pointing his twisted wooden staff towards a clearing on the earth below.

"Ah, yes." Chief Zorin agreed as he continued his circular descent and turned his head towards the clearing, "Looks like there was a battle here."

Curiously, Jacob looked down at the bodies that were scattered throughout the clearing. The faint smell of burnt flesh filled his nostrils as he frowned slightly from the stench.

"Yeah, smells like they were cooking something fowl." Jacob grunted.

"They are barbarians." King Doron said as the bodies came into focus. He wondered why barbarians would be so far out from the Kingdom.

After Chief Zorin landed on the grassy earth, the riders hastily got off and strode into the clearing, flanked on three sides by trees. Within moments Jacob found Mac lying next to Regan, his armor pierced and bloodied. But it was not that which caught his attention. It was the fact that he had a hand on Regan's abdomen. Looking closer, Jacob realized that she had apparently been wounded as well.

"Lionak!" Jacob shouted even though Lionak was not more than twenty paces from him, "Here's Mac!"

Taking Mac's hand from the woman, Jacob turned him onto his back and felt for a pulse. Jacob wasn't sure that Mac was alive after seeing all the bodies and his own wounds, but there was still a chance he was alive. Jacob was not ready to embrace that Mac was nothing more than a corpse lying in the middle of a field. He had seen too many of his own soldiers in the jungles befall such a fate.

"Does he live?" Lionak asked as he came up to Jacob.

"Come on you damn fool. You can't die. Your fucking Rambo, remember?" Jacob whispered under his breath as he waited a long moment, trying to feel a pulse from Mac's neck with his fingers. But none came.

"I don't think so." Jacob confessed as he leaned back and looked into Mac's expressionless face.

"Huh?" Lionak frowned, looking at Mac, "He has to be alive!"

"Well, I'm not getting a damn heartbeat!" Jacob lashed out.

Lionak knelt down next to Jacob and placed his hand upon Mac's cool forehead.

"Who did this?" Jacob asked roughly as he looked around at the other bodies. A glimmer of respect went through his body, realizing that Mac had stood off against so many barbarians. He knew it must have been a valiant battle. He only wished he had been at Mac's side.

"These are my men." King Doron admitted as he came up to them to see what Lionak was doing.

"What the fuck were they doing here?!" Jacob hissed out as he got to his feet and faced King Doron with glazed eyes filled with rage.

"I sent them to destroy the last war machine, not hunt these two." King Doron affirmed.

"Well, he sure doesn't look like a war machine to me!" Jacob barked. He knew King Doron probably had mean the tanks, but the King was a convenient outlet for his anger.

"Yes, I know he doesn't. But there must have been a reason they attacked. Necron had never failed me." King Doron responded steadily, sensing Jacob's anger.

That was the last straw. Even before King Doron could flinch, Jacob swung out and planted his balled fist firmly on the barbarian's jaw. Not prepared or balanced for such a sudden attack, King Doron went to his back from the strength and angle of the punch.

"I had a reason for that." Jacob glared coldly at King Doron as he took a few steps forward from the throw, catching himself.

King Doron's eyes became hot as he looked up at Jacob, ready to lurch up and pommel him with closed fists for having hit him.

"Wow here! Enough." Chief Zorin shouted, approaching them in dragon form and glaring at them with a golden eye. There was no sense in more violence, especially when it could be used against the Baron.

"Enough?!" Jacob objected, "I haven't even started with him yet!"

King Doron rose slowly to his feet, eyeing Jacob. He was ready and almost welcomed another clash. He would not be caught off guard again.

"Whatever happened here is over. Nothing can be gained by your anger." Chief Zorin stated firmly, lowering his head towards them.

"It'll sure make me feel a hell ov'a lot better." Jacob again protested, feeling his balled stomach.

"Mac is alive!" Lionak smiled as he looked up towards Chief Zorin.

Instantly Jacob spun around and looked down at Mac with raised eyebrows, "How is he?"

Lionak looked at Mac for a moment before removing his hand. Then he said, "He's weak indeed. All

I know for sure is that he will survive. His wounds appear to be healing even now, but he has lost much blood."

"Is he fit for battle?" King Doron asked easily. With barbarians it was always cut and dry.

"Battle?" Lionak smirked, "Maybe battle with a pillow."

Mac stirred.

"Then he will not be able to help us conquer the Baron." Chief Zorin said lowly through his many teeth.

"I'm afraid not." Lionak sighed as he gripped his staff in disappointment.

"What?!" Jacob frowned, "Why don't you do some of that magic on him? Heal him or something?"

Lionak and Chief Zorin both knew it could be done. Both of them had done it before to others. But neither of them wanted to risk losing any magical potency healing Mac when he would live. The Baron was already an overpowering adversary that could not be underestimated. Every thread of White Magic had to be preserved unless it was absolutely needed.

"He will live." Lionak concluded, not wanting to pursue the subject further.

"How in the hell are you going to take the Baron with your magic without him?" Jacob countered as he raised his arms hastily, "You said yourself that the Baron could only be destroyed with the two magics. Mac is the only one with the two magics."

Chief Zorin knew that Jacob was right and looked at Lionak.

"Yes," Lionak said, standing up with the aid of his wooden staff, "but he is unpracticed in the use of magic."

"Oh fuck." Jacob cursed as he looked up at the sky in disgust and then to Lionak, "Then why did you have us go through all that trouble at Mt. Reach in the first place?"

"In case one or all of us fell before the Baron." Lionak squeezed out between his lips.

"That's a pretty shitty last-ditch effort, isn't it? If he doesn't know how to use the magic in the first place, then everyone is dead." Jacob lashed out, shaking his head, "So...you can kill the Baron...right?"

"By myself, no." Lionak said as he pointed towards Chief Zorin, "But together, our combined magic may imprison the Baron until Mac is competent enough with the ways of magic to destroy him."

"Regan." Mac strained as he forced his eyes open to find her.

"Mac!" Jacob exclaimed as he rushed and knelt beside him, looking into his face.

"Jacob?" Mac asked weakly, recognizing the voice as his eyes slowly brought everything into focus.

"Yeah buddy! You okay?" Jacob asked eagerly.

"I'm...tired. But nothing to worry about." Mac replied dryly as he strained to turn his head towards Regan and continued, "Is she okay?"

Jacob quickly felt for a pulse and said, "She's alive."

"Good." Mac said, licking his dry lips, "I hoped she would live."

"What happened here, man?" Jacob asked.

"The barbarians. They tried to attack Regan." Mac said between short breaths as his strength began to return to his body, "I defended her."

"Why did they attack?" Jacob said. He wouldn't have defended the bitch for what she had done to Mac at the tavern.

"They said she was part of the Baron's plot." Mac said, although he could not remember the exact words they used.

"Huh?" Jacob said as he looked at her, "Well, is she?"

"No." Mac returned.

"Well, it looks like you whipped some ass alright." Jacob said with a proud smile.

Mac tried to smile and said, "So when are we taking down the Baron?"

426

"We will go now." Lionak said as he looked down at Mac, "You do not need to come. You need to rest."

"Bullshit! We can wait here for tonight and head out in the morning," Jacob said as he looked up at Lionak, "Then we leave. With Mac."

"He may not be recovered by then." Lionak cautioned.

"Bullshit!" Jacob snapped.

"You gonna be ready?" Jacob asked Mac.

"Roger that." Mac replied. He knew that they couldn't take the Baron without him. He was the only one with the two magics. He would have to be ready.

"He'll be ready." Jacob said, getting up and then looking at Lionak with a hard stare.

"Okay." Lionak said reluctantly. He did not really want to give more time to whatever the Baron was doing, but at the same time he knew that Mac's help could prove useful, even though he was unskilled with magic.

Having flown deep into the Southern Mountains, the Baron easily found the cavern he had been raised in by his forefathers. Vivid images flashed through his mind of his parents and all of the good times they shared, uninhibited by the White Magic and the Guardian's unrelenting quest to destroy all of the Red Dragon clan. But now things were different. He was the last surviving Red Dragon in the Realm. And he would not falter to the Guardians. If he did, his clan would become extinct.

As the torches that hung along the jagged cavern walls flickered with the faint passing wind outside, the Baron stared at the thick book of the Secret Scrolls before him. He envisioned that, by conquering the Realm, he would be able to breed a new generation of Red Dragons to again enjoy, without sacrifice, the pleasures of clan life and subjugation of everything else. And, he would be the sole master of it all.

Opening the book of the Secret Scrolls, he could feel the thick power of the Dark Magic surrounding him, as if the book's presence was amplifying something. Giving him life. It was that feeling of power that appealed to him which the Dark Magic revealed. It was almost like an unseen friend that was ready to do whatever he wished.

Even as the Baron slowly scanned the pages, that one statement from the creature of the other world still puzzled him. How could he gain the Realm from the contents of the scrolls? As far as he knew, the scrolls were nothing more than a detailed collection of the past history of the Realm along with magical spells that he really did not desire, since they pertained to life. Yet, the creature had said that the Secret Scrolls were the key.

The smell of burnt oil from the torches drifted past his nose as he continued reading the scrolls page by page, careful not to miss even the slightest detail. And there, amidst the sigils, drawing and ancient writing, the Baron found the answer as it unraveled itself before him.

Chapter Sixty-Four

The morning Sun arose, shining upon the small band of people as they rustled to consciousness. But Chief Zorin was already awake. He had been unable to sleep ever since he got that distressing message from Mildos.

Sensing that something was troubling Chief Zorin, Lionak walked over to him and asked, "What is wrong? Haven't you slept?"

"Huh?" Chief Zorin said, looking up from the large stone he was seated on in his human form.

"I said, what is wrong?" Lionak asked again as he leaned on his staff.

"Well," Chief Zorin began, unsure of how to break the news, "Mildos reached me during the night about the Baron."

Lionak frowned slightly.

"It seems that the Baron used the image of Euroc to get the Secret Scrolls."

"What?!" Lionak spurted out in amazement.

"How? I thought the keep was littered with spells against such Dark Magic?" Lionak threw out, unable to control himself.

"It is." Chief Zorin confirmed as he looked at Lionak's puzzled face, "All that I can assume is that he used the Wild Magic as some type of mask that concealed the Dark Magic from the spells." That was partially correct anyway.

"Things are getting worse by the moment, Zorin. If the Baron can unlock the secrets of the scrolls, we will fail. The Realm will fall." Lionak stated bluntly.

"I know."

"Damn it!" Lionak cursed as he shook his head, "Where is the Baron now?"

"Mildos said he had flown south. I would say he is deep within the Southern Mountains by now." Chief Zorin replied, standing up and looking south.

"We must go." Lionak urged, walking towards the others.

"Bad news?" Jacob asked Lionak as he approached them. He noticed their conversation although he could not hear them speak.

"The Baron has the scrolls. We have to confront him now if we're to have any chance at all." Lionak said, stopping before Jacob and the others.

"Then let's go!" Mac shouted as he got up and grabbed his helmet from the grassy earth.

Regan looked at Mac with a frown. If what she had heard was right about the scrolls, then they would all die against the Baron.

Swiftly she got to her feet and grabbed Mac's arm, "No! You can't go! I will not let you go off and die!"

Mac looked at Regan, into those pleading blue eyes. Suddenly part of him did not want to go. Part of him yearned to stay here with Regan. To enjoy her embrace. Her companionship. Her love.

"But I have to. I am the only one with the two magics." Mac said slowly, barely able to look into her soft eyes.

A tear of despair welled up in her eye and rolled slowly down her cheek, "Do you not love me enough to stay with me and take me for your own?"

Jacob looked over and scowled at Regan. He could not understand why she would say something like that. If the Baron was not destroyed then nobody would live to take anything.

"Oh Regan." Mac whispered softly as he glanced at her soft lips and up to her teared eyes, "I do love you. More than any man loves his most precious possession. You give me a sense of fullness I never had before. You are my life...my spring and fall."

As Mac reached over and felt her soft cheek with his hand, he continued, "But if I don't do this thing, you my love, will be threatened by darkness. And I must do whatever I can to protect you from danger and take you for my own."

Bending down slightly, Mac embraced her lips with his as their emotions entangled each other in unison and yearning for the other. Slowly Regan brought her arm up around Mac's strong neck to draw him nearer to her. She did not want to be without him.

Gradually Mac broke away from her and looked passionately upon her open mouth, resisting the desire to kiss her again.

"I love you, Mac." Regan whispered out as she opened her eyes and looked into his.

"And I you." Mac responded without hesitation as he held her warm hand in his.

"We must get ready. The other Guardians will be here any moment." Chief Zorin said, walking over to the group.

"The other Guardians?" Lionak probed, turning to face Chief Zorin.

"Yes. I have commanded all of the Guardians to assemble here. What they protected is now gone. We will, undoubtedly, need all the help we can muster to get the scrolls back and destroy the Baron."

Lionak shook his head in agreement.

"Hey! Look there!" King Doron shot out as he pointed north and withdrew his sword.

A hazy blue mist collected before them as small white globes swirled down from the sky above them. Each globe pulsated and hummed lightly as they descended, mysteriously vanishing within the mist.

Lionak looked on in silent awe. In all his years as a wizard he had never seen such a peacefully breathtaking sight as the one he stood before now.

"Could this be the work of the Baron?" Mac practically whispered to Chief Zorin.

Chief Zorin squinted at the mist for a moment and said, "No. It is the essence of the White Magic gathering before us."

"For what?" Jacob grunted with raised eyebrows, unable to take his eyes away from the mist.

Then, as the last globe found its way into the mist, the mist itself tumbled inward on itself until a brilliant white flash of light sprang outwards, temporarily blinding them.

"By the gods." King Doron whispered, unable to form any other words on his tongue as he strained to see before him.

"Jacob!" Bev exclaimed in relief and happiness to see that he was alive.

"Chief Angela." Chief Zorin said respectfully as he bowed his head in great admiration to her.

"Chief of the Guardians?" Lionak asked as he rubbed his eyes and looked at the Silver Dragon with apprehension, "I thought that she had died."

"Bev?" Jacob rattled out in utter surprise that she was in the Realm. He just could not believe it.

"Yes, wizard, great-son of Metsys. I had died. But I was bound by a promise made long ago with the rezuqia flower." Chief Angela responded with a surprising knowledge of who stood before her.

"Why are you here?" Chief Zorin asked lightly. He did not want to ask the wrong question to an entity that was much stronger than he. Even if he had known the Chief on the material plane, a wrongly phrased question could bring wrath, regardless of who the entity was.

"Beverly, wife of Jacob, commanded me to bring her to him." Chief Angela responded soothingly.

"And what more?" Lionak probed bravely as he gripped his staff cautiously.

"None." Chief Angela replied as she outstretched her wings, "I have fulfilled my promise."

With that, Chief Angela simply vanished from before them.

"What are you doing here?!" Jacob exclaimed as he felt anger swell up inside of him.

"I had to make sure that you were all right, Jacob." Bev replied with a tear of relief rolling down her cheek.

He did not understand it. He did understand why she came here, but regardless, he had given her an order, in an effort to shield her, and she had obviously disregarded it. And, now she was in danger. He already had enough to worry about, and Bev's presence did not help the situation any.

"What?!" Jacob said as he shook his head, "I told you to take care of the kids while I was gone! I told you this was a dangerous place! Why the hell didn't you do what I told you?!"

Bev took a step back in shock, unable to say anything. She just wanted to make sure that he was...

"How did you get here anyway?" Jacob asked as he threw an open hand into the air before her.

"I burnt some of your stuff..." Bev began.

"You what?!" Jacob roared out, getting more agitated with each passing moment.

Chief Zorin and Lionak turned to stare at the feuding couple anticipating that they might have to intervene.

432

Jacob turned away from her, shooting both hands into the air and said, "Never mind. I don't want to know!"

"I just…"

"Quiet!" Jacob commanded as he strode away from her, throwing an open hand up towards the side of his head where she could see it.

"Jacob." Bev said weakly with tears building around her eyes.

Mac stared blankly at Jacob, wondering what he should do, if anything at all. He had never seen Jacob so distraught before.

Jacob closed his eyes momentarily and took a deep breath, trying to calm himself.

"What do we do now?" King Doron asked as he withdrew his hand from the sword buckled around his waist.

"What do you want to do with her, Jacob?" Chief Zorin asked evenly, although he hoped that Bev would not be accompanying them to conquer the Baron. Such a move could be a way for the Baron to create leverage over them.

"Well, she sure can't come with us!" Jacob exclaimed as he turned and faced Chief Zorin.

"Very well. I will send her to Metsys keep until we are done with the Baron." Chief Zorin replied, greatly relieved by Jacob's response.

"Look!" King Doron said as he pointed north into the sky, "The other Guardians have come!"

Lionak looked into the sky and noticed the silver dotted sky. The assemblage of flying dragons converging on them was impressive to say the least. Lionak speculated what such a mass would cause an enemy to think. What fear must be struck into such hearts.

"There must be over a dozen of them." Mac said openly. He could sense the White magic emanating from them as if from some unseen wind blowing past him.

"Aye." Chief Zorin agreed with a slight grin on his face, "The White magic is strong with them. I can feel it."

Now, even Lionak could feel the surges in the White Magic flow past him.

As the Guardians flew overhead, casting their long shadows over those below, one landed a few feet from Chief Zorin.

"Mildos will see you to safety." Chief Zorin said to Bev as he pointed to the towering Silver Dragon.

Bev's heart tripped over itself as she beheld the massive Silver Dragon peering at her with a golden eye.

Lionak grimaced slightly at the Guardian. He did not understand how Chief Zorin knew that this particular dragon was Mildos. He sure didn't see any differences between any of them.

"But Jacob," Bev started, facing Jacob, "I want to be with you!"

"Get on the damn dragon! I don't need to be worrying about protecting you when I'm going to have my hands full with everyone else!" Jacob said sternly. He would not allow her to come no matter what she may try.

Mac smiled inwardly at Jacob's remark and knew he meant every word of it.

Regan clasped his arm slightly. She knew that she might be the next to go. She would not refuse Mac's wishes.

"But Jacob." Bev pleaded.

Jacob merely pointed to Mildos and said, "No buts. Get on the dragon. Now!"

Reluctantly, Bev turned and strode toward the Guardian, wiping a tear from her cheek. She could not believe that Jacob was treating her like this. She just didn't want him to die.

"What of Regan?" Chief Zorin asked, looking over towards them.

Mac looked into Regan's eyes, trying to read her thoughts and tell her to get on the dragon. But he couldn't muster the words. She would have to make her own choice.

Regan looked deep into Mac's eyes and said, "I will not leave you. If it is your destiny to live, I will bear your children...and, if not, I will die with you, my love."

"Very well." Chief Zorin sighed as he turned his head towards the Guardian, "Mildos, take her to Metsys keep and meet us in the Southern Mountains."

"Save a piece of the Baron for me." Mildos replied as he outstretched his leathery wings and began beating them heavily as he lifted himself off the grassy earth.

"You had better hurry then!" Chief Zorin shouted upwards, toward Mildos.

"Shall we go?" Chief Zorin asked as he closed his eyes and transformed into his Silver Dragon form.

"Let's get on with it." Jacob grunted as he stepped toward Chief Zorin, followed by the others.

Chapter Sixty-Five

The Baron's mouth grew into a deep smile as he gazed at the rising Sun. He now understood the very essence of power that the Secret Scrolls contained between their layers of yellowed parchment. Yet he could not help wondering why the Guardians had not used such power to their advantage centuries ago. But it did not matter now. With the rising of the day's Sun, the Baron grasped the fact that the Realm would be his. Perhaps his conquest would take no more than a few fleeting hours if he was swift and deadly against the Guardians.

Turning his head downward at the bare earth no more than twenty feet below the cavern entrance, he recited a silent prayer of victory to the vast expanse that had once been a grassy plain. When he finished, the Baron looked towards the northern horizon and crossed his arms over his chest, waiting for the Guardians to seek him out.

"Haven't we done this before?" Jacob said as they rode on Chief Zorin's scaly back, trying to get his mind off what was ahead of them.

Jacob really didn't want to face the Baron without the Sword of Dragon Slaying. And, likewise, a streak of fear gnawed at him. With no magical weapon, all he could really hope to do was be a distraction at whatever time one would be needed, since it had been decided that the tank would remain behind to defend Metsys keep. That was assuming, of course, that his rifle and keen reflexes kept him alive that long.

According to Chief Zorin, the Sword of Dragon Slaying would be useless against the Baron. Still, Jacob couldn't avoid the fact that the Sword had magical power derived from the Realm and that half of the Baron's power was rooted to the Realm as well. He thought, in that respect, it could have done some type of damage. But it was too late to find out.

"Yeah," Mac replied as he looked at the Southern Mountains before him, "and as I recall, I'm not usually that lucky."

Jacob recalled what he was referring to and didn't like Mac's attitude, "Enough of that shit! Just remember that you have the two magics now, like the Baron."

"Yeah, but I don't know how to use it."

"What are you talking about?" Jacob asked as he glanced backward with a frown, "You've already used it!"

Mac felt the cold throb of the Dark Magic grow as they neared the mountains.

"I still don't know how I did it!" Mac retorted. He was not ready to deal with the Baron and the fact that the entire Realm's well-being was now in their hands.

"Still, you did use it." Jacob pointed out with a slight smile growing on his face, "Besides, it'll keep you alive long enough so I can rush in and save your ass!"

"Thanks." Mac replied begrudgingly.

"This is it." Jacob said, feeling somewhat lighter from Chief Zorin's sudden descent.

Most of the other Guardians dove towards the earth ahead of Chief Zorin because they had no riders to be concerned with losing. Even before any of Chief Zorin's riders had dismounted after the Silver Dragons had landed, King Doron was off running before them, sword drawn.

"What is he doing?!" Jacob rattled out with disbelief.

"He's a barbarian," Mac said, shrugging his shoulders, "what do you expect?"

Noticing King Doron running towards the Baron, Chief Zorin shouted after him, "King Doron! Stop!"

King Doron sped towards the Baron, in his human form, with precise rhythm of movement and breathing as rage pulsed through his veins and fed every sinew of his large muscular body. As he closed on the Baron, his hand tightened around the grip of his sword, eager to cleave the Baron's head from his body and then open him like one does guiding a knife through a melon.

He would have the Baron's head if it was the last thing he did.

"Your head is mine, dog!" King Doron roared out with fearless, barbaric anger, his berserker trait consuming him, "You shall die for the slaughter of my people!"

The Baron always had a quiet respect of the barbarians. They were fearless and bound by honor to their clan.

Effortlessly, the Baron raised a hand towards King Doron and wove a simple spell. Instantly, twisted lightning bolts shot out of his fingers and plowed into King Doron, sending him to his back some forty feet.

"Shit!" Jacob stuttered. Indeed, it appeared that the Baron had become stronger.

After a few long moments King Doron began to stir, but he did not get up.

"Give us the Secret Scrolls and cease your magic." Chief Zorin commanded as he walked toward the Baron.

The others followed him, Guardians scattered about the lifeless expanse of earth.

Mac turned towards Regan and said, "You must stay here."

Regan began to say something but Mac gently pressed his finger on her warm lips. Then he turned and walked toward the Baron, forcing himself to keep from looking back at her.

"If you want the scrolls Zorin, they're in the cave." the Baron began as he motioned to the cavern entrance above them, "Its knowledge has made me more powerful. I have no use for them anymore."

Lionak's heart stumbled. *How could his power exceed what the scrolls had possessed? Could it be possible?'*

"Cease your magic and surrender." Chief Zorin ordered firmly.

Slowly Regan crept over to King Doron and knelt beside him.

"Are you okay?" Regan asked. A great deal of his armor was blackened and bent from the bolts. Parts even had misshapen holes, formed as if it had been touched by acid.

"Weak," King Doron whispered as he strained to sit up to no avail, "But I'll be fine."

"Good." Regan said, spotting a dagger on his belt.

"Do you need that?" Regan asked as she pointed to the dagger.

With considerable effort, King Doron raised one of his hands to the dagger and pulled it out of the belt loop, "Take it. I cannot use it."

Eagerly Regan took it and looked around as a plan formed in her mind.

Everyone stopped within twenty yards of the Baron as they awaited his response.

"I cannot cease my magic or surrender." the Baron replied confidently, "But you can surrender to me. You know, as well as I, none have hope of conquering me. So, save yourself a lot of bloodshed and death this day."

"Never!" Chief Zorin spat in defiance.

The Baron shook his head and folded his hands together before him and said, "You are unmatched. The scrolls have given me stellar elemental power. Power to create or destroy life at its very root!"

Chief Zorin was shocked. He had never seen that in the Scrolls, undoubtedly because it had been disguised.

A couple of the Guardians took a step backwards in fear. They all knew what the Baron was saying. But the Baron was not ready to stop at that.

"Name anyone who has died. No matter how long ago. From the dust of the earth you stand on, I can bring them back." the Baron said as he pointed a finger at Chief Zorin, "And, just as easily, I can take a life no matter how powerful."

Lionak thought of his father, Metsys. Images of his death flooded through his mind. Nothing he did could save his father.

"Cut the shit!" Jacob sliced coldly, leveling the rifle on the Baron.

"Shit?" the Baron grunted with a raised eyebrow, "I hardly think so. Behold death."

As the Baron opened one of his hands and then closed it, a Guardian standing near Chief Zorin yelled out in unspeakable agony as its scales somehow pulled downward through its legs and vanished into the earth exposing the Silver Dragon's meaty red flesh. But, as the scales went, so did the golden eyeballs and blood followed by its flesh, leaving nothing but a white skeleton standing next to Chief Zorin.

Then the Baron lowered his fist and the white skeleton changed into a powdery dust and rolled downwards into the earth until nothing could be seen of the Guardian's remains.

"Bastard!" Chief Zorin roared out in rage as his fire glands expanded.

"No!" the Baron shot out, "I am your god!"

"Attack!" Chief Zorin commanded as he exhaled a thick blast of incinerating fire at the Baron.

Shortly after, several of the other Guardians joined Chief Zorin and sent streams of fire at the Baron. The sudden onslaught of brute force and intense magic caused the Baron to take a few steps backward to catch his balance as the blasts of fire were repelled by an invisible globe of protection that surrounded him. He speculated the globe would not last long against such an onslaught but it would buy him enough time to raise his kin.

"Zorin!" Lionak yelled out as he raised his staff, "Red Dragons!"

Jacob turned around and saw skeletons bursting out of the earth as flesh and scales formed on them.

Mac could not believe that all those Red Dragons were rising from the earth. Alive.

Chief Zorin turned to see a few of the Red Dragons, alive, rushing towards him. Swiftly, Chief Zorin crouched as he spread his wings and leapt into the air. Beating his wings, he gained flight. Two Red Dragons followed.

"Fuck!" Jacob fumed as he ran by Mac and scaled up the rocky face to the ledge of the cavern, "It's a damn graveyard! Get up here!"

"Graveyard?!" Mac fumbled out with widened eyes, running over and climbing below Jacob.

A deep laugh rolled through the burial ground as the Baron gazed at all of the Guardians scattering about as more and more Red Dragons exploded from the earth.

Lionak, seeing the charge of a towering Red Dragon, pulled his staff before him and vanished from sight. Shortly after, he re-appeared next to the cave just as Jacob pulled himself over the ledge.

Still on his belly, Jacob outstretched his hand towards Mac and shouted, "Hurry up! Red Dragon is coming quick!"

Sensing danger, Mac reached up and clasped onto Jacob's wrist, continuing to climb upwards as best as he could manage.

"Damn it." Jacob hissed as he pulled on Mac's arm, seeing the Red Dragon racing towards them, opening its large mouth. No much time remained.

"Aarh!" Jacob roared out, using all his strength to pull Mac over the ledge.

Jumping upward, the Red Dragon sent its gaping mouth toward Mac and snapped its jaw shut, just missing Mac's foot.

"Shit." Mac heaved, his heart pounding from the sudden exertion.

"That was close!" Mac said between breaths as he got to his feet, followed by Jacob.

"No kidding," Jacob agreed as he shook his arm slightly, "You need to lose some weight."

Serrating flames crashed into Chief Zorin as he tried to distance himself far enough from the Red Dragons to initiate an attack. But the blast caused him to lose his altitude and fall some fifty feet before he could regain his senses.

The Red Dragons opened their clawed feet and collided with the lone Silver Dragon, puncturing his scales and ripping into flesh. Sharp pain ripped through Chief Zorin's body as the claws closed up around his scales. Swiping his tail backward, his body turned and sent the two Red Dragons forward, ripping their claws from his back and freeing himself. Despite the overwhelming pain, Chief Zorin sent a blast of fire at the Red Dragon. Scarcely a heartbeat later Chief Zorin dove after the tumbling Red Dragon, sending blast after blast of scorching flame at it.

"Watch out!" Jacob warned as he leveled his weapon on a Red Dragon who beat his wings, rising above the ledge.

Pulling the trigger, casings jumped out of the rifle as rounds plunged into the Red Dragon's scales. As he continued the deafening fire, a few of the scales began to fracture.

Pointing his staff at the dragon, Lionak summoned the White Magic around its tip and sent a massive volley of lightning at it. The lightning tore a giant hole in the dragon's torso, sending flesh and a mist of blood into the air.

The Red Dragon shrieked with pain and collapsed to the earth below.

"I thought we were dead for sure." Jacob said, looking at Lionak with thanks.

"Well, I can't do much more of that or I'll be swinging my staff at those damn dragons." Lionak responded, temporarily weakened from the summoning of all that White Magic in a single moment.

"What the?" Mac mumbled as he looked below at the Baron and the figure of Regan coming from behind him.

Jacob and Lionak turned to see what Mac was talking about.

The dull flash of a weapon went past them as Regan raised her hand behind the Baron.

"Regan!" Mac cried out, knowing the Baron would probably not be affected by her effort and that she would surely die from the attempt.

Her arm came down despite his cry.

"Ahh!" Lionak cried as an unseen Red Dragon outstretched one of its wings and knocked him into the cave.

Wheeling around, Jacob came face to face with another Red Dragon who had managed to get onto the ledge. Quickly, Jacob grabbed Mac around the neck and rolled him into the cave, opening a hail of bullets at the Red Dragon as he retreated into the cave.

The Red Dragon, unaffected by the bullets, moved in front of the cave and spotted his prey.

"Quick!" Lionak ordered as he stood and swirled his right hand before him, summoning the White Magic, "Get behind me!"

Although her heart raced with fear, Regan brought the blade of the dagger down on the Baron, plunging it deeply into his back. Stunned, the Baron's eyes widened, wondering where the sudden pain had come from.

Regan loosed her hand from the dagger and took a few steps backwards, wondering why he had not fallen from her attack. Closing his eyes, the Baron wove the Dark magic around the dagger and withdrew it from his back. The dagger fell and clanked off a stone by her feet. Turning around, the Baron looked at Regan with both surprise and rage.

Regan froze with fear of what would happen to her.

"Good try wench." the Baron grumbled as he pivoted and planted a balled fist firmly on her cheek with all of his might.

As if she were nothing more than a doll, Regan flew through the air and smashed onto the barren earth.

"What the hell are you doing?!" Mac roared out as they stood behind Lionak.

A blast of fire collided with the magical shield Lionak had formed from the threads of White Magic.

"Saving your ass!" Jacob retorted.

"Regan is in danger!" Mac stressed as his temper thinned.

"We have more immediate problems!" Jacob shouted out as he pointed to the Red Dragon before them.

Another ball of fire collided with the magical shield as Lionak maintained the spell.

All Mac could think about was Regan. She was all he had. And she was in danger. If he had to sacrifice himself to know that she was alive, then so be it.

"Enough!" Mac declared as the magics built up inside of him, each growing with the other.

Withdrawing his sword, Mac reeled back, pointing the blade with singular focus on the dragon. Then, just as the Red Dragon began to open its mighty jaw for another fiery blast, Mac vaulted the sword at the Red Dragon. The blade sank into the Red Dragon's upper belly. Lightning bolts grew and danced over the dragon's scaly body as it took a few steps backward before exploding into fire and falling off the ledge.

"Impressive." Lionak said to himself as he watched Mac bolt out of the cavern.

"I guess that means, 'Don't fuck with his woman.'" Jacob suspected.

"No." Mac mumbled to himself as he found Regan sprawled out on the earth below, blood trickling down her face from an unseen wound. She didn't move.

Jacob stopped next to Mac and saw Regan.

"Time to become a god." the Baron said to himself, bored with the fact that this enemies had been much less of a problem than he had expected. Easily he transformed into his Red Dragon form and began collecting the threads of both magics into his very essence.

"I'm sorry." Jacob said lowly. And, for what it mattered, he had a glimmer of respect for Regan for what she had done, despite the fact that he thought she had been using Mac. Obviously, he had been wrong.

Mac's rage boiled within himself as his eyes became nothing more than a yellowish haze. Slowly a white glow surrounded his body as he clenched his fists, turning to stare at the Baron.

Feeling the hairs on his body stand on end, Jacob frowned and looked at Mac. Suddenly his expression changed to one of surprise as he took a couple of steps back towards Lionak who had just caught up to them.

"Do you feel that?" Lionak asked Jacob, staring at Mac.

"Yeah. It's like static electricity." Jacob whispered in astonishment.

"No, no. The power," Lionak said, "somehow he's collecting the raw White Magic from the heart of the Realm itself and an equal amount of the Wild magic from your world."

"Unbelievable." Jacob stuttered. He was not sure what it meant other than what his skin felt.

"By the gods, look at that!" Lionak exclaimed lowly, pointing towards Mac's boots.

"How the hell…"

As the two magics pooled into Mac, its pureness eroded the Dark Magic from around the earth under Mac's feet. As if time were somehow sped up, grass grew from the earth under his boots, shooting upwards.

Mac took a few steps towards the Baron who had retreated several steps. Small tufts of grass appeared from where he had stepped just moments before. Although Mac's head throbbed as if it were ready to explode, he faced the Baron. The massive Red Dragon looked down upon Mac with no visible expression.

"Hey!" Mac thundered out as white clouds mysteriously began forming overhead, blocking out the sunlight.

"Asshole!" Mac continued as more rage filled his veins and the throbbing in his head worsened, "I'm going to send you to hell!"

"Too late. I am a god." the Baron countered smoothly as if to rub in his victory.

"Well god this!" Mac roared as he pointed both hands at the Red Dragon.

Thick bolts, easily as round as a three-hundred-year oak, twisted and arched toward the Baron. Deep rumbling sounds echoed through the burial ground as the combined magics found their mark on the Baron. Instantly the Red Dragon tensed up from the awesome power as Mac continued his attack. Slowly the Baron felt his scales begin to warm from the immense power of the focused magics working in unison. He had to do something from the magics that somehow equaled his.

Focusing on a near dragon, he commanded it telepathically to attack Mac. With the swipe of the Red Dragon's tail, Mac's feet were swept from under him and he fell to his back, breaking his focus and attack.

"Damn you!" Mac cursed as he got to his feet and stared coldly at the Red Dragon who had obeyed the Baron's command.

Crackling sounds filled the air as the Red Dragon froze and grayed, turned to stone for eternity. Forcing himself to look away from the stone dragon, Mac spun around only to see that the Baron had taken flight into the sky.

"No!" Mac cried out as thunder roared out from the clouds above. Flashes of light bounced around the clouds as the thunder intensified.

Suddenly the clouds began throwing out bolts of lightning at the Red Dragon, each tossing him around in the sky as if he were nothing more than a feather. Unable to control his fall and clear his vision, the Baron crashed heavily onto the flat earth with a heavy thud. Groggily the Baron got up and turned toward Mac.

"You're a god, huh?" Mac smirked, the yellowish color in his eyes deepening.

"Yes!" the Baron yelled suddenly as his head shot forward and a thick array of both fire and balls of lightning filled with both Dark and Wild Magic collided into Mac.

Unprepared for the sudden attack, Mac was pushed backward through the air until he smashed into a nearby Guardian. Before he could gain his feet, another blast poured over Mac's body. Several Guardians and Red Dragons broke off their battles and fled from around Mac in fear of being hit with all that magical power. Without a second thought, the Baron kept on pounding Mac as he got closer to the human's squirming form.

"Oh no. We're in trouble." Jacob said, seeing the tables suddenly turn on Mac. Not knowing what else to do, he took aim at the Baron's scaly head and began shooting.

"Chief Zorin!" Lionak broadcast telepathically, as he eased a few threads of White Magic to wherever Chief Zorin was, "You must come here now. Mac is in trouble."

After a few moments a replay came, "I see it. This dragon will have to be dealt with later. Join me before the Baron."

Through the serrating pain, Mac heard a familiar voice. Struggling to focus on it, he tried to comprehend what Jacob was saying.

Again, Jacob cupped his hands around his mouth and shouted, "Come on! Kill the Baron for Regan! For Regan!"

Jacob wanted to do more than shout at Mac, but his ammunition had been expended and with every passing moment he thought more and more about beating on the Baron with his weapon instead of watching Mac burn to death.

The Baron felt the two magics flow in him with increasing intensity as he focused on destroying Mac. Mac was the only barrier which remained, and the Baron sensed that he would fall very soon. Then he would claim the Realm for his own!

"For Regan." Mac whispered to himself as those words sunk into his mind. Images of Regan lying on the earth below the ledge with a bloodied face flashed in his mind. Newfound range seeped into every sinew of Mac's being as he struggled to rise and get his feet under him despite the constant attacks from the Baron. Slowly Mac made it to his knees, grimacing at the unbearable pain lashing out at him. Then the pain seemed to stop, as if someone closed a door.

"Mac!" Chief Zorin called out as he stretched his wings between Mac and the Baron, "Take him now!"

"Baron." Mac thundered deeply as he got to his feet and turned, "You missed!"

Realizing that he was now threatened by Mac as well, Chief Zorin dove away from between them as Mac brought both hands up with arcs of intense lightning jumping between them, the magnitude of which Chief Zorin had never seen before. No one in the Realm had.

"Aaahh!" Mac roared out as the two magics flowed through him and tore into the Baron. All he thought about was destroying the Baron. Nothing else, not even Regan, clouded his mind.

"Yes!" Jacob shouted as he shot a balled fist upward. Mac was attacking!

"You shall harm no others ever again!" Mac commanded as another surge of energy flowed through

447

him and hurtled towards the Baron. A fiery explosion and mighty shockwave consumed the Baron, instantly knocking everyone within sixty feet to the ground.

Slowly, Lionak got to his feet before the others and immediately searched for the Baron. But he was nowhere in sight. All that remained was a deep charred crater where he had stood. Nothing else was visible. After a few moments, a few ashened remains of a Red Dragon fell to the earth.

"Uhmph." Mac groaned as he strained to stay on his feet.

"You okay?" Lionak asked as he sprinted over to Mac.

"Yeah. Just feel like I've been through a meat grinder." Mac sighed weakly as he peered at the crater, completely exhausted as if he had not slept for several weeks.

"You destroyed the Baron." Lionak congratulated, patting Mac lightly on the shoulder, "The Realm is safe!"

"Regan." Mac said weakly as he forced his weary legs to move him forward, back toward her.

But Jacob got to her first.

"How is she?" Mac hoarsed out although he really intended to shout at Jacob who was bent over Regan, checking her head wound and a pulse.

Jacob rose to his feet and faced Mac who was only a few steps from him. Jacob was not sure how to say it, except just to say it. It looked to him like she was in a coma.

"She's wounded pretty bad, Mac." Jacob shrugged as he continued, "But she's alive!"

Catching Jacob by the shoulder as dizziness overtook him, Mac said, "Make sure she stays that way."

Then Mac collapsed suddenly at Jacob's feet.

Chapter Sixty-Six

For the next week Jacob, Lionak and Chief Zorin attended Regan and Mac back to health with a little aid from the White Magic. And, as promised, Lionak opened the portal to Earth and sent everyone through it who had come to the Realm except for Jacob who had felt it was his obligation to watch over Regan and Mac until they had recovered. But, unlike the others, Cindy was not persuaded so easily given her love for Chief Zorin. The only incentive Chief Zorin could offer was that he would come to her once Regan and Mac were in good health. And she knew that he was bound by his word and would come.

Although Lionak had felt the Wild Magic emanating from Mac's world as nothing he had encountered before, he kept it to himself. Somehow, he knew that the Wild Magic was being controlled by an evil force. Perhaps eviler than even the Baron had been with the Dark Magic. Deep within himself Lionak felt they would need all the recovery they could get for whatever threat now lurked on the other world.

The new Red Dragons that surrendered, without a master and gravely outnumbered, came to bear with the fact that they would have to align themselves with the Silver Dragon clan, at least temporarily, and end the continued bloodshed that had been spread over the centuries. Chief Zorin reluctantly accepted them into the clan, although it would probably be a very long time before he would gain any trust in them. But he was comforted by the fact that, at least for now, the warring was finally over.

"As I place this golden band around your wrists, both of you are bound to the other for eternity." a finely ornamented man proclaimed as he wrapped a small golden band around Regan and Mac's wrists.

Many of the townspeople, Guardians and the few remaining Red Dragons cheered through they were all crowded outside, around Metsys keep.

"I love you." Mac said to Regan with happiness flowing through his entire body. Since the battle Mac had aged a few decades and gray peppered the hair on his head.

"And I you, my love." Regan whispered back with a tear rolling down her soft cheek, her eyes locked on his whose eyes had permanently changed into a yellowish-gold color.

As their emotions embraced, so did their lips.

Again, the crowd cheered as hats and other things were tossed into the air.

"Jacob." Lionak said as he nudged him.

Jacob looked at Lionak with a questioning eye.

"I fear an evil power is loosed in your world. Beware." Lionak said after a long moment.

Jacob frowned at Lionak. He had no idea what he was referring to. After all, the Baron was dead, so what more was there to worry about besides the daily uncertainties of life?

Lionak recognized Jacob's expression and whispered, "We shall be in contact soon."

As the High Priest moved from in front of the wedded couple, Lionak raised his staff and opened a portal to their world not more than four feet from Regan and Mac.

"I am ready." Regan sighed as she unwantingly pulled away from Mac, "Let me bear our children in your world."

Without warning, Mac smiled and swept Regan into his arms and carried her through the portal.

Chapter Sixty-Seven

General Lowinsky's heart raced with sheer fear and confusion as he strained to force a heavy piece of computer equipment from his legs. He could not believe what had happened. He did not know what the scientists had done wrong that had caused all of this.

In the darkness the general managed to stand and look around him, still fearing for his very life. Everyone was dead, except for him. None of them, not even the most trained and armed personnel stood a chance against the being that swept over them, as if they were nothing more than scampering insects being crushed by a stone. The horrid image of the being he saw just moments after it had entered the dimensional door, opened by the scientists, was burned in his mind. Its mighty, muscular red torso and plainly powerful limbs ending with dark claws and long, leathery wings stretching on either side, towered above a normal man. Its horned head, with rows of razor-sharp teeth and deep red-glowing eyes struck a deafening fear in him. Those fissured eyes that he had only looked upon once, had sent a cold chill of death and solitude through him.

General Lowinsky tried to shake the image of the being from his mind as he moved forward toward the communications trailer, still largely in one piece. Bodies littered the ground, strewn about as randomly as all of the wreckage of split power cables, parts of the computer center, and the dimensional door. He realized that something must be done to stop this being from whatever it was here to do.

As he cleared the top of the metallic staircase to the trailer, he couldn't help but think that maybe this being had been provoked to rage when the dimensional door was opened. If the supercomputers had made some type of mistake that nobody had seen, it was quite possible that an intelligent being from some other dimension had been caught and brought here. Whatever had happened though, the general knew it was his responsibility. His problem. He knew that, with the complete destruction of the monitoring equipment, there would be no way of knowing exactly what had transpired so that precautions could be taken in the future.

Seeing a phone terminal a few paces from him after entering the trailer, General Lowinsky took a deep breath and picked up the receiver. After pressing a coded sequence of buttons on the terminal he heard the satellite link connect. A few, seemingly endless, moments passed before he heard someone speak.

"This is Kard Alpha One." the male voice said plainly, ignorant to what had just happened.

"This is General Lowinsky." the general announced as he wiped the sweat from his forehead with a shaky hand, "This is a matter of national security. I must speak to the President."

"Hold one." the monotonous voice sighed as the general stood there waiting impatiently.

After a couple of minutes, the general heard another voice. The voice of the President.

"Yes, General Lowinsky. I read your report regarding the first phase of the project. How is it proceeding?"

General Lowinsky paused. He knew the President would not want to hear what he was about to say. Nobody would.

"The project has been destroyed." General Lowinsky stated, barely above a whisper.

"What?" the President responded, clearly surprised.

"Sir, I don't have time to go into the details now," General Lowinsky heaved out as he looked around him, "but all of my men are dead. We caught something in the dimensional door. Something I've never seen before. Something bad."

There was no response to his statement.

"Mr. President, we must go on full alert. Whatever this thing is that we caught, it's very powerful and enraged." the general confessed uneasily.

There was a pause before the President said, "Damn. General, stay where you are. I'll send a recovery team to get you out. I just hope we can deal with this 'thing' in an expedient fashion."

"Yes sir, Mr. President," General Lowinsky agreed, "I hope we can."

About the Author

Wrought from the 1980's with the rise of technology and tempered by his life's journey through time to the present, Joe has forged an action-packed tale, not only of the stuff of fantasy, but also of science fiction and our modern era not so far into the future. Here, crossing into a parallel dimension to converse with dragons no longer relies on occult ritual, magic or the limitations of ancient energetic meridians and a spiritual connection of the mind. Instead, it only relies on the technological mastery and orchestration of a sentient artificial intelligence focused on moving crude matter, mind and body, across that dark bridge between dimensions.

Claim this book as your own and allow Joe to take you on an imaginative, thought-provoking adventure full of dragons, giants, elves and even the might of the modern military as two dimensions, once unknown to each other, become inseparable in their fight to endure among the ocean of stars and competition in our universe.

www.ingramcontent.com/pod-product-compliance
Lightning Source LLC
Chambersburg PA
CBHW051056030726
47504CB00006B/1656